I0603983

When the Night is Over

LILY FOSTER

SHOREFRONT BOOKS

This is a work of fiction. Names, characters, places and incidents are
either the product of the author's
imagination, or used fictitiously. Any resemblance to actual persons,
living or dead, events, or locales is entirely coincidental.

Copyright © 2020 by Lily Foster

All rights reserved. No part of this book may be reproduced in any
form or by any electronic or mechanical means, including
information storage and retrieval systems, without written
permission from the author, except for the use of brief quotations in
a book review.

First paperback edition September 2020
IBSN: 9780998916729 (ebook)
IBSN: 9780998916798 (paperback)

Cover: Megan Barker Designs

Prologue

YOU DON'T KNOW ME ANYMORE

The scenery whips by in a blur of brown branches and gray asphalt. I'm numb, so I can still think about today from the vantage point of a nameless spectator, as if it wasn't me watching you. The feelings, they'll come I guess, but for now it's better like this. I can dissect every moment, view each and every one of them in still frame.

A chance encounter? No, I can't call it that. A sighting, that's all it was. You had no idea I was there—that *we* were there. I've imagined the reunion, conjured up countless fairy-tale versions of how it would go down. But not one of my daydreams played out like today's reality: a nonevent.

What *was* that when you turned her way and smiled? And when she gave you a playful swat on the shoulder, you shook your head and laughed. Were you just giving her something in return, being easygoing and friendly, or is it her? That girl with the golden hair, is she someone to you?

I willed you to look my way. Every muscle in my body coiled tight, teeth clenched and brows narrowed in concentration. I thought my telepathic energy would zip through the air and land on you, that I still had the power to reel you in. When it didn't work, I was tempted to scream your name, to drop the bombshell. But the moment passed. You just kept on walking.

And what if you had turned your head? What would you have seen? What would you have done once you recognized me, a ghost from your past?

I caught my reflection in the lobby window after you passed without a backward glance. Couldn't help but compare myself to the shiny penny walking beside you. That girl, she is California. She's tangerine-flavored optimism, animated and bubbling over. And me, the one you left behind? I'm western Pennsylvania in the dead of winter: barren, disillusioned and weary. Not even twenty years old, yet I've experienced more than most do over the course of a lifetime.

"We should get going, Charlotte. Long drive ahead of us."

I follow, push my precious cargo while weaving around the young, carefree people crowding the narrow sidewalk. Standing tall only a moment before, now the crush of bodies, the jarring laughter, and the gut punch of loss all swirl together, threatening to take me down.

I knew seeing you again would be painful, but I truly believed I was stronger than this. What a joke. Just one look at you and I'm sixteen again.

I stab at the single tear threatening to escape, take a deep breath and soldier on. I don't have the luxury of nursing a broken heart. I've spent too many nights living in the past, back on the banks of the river with you. A summer of dizzying laughter, soft touches and whispered promises—so much in love I could hardly catch my breath. But those good memories are all buried deep in the muck of that riverbed now, and it's where they belong. When someone you love turns their back on you, it does that. It eclipses everything that was good.

You walked away and never looked back.

I should be used to it by now.

Part One

ROMEO, MEET JULIET

Chapter One

CHARLOTTE

"Why him? I don't get it."

"Hmm, what?"

"That boy you're always staring at has a giant stick up his ass. Meanwhile Adam over there, one of the few boys in this school who isn't a total Neanderthal destined to work in a steel factory, follows you around like a puppy and you ignore him." Daisy turns my chin, giving me no choice but to abandon the object of my fascination. "Earth to Charlotte Mason."

"I like to look, that's all." Flicking the strap of her backpack off her shoulder, I add, "And for the record, that Neanderthal is in the honors program...No different from you or me or Adam."

Daisy huffs out a breath, grabbing her bag up off the floor. "Is not."

"Yes, he is. You're judging him because of his...I don't know, his clothes, his attitude—"

"The fact that he never seems to be carrying a book, that he doesn't appear to own a comb, that he's twenty-four-seven surrounded by girls who I know for a fact can barely read."

"He doesn't need a comb."

We both turn to check him out. No different from any other day, he's the center of attention without even trying. Leaning back against the lockers, he offers a lazy smile to some girl. She's resting her hand on his shoulder, leaning in close to tell him something private.

Daisy's right, his hair just might be in need of a comb, but the way the longish strands shade his face, leaving just one steel blue eye visible to his adoring fans—it works.

With satisfaction, I note that this girl is vying for his attention but not holding it. Two guys in football jackets cackle while one shows him his phone screen, and he bursts out laughing along with them. The football players seem beefy, like stuffed sausages standing next to him. He matches them in height, but his muscular build is leaner.

And though I've never seen him barreling over an opponent wearing school colors, I know he's powerful and strong. I've seen the boy unload truckloads of merchandise at the hardware store—enormous bags of feed or fertilizer or whatever—tossing them as if they weigh no more than a feather. I've open-mouth stared from across the street, eyes glued to the muscles that strain and flex beneath his snug thermal shirts. Most people would be bundled up in a parka, but it has to drop below twenty degrees or so for him to wear even a fleece-lined flannel. He's tough, impervious to the elements.

He's smiling now, which makes me smile. Seeing him happy is rare from what I've observed, and it's infectious. So when his eyes lock on mine in a way that punches the air from my lungs, I know I should turn away but I can't. In that split second his smile drops and his laughing eyes turn stone cold. He makes me feel stripped down and ashamed.

"Let's go," Daisy whispers, tugging on my wrist with urgency when the bell rings. "What the hell was that?" she says on an exhale as we rush into our last period class.

I shrug, pretending I have no clue what's up, when in truth I have a fairly good idea as to why Simon looked at me the way he just did. The name Wade was never spoken in my home without a curse word preceding it. Makes sense to assume he's grown up on a steady diet of hatred for my family in return.

I was just a kid, so this Hatfield and McCoy idiocy is ancient history as far as I'm concerned. Whatever it is that happened, I wasn't there, I had nothing to do with it. He has no right to hold some stupid grudge against me, or to look at me the way he does. He's wrong.

He's wrong about me.

* * *

SIMON

I watch her every damn day, and I hate myself for it.

What is she doing here? She lives one town over, the decidedly better of the two that feed into our school district. On top of that, her father owns the only car dealership in Fayette County. She has no business working the ass crack of dawn shift every weekend at the diner.

Probably my imagination, or just my frustration and anger run wild, but it seems like every time I go to unload a delivery, to shovel the sidewalk, or to arrange whatever seasonal goods my boss wants displayed—rock salt at the moment—she picks that exact same time to take a break. She doesn't smoke, doesn't check her phone. No, she just steps outside like she's doing right now, hugging herself and shifting on her feet to keep warm, watching her breath float up as she exhales out into the cold. Not two minutes later, she fixes her gaze back to the ground, smoothes her apron and skirt down over her hips, and heads back inside.

Her mere presence ticks me off. Poor little rich girl. The way she smiles at everyone and makes small talk? It's fake as shit. I used to grab lunch at the counter during my break, but I don't anymore.

That's the kind of place where I belong, not her. The short-tempered cook and those older, world-weary waitresses are my people, but right off the bat she wormed her way in. Not a week later and she was already their little mascot, the one they watched over. I couldn't stomach it. It's the same with the customers. Rushing in from the cold, they greet her with a smile. I can see her through the plate glass window of the restaurant, pausing to laugh and joke with the regulars, or stopping to fawn over the babies in their high chairs. When it's still dark outside, the bright lights in the diner make it easy to see her every move, the expression on her face so clear it's as if I'm standing right beside her. And I can see their faces too. She thinks she's special but she's not. I've witnessed middle-aged men smiling at her in a fatherly way, only to ogle her ass like it's a medium rare porterhouse the second her back is turned.

What burns me most, though, is the little ritual she's established now that the frigid February weather has settled in. I start my workday early, but not as early as she does. I pull up outside the hardware store at six-thirty, and that's when I see her, stealing outside with a to-go cup in one hand, a paper bag in the other. Breakfast for Rudy Wallace. The guy looks like he's pushing a bad version of fifty with his stooped posture, missing teeth and roughened skin, but I know for a fact he's not even ten years older than me. Nothing but a loser junkie who—because of *her*—has recently made a habit of trolling this street. I want to knock the last of his remaining teeth down his throat for it, for forging some kind of twisted relationship with her.

Does it make her feel better? To be charitable to people like Wallace, or to work when she clearly doesn't need to? When she has everything just...handed to her? She's a puzzle I can't figure out, and at the same time, even sparing her a second thought makes me want to punch myself in the face. Why do I even give a shit?

Sometimes I catch sight of her walking across the parking lot at the end of her shift. Her head is usually cast down. She looks at the pebbles, kicking a few as she makes her way towards her car, never in a rush. And that car—a little compact thing, but shiny and new. I want to look away, but my eyes always zero in on the Mason Motors logo. It feels like a kick to my gut every time.

She carries that name, and for that alone I can hate her.

Chapter Two

CHARLOTTE

"Eyes on the road, gorgeous."

The wooly mammoth-sized jerk and his buddies have the nerve to laugh as I crouch down to pick my stuff up off the floor.

I hate Mondays.

No, usually I look forward to returning to school after the weekend, but this morning I'm dragging ass. I look up when I can still hear them cackling from a good twenty feet away.

Simon and three football players are stopped in front of Sienna's locker. Sienna is the captain of my dance team. She's kind, she's beautiful and she's a great dancer. I'm pretty sure the entire student body has a crush on her. Sienna shoots me a sympathetic smile before knocking one of the guys on the shoulder hard. He stops laughing, looks over at me still down on the ground and gives me a head nod. It's a lame substitute for an apology, but it's all I'm going to get. Sienna bestows an approving smile on her loyal subject and he beams back at her like a damn puppy. I wish I wielded that kind of power. Then she turns to Simon, but his attention is elsewhere. Ugh, his eyes are fixed on me. Hard eyes. My hands shake as I finish gathering my belongings. He rattles me. What's worse is he knows it and uses it against me.

The way he rakes his eyes over me and then shakes his head is becoming familiar. It's as if I'm being appraised, and the sum total of who I am is deemed severely lacking. The fact that I willingly risked running into him yesterday is testament to how desperate I was.

Making my way into enemy territory, I breathed a sigh of relief when I saw a different clerk at the register, a woman. I wandered around for a few minutes before going back up front to ask for help. Just my luck, it was Simon putting a fresh roll of tape into the cash register.

"Can I help you with something?" he asked as he clipped the roll into place. The smile died on his lips when he looked up to see me standing there. I wasn't smiling either. My nerves were on edge, I hadn't gotten more than two hours sleep the night before, and I didn't want help or anything else from Simon Wade.

"I need a lock, like a chain." My words were clumsy as I motioned with my hands to describe the item I was looking for.

He cleared his throat. "Something with a key? A deadbolt?"

"No." I shook my head, looking away. "Simple. Something I can install by myself, I guess."

He didn't say anything for a moment. When I looked back up, he asked, "You need to put this on a door?"

He studied me, waiting on my response, but the words were trapped in my throat. I felt as if he could see right through me, as if he knew exactly where I needed to install a lock and why. Eyes narrowed, two deep lines etched between his brows, just waiting for me to confirm what he already knew.

"Look, I'm on break…Just a basic chain lock. Do you have them?"

He was back a minute later with the lock and some extra screws. "These are sturdier than the ones that come in the package."

He rang up my purchase and handed me my change without another word. When I took the bag from his outstretched hand and our eyes met, his were cool and impassive. *Screw you, Simon.* Did my look convey what I intended, or did my flaming red cheeks and shaking hands give me away?

After work I slipped in through the garage to bypass the living room. When I pulled in, I saw my brother and half a dozen of his friends sprawled out on the couches drinking beer and watching football. Typical Sunday. I could hear my brother cursing out the referee over a blown call and Wes asking someone to grab him another beer from the fridge. I went right to work installing the lock.

Wes Keller would not be tucking me in again tonight.

Christian doesn't like my company, but he doesn't like to be alone. Sometimes my brother just has a few of his boys over, but more often than not it's a full-on blowout. When Saturday nights involve kegs and body shots, I normally hide out at Daisy's, but this weekend she was out of town with her parents. Without that option, I was stuck eating cold pizza and catching up on homework in my room, watching the clock and praying they'd clear out soon. When midnight passed and the music was still blasting, I put my earbuds in and tried my best to fall asleep.

Wes has been a fixture in our home for as long as I can remember. What's more, he's consistently shown me kindness.

I can still remember Wes helping me carry my fifth-grade science fair project to school. He made sure I got my display board into the classroom in one piece before heading off down the road to the high school. And before I started driving, Wes used to catch me at the bus stop and give me a ride home when it was raining. Sometimes he'll pop over after his tour just to hang out, entertaining me with wild stories that seem to happen on a regular basis when you're a police officer. He's the one who thinks to ask if I've had dinner, and orders take-out when he sees the refrigerator is empty. And Wes is the only person who will step in and correct my brother when he's being miserable. He's the only one Christian will listen to.

He wasn't acting all that weird. Being freaked out is crazy on *my* part. This is what I've been telling myself.

With the party still raging, Wes knocked on my door and came in, sitting on the edge of my bed as he pulled out an earbud. "What are you listening to?"

"Nothing, just classical. Trying to drown out the noise." I burrowed deeper into my comforter when his glassy eyes moved down and away from my face. "I have to be up early."

"I hear you. I'll see what I can do to clear the place out." I shrugged, knowing there was nothing anyone could do if my brother was holding court. Smiling, he asked, "How was work today?"

"Fine. I like it."

"You make good tips there?"

"Decent, I guess."

"I'll stop in next time I'm on a weekend shift."

"That's not in your area, though, right?"

He reached over and ran a hand through my hair, twisting the ends between his thumb and index finger. "It's a little bit out of my way, but I'd like to see you in action."

The way he looked at me didn't flat-out alarm me, but it did set me on edge. He was too close now. So close I could smell the beer on his breath.

"I'm beat, Wes."

"Yeah, you get to bed." He moved in even closer when he put my earbud back into place and then kissed my forehead. I couldn't hear him, but as he backed away I watched his mouth form the words: *Goodnight, baby*.

Sound travels easily through the paper-thin walls of our ranch house. Above the din of the football game, I heard Wes ask my brother if I was home from work. "Car's in the drive-way, so yeah, I guess she's here." My brother's careless reply doesn't sting the way it should. I'm used to it. More often than not, I feel like an unwelcome guest in my own home.

Staring at the ceiling, I listened to them laugh, curse at the television screen and toss insults at one another for hours. I listened for footsteps in the hallway, a tap on my door, the rattling of my newly installed chain lock, but no one came.

I don't make a habit of ignoring my intuition, but I suspect my instincts are off when it comes to Wes. I hope they are, anyway.

"How did everything work out?"

Deep and raspy—he has the voice of a full-grown man. And I know Simon Wade's voice even though it wouldn't take all my fingers and toes to count the number of words he's directed my way in this lifetime.

He's materialized out of nowhere, moving in so close that his breath tickles my scalp when he speaks. My hand shakes as I reach for a bowl of rice pudding and place it on my tray. I've never tried rice pudding but I'm pretty sure I hate it.

"This isn't your lunch period."

"Really? Thanks for clearing that up for me." He looks away with his lips fixed in a firm line. "The lock?" he asks through clenched teeth.

"Uh, yeah, it works."

"Good. I forgot to tell you that if the door isn't solid wood, if it's just hollow plywood or something, then a chain won't do shit. It'll give with a hard push or a kick."

"Um, it's solid. It took me a long time to get the screws in."

"All right."

When I turn back to thank him, he's gone.

Chapter Three

CHARLOTTE

"Let's go, girls!" Lined up center court, Sienna scans our group from one end to the other. "Now that football's over, those cheerleaders are going to be pushing in on our territory. We have the floor to ourselves during half-time tomorrow night, and I don't know about you, but I intend to wow everyone. Let's make them look like the pathetic pom-pom waggers that they are!"

We all laugh because Sienna doesn't mean any of it. Her sister Skylar is the captain of the cheerleading squad, and they're like peanut butter and jelly. Sometimes I catch myself watching them, each dressed in their own unique but trend-conscious way. They captivate everyone's attention with the way they laugh, finish one another's sentences and socialize effortlessly. It almost doesn't seem fair for one family to have so much beauty and goodness. The boys want the Perillo twins, and girls like me, still awkward and shy in the big world that is high school? We want to be them.

Looking down at my sequined blue skirt, I notice the strip of midriff visible between it and my red, white and blue sequined tank top. I wouldn't call it a full-on crop top, but the show of skin is risqué by our small town's standards. The patriotic theme will probably win over most people, but I'm sure a few old biddies will have something to say about our new dance costumes. Personally, I think they rock.

Miss Dawson doubles as our English teacher and the director of our dance program. She's young compared to our other teachers and I'm pretty sure she's not originally from around here. She dresses in tight tops, long flowy skirts and scarves, and when she wears her hair up, you can see a tattoo at the base of her neck—a blackbird in flight with some numbers underneath. Sienna told me the administration nearly fired her mid-way through her first year because she was so unconventional. Now she walks the line as best she can, but I think she still has a rebellious streak.

For example, Miss Dawson was walking a fine line when she choreographed this routine. I've seen the movies where cheer and dance squads bump and grind to the thumping bass of whatever hip hop song is topping the charts, but that would never fly here. I mean, not that the student body wouldn't appreciate it, but the townspeople would stroke out. Probably institute some *Footloose*-inspired laws banning dancing from this day forward. So Miss Dawson had to get creative. *Something Bad About to Happen* has the foot-stomping beat we need to shake our hips, but the suggestive lyrics are being belted out by Miranda Lambert and Carrie Underwood, country music's version of American sweethearts. I doubt anyone from here, the most redneck county in Pennsylvania, would be complaining—not too loudly anyway.

Dance Ensemble practice is the best part of my week. Every

Tuesday and Thursday afternoon I get to spend two hours uninterrupted dancing my ass off, dreaming up routines to my favorite songs, and hanging out with girls who are, in my opinion, the coolest in my school. Miss Dawson sets the tone for the group. There are no bitchy cliques and no barrier to entry. You like to dance, you're in. Take Daisy for example. In geometry class she's a star, but in the gym it's like she can't remember the steps to even the most basic routine. To be brutally honest, Daisy's the least coordinated "dancer" I've ever known, and I can admit to swapping spots on the line a few times for fear she'd trip me up during a performance. But Miss Dawson loves her enthusiasm, so in turn, the rest of the girls rally around her. And being a part of this group means we have older girls in the school who are like big sisters to us. Sounds silly, but when the junior and senior class girls call my name in the hallway or wave as they pass by, I have to school my expression so that I don't look like the fawning, awestruck underclassman that I am.

After practice, Daisy and I usually go back to her house to do homework together while simultaneously fan-girling over Sienna and the others. Today though, Daisy is the only one in a happy space. I mean, those girls are really nice to us, but we aren't friends, we don't pal around with them on a day to day basis. It was out of left field when Sienna hit us with the invitation.

"Tyler's having a party after the game. You two should come along. We're all bringing outfits to change into, so you can get a ride over with me." When Daisy and I stood there speechless, Sienna widened her eyes and added with a teasing smile, "You know Tyler, my sister's boyfriend, captain of the basketball team...Ring a bell?"

Ring a bell? Everyone knows who Tyler is. He's one half of Ty-Lar, as some have taken to calling the best looking couple in the senior class. Tyler and Skylar. I'd laugh at that ridiculous nickname if they weren't so damn perfect. So perfect that I'm feeling way out of my comfort zone. Did I even want to be at a senior party? I had no time to mull that over before Daisy decided for me, blurting out, "Absolutely! We're in!"

Daisy could barely contain herself. I'd taken to ignoring her by lunch on Friday when the agonizing over what *we* should wear reached borderline hysteria level. I was planning on wearing jeans, a sweater and boots, and that's not because I'm one of those badass girls who won't change to please anyone. It's just that Daisy was viewing this as her coming out party or something, while I wasn't sure I was brave enough to even make a cameo at this thing. Aside from the few spiked seltzers Daisy and I snuck from her parents' cooler last summer, I had no experience with drinking. No experience with anything, really. And from what I've heard, Tyler's parties were known to rage for the better part of the weekend when his parents weren't around.

All that noise was out of my head as the lights dimmed at half-time on Friday night, though. Daisy and I were usually second row with the other underclassmen, but at yesterday's practice Miss Dawson moved me to the front row with the juniors and seniors. I was so pumped that I spent all last night going over the routine in my room. I was so ready.

And when the lights came back on, I knew we'd kicked ass. The gym was still loud with hooting, whistles and applause when the basketball team came back out to start shooting around. I don't think a single one of us could contain a smile as we made our way back to our spot on the sidelines. And when Miss Dawson made her way down the line to tell us how proud she was, she paused in front of me, nodding when she said, "You have talent, Charlotte."

"Teacher's pet," Daisy teased, poking me in the side. Looking over and waving to her parents, she bent her head my way. "Seriously, Charlotte, you were amazing. I was right behind you, trying to freaking keep up."

"C'mon, Daisy, you were great too!"

"Whatever." She shrugged me off, smiling. "Ugh, be right back. My parents are acting like lunatics."

I looked their way, and Daisy was sort of right. They were waving her over, arms flailing, beaming like the two proudest people on the planet.

Daisy's parents are fairytale perfect. They're supportive, loving and have big plans for their child. The two of them are like Daisy's very own personal cheerleading team. And as their daughter's friend, I've always been welcome in their sickeningly happy home. If I was normal I would lap it up, take what they so kindly offer. But for some reason, being in their home is more painful than comforting.

I'm not jealous. I've never begrudged Daisy anything and I usually don't conduct play by play comparisons between my life and hers. For instance, when her father announces that he's heading out to the store to get ice cream, calling out, "Mocha chip, right?" without waiting for an answer, I don't stew over the fact that my dad never does anything remotely like that. In fact, because I've been left to fend for myself for so long, I find their brand of loving care to be oppressive, suffocating even. Daisy's parents have a tracker on her phone to keep her safe, they text back and forth all day long just to catch up with one another, and they keep one night a week sacred as Game Night —I kid you not. They are a unit, a team. Once or twice I asked Daisy about it, hinting around at whether or not she finds them overbearing, but it's clear that she's on board.

I don't know what they think of me. I'm at their house

often enough. Always looking to escape my own home, I spend a good part of my summers hanging around with Daisy in their backyard. I eat dinner with them at least once a week, but that's only because her mother will do everything short of barricading the door if I attempt to decline an invitation. But I've never been truly comfortable there and I'm sure they sense that.

Daisy's parents ask a lot of questions, and I'm just not the sharing kind.

* * *

SIMON

She's holding her friend's hair back as the girl pukes into the bushes.

It's late, today's been a total mind fuck, and I'm about an hour past being ready to call it a night.

I'm still angry thinking back to this morning. She's the first person I see when I exit my truck, and damn if I can't look away. Long hair, pink cheeks and chocolate brown eyes. She's wearing jeans and just a hoodie, hugging herself and rubbing her arms to keep warm. She's quiet, taking it all in while the older girls flirt and compete for attention. One of them is braiding her hair. I shake my head, seeing as she's taken on the role of little mascot in yet another circle.

"Si-mon." Sienna always drags it out, making my name sound like two separate words. And she kind of sighs when she says the first syllable—don't know if that's her idea of a joke or something. "Please tell me you're coming to the game tonight."

My instinct is to walk straight into school, breeze right past little Miss Mason so fast she feels the arctic chill I'm giving off, but screw that. These are my friends. Not changing my routine on account of her. Instead, I drag my eyes over the length of Sienna's body. "I'm considering it, but I, uh, might need some persuading."

Sienna pushes off the wall and walks up to me, leaving less than a foot of space between us. I glance over at Charlotte. Eyes fixed on me, she's reaching her hand up absently, a silent request for the girl to stop braiding her hair.

Like what you see, sweetheart? I've caught her checking me out once or twice. All doe-eyed and eager—she's no different from the rest. The cold look I always shoot back is meant to tell her: *Not if you were the last girl on earth.* And now I've got her where I want her: front row center, watching my performance. The cold-hearted side of me is getting off on it, on hurting her, but I'm the one who's left damn near aching.

I haven't been able to get this girl out of my head all week. Something's wrong there. I'm at war with myself, furious with the part of me that's even curious as to why she needed to buy that lock, for caring even the slightest bit.

I followed her into the lunchroom on Monday without giving my body permission to move in that direction. And when I cut the line, shooting the boy behind me a warning look, I stood so close to Charlotte that I could practically feel the heat radiating off her. She jumped when I spoke to her, stammered her words a little bit. I was rude to her, same as always, when I had no right to be.

And here I stand, having thought about her every damn day this week. Knowing there will be no reprieve once school breaks for the weekend because I'll be watching her from across the street, staring into that diner. She's turning me into something weak and pathetic.

Sienna's finger, now wedged between my pursed lips,

brings me back to the present. "I *said*, I'm very persuasive when I need to be."

I put my hand over hers, drawing her finger away gently. "I know that."

Sienna's eyes are searching mine, looking for something I don't have to give her. Once upon a time, I was into her. Sienna's a good person, kind to others as far as I can tell, she's pretty and she's got a brain in her head. Back at the start of the school year we hooked up a few times, nothing too serious. One night we were making out, stopping when it got to that point where she needed to stop. After, we stretched out in the flatbed of my truck, looking up at the moon, passing a joint back and forth as we talked about nothing and everything. Once Sienna shared her hopes and dreams with me, her version of happily ever after, any desire I felt for her shriveled up and died.

I'm leaving here.

I have it all planned out.

So anyone who thinks happiness resides in this little backwoods corner of Pennsylvania, white picket fence, two kids, chairing the freaking PTA and running bake sales? Not for me. And given that a whopping sixteen percent of people in this county hold a bachelor's degree—true, I looked it up—there's always the chance a girl like Sienna would be fixing to start in on those plans sooner rather than later.

No thank you.

"I'm sure I'll run into you at some point. Garth and I are responsible for getting the kegs over to the party later on." I mention my friend's name on purpose. Garth has a thing for Sienna, so anything I can do to turn her head in his direction, I'm happy to oblige.

"You and Garth should come to the game first, though."

Upon hearing his name, he saunters over. "Where do you want me, sweetheart?"

Sienna looks to Garth and flashes him a smile. "I *want* you boys to come see our half-time show tonight."

"Think I'd miss you dancing around in that cute little outfit?" He pushes me back square in the chest, knocking me a step off balance. "I don't know about this faggot, but I'll be there."

Garth doesn't mean to be a dick—not all the time, anyway. He's just a clumsy giant who doesn't know his own strength. And I choose to let the gay thing slide as well. Sienna is still smiling his way, meaning there's a chance she might be off my back for good, and I've recently decided that correcting someone for a gay slur in this ass backwards corner of the world generally isn't worth the effort.

I did go to the basketball game. Knew I was going even before Sienna brought it up. I heard the girls talking about it yesterday, razzing each other about whose performance was going to kill it, cheerleaders versus dance team. I talk a good game, even when I'm just talking to myself in my own head, but I knew I'd be there. The chance to see Charlotte was a draw in and of itself, but to see Charlotte dancing? Yeah, wild horses and all that.

Not that I know anything about dancing, but she was the best one out there. I was by the exit, tucked off to the side. I had a clear view of her, but she couldn't have seen me. Out there she looked confident, like she was born to move to the music that way. God, she was so beautiful I couldn't take my eyes off her.

So I was a frustrated, broody bastard by the time everyone started crowding into Tyler's place later that night, convinced I should have just stayed home. Unlike most of these clowns, I need to be up bright and early. I was having my two beers and then bailing. But then she walked in with Sienna and Skylar. She'd washed off her makeup and changed out of the little outfit she was sporting during their show, but the sight of her still made me sweat. I could feel her eyes on me throughout the night, too. It made me self-conscious. I was relieved when I looked around at one point and didn't see her. I wanted her home, safe, out of reach from the one or two untrustworthy boys here who wouldn't hesitate to look upon her as easy prey.

I'm thankful for the blast of cold air that hits my face when I leave the cramped trailer. I nearly trip over Charlotte, who's holding her friend's hair away from her face, rubbing her back and whispering soothing words as her friend dry heaves. She's being nothing but kind and generous, but I can't help myself. I'm angry. This girl is taking hold of me and I do not welcome the feeling.

"Let me guess, first party and you drank yourselves senseless. Not very original."

Charlotte fixes me with a glare and hisses, "Do you mind?" Then she gestures with her chin, dismissing me. "Keep walking."

Her friend may be shitfaced, but Charlotte is clear-eyed and lucid. Hmm. She's got her hands full because unless she drove here herself, no one inside is fit to take them home. And she's a ways from home. Has to make it all the way over to the right side of the tracks. Boo freaking hoo.

Aw, shit. I can't seem to move. I'm just standing in place, flipping my key chain around my index finger, listening to her friend make these disgusting belching puke noises.

I cave. "Do you need me to help get her home?"

As her friend flops down on the bottom step and says,

"Yeah, I gotta get home," Charlotte squeezes her eyes shut and shakes her head.

"I'm fine to drive. I wouldn't offer otherwise."

The hurt look she delivers when she shakes her head again makes me feel like a failure, like I've wounded her. I swallow the feeling down and shake it off. I don't need this. "Suit yourself."

Her voice is so small I can barely make out the words when she says, "It's just…I already called for a ride." I turn at that and she cracks a sad half-smile. "But thank you."

I imagine the expression I return is the same.

I look for Charlotte the next morning but she's missing in action. And that bum Rudy Wallace is practically pacing in front of the diner by the time Sunday afternoon rolls around and there's still no sign of her.

Chapter Four

CHARLOTTE

It's the most awkward family reunion imaginable. I think on it for the better part of an hour, but can't remember how long it's been since the four of us were in one room together.

I'm the only one who comes to see her. My father and brother have gone on with their lives. They act as if she died years ago and I used to hate them for it. I believed in miracles, and I could prove I still held on to hope by sitting vigil at her bedside, combing her hair and painting her nails.

I used to talk to her. I'd tell her what was going on in my life, ask her opinion when I had a problem. Or I'd ask her questions about our family, things I couldn't sort out on my own. All the while I knew it was pointless. She has no answers for me.

So I come less frequently now—once a month at best since I started high school. Most of the nurses are really nice, but one or two of them, with their false smiles and cheery comments— *Your momma's going to be so happy to have some company today!*

—they make me feel ashamed for the way I've been neglecting her. During my last visit I encountered one of those nurses. She passed a seemingly harmless remark about how much I'd grown, that she hardly recognized me. But it was her tone, the way she said it. She might as well have told me I'm no more than a stranger to my own mother because I don't care enough to come see her regularly. God, it burned. And she had no right. That lady doesn't know what it's like to pine for the kind of mother every other teenage girl has, only to sit here and stare at a corpse that refuses to die.

On that very day I decided to let my father and brother off the hook, realizing we all handle tragedy and grief in our own way. I was surely no better than them.

That last visit took place on my birthday. I wanted to show her my car keys, or maybe I just wanted to sit with someone on my special day. I definitely wanted something more than the casual toss of keys on the table and the *Happy birthday, kid* my father threw my way before heading off to work. After leaving the nursing home that afternoon, I went home and ate a pint of chocolate ice cream while binge-watching some ridiculous reality show where spoiled, obnoxious kids plan their sweet sixteen celebrations for the better part of a year. It's not like I wanted some over the top party where I changed my outfit three times and had a famous rapper performing just for me— hell no, I'd hate that. I'd have been satisfied with blowing out some candles on a store-bought cake.

Today we're all gathered here because my mother has pneumonia. My father got a call sometime last night, letting him know his wife might not have much time left. He was probably in bed with his secretary when he answered the call.

I cannot bring myself to step foot inside the dealership now, not since my father started dating this one. Liza is only a few years older than my brother. She dresses in tight clothes, dons a full face of makeup every day, and wears the gaudy jewelry my father has gifted her from my mother's jewelry box. I wanted to scream and rage the first time I saw a gold bracelet of my mother's on her wrist. It looked so wrong. It *is* wrong. But I don't do that. I'm quiet, I'm obedient, I don't rock the boat. Instead, I went home and sifted through all my mother's belongings, taking anything that held sentimental value. I can't believe Liza would want anything of hers anyway. If he proposes, would she *want* that engagement ring? I left it in the jewelry box, sure in the knowledge that it would curse my union if I ever did decide to go and get married someday.

He's a tall man, my father, and he's imposing, but he looks like a balding, chubby, fawning fool standing next to her. And she's ridiculous—laughs at everything he says. When she's not batting her eyelashes at my father, she's staring at her gel manicured nails as if they hold the secrets of the universe.

There is one thing that I do have to thank Liza for. Her presence saves me from having to work alongside my father and brother. The one time Dad suggested I work at the dealership answering phones, I shot back in a sweet as sugar tone, "No thanks, Liza seems to have everything you need covered." That was the end of that. Maybe it was a cheap shot, but sometimes I believe I'm doing him a service. He needs a reminder, someone to tell him he's wrong to dishonor my mother.

The air in the room is stale, and the only sound echoing off the walls is the wet, sucking noises my mother makes as she struggles to take in air. My mother was intubated, but they removed the tube earlier this morning. Her eyes are closed. Her chest rises and falls. Lying in that bed, so thin you can practically see the bones beneath the skin of her forearms and fingers, I've never seen her look so fragile.

My father has been sitting in the same chair for hours, staring out the window. My brother, meanwhile, is in constant motion. He's walking in and out of the room, pacing, making phone calls, distracting himself. They're both waiting for the doctor to make his rounds and give us some news, perhaps a timeline. Maybe he'll tell my father he can go home. He wants someone official to let him off the hook. Both of them are itching to get out of here. Can I really blame them?

I busy myself, rubbing cream into her hands and feet. I look like the dutiful daughter right now, but I'm no better than they are. I'm just going through the motions. I may be physically tending to my dying mother, but my mind is entirely elsewhere.

Daisy's parents were pissed when Wes brought us to their doorstep, having driven us home in a squad car. I've never seen them mad—not ever. I imagine Daisy isn't having a very pleasant weekend, but it serves her right. The girl took every shot handed her way. I couldn't even get Daisy's attention when I was ready to leave. No, I had to wait until she stumbled outside and spewed chunks. Then I had to call Wes when I realized we had no way to get home. He was the last person I wanted to call but my options were limited. My father was typically occupied with Liza on Friday nights, and I would have walked the five miles home with Daisy on my back in a downpour before calling my brother for help. And Wes was good about the whole thing—better than good. There was no lecture, and when I asked, he looked at me as if I'd grown an extra head when he assured me he would never tell my brother. It put me at ease, erased the concerns I still had over that weird goodnight kiss he laid on me last weekend. He was in good cop, concerned friend mode last night, and I was grateful.

At least Daisy had fun. I was too fixated on Simon to enjoy

myself. And if she wasn't all giggly and talking too loud at the party, I would have pointed out to her that Simon does not scowl all the time. No, I was watching him, watching him smile with lazy indifference and ooze charm when he was surrounded by his people.

It's weird. He doesn't play sports but he's friends with all the athletes. The girls flock to him even though he doesn't seem like the type to pursue them in return. The stoners are his buddies and I *know* focus and determination when I see it—he doesn't partake on a regular basis. He barely even drank from the red cup in his hand.

Simon is an enigma. He's at the center of everything but on the fringe at the same time. Everyone is his friend but there's something about him that screams loner. Maybe that's why I'm drawn to him. He keeps people at arm's length, like me, and I want to know why.

Is he looking for me at the diner this morning?

I hope so.

When the doctor enters the room, the three of us stand in unison like we're performing some bizarre synchronized routine. We look ridiculous. Collectively we're guilty, sad, angry and tired. The verdict? She may not last the night. My father nods his head, half listening as the doctor drones on, describing her condition in detail.

I know what he's thinking. We've been down this road before, been told she's on death's doorstep only to bear witness, mystified and bewildered, as she makes a—well, you can't really call it a recovery when you're in a vegetative state. Anyway, the last time this happened was over two years ago. Told the end was imminent, my father went ahead and contacted the funeral home to make arrangements. And I see it in his eyes now, he's not convinced. He nods his head, tells the doctor to contact him if her condition worsens, blah, blah, blah. He wants to go home. So does my brother.

I want to stay, though. Something is telling me this is the end.

"You sure, honey?"

Honey. The endearment and the tenderness in his voice are so foreign to me that my eyes mist. I swallow the emotion down. "Yeah, Dad, you guys go. There's no point in all of us sitting here. I'm just gonna hang out."

"All right." He's got his coat on in seconds flat. "I'll ride with Christian." Handing me his car keys, he leans down and kisses my forehead as I fight back the urge to weep. "You call me if you need me."

Chapter Five

SIMON

Her mother is dead.

Her mother? I sift through my memories of those days, but can't picture a woman sitting behind that smug piece of shit in the courtroom. I always assumed he didn't have a mother, as only someone who'd never experienced a mother's love could carry himself the way he did.

Christian Mason sat there for all *two* days of his sham trial, dressed in a tailored suit next to his slick attorney, smirking like the conceited, entitled asshole that he is. His father sat behind him, first row in the gallery. He never looked our way. We sat first row too, right behind the assistant district attorney who interviewed one witness after another without a trace of enthusiasm—none whatsoever.

It was clear that each and every person who took the stand was in the Masons' back pocket. No one saw anything. Couldn't be certain who it was they saw swinging the bat. Even the woman who'd dialed 911 as they were beating my brother to a bloody pulp was suddenly plagued by amnesia. And the prosecutor asked no hard questions. There was nothing akin to an interrogation and he didn't question anyone's integrity. It was nothing like those *Law and Order* reruns I used to watch, I'll tell you that.

I heard about it on Tuesday, listening in as Sienna and the girls discussed taking up a collection to send flowers. The funeral was the next morning and they were asking permission from the principal to attend.

For a split second I was relieved to hear the news. I'd nearly driven by her house after school on Monday, out of my head with worry. Two days of not showing up to the diner and then no sign of her at school. I looked out for her in the morning and then took a casual stroll through the cafeteria during her lunch period. I didn't see her or her friend. I was beating myself up for the way I acted on Friday night. Maybe if I'd been a little nicer she would have accepted my offer for a ride home. But I was being stupid. In this county, two rich girls gone missing would've been top news. Search parties would have been combing the foothills by now and they would have dragged our stretch of the Monongahela River.

Over the past three days I've had plenty of time to reflect. I've reluctantly admitted to myself that I feel something for this girl. In the end, though, none of it matters. Even if she does have an interest in me—and there's really not so much as one iota of evidence to prove that theory—nothing will come of it. I'm leaving, that's certain, and her family's hatred for me and mine is matched only by my hatred for them. Hell, even if I did want to offer her my condolences, there's no way I'd be welcome within a mile of that church tomorrow.

And I have other things to focus on.

Last week I nailed down my scholarship to Northwestern.

With the help of Mr. Vargas, my honors program advisor, I'd put together a kick-ass application. His connections also got me an interview with a wealthy benefactor, a lawyer who seemed sympathetic to my plight and impressed with my drive to improve the lives of others.

I wasn't looking to pimp out my brother's life story for my own benefit, but in a way I suppose I had done just that. But it was necessary, a means to an end. Something clicked the day I sat in that courtroom and heard the judge proclaim there was no evidence to proceed with a trial for Christian Mason. That old saying, *Money talks, shit walks*? Truer words were never spoken. I believed Christian could have bashed my brother's skull in right then and there, right in front of the jury box, and he still wouldn't have been convicted. While not one year later, my brother would stand trial and be convicted for possession with intent to distribute, the very same painkillers he was prescribed and became addicted to after he was nearly killed at the hands of the Masons.

With his court appointed attorney, he sat there and listened to his doomed fate in a threadbare second-hand suit that hung off his thin, wasted frame. So fucking unfair.

The only thing that gives me peace is to believe that someday I'll be sitting next to someone wrongly accused, fighting on their behalf. Or even better, that I'll be wearing the black robe and pounding the gavel, making sure people like the Masons don't get a free pass just because they have money and privilege on their side.

Charlotte seems like a sweet girl despite her last name, and I feel bad knowing she's hurting, I guess, but she'll survive. And like I said, I have more important things to worry about.

. . .

The drive over to Somerset takes just under an hour. My mother and I make the trip once a month. Occasionally my mother's boyfriend comes along for the ride, but typically it's just the two of us. It used to be a sad occasion, these monthly visits, but like everything else in this life, good and bad, you adapt.

He got five years when he was convicted. If he would have just toed the line, Timmy probably would have been out by now, but drugs are as readily available inside prison as they are out here. He had a year tacked onto his sentence for dealing inside, and now he'll be serving that full term, screwing himself out of any chance for an early parole.

Three down, three to go.

He's been telling us he's clean, and for the past few months, he looks it. Even earned his GED and started taking community college classes this year, so I'm hopeful.

"You're looking good, little brother."

"So are you, Timmy. How's it going?"

I don't say it, but looking around the visiting room, I see an increased guard presence, and the people, both the inmates and their visitors, are more street than I've noticed in the past. I mean, this is a prison, those of us who have loved ones in here don't typically hail from the upper echelons of society and all, but still, I don't like the energy coming off some of these people.

"Keeping my head low, staying out of trouble." Timmy looks up to see my mother still busy getting snacks from the vending machine before continuing. "As you've noticed, the clientele is changing around here."

"Yeah, and what's with all the guards? Gotta be twice as many keeping watch in here than usual."

"Getting the overflow from Lewisburg and those boys

don't play. A lot more gang bullshit in here now. The guards are so tight lately, they'll shackle you and throw you in solitary just for looking at them sideways."

"Assholes."

"I don't know, Simon," he says, shaking his head. "They're just people, people who took a real shit job...Maybe the worst job on the planet. They're taking care of their families, trying to do right, I guess. And some of the bullshit they have to deal with in here?" He offers me a tired smile. "It'd turn the Dalai Lama into a hateful man."

My mother approaches, her hands full with cans of soda and these cheese cracker snacks that my brother used to eat when he lived at home. She gets them every time we're here. Before she sits, I ask him, "So you're just keeping your head down?"

"Yeah. I'm working in the library now and spending my free time doing those online classes."

"I'm so proud of you," my mother says as she slides a soda and the snacks across the table towards him.

He smiles at my mother and shakes his head, because really? Only a mother could tell a convicted felon she's proud of him while sitting in the visiting room of a correctional facility.

"Yes, Timmy, I am. You're turning it around for yourself... Taking classes, mentoring the boys who are trying to get their GEDs."

He shrugs. "Well I'm doing it out of spite. It makes me feel better to know I'll be getting my college degree thanks to the generosity of the Pennsylvania Corrections Bureau."

"What are you majoring in?"

Sometimes things are so sad that I smile at the irony of it all. Here's my mother, talking like Timmy's heading off to freshman orientation on the grounds of some leafy, idyllic campus, while every time I look up, I take in his fellow inmates, some of whom look like jacked-up soulless killing machines.

"Earth to Simon," Timmy says as he snaps his fingers in front of my face.

"Sorry, what?"

He looks over his shoulder, taking in my view. "I'm good, I promise," he says softly. "So, I want to hear about you. How are your prospects looking?"

"I got the scholarship."

If we were home, I'm certain Timmy would've let out a whoop and grabbed me into a bear hug. In this environment, though, you condition yourself, school your expressions. You never look to draw attention, so Timmy just nods and says, "I knew you would."

He's happy for me, and for some reason that hurts like a motherfucker.

"I'm leaving mid-August. I need to settle in and find myself a job before classes start."

"Does the scholarship cover room and board?"

"Most of it," I lie. I'm seriously stressed out about the amount of money I'm going to need just to cover my books and living expenses, but I'm not letting my mother in on that. She's got enough on her plate already.

My mother takes my hand. "I'm glad you'll be near Michael. And you could always live with him if you don't like the dorms, right?"

"I'm sure the dorms will be fine." I check with Tim and see he's smiling too. "You have any access to social media in here?" I ask him.

"No, those sites are blocked. But Mike sends me letters, he's been preparing me."

"He's careful about what he posts but it's pretty obvious. I suppose he's gearing up for a big announcement."

"Yeah, like we don't already know." Timmy laughs, shaking his head. "I should just put him out of his misery...Ask him when the wedding is."

The two of us are sharing a laugh as my mother looks between the two of us, lost. "What are you two talking about?"

Tim cocks his head to the side, fixing my mother with a smile. "We're just wondering when Mike is finally going to bust out of the closet."

She closes her eyes and pinches the bridge of her nose. "I know. He talks about his good friend Brandon all the time. Does he think we're foolish?" She looks between us. "Does he think we won't accept him?"

Both of us reach out at the same time and take one of her hands.

"No, Mom," Tim says. "He knows we love him. He's just gotta go about this in his own way. When he's ready, he'll tell us."

"Well, I may be crashing at his place for a few weeks in August, so I'm thinking the cat's gonna be outta the bag pretty soon."

"I could wring that boy's neck...Running off like that to Chicago."

"Yeah, well, if I was gay, last place on Earth I'd want to live is Fayette County."

"Simon's right, Mom. People in our town made it clear his kind wasn't welcome."

"People knew in high school?"

"No one knew for certain, but people can be assholes." Timmy looks off into the distance when he adds, "Can make your life miserable if they want to."

The buzzer sounds, the deafening noise droning on for a full thirty seconds. I should be used to it by now, but it startles me every time.

"I love you," Mom whispers as I fix my brother with a brief look that tells him the same. I see his face change, morph into an impassive mask. Showing emotion won't do you any favors in this place.

As he lines up with the others, I notice a bruise blooming purple and yellow at the base of his neck, right in the back where his collar meets skin. I wish I never saw it. Knowing there's nothing I can do to protect him makes me feel worthless.

* * *

CHARLOTTE

Two days ago we buried my mother.

Two days, and the mourning period is officially over. My father announced he was taking the weekend, "heading to the casino," and Christian is throwing a party at our house tonight.

Dad sat with me this morning for an uncomfortable minute, watching as I scarfed down a bagel before school, then asked if I was all right with him leaving. The question and the concern in his voice caught me off guard. My father doesn't make a habit of asking for my permission.

And what was I to say? *Please stay, Daddy. You just buried Mom. Remember her, your wife? So yeah, it would be uncharacteristically decent of you to stay home and comfort your children this weekend instead of fist pumping at the craps table and sucking down martinis with your barely-legal girlfriend.*

Nothing would have convinced him to change his plans anyway.

The smell of his cologne turned my stomach. I took note of the brand new suit paired with leather sneakers, his shirt unbuttoned at the neck, no tie. He was going for upscale, hip yet casual. I could have laughed out loud. My middle-aged father following the trends, emulating the look his favorite ESPN commentators sported—men who were more than twenty years his junior. And stay or go, what did it matter? It's not like the two of us would be spending quality time together anyway.

"I don't mind, Dad."

"Hey," he said, waiting for me to look up. "I'm sorry, sweetheart. I'm doing my best. We've all been dealt a crappy hand, right?" The asinine gambling reference nearly sent me over the edge, but I bit my lip and fought to keep from crying. He wouldn't appreciate the melodrama. I focused on the poppy seeds dotting my plate, nodding repeatedly through the uncomfortable one-sided exchange instead. "You're working this weekend?"

"Yeah...Saturday and Sunday."

"Ok, I'll see you."

Without a backward glance he made for the door, our father-daughter moment officially over.

Now it's past midnight, the music is cranking, and the intermittent sounds of girls laughing and guys yelling above the din have me convinced I won't get more than an hour's sleep before my alarm goes off at five-thirty. I'm crying tears of loss and fatigue when I hear a knock at my door.

"Charlie?" The door opens and Wes sticks his face into the small opening the chain lock allows. "Charlie, it's me."

I throw the covers off and pad across the room. My instinct

is to lie there pretending to sleep until he goes away, but at the same time I don't want to be alone. Sliding the chain free, I turn back and get under the covers again.

"What's up, Charlie girl?" He closes the door behind him carefully and comes over to sit at the foot of my bed. "Aw, shit. I was just gonna ask how you're doing," he leans over and wipes a thumb across my damp cheek, "but I can see those tears. I told your brother he shouldn't have people over but Christian's a dumbass. Guess I don't have to tell you that." That draws a nervous giggle from me. "There she is," he whispers, smiling.

"Why are you friends with him?"

"Who?"

"My brother." I pull the sheet up, using it to wipe my eyes. "I can't figure it out. You're normal, you're nice, and he's—"

"He wasn't always this way. I've known him all my life. You were only seven when your mother had the stroke. We were thirteen. He was a different person before your mom got sick. Don't you remember how it used to be? He was always teasing you, yeah, but he was good to you, looked out for you."

"Looked out for me?" I roll my eyes. "No, can't say I remember that."

"I'm not gonna lie and tell you I don't want to beat his ass now and then. I see how he treats you and it kills me. I tell him he needs to make sure you're all right, that he needs to keep an eye on you now that you're grown." Wes looks away from me when he adds, "You're sixteen now."

I scoot up, sitting back against the headboard. "I'm invisible to both of them." And then I really start crying. No, I weep. I weep big, fat, ugly tears. He hands me a shirt from the floor to wipe at my runny nose and eyes. Catching my breath between words, I let it all out. "I'm all alone now. She's gone, my father's always gone, and Christian...I *wish* he was gone. I hate him." Wes is shaking his head, but I'm not about to listen to him defend my brother. "I *hate* him. When you're around, yeah, he's rude and bossy, but when it's just the two of us, he's worse."

"What do you mean?"

"He barks orders at me, tells me to shut up, tells me I'm getting fat, tells me—"

"Are you fucking kidding me?"

I cross my arms over myself, ashamed of the way he looks at me now. I shouldn't have opened my mouth. It's better not to rock the boat, not to make trouble. I still have two years before I graduate from high school. Two years to save every penny I make so I can get the hell away from here once I have my diploma. Why am I suddenly confiding in Wes?

"Look at me." Wes coaxes my chin so that I have no choice but to follow the command. "You're beautiful. Please tell me you know that."

I don't answer because I don't care. Whether or not I'm beautiful isn't a question I wrestle with. I'm not like Sienna or those other girls. Even Daisy fusses over her outfits and hair in a way that makes her seem foreign to me. I'm in my own head most of the time, caught in the same kind of purgatory as my mother.

And she's gone, so now what? *Now I just keep on going.* The thought leaves me feeling so empty, so isolated. My body shakes with the force of my sobs. He leans in and holds me close to his chest. His hands rub up and down my back slowly, soothing me as he whispers words I can't make out.

I turn and lean into him, wrapping my arms around his neck. At first he grips me tighter, pressing me into him, but a moment later he drops his arms and stands abruptly. I look up, the loss of his warmth like a blast of ice cold air. Wes walks to my window and presses his palms against the pane. He hangs his head, shaking it slowly from side to side.

"Wes?"

He looks at me with a pained smile before turning to leave my room. "You get to sleep. I'll get rid of these idiots."

I want to stop Wes, to warn him, but I don't. The last time I asked Christian to turn the music down during one of his parties it didn't go well. He grabbed me, and with one hand spanning the length of my jaw, he walked me in reverse, forcing me back into my room. I tripped over one of my books when he pushed me inside, so startled that I didn't put my hands out to break my own fall. I had a lump on the back of my head for a week afterwards.

Wes peeks his head in a moment later. "Get up and lock the door behind me."

I do as I'm told. My heart is beating faster, anticipating conflict. The music goes off. I hear people talking in hushed tones with a little laughter mixed in. No yelling. The front door opens and closes a few times and then the house is silent. I lie awake for some time, waiting for the fallout that never happens.

After my first trip outside to give Rudy his buttered roll and hot chocolate, I stay indoors. I take my breaks at a corner booth in the back, so tired that I rest my head against the table. Marley, the den mother of our diner crew, asks if I need her to cover my tables. I could go home early, take the next day off if I want.

I don't want to go home.

Christian was awake when I came out of my room ready to

leave for work this morning. He looked up at me, pausing as he cleared the counter of plastic cups and beer cans. His hair was messy and his eyes were bloodshot. He looked out the front window and said, "You leave this early? It's still dark outside."

"Um, yeah, the diner opens at six."

"It's not safe, you driving over to that side of town in the dark. I'm just saying, you could make extra money working with me and Dad."

"It's fine." What was with the small talk, the sudden concern for my welfare? "I'm not working there, not working with Liza. I like the diner."

He looked back down at the black trash bag nodding his head. I stood there waiting, thinking he might need me or something. He was grieving too, I reminded myself, and for a brief moment he seemed, I don't know, remorseful maybe.

I startled when his head whipped back in the direction of the hallway. "Get dressed and get out," he ordered the girl who'd suddenly materialized in his bedroom doorway. Her eyes were wide, her face smeared with last night's eye makeup. She was shifting her weight from one foot to another, wearing nothing but my brother's shirt. Clearly she had to pee. When she looked towards the bathroom door, he raised his voice. "I said I want you gone."

As she scurried back into his room to get her things, Christian looked to me, challenging me to say something. I wanted to tell him he was being an asshole, that was obvious, but I also just wanted to ask him why he was so angry all the time. I felt sympathy for him in that moment, which made next to no sense.

On the drive to work, I tried and failed to conjure up an image of a happy child, a loving brother. I don't remember the person Wes described to me. But his words ring true. My mother's stroke, although I hardly remember the actual event, changed everything and every one of us. Home was suddenly a very sad and lonely place to be once she went to stay in the hospital. I knew it couldn't have been easy on my brother. He saw it through the eyes of a teenager, so he saw more than I did. And then a few years later, whatever happiness remained was tied to his big dreams. Those were taken from him too.

A paper tablecloth, a giant tray of sandwiches wrapped in colored cellophane, paper plates, unopened soda bottles, a cake and a platter of cookies. Maybe it's the memory of that night that keeps me from turning my back on my brother, no matter how hateful he can be.

The accident left my brother with a shattered leg, his all but guaranteed football scholarship shot to hell. I was only eleven and started staying after school most days, the tension in our home too much to take. I'd hear my father giving false, cheery updates to the college coaches recruiting Christian, only to hear him slam a palm into the wall once the calls disconnected. After the surgery, physical therapists came and went, Christian and my father dismissing every one that contradicted their mandate that Christian be back on the field before playoffs. My brother hurled a water glass at one, barely missing the man's head before it smashed against his bedroom door. That therapist's crime was telling Christian he should focus on going to college, not on playing college football.

Everything was set for a party, like we were expecting a crowd, but there were only four of us in the living room. Three really—I was hiding in a nook off to the side, silently taking in the awkward scene.

Christian was showered and dressed in clean sweats, even wearing his regular sneakers. He wanted Coach to believe that it was all good, that he was just fine, that he was ready to get back out there and lead the team to the state championship.

No one ate. Christian barked at me right before Coach knocked on the door, ordering me to remove his crutches from the room, so he couldn't get up to make himself a plate even if he wanted to. But both Christian and my father were too busy to eat anyway. Too busy with the effort of plastering on their winning smiles, with making small talk, with putting a positive spin on Christian's recovery.

I almost felt bad for Coach. It was clear from his expression that he knew the score, knew he had to focus his energy on the other boys who still had a shot at being recruited. He was only humoring my father with this visit. He begged off when they both gestured for him to dig in, my father making a show of slicing open the cellophane even as Coach made excuses, something about having to take his daughter to Girl Scouts. My father didn't let up, making two plates and forcing one into Coach's hands.

I watched my father take a big bite of his own sandwich, forcing himself to chew something that probably tasted like battery acid at that point.

Christian works for my father now. He dresses in cheap suits and sells cars to people who can't afford them, offering credit with terms no sane person would ever accept. Knowing Christian, he lives for that part of the job, for that exact moment when he knows he's succeeded at putting some sucker between a rock and a hard place. I'm sure he enjoys repossessing vehicles twice as much as he enjoys selling them.

He's not a happy man, that's plain to see. Without football, he had no need or desire to attend college—that's what he tells everyone anyway. He likes to present himself to the world as Christian Mason, independently wealthy heir to an automobile dealership dynasty. As if. In truth, he had no aptitude for college, barely eked his way through high school. And our family business, while it doesn't lose money as far as I know, isn't exactly going to set either one of us up on Park Avenue.

Nowadays I try to avoid him in the mornings, leaving for school half an hour before I need to. He stomps around, cussing under his breath in a general state of dissatisfaction. Then Christian stands in front of the large mirror that hangs over the couch in our living room, yanking on the end of his tie as he works to make the knot. At twenty-two his middle has already gone soft, a small bit of fat pushing over the waistband of the pants he insists on buying. He needs a bigger size, but I'd sooner take up residence in a lion's den than suggest it.

His mere presence sucks the air from the room. If I'm around, I become a target. *The house is filthy* (Christian and his friends make the mess). *There's no reason you shouldn't be cooking dinner for the family at night...We work all day* (my father never comes home for dinner, so I'd be cooking for Christian and Christian alone). *You should stop wasting your time with that "dance shit" and start taking care of this house* (yes, at sixteen being a homemaker is my dream). I'd gladly wake up at four in the morning if it meant avoiding a run-in with Christian. He hasn't been my brother in a long time.

He's like a simmering pot of water with the lid on, always threatening to bubble over. He can spin tales to his friends and to the stupid girls who try in vain to get close to him, but I see through the act. I know him. In his weaker moments, drunk and tired, he sometimes lets it out—the sadness that threatens to crush him, the disappointment of unfulfilled dreams.

I do feel for him, but if you listen to Christian tell it, Timothy Wade is to blame for every wrong turn his life has taken. And when he gets on that thread, no one around him is safe. There are nights he sits out back with his loser buddies drinking beer. I can sense when it's about to happen, when he's about to turn. Ribbing between friends becomes personal, his voice rises above the rest, the others try to pacify the petulant baby, and bottles invariably smash. He's an angry drunk, my father says, shaking his head as I sweep up the shards the next morning. *A chip off the old block*, I'm always tempted to say back, but I don't dare.

Still in my corner booth, I stare at Simon through the window. He's loading a flatbed with sheetrock for an older man. I know the pieces are heavy, having seen my dad and brother work together to carry the same kind of materials when they started the garage renovation last year that they still haven't finished. But Simon labors alone, and waves the older man off, smiling but refusing him when he tries to press some bills into his hand for a tip.

He's being kind. I've seen that side of him before, I've witnessed his goodness. But I've also been at the receiving end when his alter ego is in charge. He's capable of cruelty. I think of the other night when he offered me and Daisy a ride home. He couldn't even be civil towards me when he was trying to do something nice.

I've never done anything to deserve his scorn. From what little I've heard, I know his family is a mess, but how is that on me? Tim Wade, I'm told, sits in a state prison cell to this day— dealing to feed his habit landed him there. I can't say I feel sorry for him, karma being a bitch and all that. The middle brother doesn't live here anymore. I've never heard the back story on him, only that he was a loner, or a "faggot emo weirdo" as my sensitive, enlightened older brother tagged him. Simon's family is poor, I'm assuming, but no one is truly wealthy here. No one has it easy. Maybe he feels sorry for himself while he sees me as some trust fund princess, even though nothing could be further from the truth.

Taking one last look at the hardware store as I haul my tired body into the car, I decide that Simon Wade can take his rotten attitude and shove it. I'm done looking his way, done pining for that sour-faced jerk. I'm just done.

I tell myself all this, knowing it's nothing but lies. There's a thread between us, fragile and shaky, but I feel it, feel the connection. I know I'd give my right arm just to have him look across the street and meet my eyes, to truly see me. I'd give anything for Simon Wade to talk to me. To share his sadness, then hold me and listen as I share mine.

Chapter Six

SIMON

March never brings springtime to this part of Pennsylvania. The winters drag on well into April, wet and cold and depressing.

We saw Timmy last weekend, knowing he was recently released from the infirmary following a fight. His arm was in a cast and he had the look of a spooked cat when he limped towards us. He doesn't say it outright because he doesn't want to alarm my mother, just plays it off as an "episode" in the rec yard, but I know he was jumped. Mom's hands shake as she takes the coins from her purse to buy him some snacks from the vending machine. She knows it too.

"What's going on?" I press when she gets up from the table.

He shakes his head. "You can't refuse your cellmate assignment and some of these guys are fucking crazy. I mean for real, they're mentally ill. The guy who did this," he gestures to the healing gash on his forehead and then looks down at his arm, "he was screaming like a crazy, strung-out motherfucker when they brought him by, introducing the two of us like we were gonna be best buddies."

"They know the guy's violent and they don't care?" Timmy raises an eyebrow, shooting me a look like I'm a naïve child. "Is there someone me and Mom can talk to while we're here?"

"No." He lets out a tired breath. "There's nothing you can do for me."

My mother doesn't say a word for the entire ride home. I'm quiet too, silently begging for mercy, for my brother's safety, for his life. Raising my prayers to a god who isn't listening.

I'm still in a funk by the time Friday rolls around. It also happens to be my birthday, but I'm in no mood to be reminded. So when I walk up to my locker and I'm ambushed by Sienna and a few of her friends bearing balloons, cupcakes and good wishes, I have to repress a sudden urge to rage, to destroy, to take the tray of cupcakes and smash them against the wall.

"How does it feel to be eighteen?" one asks me.

Fucking peachy. The words are pushing past my lips, itching to break free, but with some effort I manage a tight smile. "The same, I guess."

"I know, right?" Sienna says. "You can already drive, but you can't have a drink. What's the big whoop about turning eighteen?"

"You can enlist," Garth offers.

"*You* are not enlisting." Sienna pokes him in the chest. "Got that, mister?"

He grabs her finger and brings it up to his lips. "I'm not going anywhere."

Those two are an item now. Garth is asking her to the

prom. When he asked who I planned on taking, I told him the truth straight away so he'd back off.

The prom isn't in my budget. I truly don't know how I'm going to eat next year, so plunking down money on a tuxedo rental, flowers, prom tickets and whatever other bullshit goes into that night just isn't happening. Hell, I'm seriously considering skipping out on graduation because the school is asking for thirty-five dollars to cover the cost of those crappy cardboard caps and flimsy gowns.

"You can go to a strip club," Tyler adds, earning him a swat on the ass from his girl.

Skylar flips him off when she says, "I can go to a male strip club too, you know."

"You can vote now," one of the girls adds.

"You can gamble," another chimes in.

Gamble? My father was a gambler. More happy memories. "Gee, you're right," I deadpan. "Turning eighteen sure is swell. Thanks guys."

Garth keeps it up. "You can buy porn, you can get married—"

"You can get a tattoo!" Tyler looks to Skylar. "I'm definitely getting a tattoo this summer...Your name right across one of my ass cheeks."

Skylar smiles as Sienna scrunches up her nose. "Gross."

Garth comes in close and nods, gesturing down the hallway. "I know whose name you'd be tattooing over your heart, you big pussy."

I follow his gaze and my eyes land on her. Charlotte's fussing with her locker but it won't give. Some kid comes over and gets it open for her. She flashes him a grateful smile. He takes that as an invitation, sticking around to chat her up. Her look changes; it's subtle but I notice. She's being polite, smiling and answering his questions, but she's not into it. After my craptastic week from hell, this is the one thing that makes me feel like smiling.

As the bell rings, Garth pushes my shoulder. "Almost forgot…You can also get locked up for statutory rape now that you're eighteen."

I push back harder. "The fuck are you talking about?"

He can't contain his laughter. "I'm just screwing with you. I mean, I do notice that you stare at that pretty little thing *all* the time, but I can't figure out if it's because you're admiring her fine ass or hating on her. I'm pretty sure you'd never so much as talk to a Mason, let alone swap bodily fluids with one."

He claps me on the back and then turns as Sienna approaches. The bell rang a full minute ago but the seniors are no longer inclined to rush.

"The party is at our place tonight," she says, looking directly at me. "You're not going to freak out if we sing Happy Birthday, are you?"

"Not at all."

She looks genuinely surprised. "Really? I thought you'd be a total grump about it."

"I don't mind. I'm gonna be at work, so sing your little hearts out."

For that I take one right to the solar plexus, but she hits like she's not aiming to hurt me, so I just laugh.

"You're terrible," Sienna says over her shoulder, but she's smiling.

Garth watches her walk away. "I think I'm in lurve."

"Good luck with that," I say, heading off to see my advisor. He's got a lead on another academic grant. It's small from what he told me, might just cover my books for freshman year, but money is money and I need every cent I can get.

I go to knock but stop when I hear voices.

"No, I think you're being very proactive, Charlotte. The earlier you start working on your applications, the better."

"I need to earn a scholarship, Mr. Vargas."

Vargas hesitates for a moment. He's probably thinking what I'm thinking: poor little rich girl needs a scholarship like I need a box of tampons.

"Let's make an appointment for the end of next week. We'll plot out your schedule for next year, see what you can handle in terms of advanced placement courses, and we'll talk about some of the lesser known scholarships I've been researching. If you're willing to write the essays and put in the effort, I think we can make it work."

I hear a chair scape against the floor tiles. She's getting up. "Thank you, I really appreciate it."

"I'll see you Thursday during lunch period. Have a good weekend, Charlotte."

"You too."

She's sporting a broad smile as she exits the office, but it drops when she comes face to face with me. We shuffle, both moving in the same direction, trying in vain to get around one another.

"Sorry," I say, moving off to the side to let her pass.

She nods but her eyes won't meet mine. It kills, knowing I've given her good reason to be wary of me. Without thinking, I turn and grab her wrist. "I heard about your mother. I-I...I'm sorry."

Charlotte swallows as tears well in her eyes. "Thank you, Simon."

She looks down at her wrist then, because I still haven't let go. "Sorry," I say again, absently this time as I release my hold on her. I'm still buzzing and lightheaded, the sound of my name on her lips and the feel of her soft skin doing something powerful to me that I cannot define.

"Mr. Wade, are you out there?" Vargas calls from his office, bringing me back down to earth. I still haven't taken my eyes off her though, and now she's looking back at me. The moment probably lasts no more than three seconds, but it feels meaningful, important.

Her cheeks redden when she says, "See you tomorrow."

That night I dream of Charlotte. I picture her standing in the shallow end of the creek. She's wading in water up to her calves, wearing a sundress that skims her thighs. She's laughing and smiling at me as she kicks one leg out to splash water in my direction. I rush her and she shrieks as I throw her over my shoulder. *She's mine*, I'm telling myself, and I smile as I take us out deeper into the water, clamping one arm around her backside to keep her still. She's squirming and telling me to put her down, but she's playing with me. When I loosen my hold, she slides down the length of my body, both of us submerged chest deep now. She presses herself close and I drag her hips in even closer in response. I want her to feel me and she does, dragging in a breath when we make contact. "I love you," I tell her. And I feel it so deeply that my heart physically aches.

I wake up startled, one hand rubbing the center of my chest, the other wrapped firmly around my dick. I finish myself off before climbing out of bed. I'm tired, or sad, or maybe some combination of both. Standing under the steady stream of the shower, I understand that the dream represents reality: being close to her could bring me happiness like I've never known before, but it would most certainly bring both of us pain.

* * *

CHARLOTTE

Why do I keep dreaming of you?

That's what I want to ask him this morning. Most nights, even the night Wes held me in his arms and gave me comfort, it's Simon Wade I dream of.

In my dreams he's not the boy who shows himself to me in everyday life. No, in my dreams he's sweet. He smiles instead of grimacing, he's lighthearted instead of sullen. He holds me close instead of acting like the subtle brush of my skin burns worse than straight lye.

He's standing outside the hardware store. His chin is perched on hands that rest atop the broom he's holding but not using. He's lost in thought. He doesn't look happy or sad, just lost. I think he knows I'm standing out here too, but he won't acknowledge me. We're North and South Korea, locked into some sad, silent cold war.

I take another short break at ten and then another at one. He's always outside at the same time, it never fails. I look his way, hoping for something, but I'm never rewarded. I'm restless today though, something's off, and by the time my shift comes to a close I can feel it unraveling in me, angry and mean. So instead of turning right towards the parking lot, I march across the street and wait behind him while he moves a load of paving stones from a delivery truck. He makes three round trips to the truck, ignoring me as he hefts the stones to an area where it looks like they'll be setting up an outdoor furniture display. A patio dining set waiting to be assembled sits there with an umbrella still wrapped in plastic perched next to it. I have plenty of time to take it all in as I stand there like a fool. I don't even know why I came over here. I have no plan, no idea of what to say. I turn to go when I feel the first tear threaten.

Get it together. You are not crying over him.

"Did you need something?" He's caught up to me in the middle of the street that divides us, taking my elbow to stop me from moving, from running away.

I shake him off. "No, I don't need anything from you."

"That's for the best," he says to my back, and that pisses me off.

"Why do you hate me?"

His eyes go wide for a split second, but then he's back in control, cold and impassive. "I don't even know you or think about you, so how could I possibly hate you?"

"You hate my family," I challenge.

"I do."

"Well, I was brought up to hate your family too, but I never bought into that. No one's a saint or a sinner. You should know that better than anyone."

My bold mouth and bravado abandon me when he takes one step closer. He towers over me, his expression menacing. "What exactly are you trying to say?"

"Just," I pause to catch my breath, "that your family, I mean, your brother's no angel." I'm so scared and nervous that I hardly know what I'm saying anymore. And he's waiting me out, making me suffer, squared off and staring at me with that all familiar look of disgust. "Your brother's negligence destroyed my brother's future."

"Simon."

"Be there in one minute," he answers his boss without turning back around.

"*Your* brother's future…That's all anyone in this county cared about after the accident, as if my brother was nothing, as if he hadn't lost everything too. They were on the same football team, both had college coaches recruiting them. My brother had just as much going for him as Christian Mason."

He steps even closer and forces my chin up with a rough finger. "Your brother is a piece of shit." He nods for emphasis. "When questions were asked, he acted like my brother all but ran him over instead of admitting to the fact that they were both out drinking together that night and decided to drag race like two seventeen-year-old idiots."

He laughs and smiles then, but it's wicked the way he does it. "I think Christian truly believes his own bullshit, believes he was wronged. I guess that's what happens when you're the golden boy and everyone's been blowing smoke up your ass your entire life. My brother was in the same hospital, but while yours was being visited by friends, by their coach and by every fucking hypocrite disguised as an upstanding member of the community, Timmy was being interrogated by the cops. I think if they could have framed Timmy, staged it as a hit and run or something, they would have, but there were too many witnesses."

I was always under the impression that Tim Wade was doing drugs the night of the accident. The thought spills out before I can censor myself. "He's a drug addict."

"Little girl, you don't know shit." He turns to go but doesn't make it more than two steps before he turns back around. "You know what? You're right, princess, my brother is a drug addict. He got hooked on painkillers after your brother made sure Timmy got what was coming to him. He spent three weeks in the hospital after they beat him and left him for dead...Your brother and his boys." His shoulders fall like the heavy weight of the memory is dragging him down. "I always thought it was ironic, your brother's name...He's got to be the least Christian-minded person on the face of God's green earth."

I feel like I've been smacked, like the air has been sucked from my lungs. "I-I didn't know."

"Like I said, you don't know shit."

He leaves me like that, shaking his head, face red with anger and eyes that express nothing but disappointment.

Daisy's mom took us shopping at the mall later on that afternoon and treated us to dinner. I think I pulled it off. I kept up with their conversation, commenting when it was expected and smiling on cue, but I was somewhere else entirely.

Filled with regret, I wish I'd had the courage to cross over. I should have taken those two small steps that separated us and wrapped him in my arms. I was scared of him in that moment, for sure, but I finally saw him. And then I was sorry, so very sorry. I understood now. I understood why he didn't trust, why he kept everyone at arm's length. I understood why he saw me as some out of touch, privileged princess. I was like everyone else in his eyes: prone to think the worst of the kid from the trailer park, while accepting the false innocence of the fortunate son—the Christian Masons of the world—without a second thought.

On Sunday I keep to my own side of the street, too ashamed to face Simon. I use the back door when my shift ends, slinking into my car and driving off without chancing a look in the direction of the hardware store.

When I hear voices cheering the team that just made a touchdown, I change course and use the back entrance to the house. I can't bear to see him, to see any of them. If what Simon said is true, then my brother is a pathetic excuse for a human being. When there's no one around to impress, when he drops the act, does he feel ashamed? He must. I want to believe that he feels remorse. I want to believe, I do.

Not an hour later, Wes peeks his head in and then makes his way over towards me smiling. I didn't think to lock my door tonight.

"I hated that book," he says as he lifts the spine to see the cover. "Couldn't get through it...Had some girl write my paper for me."

I have no energy for small talk. "Tell me about the accident, Wes. I want to know what happened."

He looks back to the door that he just closed a moment ago, making damn sure my brother is out of earshot. "What are you talking about?"

"My brother's accident. Tim Wade. What really happened that night?"

"Where's this coming from?"

"I've never heard the actual story. I don't really know how it happened."

He lets out a breath. "Tim Wade crashed his car into Christian's. That's all there is to it." He takes the book out of my hand, folds the page down to mark it, and smiles. Wes has decided the conversation is over. "I'm making a pizza run... Take a ride with me."

We're in his truck riding along a stretch of highway on our way back home. Since regaling me with every tiresome detail of his latest arrest on the way to the pizzeria—lamest diversion tactic ever—Wes has been quiet. His silence is confirmation in and of itself. If there was nothing to hide about that night, Wes wouldn't be staring out into the distance with the troubled look he's sporting.

"Come on," I plead on a weary breath. "Will you just tell

me? You and I both know there's a lot more to it than what you said back there."

He drags a hand through his hair. "You're digging up some painful memories. I'd advise you not to go asking your brother about any of this."

"I'm not asking my brother, I'm asking you." I stand my ground, crossing my arms over my chest to let him know I'm serious. "If you won't tell me, I'll ask someone else to fill in the blanks."

"There's nothing more to tell."

"Was Timothy Wade on drugs when he hit Christian or were they drag racing?"

He's fidgety, shifting in his seat and tapping a rhythm out on the steering wheel even though the radio isn't on.

"Wes, answer me. Were they friends when it happened?"

"We were all friends...Played football together all through high school."

"So what, you all turned on Tim Wade and backed my brother after it happened? Acted like Tim was the only one at fault?"

He shoots me a warning look and then stares ahead. It's a full minute later when he says, "It didn't seem like it back then, but now, yeah, that seems a like a pretty accurate summary of what went down."

"Did my brother try to kill him?"

Wes slows, pulls the truck over and shifts it into park. He studies me with a look that isn't the least bit friendly. "I suggest you choose your words very carefully, Charlie."

"I want to know...Did my brother beat Timothy Wade up so badly that he almost died?" I don't wait for him to answer before letting out a cheerless laugh. "I can totally picture it. Poor baby didn't get what he wanted so someone had to pay.

Someone else had to take the blame, right? Christian couldn't accept the fact that he was responsible, that he screwed it all up."

Wes's knuckles are white around the steering wheel and his jaw is tight. I remember Simon's words and it all clicks into place. "You all did it, didn't you?" Shaking my head, I whisper, "How many of you against one?" He doesn't answer. "Did you use bats, pipes? Or did you punch and kick his body lifeless?"

Wes's face, a face I never once saw harden in my life, is now cold and unforgiving. I undo my seatbelt and open the door to, I don't know, get some air or distance or something. The truck starts to move slowly. I jump to get out of the way, staring at the tailgate like a dumbfounded fool as he picks up speed. It doesn't sink in until a few moments later that Wes has left me out here alone.

Chapter Seven

SIMON

You don't know shit.

Those are the words I spat at her. And the truth is that she didn't know, she didn't know a damn thing about what happened back then. I could see it in her eyes, the realization. I was rewriting history for her right out there in the middle of the street. I can't keep from feeling just the slightest bit guilty that I've tarnished her opinion of her brother, being that she just lost her mother and all, but that's stupid and weak on my part. Christian Mason doesn't deserve to hide behind his lies.

I don't even know if she showed up to work yesterday because I kept myself busy inside most of the day. I didn't spare one look in her direction. I can't play it off like I'm indifferent towards her. No, even after that all went down, the polar opposite is true. I feel tethered to the girl in some fucked up way. I want Charlotte more than I want my next breath, but I won't let myself have her. I tell myself nothing good will come of it—repeat it to myself like a mantra.

So Monday morning when the pale blue paper falls from my locker and floats down to the floor, I don't move to pick it up right away. I know it's from her. I stare down at it, this radioactive thing that holds the power to crush me, while studying the delicate handwriting, the way she crafts my name. I don't snatch it up until I hear the pack of them approaching. I stuff it in my back pocket and walk off without answering when Skylar teases, "Hot damn...Is that a love note, Simon?"

Dear Simon,

If you decide to rip this note up without reading it, I can't say that I'd blame you. I'm ashamed of the way I acted on Saturday. I'm ashamed of the way I judged your brother, and of the way I blindly took my own brother's version of events and accepted them as truth.

So I'm sorry, that's what I want to tell you.

I love Christian, even though we're not close anymore. I love him and I hate him and I pity him. I don't expect you to ever forgive him, especially since he's never had to pay for his sins. But I know from where he comes, and contrary to popular belief, growing up in our house was no picnic. I don't see him in black or white terms, as good or evil. I see him as someone who is flawed and struggling, and (I hope) trying to do better. I'm sure it's not too far off from the way you see Timmy.

I think I have a better idea of what happened back then, both from you and from others who have filled me in. So now I under-stand why you look at me the way you do. I wish things were different, I really do, but at least I get it now.

-Charlotte

. . .

My hands were shaking when I opened the paper folded by her hands, and now that I've read the words, I imagine our hands are touching as I refold it.

I get it now.

No, she doesn't. The girl thinks I hate her when nothing could be further from the truth. Her words confirm everything I thought I saw in her but couldn't really know for sure. Maybe no one is good or evil, there are no absolutes, but there's a beauty and goodness in Charlotte that I want her to see reflected in me.

Everything in me hurts. I want her to know that I wish things were different too. To want someone and know you can't be with them is the definition of pain. So instead of heading to class, I settle into a quiet corner at the top of the stairwell next to the rooftop exit. I write back to Charlotte, giving myself the freedom to tell her everything I know I'll never say out loud.

She'll never read it.

* * *

CHARLOTTE

I was there before the first bus pulled in, before most of the teachers arrived. My fingers trembled as I slid the letter through the top slat in his locker door, looking from side to side to make sure the hallway was empty.

Writing to Simon was either the most courageous thing I've ever done or a grave mistake. Odds are good he'll make me come to regret the decision, but right now I'm glad I did it. Writing to him felt good, lifted a burden. The note was simple but said what needed to be said. At least he knows I'm sorry.

I wanted to say more in the letter, but I'm not that brave. I want to tell him things. I want to tell him that I like watching him work, I admire his strength and the way he uses it to help people who aren't so strong. Also that I read the poem he wrote, the one about his mother that Mr. Vargas keeps on his office wall, and it made me cry. I want to tell him that when he touched my wrist the other day, it was like a shot of adrenaline to my system. I felt it everywhere—deep in my chest, the base of my spine, and out to the tip of each and every finger and toe.

Hopefully Simon will read between the lines, he'll know that I care about him. And if he doesn't feel the same, even if he never speaks another word to me again, at least he knows I never meant to hurt him.

Daisy runs into me when I stop short. "What's up, Mason? Are you trying to take me out? I'm clumsy enough without you trying to trip me."

"Sorry," I say absently. "I just need to walk." I gesture to my side. "Cramp."

"Better not let that witch see you." Daisy puts her index finger sideways under her nose and speaks in what's supposed to pass as a German accent. "Ven I vas yur age, I could run a kilometer faster zan you can say bratwurst!"

I laugh and wave her off. "Go!" I'm on a solo mission right now and need to concentrate. It's no surprise that I spotted him. My eyes always look for his truck in the parking lot, just as I always set my gaze on locker number eighty-four when I pass by in the hallway. And I probably spend more time staring across the street to catch sight of him working than tending to my own customers in the diner. I never miss a chance to get a glimpse of anything associated with Simon—I'm pathetic like that.

What is he doing? Leaning back against the passenger side

door of his truck, both hands are in his hair as he looks up to the sky. It's third period and he's not in class. Did he find the note? Has he read it? My heart sinks. I jog at a snail's pace, looking over every few seconds. Two more laps and he's still in the same position. But wait, now he's in motion. I stop in my tracks when I realize he's heading in the direction of my car with purposeful, determined strides. I can't make out his expression but considering the last time I saw him it was in a state of barely contained rage, I'm prepared and bracing for the sound of my front windshield shattering. The sound of the bell ringing from inside school and our teacher yelling at us to line up are muted in the background. I'm transfixed, watching as he lifts one of the front wipers and tucks something against my windshield. Simon is still there when Ms. Brunner yells at me to line up.

There's nothing on my car when I ask for a bathroom pass and sneak outside during fourth period. Nothing. I search the exterior of the car and even go down on my hands and knees looking underneath to see if it dropped or possibly blew away. I could have sworn I saw him place something on the windshield.

I know what I saw, but over the next few days, Simon gives no indication that he's received, let alone read my note. He passes me in the hallway without so much as a sideways glance. When Sienna calls me over to talk one day before class, he walks off abruptly, as if I've suddenly contaminated the air. During the pep rally for tonight's basketball playoff game, I spot Simon in the top row of the bleachers, his attention fixed on the girl huddled in at his side for the duration of our dance routine.

. . .

"Tonight I'm going to redeem myself, I promise!"

Daisy is bouncing on her toes excitedly when I burst her bubble. "Have fun, Daisy…I'm going straight home after the game."

"What?" I feel bad that her mood's taken a nosedive because of me, but there's no way I'm going to Tyler's party. "You *have* to come! I think we're the only sophomores Sienna and Skylar invited, and they only invited me because of you."

I shake my head to reassure her, even though I know this is probably true. Sienna and her sister are truly nice, so I'm not being entirely fair, but I notice I've been on the receiving end of a whole lot of kindness lately. I'm still riding that odd wave of celebrity that comes when some terrible tragedy befalls you. Humans are predictable. We like to feel good about ourselves, see ourselves in a positive light. And nothing works better than bestowing kindness on others, especially when there's an audience to witness your good deed.

In seventh grade some boy in my class was diagnosed with a rare blood disorder. The rumors flew, the outlook was bleak. No one paid much attention to him before, then all of a sudden bake sales were being organized to help out with medical bills, kids who never spoke to him were writing the most heartfelt *Get Well Soon* cards, and the soccer coach, who never let this boy off the bench when he was in perfect health, was now donning a *Do it for Brady* patch on his warm up jacket, same as the one his players wore on their jerseys.

I am currently wearing the crown. I am the girl who lost her mother.

Daisy looks as if she's just reminded herself of this. "I'm sorry. I wasn't thinking."

"I'm sorry too, Daisy. I know I haven't been the best company lately. You should go to the party. Most of the juniors are going and you're like a freaking social butterfly...You'll be fine."

"It *is* potentially the last game of the season."

I push her gently from behind as we walk into the lunchroom. "Way to have faith in our team."

"Please," she whispers as she turns around, "I overheard Tyler saying they have no chance of beating Lincoln."

"I think he's right."

Taking me by the shoulders with a gleam in her eye, she says, "I'm going to go."

"Good. I'd feel like a wet blanket if you stayed home because of me."

"If you change your mind—"

"Pretty sure I won't."

"Okay, okay. Think I could say I'm staying over at your house?"

I don't even reply as we roll our eyes in unison. Even though it's never been said, we both know Daisy's parents would never permit her to stay the night at my house where—gasp!—children are not supervised twenty-four-seven. If they ever knew the truth, that my father slept at home no more than two or three nights a week, they would have called child protective services by now.

"Just take it easy on the drinking this time. No shots."

"I know," she says, shaking her head. "I felt like crap for two days after that last party. I don't even know if they'll let me go tonight. Maybe if I ask my Dad to pick me up at curfew, he'll trust me to behave myself."

"Right...You're going to ask him to pick you up at Tyler's place in the trailer park? With music blasting and drunken idiots playing beer pong out front?" Daisy laughs but looks defeated. "I'll make you a deal. You can tell your parents we're going out to get something to eat after the game and then I'll come pick you up at Tyler's and take you home. But please don't be drunk, or I swear your parents will never let us hang out again. Sound good?"

My tray, still thankfully empty, clatters to the floor when she grabs me in a bear hug. "Did I tell you today that I love you and that you're the best friend ever?"

I smile and maybe even laugh a little, but her show of affection and her words make me sad. Best friend ever? I don't know much about true friendship, but I assume that close friends share things with one another. I certainly know a lot about Daisy. She shares on a near constant basis. But her thoughts and dreams are candy-coated and sparkly. The positive stuff is easy to share. On the flip side, Daisy knows next to nothing about me. I have dreams that are as bright as the stars too, but unlike Daisy, no one in my family is interested, let alone encouraging. I have a plan in place, and I'm determined to get out of here, but there are times when I feel so alone that I can't envision a future that's anything other than bleak.

Daisy is always pure of heart, happy and hopeful. I just can't bring myself to burden her with my bullshit.

Last night on the drive over to Tyler's, I started to get a little sick and tired of myself. Yes, my mother had just died and I was a hot mess in general, but I had to get on with it. I pulled up at quarter to eleven, praying that Daisy would come out at the agreed upon time. Holding up one finger after another, I rattled off all the things I had to be thankful for. I had Daisy, I did have my father if I ever really and truly found myself in a jam, I had a car, I had a job—now I was on a roll. I had amassed twelve hundred dollars in the envelope I kept tucked away in a hollowed out copy of *The Grapes of Wrath* on my bookshelf, and I also had a lead on several scholarships after meeting with Mr. Vargas yesterday. I filled my lungs with air and nodded. *Screw this Debbie downer attitude, I'm going places!* And the gods were truly smiling down from Mount Olympus, because at ten to eleven on the dot, a very perky and only slightly buzzed Daisy came walking—not stumbling—out of the party, and I got her home without so much as a suspicious look from her parents.

* * *

SIMON

I read the letter every night before I go to sleep. I don't want to read it, but somehow the paper winds up in my hands, and then I'm opening it and feeling the emotions I felt when I penned the words. The ritual comforts me and hurts me at the same time.

Instead of leaving it in the nightstand drawer like I usually do, I grab it this morning, tucking it into my back pocket before I leave for work. Pulling up a few minutes before my boss opens the store, I watch her from across the street. She's setting up tables and pouring coffee for the two or three early birds already starting their day. I recite the words from memory as I watch her, imagine myself speaking them to her. In reality, I'm a coward. I've ignored her all this week, even done things to intentionally push her away. In the predawn hour, sitting here alone in my car, it's only then that I'm brave enough to tell her how I feel.

I take the page out and unfold it. It's a long yellow sheet of legal paper crammed with words from top to bottom, filling both front and back. Looks like something Ted Kaz-whatever his name is would write—the Unabomber, yeah. It's more like a scrawled out manifesto than a letter that's supposed to express what I feel.

Just holding the paper feels therapeutic. Even though the intended recipient will never read the words, writing them lifted a heavy weight. I guess I never really talk to anyone, about anything that's real anyway. I would never saddle my mother or Tim with my troubles, Mike is far away and dealing with his own shit, and my friends aren't true friends. But that's entirely on me. Garth, Sienna, Tyler—they're good people, it's just that I'm not in the habit of letting anyone in. Talking to Charlotte through a letter she will never read might be stupid, but it feels good, or more like something I need.

Dear Charlotte,

You <u>don't</u> understand.

You think I dislike you, but I don't. You think I hate you for the sins of your brother, but I don't. You think I look the other way when you're around because something or someone else has caught my eye, but that's not how it is.

I noticed you the first week of your freshman year. Mr. Vargas had me acting like some jerkoff ambassador for the new honors program students. Do you even remember that lame speech I made? I remember thinking at the time that it was just another thing I had to do, another chance to impersonate a "young man with strong leadership qualities" for my college applications. It was another small step in my grand plan to get out of this town, this state, this life. But when I looked out into the group of no more than thirty shining stars, over half of them not truly qualified to be in any kind of honors program whatsoever, I saw you perched on the edge of your seat, looking right at me as your pen scratched out notes on your paper. You were taking notes! That made me laugh my ass off because I knew I was just repeating the bullshit standard lines—manage your time, start thinking about college sooner rather than later, take advantage of the test prep courses that Mr. Vargas offers, blah, blah, blah. But you were drinking it all in. You looked so earnest, so damned adorable. At the time, you made me wish I had a little sister or brother to guide and look after.

But this year I <u>noticed</u> you. What a difference a year makes. I saw you messing around on the field with a few of your friends, practicing some dance moves, and I asked someone what your name was. Charlotte, the kid told me. I was thinking to myself that it was a pretty name, it suited you, but then he said your name in full...Charlotte Mason. I'm used to disappointment by now, so I figured this was just fate's way of kicking me in the ass yet again.

Suddenly you weren't pretty, you weren't cute—you were one of them. And I do hate your family. I think your brother, with his nice cars and his expensive clothes, is lower than scum. And from where I sit, your father is no better.

And then there's you...

When I first saw you working in the diner, I was so angry. I still don't know why ~~the fuck~~ you work there. You don't need the money and it's on the shit side of this county. It's like you're slumming or something, and I can't figure out why. But what I hate about it the most is that the more I watch you, the more I want you. And I can't have you—it <u>can't</u> happen. So this is why I act the way I do. The reason I push you away and act like a jackass whenever you're around.

I want you to know that I hate myself for it, for the way I am around you. And it's all on me. You've done nothing to deserve it —any of it. I am the one who should be saying sorry.

You won't see this letter, so you'll never know. You won't know how sorry I am. You won't know how I really feel about you. You'll never know that most nights I drift off to sleep thinking about you, so you're front and center in my dreams. And in those dreams, my life is entirely different. I don't have a brother rotting away in prison or a brother who was run out of town because of who he is. I don't have a mother who can't afford to buy medicine when her asthma kicks in, or who feels guilty because her sons haven't seen a dentist or doctor in years. We don't live in a trailer with unreliable heat and we don't worry about paying our bills. In my dreams I'm with you and it's always summer. I am happier than I've ever been. I imagine that if I really was with you, that's what life would be like. But those are dreams, and my reality is what it is.

I see you. I see the sadness that weighs you down too. But I also see you when you dance. When you dance your happiness pours out of you and seeps into everyone watching. I can't look away when you move. You are everything I imagine a man could want. You're everything I want but can't have.

Someday you're going to be loved by a man who worships you. His sole purpose in life will be to protect you and keep you happy. Me? I'll be nothing more than a bad memory. I already hate that guy you're going to fall in love with someday, but at the same time, I'm grateful to him.

You didn't understand before, but hopefully, now you do.
-Simon

The tap on my window startles me. Mr. Roberts' face is up against my window. He's smiling, rubbing his bare hands together to ward off the cold. "Whatcha doing, son? Get inside!"

I take one last look across the street and see that she's looking right back at me. *Can't happen*, I remind myself as I switch the headlights off and take the key from the ignition. I fold the paper and tuck it into the glove compartment.

Shut it down, shut her out.

* * *

CHARLOTTE

Instead of taking my usual break outside, I bring my phone to call Daisy. I need something to focus on, a buffer, something to do with my hands and my thoughts. This morning I caught him staring into the diner again, but he turned away the second our eyes met.

She picks up on the first ring and doesn't even wait for me to say hello. "I had so much fun last night! Oh, and here's an interesting tidbit...It was a lot more fun without the mind-numbing shots." Daisy laughs so hard she snorts when she adds, "I even made some new friends because I was actually able to talk this time!"

"Good for you, freak. So how was it, who was there? Give me all the deets." *Was Simon there, was Simon laughing and having a good time, was Simon sucking face with that redhead he was sitting next to in the gym?*

Tyler, Skylar, blah, blah, blah...Zach someone or other puking on the coffee table, blah, blah, blah...Sarah Beele has the best clothes and is the coolest girl ever, blah, blah, blah. No mention of Simon.

"Charlotte, are you still there?"

"Yeah, I'm here." I go for some fake enthusiasm. "So, the party sounds like it was great!"

"You weren't even listening, were you?" Daisy isn't mad, I don't think. By now she's used to my nonsense, to the distance. "I was asking if you want to go to the mall with me and Sarah later."

"Can I let you know after work?"

"Sure, no pressure, whatever, let me know…We're leaving at four."

Girlfriends, who knew?

I decided after I got off the phone with Daisy that I need to seriously work on being a better friend. And I needed a distraction to get my mind off the moody jerk across the street, the one who was loading shrubs into the back of a small pickup truck for some lady while her teenage daughter attempted to make small talk. I felt like yelling over to her: *Good luck, honey.*

"Simon Wade is the hottest boy in the senior class. And no prom date, can you believe it?"

So much for a distraction.

Daisy leans across the table and grabs a fry from Sarah's tray. "I heard a few girls asked him but he turned them down flat."

"Shocker," I say to no one in particular.

"I think the surly thing works for him." Sarah looks positively dreamy-eyed. "I could put up with his grouchy attitude. I'd love to have a session with him."

"A session?" It takes some effort to keep the contempt from my voice.

Daisy looks at me as if I'm clueless. "A *make-out* session."

Sarah's oblivious. "Yeah, I just *know* that boy can kiss."

"Nope." Daisy scrunches her nose. "Simon's too dark for me."

"The dark ones are the most fun."

"And you would know this how?" Daisy teases back at Sarah.

"School is going to be such a drag when this class graduates. Think of the juniors." Sarah holds up her hand and starts naming boys, one for each finger, while rattling off their bad traits. "And the girls...No one's going to take me under their wing the way Skylar has."

Daisy reaches across the table and takes Sarah's hand in a comforting gesture. These two are pretty chummy all of a sudden. And while a part of me feels like a third wheel, I have to admit there's something I like about Sarah. She's light and goofy, just like Daisy. The easy way they navigate the world is something I envy.

"Defect to the dance team," I offer, wanting to add something, *anything* to the conversation.

"Yes!" Daisy leans in and grabs me around the shoulders. "Best idea ever, Charlotte!"

Sarah shakes her head. "Like hell. Cheering is easy compared to those dance routines." She looks to me. "You're amazing. I'd look like a bumbling idiot next to you."

"You mean you'd look like me?" Daisy teases.

"Ohmigod, no Daisy! You're really good too!"

Sarah laughs so hard, the soda she just sipped shoots out of her nose.

Chapter Eight

CHARLOTTE

I've never been a big fan of daylight savings, but I flat out object to the asinine ritual in the springtime when I'm deprived an hour of much needed sleep. The one upside, longer days, means nothing to me right now. No different from yesterday, it's pitch-black outside when I start my day. I console myself as I drive the deserted streets on my way to work, thinking I'm in for an easy morning. God willing, some of the regulars won't remember to set their clocks forward, so the breakfast rush won't start as early.

A girl can dream.

I run through the routine in my mind as I exit the car and walk towards the back entrance: start the coffee, fill the creamers, top off the bowls filled with single-serving packs of butter, jam and syrup.

I don't hear footsteps on gravel until the exact moment his filthy hand clamps over my mouth and my right arm is wrenched behind my back.

"I'm not gonna hurt you," he murmurs, all soft-spoken and kind as he turns and walks us back in the direction of my car. He jerks my arm back again, making it feel as if it's going to separate from my shoulder when I try in vain to kick at him. "Open the door," he commands, voice low and menacing. My free hand shakes violently as I rifle through the contents of my bag feeling for the keys. "Open it," he whispers encouragement, switching tack again, using a tone meant to persuade and deceive me. He wants me to believe the awful thing that's happening isn't actually happening.

"Get offa her!"

My face slams into the door as the man's body is hit from behind. The attack is weak, though, merely knocking the man off balance rather than taking him down.

"Get inside!" Rudy yells as the man throws him to the ground.

I stand frozen. Rudy flails, kicking and throwing his hands out in a feeble attempt to land a blow, but he's no match. Skin and bones beneath his dirty parka, a cast-off so large that the sleeves hang low and confine his hands, he retreats, clumsy, scurrying back in a crab-like crawl as the man comes after him. Rudy curls in on himself as the man kicks his boot into Rudy's face over and over and over again.

No, no, no.

I scream and rush him from behind, swinging my bag like a machete in one hand and striking the back of his head with my keys in the other.

"Bitch!" he spits out.

When he reaches for my keys, I throw them as far as I can. *Don't ever let them get you into a car*—I remember hearing that during some self-defense segment on a talk show once. And now I'm going to pay for my disobedience. Wrenching both hands behind my back, he pushes me towards the brick wall at the back entrance. I open my mouth to scream but no sound comes out. I picture our cook, Denny, with Metallica blasting as he preps the kitchen, and I know I have another twenty minutes before any of the other waitresses show up.

"You stuck-up bitch," he growls in my ear.

I'm wedged between him and the wall, my face pressed up against the brick. One of his large hands has both of mine trapped, his fingernails digging into my wrists. His breath is wet and heavy on my neck as he unfastens his belt. His weight shifts as he works his zipper.

I hear myself whimper, hear him uttering his filth, but the sounds are distant. I'm floating away from here.

Cold air hits my back once his crushing weight is off me and I fall to the ground.

"You piece of shit!" The man is on the ground now, his arms covering his face to block the repeated blows. "I'll fucking kill you, Rudy!"

Simon lifts the man's head and slams it into the ground once, twice, and then rains blows down on his midsection. Slumped against the wall, I listen, dazed, as the man moans like a wounded animal.

"Rudy."

Simon looks to me, breathing heavy. He stands but then pauses, turning once to land a parting kick to the man's side. "Rudy's never gonna hurt you again," he says softly, reaching down to pick me up off the ground.

"No! Rudy...He, he...I think he killed Rudy!"

Simon turns back to the man on the ground, nudging the bloodied face with his boot, taking him in. His eyes go wide when he turns back to me. "What happened?"

"Rudy...Rudy tried to help me, but, but he, he—"

"Okay, shh, shh." He pulls me in close, smoothing my hair. "I've got you. I'll help Rudy."

He opens the back door of the diner. "Call 911," he yells to Denny while ushering me inside to a booth.

As Simon turns to leave, I dig my fingernails into his arm. "He wasn't attacking me."

"What?"

"Please, tell them he was assaulting Rudy and I tried to stop him. That's all."

"Charlotte, you need to get checked out."

"No!" I have to make him understand. "He didn't do it. You stopped him. If-if-if you tell, I...You *cannot* tell." I bat the tears away, composing myself as best I can. "I'm fine, I swear it."

He looks me over from head to toe, pausing to assess that my clothes are still in place. He nods reluctantly as the approaching sirens get louder.

"Stay here...I'll make sure Rudy tells them the same." I nod in agreement and Simon runs back outside.

I stand on wobbly legs and make it into the bathroom just in time to throw up. I want to hide in the stall, stay crouched down on the cold tile floor, want to lean my head against the porcelain and cry, but I will myself to get up. Wetting a few scratchy paper towels from the dispenser, I scrub my hands and face, then rinse my mouth. Checking my face in the mirror, I note that aside from a scrape on my cheek that can be hidden with concealer, I look all right. He knocks and comes in as I'm putting my hair up with trembling hands.

"They took Rudy to the hospital." I nod, unable to speak for fear of crying. "I'm sorry...I just assumed it was him. He's a junkie." He jams his battered hands into his pockets, shaking his head. "The police want to speak to you."

I breathe deep, trying to mask the panicky feeling that's taking hold. "Why?"

He looks away. "Guess to confirm what I just told them… That the guy was beating on Rudy, you intervened, and when he turned on you I showed up."

"Okay."

When I don't move, he opens the door and gently takes my elbow to lead me out. "I think I saw your bag outside. Want me to go grab it?"

"Yeah, thanks Simon."

I'm grateful that I don't personally know the police officer they sent to question me. It's all quick, matter of fact. He seems to buy my version of events. He asks about Simon twice, though, which makes me angry. He finally backs off when I repeat, "He was on his way to work, just like me. I'm grateful he showed up when he did."

When I ask how Rudy is, the police officer tells me he was unconscious when they took him away in the ambulance. "And that man?"

"He's in pretty bad shape too, but he's in custody. Don't worry about him coming around here again."

"Thank you, officer."

Simon comes over with my bag. "I think I got most of it."

With the way I was swinging that bag, I imagine that money, makeup and tampons were probably strewn all about the parking lot. On a normal day I might have been embarrassed, but today I don't possess the energy give one flip.

"I can tell Mr. Roberts I'll be late if you want me to drive you home."

"No, I'm working."

The police officer gets up to go. "Is there anything else you need from us?" Simon asks.

"No, son." He shakes Simon's hand. "Sounds like you did good here today, real good. There's been a string of assaults on women in Maconsville," the officer says as he eyes me. "This guy fits the description, tattoo and all. If either of you are needed to testify, I have your information. I'll be in touch."

Simon slumps into the seat across from me. Two or three customers are clustered up by the register, looking over at us as they get the play by play from Denny. "Maybe you shouldn't work today, Charlotte."

I reach over absently and touch the cut skin on his right hand. "Maybe *you* shouldn't work."

He takes my hand and squeezes it gently. "Why didn't you tell the truth?"

Looking away, I keep my voice to a whisper. "Is there any point in having the whole damn county know that I was *almost* sexually assaulted? I'd be nothing but a sordid tale for the gossips."

"I get that."

"And I'd have to quit this job...I don't want to."

"Why?"

"Why would I have to quit, or why would I want to keep working here?" I ask, attempting to joke. Simon smiles. *He should do that more often.* "My father would make me quit."

"I can understand that."

"My alternative is answering phones at the dealership working alongside his playboy bunny of a girlfriend." I shake my head, standing up. "Not happening."

He stands. "Sure you're all right?"

"Yeah, I'm fine. And really Simon, thank you." When I meet his eyes, I have to look away. He's studying me, searching for something. "You should get your hand checked out," I say over my shoulder as I make my way back to the bathroom.

I imagine him shrugging when he answers, "This is nothing."

If there was some kind of Oscar award for good waitressing, I would have been nominated for my performance today. I was on autopilot, handling eight to ten checks at once without hitting a snag. I didn't even take a break, chancing only one look out the window my entire shift. A cold driving rain came on around mid-morning, but it wasn't the weather keeping me inside today. I didn't want to be outside, didn't want to be near that lot, and I didn't want to look across the street to see Simon's curious and worried eyes staring back at me. I wanted to forget the entire episode.

For the first hour of my shift, Denny, Marley and the other waitresses kept asking how I was. I shook my head, smiling and looking at them like they were being neurotic. "I'm *fine*," I answered each time, until finally they stopped and things went back to normal.

I'm sure they saw through my *It's all good* act. Each one gave me a hug with a squeeze when my shift was over, and Marley told me she'd be coming in half an hour earlier from now on. Two of us should be setting up, and no, she wasn't saying that just because of what happened this morning.

I bite my lip to keep from bawling as I make my way out into the parking lot. The rain is coming down in icy sheets. *Keys, keys.* I look through my bag and then shake it to listen for the familiar jingle. The visual comes on suddenly. He's closing in, reaching for me as I throw the keys across the parking lot. His face, his damp, dirty hands. *No, no, no.* I lean my head against the car door, tired and defeated.

"Hey," he calls to me softly. A moment later a jacket is draped over my shoulders, over my own coat that's now soaked through.

"My keys are gone," I cry. "I threw them so that he, so he... So he couldn't get me back into my car and—"

Through the jacket he rubs my arms. "That was smart, Charlotte. That was definitely the right thing to do."

"I can't leave my car here. They'll ask questions."

"Which direction did you throw them...Can you remember?" I gesture to the left, my body suddenly so weak I can barely raise my arm to point. "I'm gonna put you in my truck to warm up. I'll find them."

He ushers me across the street, practically holding me up as if I'm an invalid. I think the shock from this morning is just now settling in. My entire body is shaking, and once I'm seated inside the truck I begin to sob uncontrollably. I don't care that Simon is witnessing my meltdown. I'm too far gone to care. He sits beside me, fiddling with the heat, looking over at me every few seconds, his discomfort rolling off him in waves. He lets out a breath, giving in to whatever he's wrestling with, then slides across the seat to pull me in close.

"He's never coming back here. He'll never touch you again, I promise you that." Words whispered into my hair, hands rubbing up and down my back, strong arms blanketing me with a sense of much needed security. I want to stay like this forever. He pulls back a few inches and tips my chin up to search my eyes. "You sit here and warm up. I'm just grabbing a flashlight from the store and I'll find your keys."

In just a long sleeve shirt that's completely soaked, Simon roams the parking lot for at least ten minutes before coming back and tapping on the window, smiling as he holds my keys up between his fingers. When he follows my eyes and looks down into my lap, he backs up a step.

He's not smiling anymore.

* * *

SIMON

Why the fuck didn't I leave that thing at home?

I startle her when I knock on the window, but she isn't crying or looking like an injured bird anymore. I'm glad for that until I follow her nervous eyes down to what's unfolded in her lap. That big yellow piece of paper, or my soul laid bare for the whole world to see—same thing.

I want to scream at her, ask her what the fuck she's doing. Who does she think she is, snooping around and reading my private things? But one look at her face, fearful and anxious, and I know I need to rein it in.

I walk around the back of the truck, taking deep breaths, face turned towards Heaven so I can ask for strength as the cold rain pelts my skin. I don't look at her when I get in. Don't know what to say as my forehead slumps against the steering wheel.

Her voice is small, cautious. "I promise, I just went in there to look for some tissues. It had my name on it."

"It's all right."

"You almost left this for me last week, didn't you?"

"What?"

"I saw you...I saw you in the parking lot at school. You put something on my windshield."

"I never intended for you to read it."

"I'm sorry." She reaches over but stops short of touching me. "Do you want me to go?"

Do I want her to go? Yes, I do, and no, I never want her to leave me. Still resting against the steering wheel, I roll my forehead from one side to another. That's as close as I'll come to telling her to stay.

I'm tempted to blurt out even more of what I know is true, but I hold back. Moments pass as we sit in choked silence.

"Say something, Charlotte. I can't read your mind and you're killing me right now."

"I don't...I don't know what to say." The passenger door opens as Charlotte draws in a shaky breath. "I dream about you too," she says, hopping out and closing the door behind her.

I see her tucking the yellow paper into her pocket as she crosses the street.

What to do? What to do?

She's there, standing with her puke in the bushes friend and another girl. Barf girl is doing some ridiculously uncoordinated dance moves while Charlotte and the other girl laugh. The other girl is genuinely laughing, but Charlotte's smile doesn't come close to reaching her eyes.

I want to go to her, want to know how she is, but I won't approach her now. I wanted to call her last night or go by her house. Fuck the letter—I'm not going to let my embarrassment stop me from doing the right thing. But there are barriers. I won't be asking anyone for the Mason girl's phone number and I certainly won't be stopping by her house.

It's just after lunch when I see her sneaking out the side exit heading towards the parking lot. I run to catch up with her. Her body stiffens at the sound of my footsteps. She flinches and sucks in a breath when I reach out to touch her shoulder.

"It's just me." She's wide-eyed for a moment until her breath evens out. "I'm sorry. That was stupid on my part, shouldn't have come up on you like that."

She squares her shoulders. "No, it's all right. I'm fine."

"You're obviously not fine," I say, shaking my head. "Yesterday was messed up. I'm still kind of reeling from the whole thing."

"Rudy's dead," she whispers, looking down at her shoes.

"What?"

"The nurse said it was a blood clot. Blunt force trauma to the head caused it."

"Holy shit." I move a step closer. I want to hold her but her arms are crossed over her chest like a shield. "I'm sorry, Charlotte. I know you cared about him. You were good to him."

"Do you know he has family?" I shake my head, silently willing her to go on. "I met his sister at the hospital yesterday."

"You went to the hospital?"

She looks up at me like I'm dense. "Rudy was beaten to death." She adds, "He died saving me." She picks at a loose thread on her sweater. "His sister said he was depressed after serving in Iraq, that he was never the same." She lets out a heavy breath and shakes her head. "He was homeless by choice. He preferred living on the streets. Turned his sister down every time she offered to take him in and get him help."

"Everyone has a story." I feel guilty knowing I never gave Rudy Wallace the benefit of the doubt. "I just thought he was another homeless junkie...Never gave much thought as to how or why he hit bottom."

"I'm glad I got to tell her."

"You told his sister what happened?"

Charlotte shoots me a warning look. "Not everything."

Don't worry, I want to tell her. I'd never break her confidence. Does she imagine for a minute that I would?

"I did tell her that Rudy was trying to protect me. I want his family to know he died a hero."

"I'm sure they're grateful for that."

"Yeah, I think it gave her some comfort."

"Is there a service or something?"

I have a sudden urge to attend. I want to make sure Rudy's sister knows there are good, caring people in this town, people like Charlotte Mason. That while me and just about everyone else walked by Rudy as if he was invisible, Charlotte fed him, made sure he had a warm coat, and slipped him a few singles now and then.

"No service. His sister lives up in Erie and his dad is in a home nearby." She looks close to tears. "It's funny, right? There was nothing here for him, but he came back to his hometown anyway."

"That just proves he wasn't right in the head."

"I know," she says absently. "Once I get out of here, I'm gone for good."

You'd think I'd be inclined to smile at that, Charlotte being a kindred spirit and all, but the thought of her wanting to leave, to run away, leaves me heavy hearted. She should be happy and she should be safe. Charlotte shouldn't have to worry about making it into work without some sick fuck assaulting her, and she sure as hell shouldn't be buying locks to keep someone out of a place they shouldn't be.

"Were you heading home when I caught up to you?"

"Yeah, my head's all over the place. I don't think I heard one word my teachers said today." She gestures back down the hallway. "Fresh start tomorrow."

"All right." Before she makes it out the door, I blurt out what I'm dying to ask. "Is everything all right? I mean, not just about yesterday, but everything else with you?"

If she understands that I'm referring to the lock, she doesn't let on. "I'm fine, Simon...I promise you I'm fine."

Chapter Nine

CHARLOTTE

I quicken my pace, ignoring him as he leans against the squad car parked at the curb.

"Charlie, wait."

"Stop coming around when my brother isn't home. I have nothing to say to you."

"I was right behind you, trailing you the entire way. And Jesus, you were no more than half a mile from home!" When I turn and shoot him a scowl, he backpeddles. "I was wrong, really fucking wrong."

"Go. Away."

But I'm not quick enough. "I need to talk to you." He wedges his foot in the doorframe. "Why didn't you tell me what happened at the diner yesterday morning?"

"I don't see how it's any of your business."

"Come on." His eyes are pleading. "The guy who killed Rudy Wallace is a serial rapist. Do you know how lucky you are?"

"He was looking to rob Rudy. He only turned on me when I went to stop him."

"Yeah, that's what the police report says. It's how your statement reads, anyway." I tilt my head and widen my eyes as if to say: *Yeah, and?* Wes studies me but I turn away, busy myself with the stack of mail that sits on the kitchen counter. "I also read the other witness statement." He pauses. "Simon Wade?"

"He works across the street."

"He backs your story up, or you back up his story. The statements are nearly identical."

"There aren't too many versions of the truth." Looking over my shoulder I add, "Well, maybe not in the world you and my brother live in...I can totally understand your confusion."

"Dammit, Charlotte," he says, taking me by the upper arm. "I'm concerned about you. Stop acting like this!"

"Concerned? You left me to walk home alone on a dark stretch of highway and I'm supposed to believe you're concerned about me?"

He backs away from me and sinks into one of the dining room chairs. "It's not like that...That night," he trails off. "You know I care about you."

I open the front door to make my intentions clear. "I don't want you to care."

He doesn't breeze past me in the hallway this week. I get a head nod. He doesn't take off when he sees me with Sienna and the other girls on the dance team. He acts as if my presence is no big deal. When the redhead from the gym tries to flirt, I catch him looking my way as he physically extricates himself from her hold.

I'm certainly not being pursued, or heaven forbid wooed in any way, but the simple gestures are meaningful to me.

I read and reread that letter so frequently, touch the paper he held in his hands so often that I'm afraid I'll wear the ink away. *You are everything I imagine a man could want. You're everything I want but can't have.* His words warm me up, fill me with something thrilling and blissful.

My mother used to love to watch the movie version of *West Side Story*. When she first had the stroke—when my father still cared about her—he used to put headphones on her ears and play the soundtrack. I guess he thought it would jog her memory, bring her back to us. And as sad as the memory of her listening to that music makes me in one respect, I can't help but sing those songs to myself this week. Because I feel it: *Something's Coming*. And yes, the way he looks at me, even though it's no more than a passing glance, makes me want to belt out the lyrics to *I Feel Pretty* at the top of my lungs. I sing in my room, I sing in the shower, and when I'm in public I sing in the quiet of my own mind.

This has been a week of extremes, of highs and lows. I know I'm a little off, I recognize it, see my mood swings for what they are. But in those moments when I can block out Rudy, block out that man, block out everything except Simon and that letter, it's as if I don't have a care in the world. I'm downright giddy.

By the end of the week, Simon has checked on me four times. He cuts into the lunch line like he did that first time and asks if I'm all right. On Tuesday and Wednesday, he simply replied, "Good," before turning to leave, but today he actually nods and bestows a smile on me when he says, "Good. Let me know if you need anything."

I want to tell him that yes, I *need*. I *need* because you are *all* I think about.

Everyone is hopped up. It's edging up towards seventy degrees by the time the last period bell rings on Friday so people linger in the parking lot. Jackets have been stuffed into backpacks and sweatshirts have been tied around hips. It's not even that warm, but the first taste of spring in this typically bitter corner of Pennsylvania makes people act a little loco.

Daisy and Sarah are wearing tank tops—loonies must have planned it out in advance—and are practically bouncing on their toes when I meet them at my car. "You're shivering, Sarah."

"Am not!" she says, laughing.

Daisy huddles us in, looking between me and Sarah. "There's a party down at the river tonight. Skylar just told us and said we should come."

My eyes scan the lot, settling on the corner where the seniors congregate. I see him. He's surrounded by people but his eyes are fixed on me.

"I'll drive."

Sarah and Daisy share a stunned look. I'm sure they had a whole strategy worked out, figured they'd have to persuade me or wear me down. But no, nothing could stop me from going to that party tonight. I even cave when they insist on putting some makeup on me and curling my long hair into soft waves. But I stick to my guns when they try to dress us up like triplets in miniskirts, short boots and shirts from Sarah's closet.

"But they're different!" Sarah whines.

"No way! It's the same shirt in three different colors."

Taking in our trio, I manage to smile and laugh at us in the mirror. "We look ridiculous!"

There's a lot I don't say. I don't tell them that I cannot, under any circumstances, wear this miniskirt that barely skims the middle of my thighs. When I slipped it on, Daisy slapped the back of my leg, making some comment about how life isn't fair or something. The jokes and laughter fade out to a distant muffle as I fight off a wave of nausea. *Nothing happened*, I repeat it like a mantra, berating myself. But I feel the rough denim of his jeans wedging my legs apart, feel my cheek scraping against the brick wall, feel his clammy hand circling my throat as he moves in close.

Stuck-up bitch.

I'm rubbing my cheek to ease the pain when Daisy calls me back to the present. "Maybe Charlotte's right, we do look a little ridiculous."

"Well, I'm sticking with this because I look hot."

I look over to see Sarah modeling a pair of oversized sunglasses that make her look like an insect, along with the wig her mom used last year when she was going through chemo. It's a fire engine red, chin-length bob. A few tears escape when the three of us simultaneously burst out laughing. Laughing when life sucks lemons. It's just what I needed.

SIMON

Always so serious.

Her friends are giggling, bouncing with nervous energy and sucking down whatever is in their red cups. Charlotte smiles as she looks around, observing. She holds her cup but doesn't drink.

I told myself that if she did come here tonight, I'd allow myself to take. I'd forget about all the reasons why I shouldn't, and for once I'd let myself have what I want.

She's here.

I'm finding it hard to concentrate, to hold conversations or feign interest in what people are saying to me. Cora, a girl I know from honors, is asking me about Northwestern, asking me when I'm flying out for orientation. Flying? At this rate I'll be selling my truck and hitchhiking my way to Chicago in August. My orientation is two days before classes start in the fall, I tell her. Then she goes on to fill me in on her roommate search and how excited she is as she prepares to leave for Philly in September. I catch maybe fifty percent of what she's saying. Cora's a nice person, pretty and smart, but there's a different girl standing no more than twenty feet away who owns me.

My ears perk up when Cora starts in on the prom again. I told her after school today that I had no plans on going but obviously I didn't express myself clearly.

"So the prom, Simon. I know you don't have a date yet." *Crap.* Cora looks nervous and hopeful. "I already bought two tickets, so if that's the issue, then—"

"Let me stop you right there." Fuck if any girl is paying for my prom ticket. "I'm not going. It has nothing to do with that." I know I'm poor, don't need anyone reminding me of the fact. And while I know that wasn't Cora's intention, it's hard to quell the shame and anger rising up in me. "I appreciate the offer, but..." I'm about to make up an excuse, say that I won't be around that weekend, but it's a blatant lie and I won't do it. "I'm not going, Cora." Her hurt look makes me feel guilty, but I don't owe this girl my life story. "I know Dave needs a date. I'm sure he'd love to go with you."

She nods and cracks a forced smile. "Yeah, maybe I'll ask him." The ensuing silence is torture, and I breathe a sigh of relief when she finally says, "See you later," and walks away.

Garth hands me a beer, my first of the night. "Another broken heart left in the wake of the legendary Simon Wade."

"I can't wait until the damn prom is over."

"Four weeks." He claps me on the back. "And don't ruin it for me...I cannot wait until that very special night."

"People make too much of it."

"Jeez...You're like Scrooge, man. That night's going to be the highlight of senior year. I still think you should go." When I fix him with a look, Garth raises his palms. "I know, I know... I'll keep my mouth shut."

"Gracias."

"It's different for me, Simon. You're itching to leave, to get out of here." He lifts both arms out to his sides and looks around him, surveying the scene. "I just don't see why people feel that way about this place. It's like you can only see gray skies but I see the sun shining. I see everyone at Jacob's Creek in the summertime, whooping it up. I see us all camping, fishing, kicking back with the girls. I love it here, I always have."

"Nothing wrong with that. I just feel, I don't know, like I'm suffocating here, like I've got to get away. This place doesn't exactly hold great childhood memories for me." That's probably more than I've ever said to Garth about my life and I don't like the feeling that follows. I feel exposed.

I'm grateful when Sienna and some other girls make their way over. Gives me a chance to excuse myself. I dump the contents of my cup onto the ground when I see her standing a few feet from the keg. Some kid is talking to her, same kid who helped with her locker that day. I recognize him. He's a junior, plays baseball. He's clearly making a play for Charlotte but she's giving him that same distant smile she did last time. I listen in, taking my time as I pump the keg and fill up a few other kids' cups before my own. He's telling her about his stable and horses, asking if she knows how to ride.

"A few times when I was younger, but I wouldn't say I know how to ride."

"It'll come right back to you."

"You think?" she asks absently. I'm looking at her now and she's looking right back at me.

"Definitely." He's nodding his head like an eager beaver. "I'll teach you."

She turns to look at him. "Um, maybe?"

"How about tomorrow?"

"Charlotte, you got a minute?" I'm speaking to her, but my eyes are now trained on this boy. He instinctively takes a step back.

I watch her throat move as she swallows. I want to put her at ease, assure her that I'm just as nervous as she is. She looks to the boy and smiles before looking back to me. "Um, sure."

I gesture with my head for us to walk. I want to be away from everyone's eyes, from their judgement, away from the people who know about the ties that bind the Masons to the Wades.

"Do you need a drink?" I ask as an afterthought, looking back towards the keg.

She looks into her full cup. "No." Dumping the beer onto the ground, she says, "It's warm."

"You've been holding that same cup for nearly an hour... Bound to happen."

I see the hint of a smile. "You've been watching me drink, or *not* drink?"

"Yeah," I say, because the gig is up. "I've been watching you."

Now the smile is bigger, but she looks away, cheeks flushed, uncertain. Charlotte is beautiful. She's got gloss on her lips and her hair is falling down and across her back. In just jeans and a light sweater, she outshines all the other girls here tonight. We stop just about fifty feet away from the pack, but it's quieter out here and darker. She sits down on a large rock and I take a seat next to her.

"It's kind of messed up that you've got full access to my sappy innermost thoughts," I say, nudging her foot with mine. "That you have everything in writing...In your possession."

"It's not sappy to me." After a pause, she asks, "Did you mean it?"

I look right at her, but she only gives me her profile. "I don't know," I confess, and she lowers her head in response. "I mean, it's how I feel but it doesn't make sense. I don't know you all that well. We've barely spoken to one another, we've never hung out, never been in the same classes. But..." I trail off, fixing my gaze on a rusted can that rests by my feet.

"But?" she presses.

"I can't stop thinking about you. I actually try to put you out of my mind, force myself to look away. I've even done things to push you away, to make you to believe that I hate you."

Charlotte lets out a cheerless laugh. "You did a good job on that last one. You're very convincing."

"Yeah, well, I'm not proud of it."

She gets up slowly and kicks at the twigs and pebbles in her way as she attempts to put a bit of distance between us, but I follow. She leans back against a tree, studying me for a moment. "If this is just some kind of guilt or misplaced sense of, I don't know, you feeling like you have to go on protecting me because of what happened last weekend—"

"You know I wrote the letter before any of that."

"But you—"

"I want to kiss you, Charlotte. Can I?"

There's a charged energy source flowing through my system. I'm literally buzzing as I close the foot that separates us. "Tell me no, I'll understand." She says nothing, doesn't turn away. "Can I?" I ask again as I lean my head in close to hers. I can feel her breath on my cheek and I can feel my own heart thumping. She nods, and for that I'm grateful. I lick the seam of her lips, tasting the cherry-flavored gloss as I open her mouth with mine.

I've kissed before. I've traded innocent pecks with my hands at my sides, twisted my tongue around another's as hands explored, and I've mashed lips in a frenzy as clothes came off.

This is different.

This, just being close to her and kissing her gently as my hands rest on her hips, is possibly the greatest high I've ever known. Her head is tipped back, eyes closed and expression soft as she returns the kiss. I feel alive, every nerve ending stirring when she snakes her arms around my neck and begins to twist her fingers through my hair. I hear myself moan when her chest presses into mine, but I'm too lost in it to care or feel embarrassed. And she's up on her toes now, the motion pulling me closer still. As much as I want to drag her in and fit every groove of us together, I know it isn't right. I sense Charlotte will freely give what I want to take, and I won't let that happen. Pulling back just a fraction, I rest my forehead against hers.

"I'm sorry."

Her brows knit in confusion. "You didn't hurt me."

"But I will."

"You're everything I want but cannot have." My heart aches as she whispers those words, my words. "Why can't you have me? Why are you so set on pushing me away?" When I don't answer, she asks, "What do you want, Simon?"

"I want to be with you."

She lets out a contented sigh, tilting her head again, inviting me back to her, inviting me in. This kiss is slow and deep and careful. I'm making a decision. Granting myself permission to enjoy this moment, to accept the goodness that's flowing out of her and seeping into me.

Part of what I said is true: I don't know Charlotte. Don't know her favorite food or color. Don't know what makes her laugh. Don't know where she sees herself in five years, ten years. And for the first time in as long as I can remember, having everything in my life nailed down, mapped out, every action correlating to the timeline I've set for achieving my goals —it doesn't seem all that important.

I want this, her, now.

She shifts when she hears a voice getting closer, calling my name. "It's just Garth," I whisper. "Ignore him."

She shakes her head and lets out a frustrated breath as she checks her phone. "It's past eleven. I'm driving and my friend Daisy's parents are beyond overprotective. I have to get her back home."

"Is Daisy the puker?" She nods and smiles. "You're a good friend to her."

"I don't think I'd even get a B-minus in the friend department, but I'm making an effort to be better at it." She shakes her head. "That sounded stupid."

"It doesn't." I plant a kiss on her forehead when I say it. Fact is that I do know Charlotte. I know what it's like to come from circumstances that are different from all the wide-eyed innocent people around you. It makes you feel alien, makes you feel like a fraud when you do your best to try and fit in. People like Garth and Daisy—people who've never experienced the dark—they mean well but they just don't get it.

I take a step back when I hear Garth's voice again. I want to strangle that moron. She smiles and starts to walk ahead of me back to the party. But I don't want her to go, so I take her wrist and turn her back to me. "Let me take you somewhere after work tomorrow?" She doesn't answer right away. "Unless, that is, you're going horseback riding or something."

That earns me a full-bellied laugh and a push. "No, I'm not going horseback riding." She studies me for a moment before nodding. "I'll go out with you tomorrow."

Chapter Ten

CHARLOTTE

He's sitting in his car when I show up for my shift at the diner. He's half an hour early for work, parked there, keeping watch to make sure I'm safe.

Oh my Lord.

That phrase played on repeat in my mind as I drove Sarah and Daisy home last night. I didn't hear one thing they said, just their tipsy giggles. I was lost in my own blissed out fog.

I can't stop thinking about you.

I want to kiss you.

I want to be with you.

I've never had someone look at me that way before. It was desperate, the way Simon looked at me. And the way he looked after we kissed, it was as if I'd helped to settle something turbulent inside of him. As if my kiss had granted him some measure of peace.

"Good morning."

"You want to get in?" he asks, looking uncertain as he finishes rolling down the window.

"Can't." I shake my head, unable to contain the smile that spreads across my face. "Here," I say, passing him a paper cup and a muffin. "You don't have to come here early, you know... Marley opens with me now and Denny's here."

"I want to." He takes a bite of the muffin and grins as he leans his head back, talking around the mouthful. "Mmm, it's still warm."

I'd gladly trade places with that muffin. When he takes a sip of his coffee, I ask if I got it right: milk light, no sugar. He nods and asks, "You remembered? I think I ordered from you once and that was a long time ago." I try to shrug it off like it's nothing, like I remember everyone's order, even though I don't.

"Can you wait a few minutes for me today, or do you want me to pick you up at your house after I'm done?"

His question comes out sounding casual, but I read the uncertainty in his expression. We both know option number two, well, it just isn't an option.

"I'll wait." Absently, I add, "Good...I didn't know if we—"

"I didn't change my mind."

"No." I swallow. "Me neither. I brought clothes with me, to you know, to change into."

He smiles at me with tenderness. He knows I'm nervous and doesn't want me to be. "I'll see you later, Charlotte. Don't work too hard today."

I don't know how I keep myself from cartwheeling my way back across the street.

Not only did I bring a change of clothes, but I brought a toothbrush, a washcloth, make-up and hair products to transform myself after my shift. I'm aware that I often leave this place smelling like french fries, and today I want to look good without looking like I put in too much effort. I think this to myself as I rub the washcloth over my arms and neck and face, practically bathing myself in the sink.

Denny whistles when I come back out by the register, tossing my duffle on a counter stool. I still have about ten minutes to kill before Simon will be ready to go. "Hot date, Charlotte?"

I feel my cheeks redden. "If your idea of a hot date involves cramming for a Global History test at the library, then yeah…I have a hot date with Joseph Stalin."

Thumping his dirty apron with a spatula, he says, "You tell him if he gets out of line, Denny here will trample his ass." Marley doubles over laughing as Denny, truly bewildered, asks, "What did I say?"

When the bell rings to signal a customer walking through the door, the butterflies in my stomach kick it into high gear. I'm hoping that it's Simon, but at the same time, I feel fiercely protective of this new and fragile thing between us. This is mine and I'm not entirely sure I want Denny, Marley, Daisy— or anyone for that matter—in on it.

"Good afternoon, officer," Marley greets Wes. "Table or the counter?"

"Just here on business," he says without taking his eyes off me. "Wanted to check and make sure you haven't had any more trouble."

Denny answers, "No trouble. And I don't imagine we'll be seeing that piece of trash walking the streets again, will we?"

"No, pretty sure he'll never get out. He's facing manslaughter charges now, in addition to four different assault indictments."

I get up to leave. He can stay here and make small talk if he wants, but I'm out. I don't appreciate the intrusion, don't want him coming to my workplace.

"In a rush, Charlotte?"

"My shift's over."

He takes my elbow. "So, everything is ok?"

"Fine."

He lets go but follows me out, and the timing couldn't be worse. I pray that Simon understands the very slight shake of my head and my wide eyes as he exits the hardware store. *Stay put* I'm trying to tell him, but he either doesn't understand or won't comply.

Wes places a hand on my shoulder. I cringe, fighting the urge to physically shake him off. "I'm fine, Wes. Everything is good."

"You're not acting like everything's good."

"You don't need to come around checking in on me. Don't do it again."

Wes starts to say something but Simon interrupts, "Hey, Charlotte, what's up?"

"Nothing," I say, going for light and casual. "Done for the day, heading to the library."

He nods, looking to Wes. It's a standoff, and for some reason Wes, with gun in holster and badge, caves first. Walking back to his police cruiser, he says, "You call whenever you need me, Charlotte, understand?"

Simon waits in front of the diner as I walk to the parking lot and throw my bag in the trunk. I stall, making sure Wes is gone and out of sight before I make my way back over to him.

"Will you follow me to the library? I'll leave my car there."

He nods his head in the direction Wes drove. "He'll check on you?"

"I don't think so, but I can't be sure. He's my brother's friend—"

"I know who he is."

I hang my head. "I've been looking forward to this all morning."

"And he's not going to ruin it," he says, taking my hand and leading me back towards my car. "I'll meet you outside the library."

* * *

SIMON

He's my brother's friend.

There's more to it than that. The way Wes Keller looks at her isn't innocent, and that wasn't some conscientious cop or concerned family friend routine I just witnessed. He looked pained when he placed his hand on Charlotte's shoulder, like he was struggling to regain some measure of control.

He's affected by her, same as me.

Christian's pack of wolves. Not one of those boys set foot near the courthouse during his trial. They were all in on it, and I still to this day don't know how they can live with what they did. I try to imagine it, to put myself in their shoes. But I can't picture anyone persuading me to turn on a friend like Garth, or getting me to turn on the worst, least likable guy in my school for that matter. So I see people like Wes Keller as weak, easily manipulated—as less than a man.

He's a piece of shit. He doesn't get to touch her.

She looks left and right as she makes her way to my car. "Hey," she whispers, avoiding my eyes when she clicks her seat belt into place.

I wait her out, and it's nearly a full minute before she looks my way. "Hey," I say back, smiling.

She lets out the breath she's been holding. "I'm sorry, he just showed up out of the blue. He's angry with me."

"For what?"

"I know what happened to your brother. And I can't pretend. I can't just go on acting like Wes is the person I thought he was." Shaking her head, she says, "I wanted to take up where we left off last night. I didn't want all this between us again."

"None of that is between you and me, do you understand?"

"Since when?"

I take her hand and give it a gentle squeeze. "Since I said so." She nods, her mood lighter. "Let's get out of here. I feel like I've got you on borrowed time."

"Where to?"

"One of my brother's friends works at a go-kart place in Rumson. You up for that?"

"I've never tried it before, but yeah, sure."

"How do you have a license already anyway? I was wondering that the other day."

"My father got that waiver for me...To drive back and forth to work."

"But you drive everywhere and at all times of day."

She's smiling when she nods and says, "Yup."

"Friends in high places." I say it without thinking. "Sorry, didn't mean anything by that."

"It's all right," she says, but it's not. I know she's trying to change the subject when she asks, "This guy is a friend of Timmy's?"

"No, my brother Mike. You wouldn't know him. He's been living up in Chicago for the past two years."

"Oh, so you'll be near him this fall. That's nice."

"You know about Northwestern?"

Her look is shy. "I asked Mr. Vargas where you were going."

I want this girl thinking about me, asking about me. It's selfish and self-centered, but it fills me with satisfaction. "I was surprised to see you in his office that day. It's a little early for you to be thinking about college, isn't it?"

"No." She eyes me as if I've sprouted horns. "Weren't you thinking about it and planning when you were a sophomore?"

"I was, but I needed to be. You just seem...I don't know, maybe like you're worrying about things you don't need to be worried about."

"You think I've got it easy. You've made that very clear, Simon." When I go to speak, she cuts me off. "I've already been told I'm going to the local community college and that I'll work for my father while I'm taking classes. If I really dig in, I'm sure I can convince him to let me continue on, get my degree in teaching or nursing or something else he deems appropriate for a girl."

"What do *you* want?"

Her eyes are sorrowful. "I want to get away from here." Cracking a half-hearted smile, she says, "Enough with the heavy. This is supposed to be a first date, right?"

Hell yes, it's a date. For some reason, the thought fills me with joy and pride. "It's my *first* first date," I confess.

"Mine too."

"So tell me something I don't know about you, Charlotte. Something weird that no one else knows. First thing that comes to your mind."

"I like circus peanuts."

She's laughing and I love the sound of it.

"What the hell is a circus peanut?"

"They're those cheap candies they sell in dollar stores. They're pinkish and chewy and they taste like—"

"Peanuts?" I offer.

"No, they taste nothing like peanuts! They taste like an orange creamsicle."

I'm watching her, kind of dumbstruck because she's so pretty, especially when she's laughing. For some reason it feels crushing. I'm in my head, asking myself why that is, so I don't even take a moment to think when she asks for something personal from me in return.

"My brother Mike is gay. He hasn't told any of us yet, but we all know."

Charlotte busts out in a fit of giggles. "Wow, my circus peanut confession seems totally lame in comparison to that. I'll dig deeper next time."

"Please do." I'm laughing now too. "I don't even know where that came from, but whatever, now you know."

"Now I know," she says, smiling as she gives my knee a squeeze.

"Good to know you're not a homophobe like the majority of people in this town."

"Maybe you're making assumptions. You thought you had me figured out, didn't you?"

"I always knew there was more to you, just didn't want to admit it."

She breathes in slow and deep, her chest rising in time. I turn away because I really don't want to be that guy. But damn, it's hard not to stare at her, take everything in, get my fill.

"We're here," she says, stating the obvious as I park the car. "You think you can take me?"

"I mean, I don't think it's a foregone conclusion. I'm assuming you've been driving since you were fourteen or fifteen, so you'll give me some competition."

"*Some* competition, huh? Just so you know, the first time I got behind the wheel I was twelve."

"Noted." I grab her hand as we make our way to the booth. It feels natural to hold her hand.

"You sure we're good?" I question Andrew when we get to the front of the line.

He nods and then says, "Don't, Simon," shooing me with his hand when I reach for my wallet. "It's been a while, right? How's our boy Mike doing?"

"He's good. I'll be staying with him when I head up there in August."

"You tell him I said hello, all right?" It's difficult to see the hurt look in his eyes. Maybe it was a mistake coming here. When I nod, he shifts his gaze to Charlotte and winks. "And who's this?"

"Down boy." I'm fucking with Andrew, acutely aware that he's still one hundred percent into my brother. "This is Charlotte...Charlotte Mason."

He's good, barely raising an eyebrow when I say her full name. "Andrew," is all he says, extending his hand as he studies her.

The kind smile she gives Andrew makes it seem like she's somehow figured out the whole backstory, the whole tragic mess. And the look he returns says he's grateful, which makes no sense whatsoever. I'm sure it's all in my head, nothing more than another person falling under this beautiful girl's spell.

We fly around the track dozens of times, and it's good. This is stupid and fun, where it's usually heavy between us. She crashes into the hay bales trying to beat me, and I nearly flip a couple of times, because damn, she's competitive and reckless in her pursuit of winning.

"I'm giving you the win, Mason."

"Giving me nothing...I won."

She reaches over and swipes a finger across my chin, then tastes the wayward cheese from my chilidog. Just her touching me casually like this has me sucking in a breath. Every smile, every brush of skin against skin affects me. Jesus, the girl sneezed before and I found myself thinking she was freaking adorable.

Pushing her half-eaten burger towards me, she adds, "You're a decent driver, though. I'll give you that."

"Thanks, I think." The overhead lights come on and I look around to see it's getting more crowded. I was only able to get us in here free of charge during the off-peak hours, when Andrew's manager isn't around. "Do you need to get back soon? Library is probably closed by now."

She drags a fry through a blob of ketchup. "I almost laughed before when you said something about borrowed time. I basically never have to be home."

"No curfew?"

"No curfew, no supervision, no nada."

The way she says it, I suspect the hurt is deep. "It's just you, Christian and your dad at home? No other brothers or sisters?"

"It's me and Christian, with my father making an appearance here and there." She thinks on something for a moment and then tilts her head. "Maybe I'm being a baby about the whole thing."

"How do you figure?"

"I'm old enough not to need him around, and I'm used to it. And I can't stand his girlfriend, so I should be happy that he doesn't bring her to the house."

"He has a girlfriend?"

I hold back from adding the word *already* onto that sentence, but she takes it as if I did anyway.

"He's gone through several girlfriends since my mother got sick. This one's been in the picture for two or three years now."

"Wow."

"It's so embarrassing, Simon. I mean, she's practically the same age as my brother."

"Think they'll get married?"

"I hope I'm long gone by the time that happens."

"What does your brother think about it?"

"I wouldn't know. Christian and I...We're not close. I don't think we ever were, not even before my mother got sick."

"That's gotta be weird then, with just the two of you in the house."

"Beyond weird, I guess. But to me it's just the way it is. He acts like it's his house. He throws parties every weekend, has girls coming and going. I basically feel like an uninvited guest in my own home."

"That's shitty. I'm sorry about that."

"That's part of the reason I'm so happy to have a job to go to on the weekends. Being able to stash away money is the main reason, though."

"Do you have any idea where you'd like to go to college?"

"Someplace near the coast would be nice. We went to visit my grandparents in Florida when I was around six years old. I don't really remember it but I look at the pictures sometimes. It's just this feeling I have, that I'm meant to be near the sand and the ocean."

"I've never been to the ocean."

"Can you swim?"

"To save myself, yeah, but not smooth like Michael Phelps or anything. Can you?"

"I took lessons when I was younger. My mother was raised in Florida, so learning to swim was an absolute necessity in her eyes."

"So if I start floundering around in the river this summer, you'll save me?"

"Absolutely."

We take our leftovers to the trash. We're heading towards the car but I don't want to take her home just yet. "Ice cream?"

"I'm good. We can just take a drive or something. Like I said, I only have to get home at a reasonable hour so I'm not dying when my alarm clock goes off for work tomorrow morning."

"Hmm, this no supervision thing might work to my advantage."

"Right," she drawls with an eye roll.

She leans back against her passenger door with her body turned towards me as I drive, no different than if she was lounging on a couch. "You've got your seatbelt on, right?"

"Yes, Dad, and the door's locked."

"Man, never guessed you'd be such a smart mouth."

"I'm usually not. Maybe you just bring out my inner sassy chick."

I pull into an overlook parking lot on the outskirts of town. It's on the way home, of course, because I can't be driving around aimlessly, wasting gas. I immediately second guess the decision, though. It's dark out here and secluded.

"Is this all right?" She doesn't answer right away. "Maybe this wasn't a good idea, just, you know, with everything that happened last week."

"I'm all right."

I shake my head, doubting her. "Are you?"

"In this moment, right now, I'm fine." She looks down into her lap. "I feel safer with you than with anyone else."

My voice is hoarse with emotion when I tell her how good that makes me feel. It's quiet between us for a minute or two. I don't know what's running through her mind, but I'm kind of overwhelmed in a good way, just amazed, I guess, by how good I feel. Being around her, talking about my life to someone who seems to get it, listening to her in return—I'm happy.

I go to turn the ignition off but hesitate. "Want me to leave the air conditioning on?"

"You had it on?"

Her smile eases whatever's heavy in the air between us, and I'm grateful for it.

"Don't even say it...I know in this junker it probably feels more like someone's blowing warm air in your face than air conditioning."

"I love this truck, it's a classic."

"I actually like being the only guy in the county who has to roll his windows down manually."

"Like I said, classic." She's twisting a lock of hair around her finger, distracting me when she says, "We don't need AC tonight, and anyway, running it while you're idling drains the battery and wastes gas. No need for that."

"Is that so?" I need to get a little closer, suddenly grateful this rust bucket has old school, single bench style seating. "Guess you know a lot about cars?"

"I know nothing!" She squeals when I pull her close to me. "I can't change a flat tire." A flush is crawling across her collarbone and up her neck. "Or change the oil." She licks her lips and lowers her voice to a whisper. "I don't even know where the antifreeze fluid goes."

Leaning in, I whisper back, "Then I'm going to teach you everything."

I'm committed to moving at a slow pace, but she takes matters into her own hands. I suspect she wants to prove to me that she is, in fact, doing fine. She's in my lap, legs astride mine, and it's all I can do to keep my hands from deviating from the path I've made, slowly running them up and down along her sides from hips to ribs. "You're beautiful," I tell her, overcome with how much I want her, want to be anywhere she is.

"You don't have to say that," she whispers.

I pull back an inch, studying her. "I know I don't. I said it because it's what I feel when I look at you." Raising her chin, I kiss her once and then tell her again, "Charlotte, you're beautiful." Her uncertain smile cracks me wide open, physically hurts me. I pull back some more. "Hey, do you think I'm attractive?"

"What?" She's stalling.

"Do you think I'm handsome, good looking, easy on the eyes, guapo?"

"Ugh!" She leans back, both hands braced on my shoulders. "You know you are!" Shaking her head and frowning, she adds, "You know every girl in the school would kill to be with you."

"I seriously doubt that, but I don't care about them...I want to know how *you* see me."

Her eyes soften. "I think you're the most beautiful boy I've ever laid eyes on."

"I'm gonna have to agree with you." I trap her wrists in my hands as she goes to beat on my chest, her effort weak as her body shakes with laughter.

"Are you seriously that conceited?"

"No, I'm just proving a point." I draw her hands up to my mouth, inhaling her scent before I place a kiss on the inside of each wrist. "You told me you like what you see and I believe you. I need you to believe me when I tell you what *I* feel and what I see when I look at you."

She nods. "I'll try."

"Do you really not see what I see? Hell, every guy I know thinks you're hot. It's not like it's even something that's up for debate."

"Stop," she pleads, cringing.

"No," I whisper, leaning my forehead against hers. "I can't look away. Do you understand?"

She moves to slide in closer, but I shift her hips back before taking her face in my hands and bringing her lips back to meet mine. This, where we are right now, this will be enough. I'm leaving in less than three months, and I'm not taking this so far that we'll both be worse off for it after.

We head back towards home a few minutes later, her hand in mine as I drive. And it's good, it's easy with her. I don't think I've ever wanted to talk or to listen the way I do when I'm with Charlotte. She wants to know everything: my favorite bands, whether or not I like working at the hardware store, what my mother's maiden name is. She's full of questions, and for the first time in my life, I want to answer.

"Where exactly do you live?"

"Not far from Tyler. We're on Dutch Lane."

"And *we* refers to?"

"It's just me and my mom at home."

"Oh." Her brow furrows. "And when you leave?"

"She has a boyfriend, Henry. He's a nice guy. And she'd never leave this place anyway...Not while Timmy's still here."

"How long is his sentence?"

"He has three years left...No chance of early parole." When she drops her gaze, I look over and lift her chin. "That's not on you, ok?"

"Can't help it, I feel guilt by association. But I want you to be able to talk to me about Timmy, about your family, about all of it."

"I hate that he's in there. The place is an absolute shithole and the system sucks. Sometimes I just need to put it out of my mind. Other times I use it to push me, to reach for things that I hope one day can help him, help my family."

"You want to be a lawyer." It's not stated as a question.

I turn the ignition off when I pull into the spot next to hers. Charlotte's car is the only one left in the library's lot. "I'm majoring in economics because I think it will give me the broadest education and best preparation for the LSATs. My plan is to take summer classes and winter break credits also. I plan to finish my undergrad in three years, then on to law school."

"You've got it all figured out."

"I guess Freud would say I crave security and stability?"

She pinches her thumb and forefinger close. "Maybe just a little."

"Do you know what you want to do?"

"Not yet."

"You're a talented dancer. Ever thought about making a career out of it?"

She tilts her head in the most adorable way. "I enjoy dancing but I don't see a future in it."

"I do."

"My mother was a theater major. I'm not about to hang my hopes on a dream." I understand that I have no place sticking my two cents in when she adds, "I need a degree that will allow me stand on my own two feet."

"I get that, I do."

We're quiet for a bit, but it's a comfortable silence.

"Chocolate chip or blueberry tomorrow?"

I lift her hand up and kiss the back of it, grateful for her caring nature. "I'm not working tomorrow. I'm visiting Tim with my mother."

"Oh," she says, looking down at the hand I just kissed.

"I've been picking up some shifts after school lately too, trying to save more. Normally I'd never give up a weekend shift, but my mother wanted to squeeze in an extra visit this month and I don't like her going there alone."

"You're a good son."

Her praise makes me uncomfortable, because a good son wouldn't be deserting his mother, leaving her here to deal with everything alone. Come August, I'll be doing just that.

She nudges my knee with hers. "So I'll see you at school on Monday?"

"Meet me by my locker before first period?" She looks surprised. Does she think I'm planning on hiding this, hiding her? "Hey," I pull her in closer, "I can't just drop by your house, or even walk down the street in your neighborhood holding your hand. When I can be with you, I'm going to be."

She nods, looking at me with those big brown eyes. "I'll be there."

She's the one who leans in first and kisses me. I'm the one who breaks the kiss a minute later, holding her to me, breathing in as I nestle into her hair. "Charlotte." I say it just because I love the sound of her name.

We stay like that for a minute, just holding on, before I go around to her side of the truck and help her out. "I'll follow you home."

"Don't be silly." She's grinning and so am I. We probably look like two lovesick fools to anyone passing by, but I couldn't care less. "I'll see you Monday," she says, getting into her car.

I already know I won't be able to wait that long.

Chapter Eleven

CHARLOTTE

I sit in my driveway, reading through several texts from Daisy. *Do I want to go to the mall later?* It's later already. Much later. *And BTW, Sarah's coming too.* Thank the Lord for Sarah. *We're getting burgers at The Ground, meet us.* Nope, still full from the burger and cheese fries I had before. *Sienna and Skylar are here. All the seniors are here.* No, not *all* the seniors. Simon isn't there. Simon's been with me. And then I get to the best text, the one from Simon that just came in:

I should be back by four. Can I see you tomorrow?

I type back *yes* without hesitation.

Maybe I should be playing this whole thing with Simon smarter, but the truth is that I don't know how to play. I don't know the best angle, don't know how to play hard to get, don't know how to make him fall at my feet. I know nothing except that I want to spend every minute with him. And when I'm not with him I'm thinking about him.

I should be wary. We've gone from avoiding and dancing

around one another for months, to diving right in head first. I don't know much about relationships—correction, I know nothing—but I'm afraid that moving at this breakneck pace has crash and burn written all over it.

But I can't stop what's already started. I don't want to stop it, or slow it down for that matter.

And I don't want to think about how this will end.

I smile my way through the Sunday morning shift. And I don't even care that the living room is filled to capacity when I get home, Wes among the crowd. I bring my change of clothes into the bathroom, lock the door and ignore the people who are knocking, too lazy to use the bathroom on the other side of the house. I take my time in the shower, blow my hair smooth and straight, dress in my favorite jeans and a snug tee, and put on some lip gloss.

I'm at the end of your street. Which house is yours?

I figured I'd be meeting him someplace neutral again, hiding. But no, Simon came here, right into enemy territory. I drag in a breath, scared for the both of us, but at the same time I'm on cloud nine. He's fearless and I love it.

I'll be right there.

I'm excited and breathless and happy when I see him smiling at me from inside of his truck. "Were you about to knock on my front door?"

"I was taking my lead from you."

"Today? Maybe not such a good idea."

"The whole gang's there?"

"Afraid so."

"Want to hang out at my house?"

"Um, sure."

"My mother's making lasagna."

"You think she'll be good with—"

"I told her about you," he says, taking my hand as soon as I click my seatbelt into place.

"You did?" I can't mask my surprise. If he told his mom about me, then he likes me. Like, for *real* likes me.

"Yeah, you goof."

"How did it go today?"

He shifts his attention back to the road. "You don't want to know."

"You don't have to leave me in the dark. I really do want to know."

I was feeling brave when I said the words, but the ensuing silence and the hard set of his jaw seems to suck the air from small space we're sharing. He scares me when his mood shifts. I can't think of anything to say, and I hate the chill in the air as much as I hate my own insecurity. I feel small next to him.

A minute passes before he slows at the intersection and turns to me. "I'm sorry. It's just that there's no way to put a positive spin on it. He's got his arm in a sling one time, eye swollen shut the next. That place is hell on earth."

"Can you—"

"There's *nothing* I can do."

* * *

SIMON

I'm poisonous. Or it's this thing, the scarlet A, the shitty circumstances that come along with being born a Wade in this town. The past and the actions of others are capable of ruining everything good.

Me and Charlotte? We haven't even started and I feel it's got the power to end us.

I don't want it to. I want this girl sitting next to me to smile and be carefree. I want to be the one who makes her feel that way. I want to be unburdened and relaxed, like everyone else my age. But today was a shitty day.

Timmy's using again. Maybe it started with painkillers prescribed by the prison infirmary, but prescribed or contraband doesn't matter—he's using. He was shifting in his seat and acting distant today, looking over his shoulder every few seconds, on alert, paranoid. His fragmented attempts at conversation were dominated by pie in the sky bullshit. Today it was some absurd "business plan" he came up with to open a bike shop. I have to hold back from smacking my own forehead when he asks my mother—dead serious—if she wants to be an investor.

I hate that fucking place. I hate every guard, I hate the warden I've never laid eyes on, I hate the governor, the president—I just exist in a state of hatred.

I don't know how to compartmentalize this part of my life. I want to keep it from her, and I can't help but feel angry when she pries. But I know the anger is because I feel so damn weak, so powerless to do anything about it. There is nothing I can do to help Timmy right now, and that makes me feel pathetic.

"There's *nothing* I can do."

She doesn't say anything, just reaches over and eases one hand off the steering wheel, lowering it down onto the seat and covering my hand with her own.

"I'm sorry...I didn't mean to snap like that."

Her thumb drags back and forth over the top of my hand, soothing me. "It's all right, Simon. I understand."

And I know she does.

The air is still heavy between us when we pull up outside my place. Seeing my home through her eyes doesn't do anything to get me out of my funk. Most people in our development keep their places tidy, but a few have given up. Being house proud in a trailer park is sort of ridiculous, I get it, but in that moment I want to hide the cinderblocks and discarded tires that litter the area in front of a neighboring unit. Then I take in the welcome mat, the flowery curtains and the wreath on our front door. The homey touches used to please me, but right now it looks like lipstick on a pig.

She pulls me out of it. "I'm excited to meet your mom."

I smile at her because I know Charlotte is more nervous than excited, and she's doing a shit job of hiding it. "My mom baked an apple pie in your honor."

"Really?"

"Yup. This is monumental...I've never brought a girl home for dinner."

She side-eyes me, grinning. "So I'm the first?"

"The first." I'm dead serious but she laughs as she hops down out of the truck.

I guide her up the steps but then pull her back against me once we reach the landing. Before I open the front door, I rest my chin on her head and exhale. "Thank you for that...You make me feel better when all the bad shit starts weighing me down. I just don't want you to have to bear that for me." I turn her to face me. "I'll do better."

She shakes her head and swallows. "You saved my life, Simon, so please don't ever apologize or think your troubles are some kind of burden."

"I didn't save your life."

"You did" She leans over and kisses me softly. "That day and every day since."

Chapter Twelve

CHARLOTTE

Daisy is drifting away, and I'm a terrible person because I've barely given our disintegrating friendship a passing thought. I've officially become *that* girl—the girl who drops her friends once a boy comes into the picture.

Sarah and Daisy practically had to scrape their jaws off the pavement that first Monday morning when Simon snuck up behind me and kissed my cheek in front of everyone. Everyone. My knees nearly gave out, but I somehow managed to keep it together, sucking in a breath as a smile stretched clear across my face.

She wanted to know. And while Sarah breathlessly asked question after question, Daisy said nothing, quietly studying me. When we were alone during our last period class, she stopped me when I started talking about a paper due the following week. "Are you going to tell me what's going on?" She looked more hurt than curious.

"He, um, kissed me at the party Friday night, and well, I've gotten to know him since I've been working at the diner and everything."

"You looked...together." Shaking her head, she said, "Like, it's three days later and you're a couple?" I didn't answer. Didn't like the line of questioning. "I mean, I always knew you had a thing for him, but," Daisy met my eyes and smiled, "he looked like he was positively on cloud nine when he kissed your cheek this morning."

I let out a breath, thankful that she wasn't looking to challenge me or question the very idea of Simon being into me. I was doing enough of that myself. *What does he see in me? Does he really think I'm beautiful? Is any of this even real?* I was self-doubt central, so I certainly didn't need anyone else chiming in with more skepticism

"What is it like?"

"What is *what* like?"

"What is it like when Simon kisses you?"

I told her inconsequential things, let her in a little but not much. And Daisy was easily entertained because she knew nothing of boys. I used some generic word like amazing, selling it by whispering the word as I moved in close so that no one else could hear. But I didn't tell her what it *really* feels like. That was mine, something I wanted to lock in a special box and hold close to my heart. And how can you explain the feeling anyway? It sounds crazy and dreamlike because it feels that way too. A feeling in your chest, a tingling sensation that extends out to the farthest point of every limb and beyond. Light, like your body is hovering above ground. Weightless, carefree and... happy. How can you explain it to someone who's never been there herself? You just can't. After that first kiss I was older than Daisy, years older. And we could never go back.

I floated away from Daisy and Sarah. I sat at the same lunch table but couldn't focus on the conversation. One day Sarah called me out for smiling while she was talking about the very real possibility of her failing Spanish. I'd been in my own head yet again, thinking of the person responsible for making me smile more than I ever had.

In the weeks that followed, we spent nearly every free moment we had together. I was Simon Wade's from the moment his lips first touched mine, and from that moment on, no one else mattered.

"Are you sure you're not disappointed?" He looks pained and I don't want him to be. "You know I'd take you if I could."

"For the one hundredth time, Simon, I am not disappointed. I'd much rather be hanging out with you at the river tonight than cooped up in that sweaty gym for prom."

"Thanks for saying that."

There's a lot we aren't saying. For one, I get the feeling Simon would love to be driving towards the school gym right now instead of in the opposite direction. These past few weeks it's as if brooding, serious Simon has changed places with a new and improved, lighthearted version of himself. He jokes around more, smiles, and wants to spend time with his friends with me tagging along. Nearly every night they meet up, and Simon will ease me onto his lap whenever we sit around a bonfire out in the woods or in the field behind Tyler's place. The closer he gets to graduation, the more a sense of nostalgia takes hold. Garth will sometimes pass a wisecrack, something along the lines of me casting a voodoo spell over Simon. I know that's his way of saying he thinks I'm good for Simon, and I hope he's right.

He should be there with his friends tonight. I want that for him, and I want to be dressed up for him, standing right beside him. Offering to loan him the money had crossed my mind but I knew better than to voice that proposal. And how would I have pulled it off, anyway? This is a relatively small town. Charlotte Mason shopping for formalwear and showing up on Simon Wade's arm would have gotten back to my family somehow, and that had disaster written all over it. I envision my brother storming the gym with shotgun in hand.

As it stands now, far as I can tell, Christian is oblivious to my newfound happiness. He goes on ignoring my very existence, same as always, and I'm glad for it. I just want to keep on existing in this bubble with Simon, even though I'm acutely aware that we are on borrowed time. There are barriers that stand between us and the things we want, but in my mind this is only a temporary situation.

Simon has plans, but so do I.

In my version of Simon loves Charlotte, our love will grow stronger with each passing day, distance be damned. We will speak on the phone every day and write letters like those first ones—letters where we bare our innermost thoughts and dreams. I'm already hatching plans to sneak away to visit him every few months. Not exactly clear on how I'm going to manage that, but I'm floating some ideas along the lines of class trips, dance team competitions and college tours. I've been forging my own absence notes and permission slips since the fourth grade anyway, so it doesn't seem all that far-fetched. And then I'll finally graduate, accepting the full ride offered to me by the very same university Simon attends. I even have a fully furnished image of the tiny but cozy one-bedroom apartment we'll share off campus. There's a small round table tucked into a nook off the kitchen. Our books are spread across the surface, the two of us studying late into the night after a dinner of ramen noodles or the leftovers I take home from my job at the diner near campus. Life isn't easy in my fantasyland, but I am blissfully happy. We both handle a full course load and work part-time jobs, struggling to make the rent each month. But in this life, in our bed that is a simple mattress on the bedroom floor, Simon curls up next to me every night and holds me close.

Sixteen and in love, you couldn't tell me there was no such thing as forever.

Part Two

PLAN B

Chapter Thirteen

CHARLOTTE

The brown paper bag taunts me from across the room. Perched on the dresser next to a picture of my mother, it's staring me down. It's been sitting there for weeks.

A parting gift from Simon.

A cold, impersonal *fuck off* is what it feels like.

Just yesterday I stood in the family planning aisle, shaking as I looked over my shoulder every two seconds, praying I wouldn't be spotted in a pharmacy twenty miles away from home. I quickly filled my basket with nonsense to obscure the pregnancy test I'd buried at the bottom. Shampoo, dental floss, nail polish—yep, just another day, nothing to see here, folks. My eyes took in the water-stained ceiling tiles, the candy display, the headlines on the tabloids—anything to avoid the eyes of the twenty-something year-old guy ringing up my purchases. I might have read more into his tone when he handed me my change and asked, *Is there anything else I can help you with?* But I'm pretty sure a knowing, sympathetic look accompanied those words.

Take within 72-hours after unprotected sex to prevent unwanted pregnancy.

That ship had sailed.

I took the bag from Simon that morning, still half asleep and confused. Why was he banging on the door so early, and when exactly had he slipped out? He fell asleep curled around me last night, the two of us crowded into my twin bed. I didn't care that all hell would have broken loose if my dad or brother caught him in my room, didn't care about the risks. He needed me last night and I was there for him.

Simon wouldn't look me in the eye. "You need to take this." When I didn't answer, he squeezed my free hand. "Promise me."

When I looked up, his eyes were fixed over my shoulder. "Don't worry," I assured him, "my brother's not home."

"I don't give a fuck about Christian." When I flinched, he pressed his thumb and forefinger against the bridge of his nose and looked off to the side as he let out a breath. "I'm sorry."

Look at me, I begged silently. *Say my name.* But when he did finally look at me a chill ran through my body. I knew what this was, knew what he was doing before he even said it.

"I'm leaving today."

I coughed like I'd taken a direct hit to the chest, as if the air had physically been knocked out of me. "Today?"

He nodded. "We're heading up to Somerset and I'm leaving straight from there."

"I can go. I'll drive your mom home."

"No. Henry's coming. We're good."

"But I want to—"

"What?" he barked.

All I could do was shake my head in stunned disbelief. Last night I was his world. It was *me* he came running to. *I* gave him comfort when he was suffering. Now, just a few hours later, he was speaking to me as if I was no more than a needy child testing his patience.

"There's not going to be a service, Charlotte. There's no mahogany casket, no priest, no flowers."

"What's happening?"

With his eyes cast down, he shoved his hands deep into his pockets. "I have to go."

Simon was pleading with me to understand. But I was selfish, foolish, and just wanting so badly to hang on to him. "You're leaving me."

"You always knew I was leaving."

"Not yet, though. And I just...Last night you said—"

"Do not do this to me."

I stood there, numb and wordless, watching as he turned his back on me, got into his truck and drove off. It was a good five minutes before I managed to step back and close the door, the realization finally setting in.

He's not coming back.

* * *

SIMON

It burns on the way down. I imagine the cheap liquor eating away at my insides as it winds its way through my system. *Just one more*, I pledge as I take another swig. Only weak people numb themselves with booze and drugs.

Timmy was weak.

I'm not.

I know this. I know that when this bottle is empty, I'll fall into a deep sleep that will help me forget, but just for tonight. I know I won't be looking for a crutch tomorrow because I can't.

I cannot fail.

But tonight I let it all crash down around me: the careless, mechanical way the prison administrator expressed his condolences, the apologetic look the clerk gave us as he handed over the manila envelope with my brother's meager belongings, the sorrow that will weigh my mother's shoulders down for a long time to come, and Charlotte.

I walked away from her, couldn't look her in the eye. In the light of the morning after, I hated myself for using her body as a vessel for mine to grieve. Drunk and lost, I went to her after we got the call. Climbed into the bedroom window she opened for me. Climbed into her bed and cried like a damn child as she held me. Pressed into her soft body and lost myself in her goodness. Told her I'd love her forever.

I handed her that paper bag before turning my back on her, getting into my truck and peeling out without a glance backward. *Tying up loose ends*, I told myself. As if she was just something I needed to cross off my to-do list before I left this town for good.

Do not do this to me.

Those were the last words I spoke to her. Do not make me feel bad. Do not pretend like you thought I was going to stay. Do not act like last night changed anything. Do. Not. Cry. *Please*, I wanted to beg her. *I have to go*, I pled in silence.

Follow me, I'll wait for you. That's what I wanted to say, what I should have said. But instead I went with coldhearted and cruel. The words and the way I delivered them were meant to sever, meant to make a clean break.

I'm not in the business of making false promises, and my life thus far hasn't set me up for believing that tired line of bullshit everyone seems to throw out like confetti: *Just have faith and everything will work out fine.* I don't think so. Charlotte is sixteen. She has two more years in this town, a town I'm never setting foot in again. So I don't want her believing that we have a future, even though I've spent countless nights dreaming of just that.

I cap the now empty bottle and put it aside, sinking into the mattress. I'm sure most people would complain about the accommodations at this crappy motel midway between Pennsylvania and Illinois, but this is the first time I've had the luxury of stretching out across a full-sized bed. The spare pillow isn't soft. The cheap polyester case is scratchy and the filling is clumped in sections, but that doesn't stop me from pulling it close to my body and wrapping my arms around it as I roll onto my side.

Now I can pretend, imagine I'm back on the bank of the river. Charlotte's eyes flutter and then close, her contented smile telling me that I'm good and worthwhile. I kiss that spot on her neck just below her jawline, letting my lips linger, feeling the steady beat of her pulse. I pull her in even closer so that I can feel the rise and fall of her chest with each breath. Holding her like this gives me a solid kind of peace that I've never known.

I've never felt this way about anyone, never felt intense emotions over a girl. Just the thought of her makes me so happy that I'm pretty much sporting a ridiculous smile all the time. I'm so proud to have her by my side that I draw her close to me whenever I can, leaving no doubt in anyone's mind that she's mine. And I feel protective over her in a way that feels irrational—territorial and violent. I will shield her and rage against anyone who would set out to harm her. She is still mine. I can dream it any way I want in this near-sleep state.

She is mine and I love her.

My mind drifts back to last night, but I want to relive it, change reality, make it so that it went down in a very different way. It wasn't the sad and desperate plea of a grieving boy. It wasn't rushed. I didn't forge ahead and take her before she was ready. I didn't collapse on her and then roll away after I was spent, trance-like and despondent. God no. In my current drunken state, I grant myself a do-over. I can kiss her tenderly, the way I always do. I can be grateful for what she gives to me and I can cherish her, taking time to make it good and memorable for her. I can hold her after, hold her close the entire night. I can stay with her and hold onto this mind-blowing goodness day in and day out.

Forever.

Fuck me...I told her I'd love her forever.

I looked away from her like a coward this morning. I didn't need to see her face to know that I'd devastated her, ruined everything good that had ever been between us.

I hate myself for using those words. A lie would have been better, would have made it easier for her to move on, to leave me in her rear view mirror.

In this moment, clutching the pillow that serves as a pitiful substitute for holding my sweet girl, I feel like it's going to be the death of me. Because what I said is true. I will love Charlotte forever.

* * *

CHARLOTTE

I exist in my memories. Hold onto them for dear life. I spend the weeks following Simon's cut and run in a sort of fugue state, going through the motions but not truly present.

I need you.

In my head he says it to me over and over again. He's hovering over me, resting his weight on one elbow as his other hand grips the flesh of my hip. He holds back like he always does, but I feel his body pressing into mine, I feel his need.

I am a grown up that night at the river, I feel bold and sure of myself. I lead him, push him, whisper in his ear that I've taken care of everything. I untie the strings myself, shift until I'm out of the suit that's still wet from swimming. I open myself up like a gift for him.

He shakes his head and kisses me softly. "Can't."

"I'm on the pill." My cheeks flush with embarrassment.

"What? Why?"

Don't cry, don't cry. "Because I—"

"Because you want to give this to me." He leans closer and lays a gentle kiss on one eyelid and then the other. "And I love you, but I can't."

The first time he told me he loved me, I cried. He kissed the tears as they slipped down my cheeks, apologizing to me as if he'd done something wrong. He didn't understand. How could he understand the ache I felt, the hollow place that those simple words filled inside of me? How could he know that it had been years since my mother spoke those words to me, and that no one else had done so since? I drew his lips to mine and kissed him, whispering on a breath that I loved him too.

But that night I don't hear *I love you.* I hear rejection and it stings. I go to sit up, covering my breasts with both hands in embarrassment. "And when you're in Chicago? Will you turn *those* girls down when they make you an offer?"

"Don't," he pleads in a soft voice. He drags his discarded shirt over my hips and eases me back down onto the blanket, raising my wrists over my head. "Be with me like we always are...It will be enough."

His breath ghosts over my jaw as his hands explore my body. This time he goes further, allowing himself to rut his naked hips against mine, touching me and losing himself in the sensation. I suck in a breath at the feel of him hard against my belly and silently will him to slide lower, will him to lose the self-control that holds him back from taking me.

When I made the split-second decision to swipe those sample packs from Sarah's bathroom a few weeks ago, I lied to myself. Her older sister won't even know they're missing—that was the first lie. I'm an adult, and responsible adults take birth control pills when they're in a relationship. That was more than a lie, it was a downright joke. Responsible adults go to the doctor and actually get information on how to properly take said pills—they don't steal them and start taking them without even reading the damn directions or warning labels. And all along I told myself that he was leaving come fall, and that I was fine with it because down the line it would all work out for us. That was the biggest lie of all. Deep in my heart, I hoped that once I gave him everything he'd never be able to let me go.

I gave, and on that last night we had together, broken and grieving, he took from me.

It didn't make him stay.

Chapter Fourteen

CHARLOTTE

"Throw your shit in the back and get in the car."

The way he swerved close to the curb and then slammed on the brakes should have me fearing for my life right now, but my survival instincts aren't what they used to be. I'm simply too wrung out to cower in fear.

I'm pretty sure my brother has always been this way. I imagine he didn't even cry when he entered the world. No, I can envision him exiting the womb and fixing the doctor and nurses with a scowl. *What are you waiting for, dipshits? Clean me up!* A similar look of annoyance directed at my mother when she paused to look on at him in wonder. *Stop gawking, lady, I'm hungry!*

He is a man of few words, and the words he directs my way are rude and clipped. Since Christian got caught nailing my father's girlfriend a few weeks ago—shocking, given his reputation for honesty and integrity—he's been on thin ice around Mason Motors.

My dad ditched Liza, which hasn't turned out to be the positive development I once thought it would be. He's home more often now and walks around in a constant state of pissed-off. Christian is on his best behavior when my father is home, but then reverts to an even more twitchy and disagreeable version of himself when he has the run of the house.

I've been avoiding the place like the plague. I've taken on one extra shift at the diner after school on Wednesdays, and when I'm not working, I hole up in the library until closing time.

I'd like to say I'm being productive, catching up on homework or prepping for my college entrance exams, but I'm not. Most days I can barely stand upright, the combination of pregnancy hormones, shock and misery knocking me for a serious loop. I've fallen asleep in those uncomfortable chairs, drooling with my head down on a table more times than I can count. On those rare afternoons when I'm not doing a spot-on impersonation of Sylvia Plath, I scan the stacks like a spy on a covert mission and then tuck into a corner to read. There's nothing to do but shake my head in disbelief, stunned by the fact that I am now no more than a grim statistic.

A whopping 38% of teen mothers earn a high school diploma.

Only 2% earn a college degree by age 30.

Less than 20% of teen fathers marry the baby's mother.

That last one hurts the most.

I've written him three different letters, but I never get it quite right. I start off by asking how he is. It's an awkward opening line, given that we didn't exactly part on good terms. In one draft I go on to ask what college is like, figuring small talk is the way to go, a way to lessen the impact of the bomb I'm about to drop in paragraph two. And after that little nugget, I reassure him that I've got this, that I expect nothing from him. I can't read over the words without shaking my head —it's a total crock of bull.

I want to tell him I'm scared, that I'm lonely for him, that I can't breathe. I want to ask him to hold my hand through this and help me make a decision, to take this burden on and shoulder it with me. But I won't do it. I won't trap him, won't saddle him with a responsibility he surely doesn't want. I won't keep him in a place that has done nothing but torment him.

I make an executive decision: I'm not going to tell him. And the joke is on me, because I couldn't mail the letters even if I wanted to. Simon left no forwarding address.

Christian has found me on a bench, waiting for the morning bus bound for Pittsburgh. The grand plan was to make my way to Florida. My mother has a sister near Tampa. Her name is written on a scrap of paper in my pocket. It's got her phone number and address on it too, all written in my mother's hand. I met her just once, years ago. I don't know her, and I don't know if this decade-old information will lead me to her. The only thing I do know for sure is that I have twelve hundred dollars saved up and no future here.

Main Street is a vision of suburban blight, with approximately half of the retail properties shuttered, but it's still the heart of town. Christian Mason, upstanding businessman, won't make a scene by backhanding me in public, so I've got that going for me.

Slamming the door, he circles the back of his car to loom over me. "Simon Wade...Really? And where is Simon now?" He lowers his voice to a menacing whisper. "Gone now that he's had his fill."

"No," I whisper.

"Yes, yes, yes," he barks back, mocking me. "Maybe this'll teach you to keep your damn legs closed."

He knows.

I flinch when Christian leans in closer. "Yeah, I *know*," he sneers as his gaze shifts towards my middle, "and so does Dad." He grabs my small suitcase and hurls it into the trunk. "Now get in the fucking car."

Welcome to Ohio the sign reads less than an hour later.

"Where are we going?"

"You're going to live with Dad's sister, Janelle."

I feel dead. No energy or desire to protest the arrangement, the plans made without my consent. And as a girl still shy of her seventeenth birthday, pregnant with a baby whose father has just traipsed off to some fancy college I can now only ever dream of attending, I know I don't have much in terms of bargaining power.

Aunt Janelle? I've never met the woman. She's no more than a mythical being. What does it matter anyway? Nothing matters anymore.

He looks over to gauge my reaction. I give him nothing. It's what I do when he's itching for a fight. "You think Dad wants you shaming us in our community?"

Shaming us? Right, because we're so upstanding. A father who whored around the entire time his sick wife lay dying in the hospital, and a brother so used up and angry at the age of twenty-three that if I didn't hate him so much, I'd pity him. Sad state of affairs, but my father is one of the few business owners in the county who actually does manage to turn a profit, so I guess he feels justified in viewing himself as a pillar of the community.

I keep my gaze fixed out the passenger side window, taking in the all too familiar landscape, the evidence of small town life along the side of the road. Desolate stretches of highway broken up by the occasional truck stop or Walmart supercenter. Billboards for adult entertainment shops, antiques or fireworks. Clusters of houses dotting the hills, recently painted and well maintained near some exit ramps, but those are the exception to the rule. Most towns look like replicas of my own, the majority of the homes dilapidated and neglected.

"I have to use the bathroom."

"Of course you do," he mocks, voice sweet and laced with sarcasm.

By the time he pulls off at the next highway rest stop, I'm about ready to wet my pants. He takes a spot near the entrance. "I'm gonna use the bathroom quick and then get gas. Get us something to eat and I'll meet you back out front."

I pause for a second. "I need some money, Christian."

He eyes me suspiciously. "You don't have any money?" I do my best to look embarrassed as I shake my head and lower my eyes to my lap. I am bone tired but I've been conditioned from years of experience to never to let my guard down. I know my brother. If he thinks I have more than a few bucks to my name, he'll be pulling off to the side of the road and rummaging through my things the second I nod off. "What have you been doing with all your tip money?"

"Used it all," I whisper, covering my flat belly with one hand. "He—"

Christian runs both hands through his hair, tugging on it. I brace myself, waiting for the blow. He shoves my shoulder once, so hard my head hits into the window, and then reaches over and jerks my head back, tugging on my ponytail. "He what, Charlotte? He said he'd take care of you? Are you really that stupid?" He's hollering now. "He's a Wade! They're all trash!" Christian gives me another shove, but this one has no power behind it. He digs into his pocket and fishes out a twenty, tossing it in my direction without looking at me. Stroking his left knee absently, he stares straight ahead. "If I had my way, all three of them would be in the ground."

"Where are we?" I ask, rubbing the sleep out of my eyes.

"Michigan."

Looking at the dashboard clock, I figure we've been on the road for over ten hours already. "Where does Aunt Janelle live?"

"Michigan."

Asshole. I'm not going to get more than that out of Christian, so I dig my phone out of my bag. No search results for a Janelle Mason in Michigan. She's probably married though; we wouldn't share the same last name. *Where in the hell am I going?* The anger comes on like a flash, but quickly morphs into a sadness that's now firmly lodged in my chest.

Checking my messages, I see only one text from Daisy. It's not like I'm expecting anything from him. No, Simon has been in full-on ghost mode. Not a word since August fifth, the date I think about twenty-four seven. In the predawn hours of August fifth I gave him everything, and since coming to realize that something was most definitely not right, I've been in the habit of counting the days and weeks from August fifth obsessively.

What's up stranger? I don't reply because I cannot even fashion an answer to that question right now. We've barely spoken all summer, but now that school is back in session Daisy is reaching out to me again. She knows how to do this, knows how to make friends and keep them. But I'm a hopeless case, more content to sit alone in the library than to socialize with her and Sarah in the cafeteria or study hall. She probably thinks I'm just heartsick or something, just missing Simon. And I am heartsick, but my sadness is compounded by terror, panic and bouts of anger. So it's better if I just stay away. It's not like she can be my confidant. I can't go to her for advice or a shoulder to cry on.

I wonder what Daisy will do when Monday turns to Tuesday, when this week turns to next week and then next month. Will Daisy ask questions, look for me? Will anyone?

At that moment it clicks into place. I see Miss Dawson walking into Mr. Vargas's office. Did she set this all in motion? On Friday morning she called me down to her classroom. I didn't bother to show up for Dance Ensemble tryouts the first week of school, and she's been on my case ever since.

When I explain for the third time in two weeks that I have too much schoolwork to do, she confronts me. "Schoolwork, huh? I'm not buying it. With all that extra study time you should be acing your classes, but you're not. We're only a month into the school year and your teachers are expressing concerns." I meet her eyes, nonplussed. I simply do not give a flip because I am so damn tired—*all* the time. "Your math teacher says you've barely scraped by on the first few quizzes and your English teacher says you haven't handed in the last two assignments. What the hell is going on, Charlotte?"

I tug on the bra strap digging into my shoulder—a tactical error. My stomach is still flat, but I think my boobs have grown a full cup size over the past few weeks. She looks to where the fabric of my shirt strains over my chest and then her eyes soften.

"You can trust me."

I can't trust or depend on anyone but myself. I've long since believed that, but the past several weeks have confirmed my views on trust. I breathe in through my nose and look out the window. The silence is thick.

"All the girls ask me about this tattoo, everyone except you." She reaches back with both hands and fixes an elastic around her long hair, making a top knot. One finger traces over the spot on her neck, the bird. "I always feed them the same generic line…That's it's about change, taking flight, and that the date signifies a turning point in my life." Now she has my attention. "I don't tell them anything more." She pauses, her finger still caressing that spot. "During my sophomore year of college I got pregnant."

I'm surprised but I don't show it. My face is stone. Sure, I've been more emotional these past few weeks, but I am still Charlotte Mason through and through. I typically don't wear my heart on my sleeve. And knowing Miss Dawson is just aching for me to break down and confide in her? That alone strengthens my resolve to give her nothing. Still, this decision is weighing on me like a ticking time bomb, so I don't hold back from asking, "What did you do?"

"I felt like I had no one…Couldn't tell my parents." She's working the similar circumstances angle. *Nice try, lady.* "And the guy…Let's just say I didn't know him all that well." She cracks a sad smile. "I'm counting on you not to judge me." I shake my head, reassuring her. "So…I fretted and waited until my days were literally numbered. I knew I had to make a decision. I considered everything, and I was very close to having an abortion, but I wound up carrying the baby to term. I lied to everyone. I told my parents I was cramming in extra classes and stayed in my off-campus apartment alone for the summer." She rubs at her eyes. "I had to call myself a cab for the hospital when my water broke." She looks to gauge my reaction, and even though I can barely draw breath I hold it together. "My baby...I gave her up for adoption."

I am furious with myself as I reach up to bat one hot tear off my cheek. Just the word *her* does it to me. What is growing inside of me? A boy or a girl? *Stop it*, I tell myself as I school my expression. "I'm sorry, Miss Dawson."

"Call me Grace."

"Um, okay. I'm really sorry for what happened to you, but why are you telling me all this?"

"I just want you to know that if you need someone to talk to, I'm here."

"Thanks," I stand, "but really, I'm fine." Miss Dawson stays in her chair, studying me. As I reach for the doorknob, I turn back to her, unable to curb my now desperate need to know. "What happened to her, to your baby?"

"She lives with a family in New Jersey. The parents seem very nice. They're wealthy from what I can tell. You know, the kind of people who can give a child every advantage." In response to the question in my eyes, she says, "The adoption was open, and I spoke with them several times before I made the decision final. I know where they are but I've promised not to interfere in their lives. She's growing up knowing she's adopted but it will be her decision whether or not she wants to find me someday."

I turn back towards the door, unable to face her when I ask, "Did you make the right decision?"

She barks out a cheerless laugh, and it feels like a direct hit to my gut. "I don't know. I've had a decade to reflect on it and I'm still not sure. Maybe there is no *right* decision. Every option has consequences that weigh on you for years. It's still painful, I can tell you that much. I just know I would have been better off if I had someone to lean on at the time."

She lets that last sentence hang in the air. I want to tell her. The words are rushing up with my breath, pushing against my lips, begging to be let out in the open. I don't dare turn back to face her. "Like I said, Miss Dawson, I'm fine."

No, she couldn't know for sure that I was pregnant, and even so, I can't bring myself to believe she would out me to my guidance counselor, to my father, or to anyone else.

"Christian, how did Dad find out?"

He makes me wait. He bites into his candy bar, chewing it open-mouthed like a donkey. After the third or fourth bite, he finally speaks around the mouthful. "He found the love letters you wrote to your baby daddy, moron."

I stare out the window, my heart hollowed out and vacant as we continue our northbound ascent into the Upper Peninsula.

* * *

SIMON

It's been nearly two months since I left her.

Thankfully my brother Mike doesn't question my shitty outlook on life, my silence, or my poor appetite. He probably thinks I've dropped nearly ten pounds because I'm still grieving. And I am still torn up over Timmy, and also homesick for Mom, but it's the loss of Charlotte that has me this way.

I wish I could put her out of my mind. I really do, because this hurts too damn much.

During the day it's not as bad. I'm busy with classes, playing catch-up a lot of the time because my school district didn't have the kind of enrichment programs that most of my fellow freshmen have benefitted from. I'm struggling in Calculus, and my Microeconomics class, while it seems like a refresher course to my peers, is full of language and concepts that are entirely foreign to me. So I read the assigned text twice, take copious notes during the lectures and then review them over and over. I read in between classes and during the few breaks I get at my part-time job.

I get back from the warehouse by midnight—quarter to one at the latest. I feel filthy by the time my shift's over, so I slip in and out of my dorm room quietly to shower, trying my best not to wake my roommate. Then I collapse into bed, weary knowing that I'll be repeating the same routine tomorrow.

That's when it hits.

Sleep should come quickly but it doesn't. I toss and turn, willing myself not to go *there*. But I do, every damn night.

The opening scene is always the same, a need to quench the desire I feel for her, to be with her the way I used to be. Sometimes that morphs into a fantasy, one where Charlotte is here with me. We struggle through classes side by side, both of us working hard and barely making ends meet, but we're happy. We laugh sitting across from each other as we eat dinner off paper plates, we tease and play in that way people in love do, and we fall asleep at night with our limbs tangled together. When it's good like that, sometimes I can manage to drift off in the middle of it. But then there are the other nights, the ones when my thoughts take a dark turn. And I fall asleep eventually, but the nightmares can wake me up, sweat pouring off my body, teeth clenched and my fists pounding the mattress. In those dreams Charlotte is crying. Someone is hurting her because I've left her alone and defenseless. Sometimes it's a faceless monster, sometimes it's Wes, and sometimes it's her brother.

Charlotte always denied it, but I know her brother. He's an angry fuck and I'm convinced he lays hands on her. She swore up and down that it was only words, he never hit her, but her denials never sat right with me. It wasn't a regular thing, but there were bruises, ones she couldn't explain away. Bruises that ringed her upper arm like someone was squeezing, or the kind of black and blue you'd get if you took a bad fall on your ass. She wasn't clumsy so I didn't buy the trip and fall stories, even though she delivered them stone-faced.

The worst part is the helpless feeling. It's like my hands are tied behind my back in those dreams. She calls for me but I can't find her. She's scared and she's lost. I can hear her voice but it's getting farther and farther away. I can't get to her. I never reach her. I've lost her forever.

It's after one of those restless nights that I break down.

I decided when I left that a clean break was the only way to do this. I wouldn't contact her. Even though I knew it was cruel and she'd wind up hating me, it was better that way. It was the only way she'd move on, forget me. So I got a new phone with a brand new number. Chicago area code—big, important man I am—and wiped my memory clean of every friend and acquaintance I'd ever made back home. Knowing my mother and Henry were out of that town made cutting ties even easier. But I can't rid myself of the memory of Christian Mason or the lock on Charlotte's door.

Early that morning, as I was fixing to open the bedroom window and crawl out the way I came in, something drew me back to her bedroom door. The screws weren't flush against the wood. You could see Charlotte had put in some effort, but she wasn't strong enough to secure them all the way in. I walked into the hallway, hoping for a confrontation, but it was still dark outside so it was an empty gesture. I knew that.

So today I dial the number and ask to be put through to my one and only hope's extension, not exactly sure what it is I'm going to say.

"Guidance office."

"Mr. Vargas?"

"Yes. Who's calling?"

I pull my collar away from my neck, even though I'm sporting an old, stretched out tee. "It's Simon Wade," I say, trying to calm my nerves.

"Simon! How are you, kid?"

"I'm doing all right."

He sobers, morphing into concerned mental health provider mode without delay. "You're settling in, doing all right? Tell me about life out there in Chicago."

"It's good. Different. Classes are hard."

"The workload is heavy."

Vargas is still using that mirroring technique. I don't call him out on it, or even mind the slightest bit, because he's good, doesn't sound like a damn parrot. He's nothing like the counselor I saw for a few sessions as part of some sham family support program at the prison.

"I'm handling the work, Mr. Vargas. And thanks for hooking me up with Professor Westfield. He's been checking up on me, making sure I have everything I need."

"I'm glad. He's a great contact to have, Simon."

"Yeah."

He lets us stew in silence for a few moments before prompting, "Tell me more."

"Just working my ass off, that's all. It's good, really."

"Ok." He lets it hang in the air, waiting on me to elaborate.

When I don't, he says, "I'm glad to hear it. No pressure, but I'm counting on you to be my success story. I've got my hands full with college applications now. Hoping we'll have another graduate heading your way in September." He chuckles. "Next September's more likely. The talent pool isn't too promising this year."

"Oh, yeah?" I press, praying I'll be rewarded with some mention of her name. "Who's talking about Northwestern?"

"The only one who has a shot is a junior...Adam Brown. You know him?"

"No, doesn't sound familiar." What the hell? I know she has the grades to make it in here. "No one else?" *Oh, fuck it.* "Charlotte Mason isn't looking to apply?"

"Ah...Charlotte moved. I didn't know you two were... friends."

"Moved?"

"You heard me right."

Now I'm the one who goes silent as I process what he just said. "When did she move?" He gives me nothing. "Look, Mr. Vargas, I'm not asking you to break confidentiality or anything, I just want to know when...It's important."

"I believe it was a few weeks ago...near the end of September."

"After the school year already started? Where did she go?"

"I don't have that information. And even if I did, you know I wouldn't be at liberty to share it with you."

"I just...That's weird, right? To leave a few weeks into the school year?"

"Well, it's not typical but it happens."

"So her family up and left? Sold their business?"

He sighs. "Simon..."

"I know, I know." I take a deep breath, still reeling from the shock. "Mr. Vargas, can you do me a favor?"

"I'm not sure."

"Please, can you just make certain that she's all right?" He doesn't answer. "Please?"

"Is there something you aren't telling me?"

"I...I don't know. I just have a feeling something's wrong. Can you just do this for me?"

"You don't have a way to contact her?"

Yeah, I could call her, but I'm an asshole. "No, sir, I don't."

"I can try to reach out to her. I'll try, that's all I'm promising."

After taking my number, he ends the call. And I can't wait any longer. Fishing my phone out again, my hands are trembling and my mind is racing as I struggle to remember the number I purposely didn't put into my new contact list. It rings once before I'm hit with the standard *no longer in service* message.

That night, the vision is devoid of shadows or murky details. Charlotte is there, clear as day. She's looks to me with fear in her eyes before being pushed up against the brick at the rear entrance of the diner back home. I can hear her gasping for air and crying. He has her caged in with his body, pushing his face up into hers, one rough hand on her jaw. I growl and go to pull him off, but I can't move my arms or legs. He turns around to laugh at me. I wake up with my heart pounding, mouth bone dry and pulling for breath.

The face that turns to laugh at me is my own. I am the one hurting her.

Chapter Fifteen

CHARLOTTE

"How far along are you?"

My aunt wears her gray hair in a braid that reaches the middle of her back, and she dresses like a cross between Pocahontas and a folksinger circa 1968. She wears a Native American-style poncho, a long flowy skirt and earthy-looking sandals. Several beaded bracelets circle one wrist, and a cigarette dangles from the fingers of her other hand.

Christian just asked her where to leave my bag without saying hello first, and Janelle is busy ignoring him, looking me over from head to toe instead.

"Seven weeks."

Janelle nods and takes a long drag off her cigarette before stubbing it out on a plate. She looks in Christian's general direction but not at him. "Put it upstairs, last door on the left." Janelle's lack of interest in getting to know her nephew is beyond odd, and I figure this doesn't bode well for me.

We stand in silence as we wait for Christian to come back

down, listening awkwardly as the heavy stream of his urine hits the bowl and the toilet flushes. I notice the faucet never turns on to indicate that he's washed his hands, and his lack of manners embarrasses me in front of this stranger. Christian, vulgar and unashamed as per usual, is still zipping his fly when he hits the bottom stair.

He looks to my aunt, lifting his chin. "I'll be heading out now."

She stands back, nodding once.

He turns to me then, shaking his head and smirking. Palm up, he demands, "Give me your phone."

"What? It's mine...I paid for it." My plea is whispered even though I'm itching to scream out in protest.

He reaches around me and snatches it out of my back pocket before I can react. "Be good, Charlotte."

God help me, but I wish a fiery car crash, a flesh eating disease, or death by a pack of crazed pit bulls on my hateful excuse for a brother. I hate him for the years of indifference, for the cruel comments he's directed my way, and I hate him for leaving me here with this cold woman.

And then there were two.

As we stand there staring at each other in silence, I wonder if Janelle is fixing on going the duration of my stay without actually speaking to me.

The standoff ends when she crosses the room, turning the lock once Christian is good and gone. "You should get on up to bed now," she says, surprising me when I take in her soft smile. "You've had a long drive. Tomorrow you and I will sit. Don't worry," she adds, "we'll get this all figured out."

I'm sure my mouth hangs wide open before I have the sense to reply, "Yes, ma'am."

· · ·

I attribute this sudden onset of morning sickness to my new surroundings rather than pregnancy.

"Ginger ale is in the fridge, I'll get you some crackers." Handing me the crackers and gesturing with her head, she says, "Head on out to the deck and try to eat a little bit. I'm a caffeine junkie, can't start my day without it. I imagine the smell will turn your stomach right now, though."

When we arrived last night it was dark and I was shell-shocked, so this is the first time I take notice of my surroundings. Janelle's small kitchen is all knotted pine with homey accents. I notice a glass-domed cake plate with scones on it, plaid curtains that match the cushions on the chairs, around a dozen cookbooks lined up neatly on a shelf, and a sign hanging above the window that reads: *Lord, give me COFFEE for the things I can change, and WINE for the things I cannot.* But nothing could prepare me for what I see when I approach the screen door. Stepping outside, my eyes go wide as I take in the expanse of water. The sun is dancing off the small ripples formed by a passing rowboat, and the man in the boat pauses his rowing for a moment to wave to me. I wave back on instinct then retreat from the railing, flopping into a deck chair. The beauty of this place leaves me awestruck, my upset stomach forgotten.

"I take it you like the water?" Janelle asks, a chuckle escaping as she takes in my expression.

"I-I guess so."

"Lake Superior," she says as she settles into the chair next to mine, sipping on her coffee. A few moments later she says, "Do you know I haven't heard from your father in nearly ten years?" I steal a quick look her way, unsure of whether the question is meant to be rhetorical or not. "Then I get a call from him two days ago, *telling* me you're coming to stay with me, not asking me."

"I'm sorry."

She shakes her head. "Nothing for you to be sorry about. That brother of yours looks like him...Acts just like him too." Janelle looks out over the lake again. "So, what are we going to do about this?" She continues like she's not expecting any input from me. "Your daddy instructed me to take you somewhere and get this taken care of. I assume he was suggesting an abortion. Not man enough to say the word, I guess." She raises her cup and blows on the drink to cool it. "Is that what you want?"

"No! I mean...I don't know."

"We'll have a hell of a time finding a provider up here if that's what you decide to do." I rub at my eyes, feeling so very alone in all this. "Let's leave the decisions for later," she says, shaking her head. "First things first. We're taking a ride into town later so we can get you registered for school."

"I'm going to school here?"

"Did you even speak to your daddy before you got in that car yesterday?"

"No."

I hear her mutter the word *asshole* under her breath. "Yes, for the foreseeable future, you're here with me. He's not taking you back in. I'm sure I don't have to tell you, but he can be harsh like that." She reaches over tentatively and pats my hand. "It's not so bad here, Charlotte. I promise. Just like you, I landed here a long time ago when I needed to escape. I've made this place my home."

I haven't been touched by another person since Simon up and left me. I wasn't comfortable in my new surroundings, and she was still little more than a stranger, but I appreciated

Janelle's small gesture of kindness more than she could ever know.

"A beautiful girl, new in town. Dis'll give 'em sometheen to talk ah-boat."

It takes me a moment to understand what the waitress is saying. Unlike my aunt, the waitress and the school secretary we encountered have an unusual way of speaking. After the woman I now know as Carol Ann takes our order, I catch my aunt smiling at me.

"I'd say about a quarter of the townspeople speak like that, more so the farther away from the coast you venture. A lot of the early settlers up here were Scandinavian. They call it Yoopanese. This and them are pronounced *dis* and *dem*, nothing is noth-*een*, and about is, yes, ah-*boat*."

"I'll get used to it," I offer, trying my best to be a good guest. Let's face it, I have nowhere else to go. I go to reach into my back pocket for my phone and realize, for the third time today, that I no longer have a means to access the outside world.

She blows on a spoonful of chili. "Reception is spotty up here anyway."

I make a mental list. First order of business is to get my hands on a computer. "Is there a library in town?"

"Powell shares a library with Ishpeming. You have your license yet?"

"Yes, but—"

"Best way to learn is by doing." She looks to me after gesturing for a refill on her coffee. "Let's take a tour around town, see the sights, and then we'll drive the route between my house and school. I imagine you won't want to be riding the bus once you start to show. I mean, *if* you to start to show." Gulping down my shame, I nod. "I work from home most days so you can take my truck. When I need to be somewhere, I'll drop you off at school."

"Thank you, Aunt Janelle. I really do appreciate everything you're doing for me."

"It's my pleasure."

And the way she says it, I start to believe that maybe it is.

I take the "sights" in again as I make my way to and from school the following Monday. Powell is a one stoplight kind of town. There's basically a diner, a general store, volunteer fire department, post office, sheriff's office and a sad excuse for a gift shop.

My first day of school wasn't entirely awful, even though each and every teacher felt the need to introduce me at the start of class. Halfway through the day, after breezing through trig, history and chem, I was confident I'd happened upon a school system less challenging than my own. By the time I sat down at a deserted table in the cafeteria with a well-worn copy of *Jane Eyre* to keep me company, I was digging this new state of anonymity and starting to believe the affirmation I'd been repeating since sometime in late August: *I'm going to be okay.*

No one approached me. Not that first day or in the days that followed. My wardrobe earned me a few envious side glances from the girls and a few lingering looks from the boys, but for the most part no one seemed to give a flip about the new girl. *Ah-boat* the new girl, I should say. God, the accent took some getting used to, and every time someone ended a question with *yah?* or *eh?* I wanted to smack myself in the forehead. I didn't really mind, though. The accent gave me the giggles, and I was sorely in need of amusement. And I liked listening in on their conversations, observing the body language, watching the way the kids interacted with one another. I was comfortable in my role as an outsider.

The time alone gives me time to think. I sit in the library, settling into a corner so that no one can walk up behind me and get a glimpse of the flow chart I'm drawing. My three choices are written as headings: Terminate, Adoption, Keep Baby.

Under Terminate, the pen shakes in my hand when I write: *Have to do it this week*. I am now dangerously close to the ten-week mark that's considered the cut-off for the non-invasive pill option. Just swallow a little pill—simple, clean and easy. It's obviously what Simon would have wanted me to do. He'd be none the wiser and I could go on with my life. Hopefully I could stay on here and get my high school diploma in this newfound state of obscurity. I could study my ass off for the college entrance exams and get a scholarship. Then I could head anywhere. I could head south to Florida or west to California. Hey, I could even plant my ass at Northwestern the September after next. Suddenly filled with rage, I picture myself standing tall, squaring my shoulders and spitting on Simon Wade as I pass by him on the quad.

My feelings are all over the map when it comes to him. I'm obviously not rocking a loving or conciliatory vibe at the moment.

When I move onto the Adoption heading, my thoughts go to Miss Dawson. A decade. She has a ten-year-old daughter out there somewhere. I write: *Find a nice family*. When I conjure up an image of my prospective parents, Blake Lively and Ryan Reynolds come to mind. I aim high. They're a golden young couple, well-dressed, and they obviously have the means to provide a child with every advantage. A lump forms in my throat when I envision their tears of joy as they look down in wonder at the precious bundle they cradle together. The scene unfolds with me snatching my baby back from them and running down the hospital corridor in the opposite direction. Ugh.

I go to town under Keep Baby. First order of business: *Get GED in January.* I'll be turning seventeen then. *Ask Janelle if she'll let us stay.* The two of us have fallen into a comfortable routine, but I really don't know how she'd feel about housing both me and a baby for the foreseeable future. *Get a job. See about online college courses.* I keep adding items. *Buy crib, baby clothes, diapers.* I still have twelve hundred dollars stashed away, and I'm proud knowing I can cover some of the basics on my own. This list is daunting, though. *Apply for medical insurance.* As I jot question marks next to *food stamps* and *welfare benefits*, I remember about the small investment accounts my mom insisted on opening for me and my brother with money from our Baptism and Communion gifts. That's what capable parents do. *See about legal emancipation*—I underline this last item on my list. I don't want my father or Christian getting their filthy mitts on that account.

"We've got an appointment in Marquette tomorrow after school." Janelle takes a spoonful of mashed sweet potatoes and then passes me the bowl. "They have a clinic there." I don't even realize I've dropped my gaze to the table until I feel her finger on my chin coaxing me to look at her. "Hey now, it's just to meet with a counselor to talk things out. Shoot, I shouldn't have phrased it like that."

"No, Janelle, it's okay. I just..."

"What? Have you come to a decision?"

"I don't want to get rid of it."

Before I blurted out those words, I really hadn't come to a decision, but now I feel some measure of relief in knowing my three choices are reduced to two.

The ensuing silence makes me uneasy so I fumble for something to say. "I mean, I don't know if you..."

"If I what, child? You have to speak. I can't read your mind."

"Do you mind if I live here until I deliver the baby?"

She sets about cutting into her steak. "Not at all." And without missing a beat, she adds, "Pass the biscuits, sweetie, will you?"

Chapter Sixteen

CHARLOTTE

After that first trip to the clinic with Janelle, I make the drive for my monthly appointments on my own. Sometimes I pass the time checking out the other girls in the waiting room, guessing as to what each one's story is. Some are there to get birth control, you can tell by their no-nonsense attitude or the bored way they flip through the reproductive health brochures. Some are teary-eyed. They're the newbies, fretting over the pregnancy test they're about to take—the one that will confirm what they already know. Then there are the girls who stare straight ahead wearing a blank expression. Decision made, keeping it or not keeping it, accepting of their fate. When I'm not busy judging everyone else in the room, I imagine it's how I look.

Every other month I also meet with Penny, the social worker assigned to my case. *The Case of the Wishy-Washy Unwed Teen Mom*—that's the title I'd pick for this caper. She does her best to cover a variety of topics with me, but I know the real purpose of these sessions. Penny is dedicated to the welfare of my unborn child. Her job is to determine if I'm mentally stable, if I'm prepared and able to provide a good quality home for this baby. If she deems me lacking, it's her job to steer me towards adoption.

I'm not painting her in a flattering light, even though I like her. I appreciate her candid nature, the way she gives it to me straight. She warns me that no matter what I decide to do, nothing is going to be easy. She doesn't treat me like an idiot, even though I often feel like one for getting pregnant in the first place.

Now seven months along, I earn curious looks on a daily basis in the halls of my high school. I don't care. Not most days, anyway. I wear my indifference like a shield. I notice two girls in the senior class who are in the same predicament, but feel no compulsion to swap war stories with them. They aren't looking to befriend me either—cue my *not* disappointed sigh.

Janelle helped me fill out the waiver form to take the GED exam early. I plan on acing it this coming Thursday. The legal emancipation business is going to have to wait, though. Apparently my father needs to sign off on it to forego court proceedings, so Janelle and I agreed it was best to let it lie. Hopefully he won't remember about that bank account until after my eighteenth birthday.

My back is hurting as I heft myself up onto the exam table today. "Shirt up, princess," the ultrasound tech teases. Shirt up —I know the routine. I cringe as that goo is spread over my middle. "You'll get a clear look at the baby today. You ready?"

My gaze shifts to the monitor. "I guess." It's a blurry image. "I thought these things were super clear now."

She chuckles. "We don't have those fancy three-dimensional machines here at the clinic. But you can still make everything out just fine."

"If it's a boy or a girl? You can see that?"

I ask the question, even though I know the answer. No one asked if I wanted to know the sex at the twenty-week sonogram, and I can tell my nurse isn't about to just offer it up today. The doctor will tell me if I ask, but I'm not sure I want to know just yet.

"Hmm, depends if this little critter cooperates. Here we've got some nice little fingers and toes...Spine looks good." She looks pensive for a split second and then starts taking screen shots, one after another. Seems like a lot more than she took the last time. Back and forth she goes with the probe over my belly, then more images. She has her smile back in place, but now it seems toothy and forced.

"Everything good?"

She gives me a kind look but says nothing as she hands me a wad of paper towels and gestures for me to sit up. "Doctor will be in shortly, honey."

Within an hour of the ultrasound, I'm being transported to the Children's Hospital in Ann Arbor. The fetal echocardiogram revealed a severe obstruction of the aortic valve. My *son* has a heart defect that may prove to be fatal if left untreated.

The course of your life can change in the blink of an eye. Instead of tackling the GED this coming Thursday as planned, I'm now scheduled for surgery.

When the doctors begin throwing around phrases like *long-term prognosis* and *best chance at a normal life*, I struggle not to zone out. I force myself to nod, making every attempt to keep up when I'm told the problem has to be repaired in utero as soon as possible.

Janelle is the one who stays tuned in, writes down everything the doctors say, researches the procedure and then explains it to me.

The night before my surgery, I wake from a nap to see Janelle crying softly as she sits in a chair at my bedside.

"The baby has a good prognosis, right Janelle?" I'm suddenly worried that the adults haven't shared the whole truth with me.

"Yes, and we're in one of the finest hospitals in the country. You and the baby couldn't be in better hands." She wipes at her cheeks and takes a deep breath. "Did your father ever tell you about my husband?"

"You were married?"

She laughs. "Is that so hard to believe?"

"No! I mean, Dad never mentioned that you were married."

"I'm sure he rarely spoke my name aloud." I don't feel the need to confirm that truth. "I shouldn't be so hard on him. He had it tough, I guess. My father died when he was just sixteen. That's pretty young to take on the responsibility of an unstable mother and a younger sister."

"He never talks about his childhood."

"I think he feels ashamed about running out on us when he finished high school. He was young...I never blamed him. I was sent to live with an aunt when my school called protective services on my mother." In response to my gasp, Janelle shrugs in a matter of fact way. "She drank heavily after my father died."

"My dad enlisted in the Navy."

"Yes. It was his way out. And I didn't see him again for another eight years. I was shocked he even came to our mother's funeral. By then he'd gone and married your mom." Janelle smiles. "She was beautiful and entirely too good for my brother. But he loved her. I'll always remember the way he looked at her as she held Christian. It was like his entire world resided in her."

"I barely remember what they were like together."

"You were so young when she had the stroke. I came to stay and help out for a few days. Do you remember?"

I wanted to tell her that I remember, but I don't. "No."

"You were so sad. I could barely get you to come out of your room. And your brother..." She looks up to the ceiling, shaking her head. "God forgive me, but he was a monster." I laugh at that. "He rolled his eyes and walked away from me when I introduced myself. He spit the homemade lamb stew I made back onto his plate after one bite—said it tasted 'like ass.' On day three I threw in the towel when he told me to fuck off and your dad didn't correct him." In response to my wide eyes, she nods and puts her hand over her heart. "Swear to God."

"I believe you."

"I always felt alone growing up. Your dad and I were never close, and my mother was not up to being a mother. After my visit, I'd wonder about you from time to time—hoped you had an easier time of it."

"Christian and I aren't close, never were. My father was always closer to Christian. They had football in common."

"Your dad and I were never close either. He did give me away at my wedding, though." Janelle shoots me a sly grin. "Turned out to be a bad omen, I guess."

"What happened?"

"Paul was a really nice guy...He still is. I ended things after nine years. I just couldn't stand disappointing him anymore, even though he never acted like having children was a make or break situation."

"I'm so sorry."

Janelle sips at her soda. "It was a bad time. I just wanted to set him free, let him meet someone new, someone he could start a family with."

"You couldn't adopt?"

"Before I met Paul...Well, let's just say I made a few bad decisions. I had a boyfriend, a real wild one." When I smile, she shakes her head. "Not the good kind of wild. He was a small-time dealer with a temper. Yeah, and it turns out his idea of a good time was armed robbery. Two weeks after my eighteenth birthday I was driving the getaway car. I was tried as an adult of course."

"You went to jail?"

"For two weeks. I mean, I knew the boy was no angel, but I truly didn't know he walked into that convenience store fixing to hold a gun to the cashier's head. I testified against him... Didn't see how I owed him my life after what he put me through. I was found guilty but the district attorney and the judge were sympathetic. I was sentenced to five years of probation." She shakes her head. "I can still hardly believe it happened."

"I can't picture you meeting with a probation officer."

She nods. "Month after month after month. It's sobering, I'll tell you that."

"So how did you meet Paul?"

"One of the conditions of my parole was steady employment. I was hired as a temp and Paul was my boss." She smiles and shakes her head. "He saw something in me. Went to bat for me when I applied for a permanent position at the firm and my record became an issue. Pushed me to start junior college, encouraged me to apply for promotions...He taught me everything I know." She reaches over and takes my hand. "You never know what lies around the bend, you know? Here I was, in the worst predicament possible, and something very good came of it. I met Paul, who showed me how to stand on my own two feet."

"But?" I ask, having not gotten an answer to my question.

"Long story short, no one was giving us a child to raise with a felony conviction on my record. I bet it's different now, at least I like to think the world is a more accepting place...That a dumb split-second decision you make when you're a kid doesn't brand you for life."

"Where is Paul now?"

"He stayed in Philadelphia. Started dating someone I'd introduced him to years before. When he called to tell me he was getting married, I ran. Had to get far, far away from the pain. Would have sailed to the Arctic Circle if it was possible."

"Powell is a close second," I offer, trying to ease her sadness.

"Damn straight it is. Those first two winters I wondered if I'd truly gone nuts, upending my life like that and heading off to no man's land. But I found peace in the snow, the lake, the silence."

"You've built a nice life for yourself there."

She takes in a breath and straightens up in her chair. "I have. I have my band of misfit friends—"

"The book club."

"Yes, my book club that reads roughly one third of the books assigned. And Lawrence isn't half bad. I think I'll keep him."

Lawrence is Janelle's boyfriend. She didn't let him come around for the first two months I was living with her. She told me afterwards she didn't want to upset the apple cart. I've gotten used to her animal and agriculture-related adages. I now try not to put the cart before the horse when making decisions, I know there's more than one way to skin a cat, and I realize that leopards generally don't change their spots. Sometimes I amuse myself trying to come up with ones that apply to my life. Like I didn't give Simon a reason to buy the cow, you know, having given the milk away for free, and as a result, the chickens have come home to roost. Yes, I have that much time on my hands. Five months later and Lawrence has yet to stay overnight. But I watch them, they're affectionate with one another. I figure they probably get it on while I'm at school during the day. As they say, while the cat's away, the mice will play. Yeesh.

Our smiles fade in tandem. "So..."

She looks at me square, reading the question on my mind. "Paul and his wife have three children." She rolls her eyes. "Amanda *loves* posting dorky photos." She adds, "He looks happy and that's what I wanted for him."

I reach out and squeeze her hand. Every single person has a story, and I feel closer to Janelle knowing hers.

I don't get much sleep the night before the surgery. My aunt is wonderful, so wonderful, but she's no substitute for Simon. When I first got the news, I wailed like a wounded animal, faced with the prospect of losing our child, our son. Up until that moment I was so undecided, ambivalent at times even. But now I feel as if I would surely want to die myself if my baby doesn't survive. God, I want Simon to hold me, to tell me it's all going to be all right. I want him to *know*.

But he doesn't know because he never came looking for me. It pains me to admit that I believed he would. After every-thing, after the way he left and the deafening silence in the weeks that followed, I still believed that I was special to him, that he must be suffering, missing me and what we shared. I believed he would find me, sweep me up in his arms and tell me he was sorry. He'd hold me and tell me again how he'd love me forever.

As they roll me towards the operating room, I wonder where he is at this very moment. Is he just waking up, thinking about an assignment due later this week? Or maybe he's eating breakfast with his new friends in the dining hall. He might even be on his way to class walking alongside some new girl—flirting, laughing, entirely oblivious to what is going on.

Simon.

He is my last coherent thought, the last face I see before the anesthesiologist places the mask over my face and instructs me to start counting backward.

One hundred, ninety-nine, ninety-eight...

Chapter Seventeen

SIMON

"You'd be up shit's creek if I fell for an accountant."

"Brandon enjoys working on my truck. You like the challenge, don't you?"

"It's not a challenge, it's just an old piece of crap five years past its expiration date."

Mike comes over to the kitchen island and hands both of us a beer. "Is it running?"

Brandon smiles at my brother the way you smile at someone you love. "It'll get the job done." Looking to me, he adds, "For now."

"For now, my ass. I need that baby to get me back and forth to my job."

"How is that working out?" Mike clearly doubts my ability to keep up with classes while holding down a night shift. "You know I can lend you some money."

I take a long pull off my beer and shake my head as I swallow it down. I'm exhausted, and I've been questioning my decision making skills lately too, but I'm not taking my brother's money. "My classes are manageable and the workload isn't too bad."

In truth, I feel like I'm drowning sometimes. The kids here are different. Their mothers and fathers are research scientists, prize-winning novelists, corporate titans—they come from the land of success and they speak the language of privilege. I retreat to Mike and Brandon's place sometimes when it gets to be too much. I don't have to pretend like I have my act together when I'm around these two. I can be myself, let my guard down.

Brandon grabs a sweatshirt from a hook by the door. "I forgot the arugula. I'll be right back."

Mike gives him a lazy salute. "I'd say screw it, but I'm making broiled salmon over a bed of arugula. It's kind of necessary." When we're alone, he asks again, "Sure you're all right?"

"I'm fine. It just takes some getting used to."

"I know what you mean. I felt like Chicago was some giant, scary, alien metropolis when I stepped off that bus." He stops in the middle of chopping some scallions. "Sometimes I think about those first few days here, scared out of my mind, and I can't believe I was stupid and desperate enough to do what I did."

"It all worked out."

"By the grace of God." He goes back to work prepping the fish. "I'm lucky I didn't get killed."

"You never really told me the story behind what happened."

"Same story a thousand other gay teenagers could tell. Got outed by some Neanderthal, his homophobe friends made my life miserable, I thought about killing myself, and then finally got the fuck out of that town before I did wind up dead, either by their hands or my own."

"People suck." He nods in agreement. "Did I tell you I ran into Andrew a while ago?"

"When?" Mike asks, a smile spreading across his face.

"Last spring. He let me and a friend into the go-kart place for free. He asked about you."

He nods and chuckles. "You knew about us?"

"I followed you two when you snuck off into the woods one afternoon."

He winces. "Sorry, little brother. Did I scar you for life?"

"Me?" I put a hand on my chest, pretend I'm offended. "Hey asshole, I'm open-minded."

Brandon comes back in as Mike says, "I always feel bad when I think about him. He's still living there, probably still taking shit from those ignorant clowns."

"What did I miss?" he asks as he puts the grocery bag down on the counter.

Mike says, "Just talking about Andrew." Brandon squeezes his shoulder as he passes by on his way to the fridge. "They kicked his ass when it was just a rumor. Can you imagine if they actually caught him in the act?"

"They would have killed him." I state it as fact.

"And me right along with him."

"You think it's still the same there?" Brandon asks. "I mean, so much has changed in just the past five years."

Mike smirks and shakes his head, but I'm not so inclined to agree. "Maybe it is better. I mean, I don't think it's as safe to come out there as it is in New York or Chicago or any other big city, but I also don't buy into that stereotype that the majority of people who live in rural areas are intolerant."

Mike pauses on his way to the stove. "I don't either, but it's the minority sometimes, the select few who tend to talk the loudest and punch the hardest."

I nod, acknowledging what sucks but is often true. "They did make Andrew's life a living hell for a while there."

Brandon wraps and arm around Mike's shoulder. "I work with a mechanic named Danny. Nice guy, but Brandon hates him for no good reason."

My brother and I look at each other and say in unison, "Danny Duncan." Mike adds, "Yeah, and take note...If we have kids someday we won't be naming any one of them Danny, Blaze, Wes or Christian."

Brandon is wide-eyed. "Blaze?" I can't help but laugh, even though those names don't exactly conjure up happy memories for the Wade family. Brandon cocks his head. "Maybe living with that name made him mean."

When Mike plates our dinners at the small kitchen island, I say my version of grace, "Thanks again for having me over. This looks great."

"You're always welcome," Brandon says as Mike nods with a mouthful of food.

I clear the plates after we finish. Mike sits back looking on, sipping the last of his beer. "Are you sure nothing's up? You don't seem right."

"I'm, uh, a little homesick if you can believe it."

"Funny, as we no longer have a home to return to in our hometown, but I guess I can understand missing what's familiar."

"Did Mom tell you I was dating a girl?"

"Ah, a girl." He smiles. "No, she didn't mention that. But in fairness, she's been a bit of a hot mess lately between Timmy, packing up the trailer and moving to North Carolina." He waits me out for a minute and then says, "Tell me about her."

I have my back turned. "I was going out with Christian Mason's sister, Charlotte."

"Really? That must have been interesting. Is he still— "

"Yes, he's still a smug, mean-spirited punk."

Mike's eyebrows are practically at his hairline. "Did you hang out at her house, get to know her family and everything?"

"Are you sniffing glue, brother?" I keep my expression neutral, but that ache is coming back, the one that hits right in the center of my chest. "I never stepped foot in their house." *Except for that one time.* "I don't think Christian or her father even knew about us."

"That's probably for the best."

I nod, but can't help wishing that her brother did find out. Maybe we would have fought. I could have landed a few hits for Timmy, for Mike and for Charlotte too.

"Do you know Wes Keller is a cop now?"

"That's like the opposite of reassuring. I mean, he wasn't the worst out of that pack, he didn't torture me and Andrew as bad as some of the others, but he was a piece of shit. Another one of Christian's lapdogs."

"I think he has a thing for Charlotte."

"You still haven't told me anything about her."

"She's not like them, not at all." I try to describe her beyond that but I can't. It hurts too much. "I just miss her."

* * *

CHARLOTTE

"Are you ready to fill out the paperwork? It's a big hassle with social security and everything if we don't file them before you're discharged."

"Discharged," I joke. "I don't live here?"

"For real...I don't know what I'm going to do with myself when you're gone. No one else watches *The Bachelor* around here."

Mary is my favorite nurse, but I love them all. I have a tremendous level of respect for the profession now, seeing first-hand how hard they work and how concerned they are about the well-being of all of us under their care. I'll miss them, but I'm eager to get home. Weird...I now referred to Janelle's as home.

"I only watch *The Bachelor* because there's no Netflix in here. It's either that or watching those creepy *Nightline* mysteries."

"So...Any ideas?"

When I wasn't busy gazing at my beautiful son with awe and adoration, or fretting every time a specialist came in to speak with me and Janelle, I was considering what name to bestow on this little man. Every single day someone reminded me about filling out the birth certificate. Who knew one flimsy little piece of paper could be capable of causing so much strife?

The first name took me a few days. I thought I'd see his face and immediately come up with the name that suited him best, but it didn't happen like that. No, the only words that came to me when the nurse placed him on my chest were *Thank you, God* and *I love you*.

I spent hours staring and smiling at him. He deserved a special and wonderful name. I tried out Simon, whispering it to him as he fed at my breast, but it just didn't sit right with me. And I wasn't naming him Bradley after my father, or Christian—hell no. I didn't know either one of my grandfathers, so naming him James or Peter seemed ridiculous. What did I want for my son? Happiness, of course, and love. But looking on at him in the neonatal intensive care unit, I realized strength is what the both of us needed. I looked up boy names associated with strength. Maximus —*hah*, Aaron—*not bad*, Jerry—*really?*, and Ethan—*hey, I like that.* And even though I didn't know James Caldwell, my mother's father, I wanted this child to have some tie to her. Ethan James.

I assumed I'd write Simon Wade down as the birth father, even though I had no intention of reaching out to him, but the state of Michigan had different ideas. Naming Simon as the father required establishing paternity. I'd have to contact him— *Surprise, you're a daddy!*—and have him sign a form in the presence of a notary. Not happening.

But leaving the line blank didn't seem fair to my son and it made me feel cheap. It made me feel like one of those girls on those stupid talk shows who can't figure out which one out of the three dudes she's been sleeping with has impregnated her. To be fair, maybe that's how people see me: careless, young and clueless. But that's not how it is. Maybe our time together had been brief, but I did truly love someone in this life, and that someone had loved me too. We meant something to one another, and the two of us together created this child.

"I'm just going to give you something to chew on." Mrs. Ryan was the social worker assigned to me when I was admitted to the hospital. This morning she eased into a chair holding my baby, looking down at him smiling as she spoke to me. "He's going to know about this beautiful child. You might tell him this week, you may reach out to him next year, he may find out on his own at some point, or this boy will seek him out when he's a young man." Every scenario made my stomach churn with anxiety. "It's never going to be easy, never going to be the right time."

"I can't tell him now."

"Is there a time in the future when you can envision yourself reaching out to him?"

"Maybe once he finishes school?" She looks to me, asking for more. "He has a plan...His undergraduate and then law school. He's brilliant, Mrs. Ryan." I can feel myself blush as I say the words, bragging about Simon, knowing I sound like a fawning fool. "He's on a full scholarship at Northwestern." Shaking my head, I add, "I'm being realistic. Telling him now would ruin any chance he has at getting an education. He's had a pretty hard life and this is his only shot."

She glances over at the television, where the Real Housewives of who knows where had been muted upon her arrival, and then looks back to me. "Everything aside from your questionable taste in television tells me that you're every bit as brilliant. I meet a lot of girls your age, Charlotte. Not many of them pass the time reading *The Jungle* or *Blood Meridian*. What have you got on your nightstand now?" she asks, tilting her head to look. "Ah, *Tess of the d'Urbervilles*." She smiles. "Another light and easy read."

"Tess is my girl," I joke.

"Yes, I'm sure you can relate to her." She shakes her head and the smile drops. "Charlotte, don't be one of those girls, the stoic ones who suffer in silence and don't reach out for what they deserve."

"I'm not."

"*He's* brilliant, *he* needs to finish school, *he* deserves a chance at a better life. What about you? What do *you* deserve? What do *you* want?"

"Are we back to this?"

She looks confused for a moment and then lets out a breath, shaking her head. "No, I'm not talking about your options anymore. This baby is going home with you. I know you'll be a good mother to him."

"So what are you saying?"

"I'm just trying to make sure you don't leave here thinking only in the short-term." She looks down and caresses Ethan's cheek. "I want you to start now, start setting and reaching goals. I want you to set a date in the near future to ace the GED, I want you enrolled in an online college entrance exam prep course, and I want you taking college credits come next September. Local community college, online through University of Michigan, whatever. I just want you to keep moving forward."

"I want that too."

"Be the exception. The most depressing part of this job is meeting so many young women like you, women with unlimited potential who get caught up in the struggle and stop pushing themselves." She seems to weigh her next words. "I feel like I can shoot straight with you and be brutally honest. Do you know that only two percent—"

"Of unwed teen mothers earn a college degree before the age of thirty?" I can't help the sarcastic edge when I add, "Yes, I'm well aware."

She has the nerve to laugh. "Of course you know. You just proved my point. And don't get defensive, Charlotte. My job is to help you."

"I know what I need to do."

"I know you do, sweetheart. But you're seventeen, and motherhood is hard, even when you have resources. I keep in touch with my young mothers. More often than not, that gung-ho attitude falls by the wayside after weeks of midnight feedings. The realization that your life is forever changed is too much for most girls to handle. You go from having a social life, dreaming of a bright future, worrying over clothes and boys one day, to filling out paperwork for food assistance and medical benefits. Dating seems ridiculous when you're leaking breast milk on and off during the day, and your baby is going to cry nonstop at the most inopportune times."

"Don't sugarcoat it, Mrs. Ryan."

"Oh, I won't. Not for you I won't." She stands and rests my sleeping baby back in his bassinet, smiling down at him for a moment before turning back to me. "I told you what the worst part of this job is, but the worst actual moments? That's when I get a call or an email from one of my young women telling me they're pregnant again. They're back with the baby's father or they met a nice guy." She rolls her eyes. "He loves them, he wants to take care of them. They give up on the idea of taking care of themselves. I picture the double-wide on cinderblocks as they're telling me about how *great* everything's going to be."

"Simon grew up in a trailer."

She pauses. "I see."

"Father took off when he was just a baby, had an older brother in jail." I meet her eyes. "He's destined to fail, he's the personification of a hopeless case—except that he's *not*. He has an opportunity now and he's worked so hard for it. I won't take it away from him."

"You believe in him and you want what's best for him. I get it and I respect you for it." She takes my hand. "But I want you to know that I believe in *you* and so does Janelle. So make a pledge to your baby. Promise him you're going to get an education, and that you're going to provide a good life for him. And if you ever find yourself struggling, lean on the people who care about you. You *can* do this."

I turn over onto my side after she leaves my room, not

wanting anyone to catch me crying. Later that evening, with Ethan resting peacefully on my chest, I fill out the birth certificate application one-handed. Ethan James Mason. I fill in my information and leave the other side blank. Looking the completed form over, I can't help but feel as if I'm cheating my son. Will he ever meet his father? Will he ever know how strong, or how smart, determined and brave he is? Will he forgive Simon for not being around? And when Ethan is old enough to hear the truth, will he understand my decision? Will he be able to forgive me?

Chapter Eighteen

SIMON

"Everyone meet back here at five o'clock and we'll head over to Elder. You have to suffer through one dinner with your RA and then you're free to tear up the campus."

I get smiles from most, and a few nervous giggles from the more pensive freshmen I am now officially somewhat responsible for. I hope they aren't a needy bunch. I'm taking eighteen credits this semester and don't have time to be drying tears or wiping anyone's ass. One father actually tried to hand me a syringe pen device for his kid's peanut allergy when they were getting his dorm ID card. "I'm just the RA, Doug's in charge of his own meds." The guy looked offended, but I have to make my role clear from the beginning. I'm here to help ensure that these dipshits didn't drink themselves to death, light the dorm on fire or commit any crimes against humanity. The operative word being *help*. I'm not their warden or their mama.

Being a resident hall assistant gets me what I need: free room and board. Even better, my room is a single. No walking in on my roommate screwing his girlfriend in the middle of the day, no listening to him play video games so loud his head-phones do little to muffle the artillery fire, and no worrying about waking him up when I come home from work late at night. I regret that I ever troubled myself being courteous to that asshole.

Classes are starting in two days, but I feel itchy, like I'm already behind schedule. I took the standard fifteen credits last year for fall and spring semester, tacked on three during winter break and took six credits over the summer. I have to up my game if I'm going to graduate a year early. I know I can't work as much this year, but the RA gig and the two shifts I have stocking the bar at an off campus favorite will hopefully keep me in the black.

"Knock, knock."

Her lilting, sing song voice should lift my spirits, but the sound makes my throat constrict and my shoulders tense. I turn to see Samantha standing in my doorway with a hopeful smile, and struggle with the effort it takes to smile back in a way that at least looks genuine.

"Hey, I thought sophomores weren't moving in until tomorrow."

"What can I say? Having a department chair for a father works to my advantage sometimes."

Samantha moves through my room, straightening the corner of my bedspread, arranging my textbooks into a neat pile and tossing a wayward sock into my hamper. What the fuck?

"What are you doing here?" I don't intend for the words to come out in the clipped way that they do, but her incessant need to look after me, to situate herself into my life, to cling—it drives me freaking batty.

"Figured I'd come to dinner with you and your freshmen. You know...keep you company."

Let me clarify. Samantha isn't some pathetic hanger on. She's a gifted writer, smarter than most people our age, she looks like a model and she's basically good natured. But she set her sights on me the moment I walked into Professor West-field's home for dinner last October, and she doesn't take no for an answer. Her father is my mentor, which makes this all the more awkward.

Last fall, when my head was in such a bad place over losing both Timmy and Charlotte, I was crystal clear with Samantha about my lack of interest in dating. She swore that she under-stood and was just looking to be friends. To prove her point, Samantha dated a few guys, discussed her love life with me, and even made sure to bring them around. Please. She couldn't have been more obvious if she tried. If she were any other girl I would have resorted to being rude just to get her to back off, but I couldn't play that card.

At her core, I believe she's a good person, but this subtle campaign she's been waging to win my heart is fucking tire-some. And I don't do well with feeling manipulated. It's common knowledge that her father is the one who makes my scholarship possible, but Samantha also understands how I've come to rely on his guidance as well. I'm the first Wade to ever step foot on a college campus, and the learning curve for stuff other than academics has been steep. It's thanks to Professor Westfield that I know how to carry myself in a room full of well-educated undergraduates, law school students and successful attorneys. I know which fork to use when the salad course is served at a formal dinner, and I know to maintain eye contact and give a solid handshake when I meet someone new. He talks about my bright future in law as if it's a foregone conclusion. He says he admires *me*, and praises my determination and work ethic. His brand of positive reinforcement is the reason I finally feel like I kind of have my shit together.

So Samantha will tag along tonight, and she'll wedge her way into the same study groups this fall, and she'll make sure she's at the few parties I show up to this year. But she won't ever get what she truly wants. I'll never lie awake at night thinking about her. I'll never miss her or rub my chest trying to ease some phantom ache because of her. I'll never reach for her in the middle of the night because she's invaded my dreams.

She will never be Charlotte.

Chapter Nineteen

SIMON

I shake my head and smile every time I pass by one of the campus tour groups jamming up the pathway in front of Deering Library, holding back when I really want to call out to these idiots: *It is called the Windy City for a reason.* It's November, and while the parents are bundled up in wool coats with scarves and gloves to ward off the icy nip in the air, their offspring are shivering. They fall into two categories. You have the eager beavers who insist on wearing the Northwestern sweatshirt they purchased at the campus bookstore just this morning, and then you have the rebels without a cause. They typically sport nothing warmer than an unbuttoned denim jacket, convinced it makes them look cool and unaffected.

It's cold where I'm from, but it's a different kind of cold here. The air that whips off Lake Michigan is wet and hostile, chills you right to the bone. The admissions brochure is filled with pictures of tulip-lined green spaces and coeds sprawled out reading on the sandy lake shore. And it is beautiful here—

don't get me wrong—but that beach is comfortable for the first two or three weeks into September. That's it. It'll be snowing here before you know it, and you may not see the ground again until a few weeks before final exams this spring.

The badass who captures my attention today is a white girl with dreadlocks wearing a black leather moto jacket. It's unzipped over the Baby Gap-sized tee that's exposing her midriff. She mistakes my smile for interest and proceeds to do her best Britney Spears circa 1998 impression, wetting her finger and dragging it across her bottom lip. I shake my head, feeling embarrassed on her behalf. I want to pull her aside and tell her that's the wrong way, but I don't know her or any of the other high school juniors and seniors packed around the bored looking tour guide.

Shoving my hands into my pockets as I pick up the pace, I can't get that girl out of my head. But it's not her I'm thinking about, I know that. Just as I know there's a reason that I scan the face of every person in every tour group that I come across. I look for her. She's nearly eighteen now. She's a senior in some high school in some city in some state.

I don't know where she is.

Mr. Vargas sort of came through for me last year. He did what he promised and no more. He called me back, assured me that he'd personally spoken to Charlotte's new guidance counselor. Told me she's living with extended family and she's adjusting well to her new school. Vargas wouldn't tell me if she was still in Pennsylvania, wouldn't tell me if she was in the north, south, east or west. I knew he wouldn't, but I tried and failed to get more info out of him anyway.

Faced with knowing next to nothing, I broke down and called Garth. He wasn't even aware that she'd left town, so he was no help. But a month later he called me back. At first I thought he'd just called to tell me the craptastic news that he'd proposed to Sienna and—wait for it—she said yes! And, *Oh yeah bro, you better be coming back for the wedding.* As I was hedging my way around the invitation, he changed the subject and told me about the sweet new truck he'd just bought. He took my old job at the hardware store, so I knew how much he was raking in and it wasn't much. I felt sad in that moment thinking of Garth, with his high hopes and low expectations. Satisfied with a dead-end minimum wage job, and at nineteen, already making bad decisions that will leave him sinking in debt for years to come. But he's so damn optimistic, wants so little out of life.

"Yeah, her dad sold me the truck, and Sienna's there with me so she starts asking questions."

"What?"

"Mr. Mason. He sold me the truck."

"You asked about Charlotte?"

"Sienna did, but we didn't exactly crack the case for you. Just said she's doing great, going to some school for academically, uh, really smart kids. Sienna asked where exactly she was, but you could tell he didn't want to tell us, which is weird if you ask me. So he just says she's living with her aunt in a way that was kind of, uh, end of story like. Know what I mean?"

"Yeah, he's a dick."

"And at that point, I didn't want him tacking any more points onto the interest I was paying, so I gave Sienna a look and we let it go. Sorry man."

"No, really, thanks for trying." I was replaying everything he'd just told me, but it got me nowhere. She never spoke of family, never mentioned an aunt. "Hey, did you see her brother there?"

"Yeah, I saw him." Garth let out a chuckle. "Heard he got

his ass kicked a few weeks ago. Got caught messing around with a married lady."

"Good...I hope it hurt."

So aside from doing weekly searches that led me nowhere except back to the damn website for the family car dealership, I had nothing to go on. I toyed with creating a page for myself, in the hopes that maybe she was trying to find me, but I didn't because I knew she wasn't looking. She knew exactly where I was, could look me up in the school's directory, could contact me through my brother Mike—she could find me.

I tried to erase her from my memory, but I knew I'd never be able to do that. Knew I didn't want to. Some of the best nights of my life were spent with her down by the river, lying side by side on our backs, fingers laced together, shooting the shit about nothing and everything. Sometimes I have to remind myself that I was with her for just four months. It doesn't seem possible.

It's been well over a year since I ran off. Maybe it's the shitty way I left—maybe that's why I can't let this go. Some sick need to set things right, to make sure she knows it wasn't easy to do what I did. That I'm not some callous prick who got what he wanted and then discarded her. I want Charlotte to know that in leaving her behind, I might have hurt her, but I destroyed a part of myself that I don't know or even care if I can ever reclaim.

Mostly I think about the times we were together. I try to remember what touching her felt like. I think about that day she got so mad at me, the day she wanted me to and I denied her. I want to be back there again, lying on that blanket with her. I want to run my hands over her soft skin and kiss her. I want to be tender with her and show her how a man should love her. Those memories turn into daydreams that always end with me moving inside of her. And it hurts, because fuck, I'd give anything to see her again.

When I let myself go back to the very last time I saw her, pained and devastated, I'm overcome with guilt. And the only way I can make myself feel better is to imagine what her life is like now.

I see her living a good life. She's living with family, with an aunt who loves her and takes care of her the way her mother would have. I hope it's warm where she is. Hope she's somewhere like Florida or the Carolinas because she told me she hated Pennsylvania in winter—said the gray sky and the howling wind made her feel lonely. Yeah, I can picture her in some sunny place. I can hear that tinny singing voice of hers trying and failing to hit the high notes along with Adele as she drives down some coastline. I bet she still dances all the time, moves her hips in that way that used to slay me. In my fantasy she's at an all-girls school, but in reality I know she's probably the new girl in town that every boy wants to get to know. But the girl I knew had her priorities straight, so I'm sure she's focused on kicking ass in school and finishing up her college applications right about now.

Smiling to myself, I can picture Charlotte Mason getting ready to take on the world.

* * *

CHARLOTTE

If you go out our back door and walk about a hundred paces to the left, there's a boulder with a flat surface big enough to lie down on. It's where I'm curled up right now on this chilly

November afternoon. It's four o'clock. Janelle has come to call it the witching hour.

Ethan will be seven months old tomorrow. And it's not like he cries all day, he doesn't. In fact, he's a dream most of the time. But there's something about this time of day that frays his nerves, and as a result of the high-pitched squeals that will not stop, it frays mine too.

About ten minutes ago I gave Janelle a look, grabbed the afghan off the back of the couch and walked outside, leaving Ethan in her care. My head and body are resting on solid rock and it's the most relaxed I've felt all day.

Everyone tells you motherhood is hard. In fact, you hear it so often that you begin to ignore people when they start droning on about the lack of sleep, the anxiety, blah, blah, blah. I am currently wearing the baggy sweats I fell asleep in last night, I'm sure my hair looks like I fixed it with an egg beater, and my nostrils are being assaulted by the smell of stale breast milk. Ethan spit up on me earlier today. Several hours ago, in fact, and I still haven't mustered up the energy required to shower or change.

Not every day is like this. Usually I get four hours between feedings, and after Ethan burps I fall back into a coma-like sleep right along with him. But last night I woke up off and on all night.

There are times when I'm plagued by anxiety over things that truly should worry me, and other times when I know I'm worrying over nothing. Last night I kept waking up breathless, thinking the baby was in bed with me and I'd rolled over onto him and he'd suffocated. He was safely in his co-sleeper each and every time. There are other nights when I lie awake fearful that he'll die in his sleep—that the operation didn't work and his poor little heart can't pump blood the way it needs to keep him alive. I worry that he won't be able to run around and play sports when he's older, making mental notes at four in the morning to sign him up for lessons so he can learn to play a musical instrument. I worry that I'm not producing enough breastmilk, even though I'm leaking like a damn faucet and Ethan's gaining weight at a healthy rate. I worry that we're too far away from a decent hospital if and when something does go wrong. I worry that I'll drop him. I just worry.

It's days like today that I thank the Lord above for Janelle. I'm convinced she's my fairy godmother. We are a team taking care of Ethan together. Since I'm breastfeeding I have the night shifts, but she makes sure to give me plenty of opportunities to rest throughout the day and she takes care of basically everything else. I feel bad when I see her hauling the laundry downstairs or cleaning out the diaper pail, but the guilt is offset by the delight I feel every time I see her rocking Ethan in the comfy glider chair she bought for us. Janelle looks blissed out and content when he is in her arms, looking up at her smiling.

Just a few more minutes. That's all I need to recharge before I go back in there.

Sitting up, I see my name and think back to the day I etched it into the surface with my pocket knife. I was mad as hell that afternoon. For the most part I was completely ignored during my short stint at Franklin Murphy Memorial High, but that day some girl yelled out the word slut as she passed me in the crowded hallway. I was never a fighter to begin with, but you really can't throw down when you're sporting a baby bump. I held my chin up and kept on walking, silently cursing the heat and color creeping up my neck and across my face as her friends and a few other morons laughed.

I wasn't angry at her as I stabbed at the stone, doing a messy job of scratching a C into the surface. My fury was directed at him. He should be here. He should be enduring this shit storm alongside me.

There I sat, wearing the ultimate mom jeans: faded blue denim with an elastic panel that pretty much stretched from my waist down to my crotch—so hot—topped off with a baggy flannel button-down of Janelle's because my boobs now looked obscene in my own shirts. I never cared much about how I dressed or looked before, but maybe that was because I never had to. It takes carrying a watermelon around every day to appreciate how rocking your body was before pregnancy. And though I really wasn't looking to make friends in this new town, the loneliness had been getting to me. Back then, Janelle and I were still feeling each other out. We weren't relaxed around one another the way we are now.

I remember feeling so alone that day. Simon was more than just a boyfriend, more than the first boy I've ever loved—he was my friend. I missed him, but the longing quickly morphed into anger and resentment.

What is he doing today? It's a game I play now and then. Is he at the library studying? On his way to catch dinner at Mike and Brandon's place?

As I make my way back across the yard towards the house, I think about how tragic and wild and awful this whole state of affairs is. He's oblivious. He's going to classes, study sessions and parties, ignorant of the fact that he is the father of a beautiful seven month-old boy. A fighter who braved five weeks in the hospital after his momma was discharged. A tough little peanut who lets doctors and nurses hook him up to machines that beep and buzz on a fairly regular basis. A sweet little trooper who laughs, coos, farts, burps and smiles his way through each and every day.

Janelle is singing James Taylor's *You are My Only One* as

she rocks from side to side holding Ethan in one arm while she stirs a heavenly smelling venison stew with the other. The storm has passed. Ethan is content, holding her long braid in both of his chubby fists. He stares at her face as she sings those sweet words to him, studying her.

I'm smiling as I reach for Ethan, but the sorrow is heavy as he wiggles his body towards me and stretches his little arms out. As I snuggle him in close, I pray that I haven't made a colossal mess out of everything.

Simon will find out someday. He won't be able to turn back time, won't ever get to experience this. He'll never know what it's like to have a newborn Ethan sleep in his arms, never look on in wonder like I do when he feeds at my breast. He'll never feel the rush of emotion that comes when Ethan looks right at you and smiles.

I'm pretty sure Simon will never forgive me for this, even though everything I've done has been for him.

Tomorrow we head back to the apartment Janelle has leased for the year. It's just a few miles away from the hospital. We stayed there after I was discharged, visiting Ethan daily while waiting for him to get the green light to come home with us. Janelle says it makes sense to keep it for a while, as we have to be at the hospital every few months to meet with Ethan's specialists.

His echocardiograms have come back clear at every check-up so far, and his doctors use the phrase *cautiously optimistic* when they discuss his long-term prognosis. But I know he's not out of the woods. There's always the chance of a setback, so I pray for him nightly with the fervor of a zealot. And I'm like the germ gestapo, barring anyone from our home that so much as sniffles. The parish sponsored mommy-and-me group one town over? Over my dead body. There are so many things that are out of my control, like whether or not his aortic stenosis will rear its ugly head again and require some difficult, risky procedure. So anything that I can control, like keeping Ethan from getting some random infection, I'm going to do my best.

During those first few months in Ann Arbor, especially right after Ethan was born, I'd cue up the driving distance between Evanston and Ann Arbor on my phone. I wanted to see how close they were on the map, to study the line connecting us.

I used to think that time would lessen the pull he had on me. And maybe if there wasn't a child involved that would have been the case, I would have moved on. But every time I look at Ethan I see Simon, and I'm not sad about that. Maybe I'm a glutton for punishment, but I don't ever want to forget him.

Chapter Twenty

SIMON

"You're like a machine." Finished with the meal, Professor Westfield lays his linen napkin back on the table. "And I'm not sure this is a good thing. What's the rush? You have a four-year scholarship. I'd advise you to slow down and take the four years." When I don't answer, he adds, "Law school's not going anywhere. It will still be there waiting for you."

I was asking for suggestions on prep courses for the LSAT. And really, I should have turned it off for tonight. The topic wasn't fitting for a holiday dinner, when normal people are feeling all sentimental and joy to the world-ish, but I'm not like them.

Yeah, I was already prepping for the LSAT because I was on track to earn my undergraduate in three years. Maybe other kids my age could stop and smell the roses, but I need to kill it on that test. No scholarship, no law school—it's that simple.

"I'll talk to you about it some other time."

Brett raises an eyebrow and smiles at me as if to say: *Nice going*. He's only a year older than me but acts like he already has the keys to the kingdom. He's of the fake it 'til you make it school of success. His "vintage" beamer and the upscale castoffs he wears from the thrift shops he trolls in Lake Forest don't fool me—he's another kid from the wrong side of tracks. Westfield seems to pick one golden child from each incoming class. We're his lab rats, his nature versus nurture thesis project.

Across from me sits the freshman pet, an insanely smart girl from West Virginia who is only half-listening to the conversation as she studies Samantha. I can't figure out if she has a thing for Samantha or if she's looking to emulate her. I imagine she's beating herself up over the misstep she's made tonight. Everyone is in decked out in stylish holiday-themed threads, while West Virginia, dressed in black pants, a black button down and black sensible shoes, could easily be mistaken for a member of the catering staff. She's a transplant, a gatecrasher just like me, whereas Samantha so obviously belongs in this room. Her sense of style, her cultured mannerisms and the easy way she navigates social situations leave no doubt that she was born into this. I want to lean over and whisper to the new girl: *Don't worry, you'll get there.* I know how intimidating this world can be to a newcomer.

"Samantha, are you still thinking of doing a semester abroad?"

"I'm considering it."

"You should. I got so much out of studying in London this summer."

"I know, you told me…That's great."

I want to tell Brett to save his breath, that Samantha wants no part of him. She's not showing any interest in the senior who has Professor Westfield's ear at the moment either, and unlike Brett, he is a genuinely good guy. No, Samantha is still dogged in her pursuit of me.

When we first met, I swear she got a gleam in her eye whenever she'd catch me leaving for my warehouse job wearing battered carpenter's pants and my old, worn thermal shirts. She liked the uniform of hardship that I wore, liked that I was rugged in comparison to the boys she grew up with—the ones who played squash and got their first Brooks Brothers suit at age fourteen. Both of my hands clench into fists when I think back to that one night when she casually asked if I had any tattoos. *Sorry to break it to you, sweetheart, got no tattoos or dick piercings to entertain you.* Instead of saying what was on my mind, I just stared her down for a moment and shook my head. "Sorry to disappoint."

She looked truly embarrassed and has since gone out of her way to make certain that she does absolutely nothing that might offend me. She doesn't challenge my opinions, she adopts my point of view in political discussions, and she praises me, both to my face and to others.

I can't take it.

I decided that hooking up with some other girl is the only way I'll be able to get rid of her. So next to me sits Diana, a pre-med student from Akron, Ohio. She'll be leaving after finals are over next week for winter break. She asked me to come, knowing I have no home to return to, but of course I declined. She's a nice person, but I'm not even remotely smitten. Diana puts an insane amount of pressure on herself, which leads to a schedule packed with study sessions and research. As a result, she makes very few demands on me. It's perfect. We got together about six weeks ago at a party. Samantha was there. I don't know if it was the shots or Samantha's excessive fawning that led me to dance with Diana and then make out with her in full view of everyone in the room.

Samantha studies Diana at the table, and I can tell from her expression that she sees herself as superior to her competition in every way. Satisfied, she looks back to her own date and makes a show of interlacing her fingers with his and resting them on the table. I'm not even the slightest bit jealous.

As I'm helping my date with her coat, Samantha calls and then waves me over. "I'm so disappointed we won't be here for Christmas."

"Why? Kicking back on a beach sounds like a great way to spend break."

"I know, but I had fun last year. I'll miss the two of us hanging out." When I don't respond she plasters on a winning smile. "Here...It's nothing. I just thought of you when I saw the post online."

I shake my head. "Samantha, I didn't—"

"Stop...I wasn't expecting a gift, and like I said, it's nothing."

But it's not, and suddenly I feel like a total shit. I feel the same way I did when I made a show of macking on some girl in the high school gym back when I wanted to shake Charlotte off.

It's a small green envelope with my name written across the front in gold. The envelope holds two tickets to an Avett Brothers show. I knew they were coming to Chicago this February but never once entertained the idea of seeing them. Concerts, along with most other luxuries, are not in my budget.

I can't look at her. "Samantha—"

"I know you like them. You listen to them all the time. I

just wanted to do something for you." When I go to speak, she cuts me off. "You can take Diana."

That all but guts me. "I appreciate the thought you put into this. Do you like them?"

Her tone is cautious. "I'm a fan. My favorite of theirs is *I and Love and You*."

It's every non-fan's favorite song, but whatever. "Then come with me. I wouldn't feel right taking anyone else."

She looks over at the front door where Diana is talking to Professor Westfield. "Will your girl be down with that?" She's teasing me, knows I'm not hopelessly devoted.

Her mother, a woman who has welcomed me into their home and fed me more times than I can count, shoots a hopeful smile my way as I slip the tickets into my coat pocket. "It will be fine."

When I get back to my place, I cue up *I Wish I Was* instead of Samantha's pick. That song is everything—it's my absence, my longing for Charlotte, and my desire to make sure she knows how sorry I am. Sometimes I play it on repeat, and when I do, I get lost in a familiar fantasy. It's the one where me and Charlotte are together in our simple home, making a life. It's not always easy, but every struggle is worth it because she's everything to me.

* * *

CHARLOTTE

"What do you say, little man? Think momma's gonna do well on her big test today?"

"Are you serious? You're going to ace this thing. Your score was nearly perfect on the other one."

"That was the GED, Janelle, this is the college entrance exam…Apples and oranges." I was starting to speak her fruit, vegetable and animal-based language. "And I've only been studying for one month. Most kids prep for the better part of a year."

This whole plan is ridiculous and rushed and crazy.

The first person to greet me when we arrived at the hospital last month was my pitbull of a social worker, Mrs. Ryan. I'm reduced to a naughty kid sitting in detention when she approaches with purposeful strides and a smile that could only be described as borderline menacing.

"You haven't answered my emails."

"You were right…This motherhood thing takes up every minute of every day. But here's Ethan." I hold him up in front of me like a shield. "He's doing great."

She softens immediately, smiling at him. "He's perfect." With a generous pump of hand sanitizer from the wall dispenser, she rubs her hands together as if she's prepping for surgery. "Can I?" she asks, reaching out for him.

"Sure."

She closes her eyes and smiles as she breathes in his scent. He's drowsy, thank goodness, otherwise he might not be cool with a stranger holding him. "He's delicious, Charlotte, and it looks like he's thriving. What are you here for today?"

"Routine check-up. They still want to see him every two months or so."

"So how has it been?"

"Good, but hard like you said it would be. I honestly don't know what I would have done without Aunt Janelle."

"Where is she?"

"Just getting coffee downstairs."

"Good. It's important that you have someone here for support. I always say it's good to have a second set of ears when you're speaking with doctors."

"My niece has read everything there is to know about aortic stenosis." Janelle blows on her coffee before taking a sip. "Sometimes I have to remind myself that she's not a cardiologist."

"Good to see you, Janelle."

"You too."

I feel out of the loop when a look passes between the two of them.

"So," Mrs. Ryan starts in as she passes Ethan back to me, "I have some things I'd like to discuss before they call you in."

I sound ridiculous to my own ears when I pipe up, heavy on the enthusiasm. "I took the GED!"

Why oh why do I feel this pathetic need to defend myself to her?

"And I'm sure you passed, so let's move forward. University of Michigan's admissions deadline is February first. That gives you a little less than three months to get your application together."

"What?"

Mrs. Ryan shrugs her shoulders and shakes her head. "The GED is behind you, so now we take the next step."

"I-I'm busy taking care of Ethan. I can't do this right now."

She rests a hand on my shoulder. "You won't actually be doing anything right now, but you have to take care of some details if you're going to be starting classes next September."

I look back and forth between her and Janelle. "Here? This is like six hours from home. I can't do that!"

"Take a breath," Janelle says in a voice that calms me. "You haven't made any concrete plans yet, and that's fine. Mrs. Ryan is just suggesting that you meet some deadlines so that if you *do* decide to enroll in school next fall, you'll be able to."

"And wouldn't that be impressive?" Mrs. Ryan beams. "You'd be starting your freshman year of college right on schedule."

"And no pressure at all, Charlotte, but I want you to know that you have options. Ann Arbor has grown on me and I have the means to keep the apartment. I can care for Ethan while you're in class and while you're studying." In response to the look of shock I'm sure I'm sporting, she adds, "Or you can go to community college up by us for a year or two before you enroll in school full-time. Nothing's written in stone."

"I could never ask you to do that for me."

"Why not?"

"You'd be leaving your home, your friends. And what about Lawrence?"

She rolls her eyes. "You act like we'd be moving to Bora Bora. We would go home for weekends and school breaks. We'd spend the summers back up north. I already talked it over with Lawrence, and not that his opinion would dictate my decision, but he's fine with it."

"You've already discussed this with Lawrence?" When Janelle looks over to Mrs. Ryan for the save, I know I've been left in the dark. "Seems like you two have it all figured out, but I need a little time to think this through."

"Of course!" they say in unison.

A nurse comes out and calls Ethan's name. As I gather his things, purposefully avoiding any further discussion on the matter, Mrs. Ryan chirps, "Time waits for no man, Charlotte Mason. Carpe diem!"

. . . .

Ethan sits in his high chair, ignoring me as he focuses on feeding himself the bits of cereal on his tray. I lean over to kiss his forehead. "Wish me luck, little fella."

"Got your number two pencils?"

"Check, Janelle."

"Graphing calculator?"

"Got it."

"Admissions ticket for the test? Identification?"

"Yes and yes."

"Good luck, sweetheart."

I walk over and hug her tight. "Thank you. Really, Janelle, thank you so much."

It's a total long shot. Even if I do ace the exam—and that's unlikely given that I've pretty much taught myself Algebra Two and the very basics of Calculus from outdated textbooks—my application has more holes in it than the ozone layer. I don't have any teacher recommendations, having not finished a full year at this high school. My one and only recommendation is from Mrs. Ryan, who knows squat in terms of my scholastic aptitude aside from what she saw on those old transcripts from Pennsylvania. And I'm applying with a GED instead of a high school diploma. My essay is pretty solid, if you ask me, but my answer to the question: *What obstacles have you encountered in life and how have you learned to overcome them?* underscores the fact that I am a teenage mother. I don't know what the admission committee's opinion on that will be.

But even with the uphill climb I'm facing, I'll admit, something old but familiar has been sparking to life inside of me. Opportunity is knocking, and while caring for Ethan fills me with a sense of joy, this is different. For the first time in a long while, I'm excited about the idea of me.

Walking back over to my son to give him one more quick kiss, I whisper, "You and me baby…We're going places."

Chapter Twenty-One

CHARLOTTE

The summers are the only thing the Upper Peninsula has going for it. Sounds harsh, but I'm officially sick of freezing my ass off. Bringing logs in for the fireplace seemed quaint the first time I did it, but the novelty has worn off. So I'm beyond pleased to see the green buds on the sugar maples dotting Janelle's property. And looking out over the sparkling expanse of water, I'm excited for Ethan to discover the rocks and cool little critters that inhabit the shoreline in the years to come, even though it's pretty much mid-August before you can wade in up to your ankles without risking hypothermia. Lake Superior is no joke.

It's not like Ann Arbor boasts a comfortable climate in the winter, but the busy college town is far more welcoming. I've kind of come to love it this spring. Janelle and I have gotten in the habit of staying on a few extra days when we venture down for Ethan's appointments. We take the baby for walks down Washington Street and always hit the farmers' market on Saturdays when we're in town. We walk the campus. We explore the museum, the arboretum and the quad with its Hogwarts feel. I have to pinch myself, still hardly able to wrap my head around the fact that I'll be a member of the incoming freshman class this September.

Janelle surprised me when she offered to pay for my schooling in full, insisting that since I was now a state resident it wouldn't be hard to swing. But I turned her down. In addition to everything she's already done for me, she was going to be covering housing and childcare. I was determined to pay the tuition on my own. It was time to get my hands on my money.

I could have arranged for the bank in Pittsburgh to transfer my funds to the small savings account I'd opened in Ann Arbor—that would have been the easiest and smartest thing to do—but I think there's a glutton for punishment inside all of us. So Janelle and I set out at six that morning in July, taking the four hour connecting flight through Detroit that would land us in Pittsburgh. Lawrence stepped up to watch Ethan, and although I hated leaving him in anyone else's care, I left that morning free of worry, knowing Lawrence is just as safety conscious as I am.

Ethan wasn't out of the woods, but now at nearly fifteen months, his doctors are pleased with his progress. He's scheduled to see his specialists every four months now, and if all goes well this year, he'll graduate to six-month follow-ups. He's on the small side for his age, was slow to sit up independently, and is now just beginning to pull himself up to a stand using the coffee table for support, but he's been meeting his language and learning milestones right on target—I've been studying those child development books since the day he was born.

The car rental was ready when we landed, and the business at the bank in downtown Pittsburgh took no more than an hour. I walked out with a check for fourteen thousand dollars tucked into my wallet. Along with a grant for single parents that Mrs. Ryan helped to secure, and a "nontraditional family" scholarship of one thousand dollars I got for writing an essay of the groveling variety, I would now be able to cover my freshman year. I planned on earning merit scholarship money with my kick-ass grades and taking out loans when necessary to finance the rest.

It takes less than an hour to drive from the bank to Mason Motors. I was going to do this alone, but when I told Janelle about my plan to visit my father, she insisted on coming along for the trip. Solid move on her part, knowing full well that seeing him was not her idea of a vacation. It wasn't mine either.

The building was massive in my memory, with its endless sea of shiny new trucks and cars surrounding it, but now it seems less imposing. Compared to what I've seen outside of this small town, my dad's business doesn't impress. And I guess Liza was the one who handled the seasonal landscaping and other decorative touches, because Independence Day is just around the corner, but unlike years past, you'd never know it. There are no red, white and blue displays of patriotism to be seen.

I take a deep breath to calm my nerves when we pull into the lot. It's the middle of the afternoon, and I'm praying I don't see any familiar faces when we walk in. I love my son more than anything on this earth, but the idea of making his existence known to the people of my hometown coats me in shame. In that moment, I am not an incoming freshman at one of the most competitive state universities in the country. I am not a competent young woman who has taken on the responsibility of raising a medically fragile child, and done a damn good job of it too, thank you very much. No, I am nothing more than an unwed teenage mother. Nothing more than that sixteen year-old girl who was too stupid to know that taking antibiotics to combat a mild case of back acne would render the stolen birth control pills she was taking all but useless. I fight off my insecurities and take strength from Janelle when she squeezes my hand.

Christian is on the phone. His mouth hangs open, momentarily stunned when he sees me. He resumes talking with his eyes fixed on me. His look isn't angry or shocked. No, he plays it off like he's devoid of emotion. I mirror his expression as I take him in. He looks the same: a good looking man but one who isn't putting enough effort into his appearance. He's still got the makings of the pot belly he was growing before I left, and he looks like he could use a woman to shop for him. His tie clashes with his shirt, and he's wearing a brown belt in contrast to his black shoes. He presses a device on his desk, and within a minute my father appears.

Like the business itself, my father seems less imposing as he walks over to greet his daughter and his sister with a smile. It's the same smile he uses to greet prospective customers. I'm expecting him to say, "What can I help you folks with today?" so I'm surprised when he hugs me. It's a stiff hug. He doesn't pull me in close.

"Charlotte," he says as he pulls back to look at me. "Why didn't you tell me you were coming?"

I smile back at him and shrug my shoulders.

"Janelle."

"No hug for me, big brother?" She teases with a smile, but there's an edge to her voice.

He gives her the same awkward hug. "So what brings you two here today?"

What a weird question. It's as if my father has never considered the possibility that I would someday come home. He carted me off without even saying goodbye, has gone almost two years without once making contact, and now stands here and acts like everything is copacetic. He doesn't ask about my life, or ask: *Hey, what'd you ever do about that pickle you got yourself into last year?* His refusal to acknowledge me pisses me off.

"We came back to clear out that bank account mom started for me."

"The account *we* opened for you?" Talk of money piques Christian's interest. He's still on the phone, or pretending to be, but he's listening. "That was money I put aside for you. Money I wanted to go towards your education."

"It is going towards her education." Janelle looks to me and winks before looking back to my father, her chin raised in defiance. "Charlotte's going to be a freshman at the University of Michigan this September." There's an awkward pause before she prompts my father, "You should be proud."

He doesn't hold much love for his sister, that's as plain as the look on his face. "Don't *tell* me what I should be, Janelle." Turning to me, he says, "I am proud. And I'll see about the account. I need a few days to look into it."

A few days? There's one person in the dealership at the moment, so some mad spike in sales isn't tying him up. What an ass. He thinks he still has control, has some power over me, when he has none whatsoever.

"You don't need to look into anything. I've already been to the bank. I turned eighteen in January, remember?"

He smiles but his jaw is visibly tight. I want to press him: *Did you remember my birthday?* It shouldn't hurt but it does. He wasn't a terrible father—I never went without, I wasn't abused—but he wasn't a good father. He's not a good man.

And looking over to Christian, I recognize the same qualities in him, and know I'll never reach out to either one of them again. I don't want them in my life, don't want them near my son. I don't want Ethan exposed to their warped brand of masculinity.

I look my father in the eye and take a deep breath. "Just figured we had a few hours to kill before we flew back, so I wanted to take a spin around the old neighborhood. It was good to see you again, Dad." Christian still hasn't greeted me. He's doing his best Mark Cuban in the middle of some epic deal impersonation. To spite him I call out, "Good to see you too, Christian," before turning to walk out the door.

I hold my breath until I reach the rental car. I need three tries before successfully jabbing the key into the ignition with my hand trembling. I see Janelle exit the building then, her face hard as stone as she makes her way to the car.

"I'm not gonna say it," she says as she buckles her seatbelt.

"He's an asshole," we say in unison a moment later and then turn to each other laughing.

"I cannot believe that man's sperm had anything to do with producing you."

"Eww, Janelle. Don't mention my father and sperm in the same sentence."

"Can you believe how arrogant he is? Acting like he had to give you his blessing and permission to get your own money?"

"I want to deposit that check the minute we get home."

"Charlotte, the funds were electronically transferred. That paper is just a receipt. Don't worry, he can't get his hands on the money."

"Thank God. He still has that way about him, you know?"

"Intimidating?"

"Yeah."

"He's all about the show, there's no true substance there." She rests her hand on mine as I shift into drive. "I shouldn't talk that way about him to you. It isn't fair."

"It's all right, Janelle. I'm not exactly his biggest fan right now. Can you believe he never even asked me what happened?"

"He knows."

"He does?"

Oddly, I'm not shaken up by the news. I'm focused on driving now. I have several places I want to see and checking those places off on my list is of greater importance to me than my relationship with my father.

"I called him when you were in the hospital, the night before you and Ethan were having surgery. It didn't feel right not to let him know. I didn't know what was going to happen."

"What was his reaction?"

"He was mad at me, of course!" She shakes her head. "He does love you and your brother, but he doesn't have a healthy way of demonstrating love. I'd like to say your mother's stroke was the reason, but he was never an emotionally giving person." Janelle looks over to me to gauge my reaction when she says, "I gave him a picture of Ethan before I left just now. Pisses me off that he hasn't asked about him once in all this time." She lets out a cheerless laugh. "I guess I have a flair for the dramatic...Handed the picture to him and said, 'Just in case you've been wondering about your grandson. He's healthy and doing well, by the way. And Charlotte's a great mother to him.' I added, 'You raised her well,' just to stick it to him."

"You're badass, Janelle."

"Damn straight." She turns to me again. "You're not mad I gave him a picture of Ethan, are you?" When I shake my head, she lets out a relieved breath. "Now where are we heading? I hope there's a DQ in this backwards town."

"There is, but you're bringing my cone out to the car. I want to stop by a few of my old haunts, not walk into an impromptu reunion."

We drive by my house, even though no one is home. I don't even know why I want to see it. Looking at the flaking paint and the dead flower beds makes my father's stiff hug and Christian's cold reception cut even deeper. *I don't care, I don't care.* I've been repeating the words to myself the entire ride over here, knowing the need to say the words is proof that I'm lying.

Next stop is Daisy's. She lives just a few blocks over. There are no cars in the driveway and the mailbox is stuffed with flyers, envelopes and magazines keeping it propped open. Was I planning to knock on the door if someone was home? I'm not sure. I want to know how she's been, who she went to prom with, where she's going to school. I want to know if she's still close with Sarah. I hope she is. I hope Sarah is the friend Daisy always deserved. I miss her. I wonder if she ever thinks about me.

Janelle sits quietly as we make our way over to the other side of town. I pass the turn off for the dirt road that used to take me and Simon down to our secret spot by the river. I pass Tyler's trailer, speeding up slightly when I see the door open and Tyler steps out onto the landing with some girl who is not Skylar. I have to remind myself that it's been nearly two years—things change. I slow to a stop when we approach Simon's trailer, pulling over a good twenty feet away.

"Who lives here?"

"Simon." I correct myself. "He used to live here."

Should I knock? Say hello to his mother? I won't tell her. I'll just make like I'm passing through town. Just ask her to tell Simon I said hello the next time she talks to him.

"Just give me a minute," I say as I go to let myself out of the car. I'm not kidding myself. I'm knocking on his mother's door in the hopes that I'll get something, some nugget of information. Wondering about what he's been up to and who he's with has been gnawing at me since the day he left. It's too tempting. I can't leave without at least trying. But as I go to close the car door behind me, a man and a young child step out. A woman with a swollen belly follows. I take in the scene, noticing for the first time how different it all looks. Trash bags are piled up on the side of the trailer with gaping holes in them, proof that the local raccoons are being well fed. A bent and discarded screen lies in the dirt below the window. The wreath that used to hang on the door is gone.

"Excuse me...I'm looking for Mrs. Wade. Does she still live here?"

He doesn't answer, just eyes me with suspicion. His woman pipes up, "I've never heard of her. We moved in this past winter."

I smile at her and then smile at her surly man, hoping to soften him, willing him to be kind to his child and to her. "Thank you. You have a nice day."

She gives her man a cautious glance and then smiles back at me. "You too now."

It's ridiculous, feeling sad for this pregnant woman, someone I've never laid eyes on before today. Maybe I see myself in her, see my personal worst case scenario. But no, even if I'd told Simon, even if he was trapped here and life became only work and raising Ethan with me, I could never see him turning into a version of that man. Poverty never defined Simon. His quiet dignity was one of the many things I admired about him.

Pulling into the DQ parking lot, I tell Janelle not to get me anything. My eyes follow as she walks inside and orders at the counter. I don't recognize the girl at the register, who looks to be no more than fourteen. And Janelle is the only customer. I came here telling myself that I didn't want to be spotted, but now feel an overwhelming sense of disappointment.

I am invisible, a ghost wandering through the streets of my hometown. It's as if I fell off the face of the earth and no one cared to ask why. Deep down, I was hoping for someone, for Daisy or Garth or Sienna to see me, to press me for details about my life. To grab me in a bear hug and ask: *Where have you been, girl? We've missed you!* I'd hug them back, no matter who it was, happy for any link to my past. Then I'd give them the heading off to college highlights, not the baby with a congenital heart condition tale of woe. And voilà, the people of this town would know that I still exist. Maybe someone would get word to Simon. Tell him where I was going to school, give him something to go on. Give him a way to find me.

Sulking, I text Janelle to get me a chocolate dipped cone, needing to drown my sorrows in some ice cream now that I've fully acknowledged what this trip was all about. And if connecting with Simon in a cowardly, through the grapevine-kind of way truly was my end game, I didn't accomplish a damn thing.

* * *

SIMON

Our bodies don't line up the right way. It's a petty observation I make nearly every time I'm with Diana. It's the weirdest relationship and it endures. I have no real feelings for her, and I don't get the impression that I'm anything more to her than someone to eat lunch with and occasionally fuck.

I haven't tried to go deeper with her, and she's never once asked about my past or my dreams for the future. I used to think it was exactly what I wanted, but it feels crappy. The just sex-thing serves an obvious purpose but it's not truly pleasurable.

Samantha looks on with an amused expression every time the three of us share the same space. She plays the role of *friend who just happens to be a girl* very well, but it's just that, an act. She's biding her time, subtly persuading me with her beauty and goodness, just waiting for that day when I wake up and knock myself upside the head. *Gee whiz, Samantha...You're the one I wanted all along! How could I have been so blind?*

After the concert, I took Samantha to an all-night diner and I was brutally honest with her. I know she has feelings for me and said as much. She didn't contradict me. I didn't want to hurt her. I wanted her to understand. So I told Samantha everything. Told her about my childhood, told her about Timmy, told her about Charlotte. Everything. Told her what I did, how I left. Told her I'm still in love with Charlotte.

"Can I see a picture?" she asked. I lied and told her I didn't have one. Samantha's one fault is the high opinion she holds of herself. I'm all for confidence, but it's obvious that Samantha sees herself as a cut above the company. I didn't want Malibu Barbie comparing herself to my girl.

It always made me sad, the way Charlotte saw herself as a plain Jane when nothing could be further from the truth. Is it just something you go through when you're still figuring things out? When you're young? The kind of confidence Samantha carries herself with, does it come with age? I wonder how Charlotte sees herself now.

I study the picture. The one I went to the trouble of printing out at the drugstore before I traded in my phone. It's a selfie, the two of us sitting on the tailgate of my truck. We were just out of the water, Charlotte in her bikini. Her face is turned. She's looking up at me and smiling. How could anyone see anything but the most beautiful girl on the planet in this picture?

Where is she now? I haven't spoken to Garth since his wedding, when I called to congratulate him. I told myself that I wouldn't but then caved in and asked about her. He had nothing new to report. There have been a few times I've broken down and seriously considered calling her father, but I know it wouldn't get me anywhere. And I know I wouldn't be doing it for her benefit. It would be selfish on my part.

We break for the semester next week, or most students do anyway. I have just a few days off before the summer session starts up. Between classes, work and cramming for the law school entrance exam, the fact that it's summertime will barely even register. The Westfields invited me to their cottage up on Lake Superior in August, but I declined, thankful that test prepping gives me a valid excuse. I'm extra careful to avoid giving Samantha mixed messages. I think her parents get it, but while doing her best to be subtle about it, she's still as rabid as a bloodhound.

The cottage, the cottage. She goes on and on about the damn place. The word grates on me. Only uppity people use that word, people who say they "summer" somewhere. Garth lived in what could only be described as a shack, and most of my friends grew up in trailers, some on farms. Just Charlotte and the Perillo twins, they were the only ones I knew fortunate enough to grow up in bona fide houses. But the world I now inhabit is completely different. I'm sure Professor Westfield's "cottage" is a sprawling lakeside mansion fashioned to look like a log cabin or some shit.

"It's so charming up there. The people speak and dress like absolute hicks, but their way of life is quaint in the Upper Peninsula. It's like going back in time."

I make a mental note to kick my own ass if I ever use the words quaint, charming or cottage in conversation.

"From what I hear, that area is going through tough times. Their economy is shit and the unemployment rate is sky high."

"Really?" Samantha's nose is scrunched up. "Marquette looks booming in the summertime. And the locals always seem so happy."

Do I really need to explain it to her, that people who live in tourist destinations are reliant on the benevolence of people like her, people who waltz into the shops decked out in Vineyard Vines and spend money like tomorrow is their last day? Acting happy is a necessity. Those storekeepers and restaurant owners are desperate to make the experience Disneyland-wonderful for their summertime guests, lest they find somewhere else to spend their disposable income next year. No, she knows all this and obviously doesn't care; she's not a stupid girl.

And shit, why am I being so tough on her? She has no reason to spend her days thinking about economic disparity and hardship. Neither do I, but I can't help it. I'm different from her and from the vast majority of people I now interact with on a daily basis. In the summer vacation scene Samantha paints, I'm the clerk stocking the shelves in the store, not a customer like her. I'm the waiter who smiles when people like her ask if today's catch is wild or farm raised, and then calls her a twat under my breath as I walk into the kitchen to ask the pissed off line cook her asinine question.

Maybe I dwell on depressing shit because poverty and adversity are in my blood. Whatever the reason, I know I'd rather sweat my balls off in Chicago than spend a week at the Westfield cottage this summer.

I'm suddenly so over this bullshit, want to shake everyone and everything off. Looking over to my bedmate Diana, I say what should have been said months ago, "We need to talk."

Chapter Twenty-Two

CHARLOTTE

Ethan toddles across the yard, giggling as he chases after Lawrence's dog. Looking on, my heart is full to capacity. It's warm and familiar, that surge of pure joy I get when I look at my son.

He'll be two and a half next month. Every birthday, every season, every successful follow-up appointment seems like a milestone, a hurdle he's successfully navigated.

"Careful," I say as he goes to grab Moe's tail. It's a word that's become a reflex for me, and one that's unnecessary in this moment. Moe is the sweetest creature on the planet, much like his owner, Lawrence. He humors Ethan, lets him tackle him, grab at his wagging tail, even lets him take a ball straight from his mouth so that Ethan can throw it for the umpteenth time, only to fetch it for him and bring it right back. One day last week he was barking loudly, making such a commotion. When I looked over, I saw Ethan making his way towards the shoreline. And while Ethan was still a good ways from the lake, it served as a stark reminder that turning your head, even for a split second, is dangerous when you're responsible for a toddler.

I crouch down and pet my son's protector. "You are such a good boy, you know that?"

"Good boy," Ethan parrots as he rubs his chubby little hand along Moe's head.

"Moe's going to miss his buddy."

"Ethan will miss him too. He'll miss you even more, Lawrence. You are going to come down and stay with us in Ann Arbor sometimes, aren't you?"

"As long as the boss says it's all right."

"Puh-lease, she'll be lonesome for you, even if she has a hard time admitting it."

Tomorrow is moving day. Lawrence is watching Ethan while Janelle and I busy ourselves with packing. He plays it off like he's all good with this plan, but I know Lawrence has come to rely on Janelle in the same way she gets comfort from his presence.

"That woman is stubborn, but she's already planning to come back here for your fall break, so," he nods his head in the direction of the house and winks at me, "the gig is up...I know she loves me." Lawrence whistles then and Moe comes running to his side. "C'mon Ethan, I'm going to teach you and Moe how to make sun tea and then we're going to pick some wild blueberries for Aunt Janelle."

"Don't the bears up here like to hunt for blueberries this time of year too?"

Even though Lawrence has assured me on more than one occasion that Moe is a Karelian Bear dog, a breed that's loving towards people but known as fierce hunters who don't cower to bears twice their own size, I'm not having it.

"Tell your mama that us Finns are tough. The bears are scared of you, me and Moe."

To that, Ethan giggles, but I stand my ground. "The two-year-old stays with me while you and Moe fight the bears for the blueberries." Looking to Ethan, I say, "Come on, you can help Mommy."

He's not happy until I put him in one of the boxes I just assembled and pull him around the yard. He laughs and that sets Lawrence laughing too. "Okay," he says, waving. "When I get back with the blueberries, I'll teach you how to make ice cream too!"

This kid has three adults literally wrapped around his finger.

"Charlotte?" Janelle calls up the stairs in a quiet voice. She knows I've just put Ethan down for his afternoon nap.

"He's asleep," I whisper back as I make my way downstairs. "What's up?"

"You have a visitor." She looks apprehensive when she gestures towards the couch.

I nearly stumble back when I see him. "Wes?"

"Hey, Charlie." He stands and takes a few steps in my direction. "How are you?"

"I'm, uh, I'm good. How did you know where to find me?"

Wes looks over to Janelle and Lawrence, who are standing side by side, eating ice cream in slow motion. Their spoons are moving in freaking tandem as they watch this unfolding scene with rapt attention. "Can we take a walk or something?"

"Sure."

"You all right, Charlotte?"

I nod, finally getting it. Janelle thinks this is Ethan's dad, even though I've told her all about Simon. I know I've mentioned him by name. "*Wes* is an old friend."

She narrows her eyes at Wes but nods her head. After Wes steps outside and I turn to close the door behind me, I shake my head and mouth the words: *He's not the dad*, to make sure there's no confusion.

"That was a little awkward."

"I don't have friends popping over for visits, like ever, so Aunt Janelle and Lawrence are probably a little shell shocked right now." I'm not offering up the real reason Janelle and her gentleman friend were acting like total freaks back there.

"I'm sorry I just barged in, didn't call first or anything."

We start down a path that leads back towards the lake. "It's fine, really." My head is spinning with questions. I ask again, "How did you find me?"

"Wasn't easy. Your brother's been feeding me the same line of bullshit for the past two years...You went to live with an aunt, you're doing great, all is well. It's like you just up and disappeared, and when I ask why, he tells me you wanted out of there." He stops and turns to look at me. "One night last month he was really drunk...Tells me you came back, stopped in at the dealership acting like..."

He trails off, so I finish for him. "I'm sure he said I was acting like a little bitch."

He doesn't reply, so I know I've hit the nail on the head.

"Anyway, he starts talking about driving you up and dumping you with your dad's sister in Michigan. Then he starts ranting about the Wades, and how if he ever gets his hands on Simon Wade he's going to do to him what he did to Timmy." He lowers his head in shame. "I hate myself for it. You know that, don't you, Charlotte?"

I look away and nod.

"He wouldn't tell me anything more specific, but once I had a little information to go on, I was able to use the database at work to get your aunt's address."

"This is a long way to come just to say hello, Wes."

He reaches down tentatively and grabs my hand. He squeezes it gently before releasing me. "I had to see you with my own eyes, make sure you're safe and doing ok. It never sat right with me, you just up and leaving out of nowhere."

I nod. "It wasn't by choice, but it turned out to be a good thing."

"Who was upstairs sleeping?" When I don't answer, he says, "You had a baby, didn't you? You left because you were pregnant?"

"My son's name is Ethan." I face Wes. "He turned two in March."

He scrubs his hands up and down his face. "Wow."

We walk side by side in silence for a few moments.

"Aren't you going to ask me who the father is?" And I'm nervous now because this cat has been safely secured in the bag for quite some time now.

"I'll go out on a limb here and guess that Simon Wade's the father?"

"Bingo." I attempt levity even though I'm shaking like a leaf.

"How are you?" He adds, "How is it, being a mother and everything?"

"It's, I don't know, everything. It's the best thing in the world, the hardest thing in the world, it's rewarding, it's nerve-wracking, you name it." I stop at the water's edge and look Wes in the eye. "No one from home knows." I breathe in deep and add, "Simon doesn't know."

He looks down at the water, shakes his head and lets out a cheerless laugh. "Good."

"Huh?"

"If he knew and then left you to do this on his own, I'd want to kill him...same as Christian."

"He's a good person, Wes."

"Then you should probably tell him."

"It's complicated...I can't."

"Are you ever going to tell him?"

"I don't know."

"So you're just taking this all on by yourself? Doesn't seem right...or fair."

"He's not a burden. I'll never see Ethan as anything but a gift."

He tussles my hair like he used to when we were kids. "You were always good, Charlotte. I bet you're a great mom."

At that I tear up and my lip trembles. "I hope I am."

He sits on the grass and pats the space beside him. "It's really beautiful here. How could our parents ever settle in a landlocked shithole like our town when places like this exist?"

I laugh through the emotion clogging my throat. "I know, right?"

He nudges my shoulder with his. "Hey, your secret is safe with me."

"That's the worst part. I don't like thinking of my situation as a secret. Ethan is nothing to be ashamed of."

"You're right." He turns to me. "Can I ask you something?"

"Sure."

"Are you afraid to tell him? Afraid he won't want to be a part of Ethan's life?"

The question breaks something that I've kept buried deep

inside of me. All I can do is lower my head and nod as a few hot tears fall. I wipe them away and breathe deep for a few minutes to steady myself.

"Do you know why I really drove out here?"

Before he gets a chance to tell me, Janelle calls out for us and rings the freaking dinner bell. I know for a fact that bell hangs in her kitchen for decoration only.

I stand and reach down to give him my hand. "You heard her, it's dinner time."

Over dinner, with Janelle in investigative reporter mode, I learn several interesting tidbits. Wes has quit the police force. He tells Janelle and Lawrence he's realized it's not what he wants to do with his life, so he's going back to school and getting his degree. He shoots me a look, telling me what I already know: there's more to that story. He's also leaving town. He's moving east for school come September, and he'll be working part-time for his uncle, a contractor in Yardsley.

"It's not Philly," he says, looking to me, "but Yardsley is downright cosmopolitan compared to where we come from."

I'm reeling, feeling the effects of this time warp, so I haven't added much to the conversation. Ethan, on the other hand, is hamming it up for our dinner guest. At the moment he's putting his finger into his mashed potatoes and placing a blob of it onto his nose.

Janelle reaches over with a napkin and wipes his nose. "Are you wasting my good food, young man?"

Ethan is busy entertaining Wes, who is laughing at his antics, and also knows he has Janelle wrapped around his little finger, so he doesn't let up. I lift him out of his chair when he ups the ante and pretends he's farting, complete with the lifting butt cheek gesture and sound effects. "That's enough, my little comedian. It's time for your bath."

"I'll do the honors," Lawrence offers. "You catch up with your friend." As they head upstairs, I hear the two of them making fart noises.

"Guess that solves the mystery of where he learned that behavior."

"Ice cream, Wes?" Janelle is making two bowls before he has a chance to answer. "Ethan and Lawrence just made it today."

"Thank you, Janelle. And thank you for dinner. The chicken was delicious."

"You're welcome."

"Come on, Wes, we'll sit out on the deck."

I look over and watch as he takes it all in. A few sandhill cranes fly in formation close to the surface of the water, and the sunset has given the sky a pinkish hue. When you see it every day you forget how spectacular it is. I settle into my chair, struck by a feeling of contentment. This is nice. Having a friend is nice.

"This is some view."

"We sit out here and have dessert every night when it's warm enough. Ethan loves playing out here with the dog. It tires him out before bed."

"He's adorable, Charlie." He takes my hand and gives it a gentle squeeze. "You're doing a great job. I hope you know that."

"He's the best thing in my life. And thank you for saying that. Sometimes I question everything I do and just pray I'm not screwing up too much."

We eat this amazing blueberry ice cream in companionable quiet for the next few minutes. As I scrape the last bit from my bowl, I work up the nerve to ask, "So what's the real story behind the career change and the move?"

"The part about law enforcement not being my true calling isn't a lie. I never loved my job. But after you confronted me about Timmy, about my part in all that...It just left me with a lot to think about."

He puts his bowl down on the deck and sits back, fixing his gaze over the water. "I'm not a good person, Charlotte."

"Wes—"

"Let me speak," he says quietly. "I'm not going to walk into the precinct and turn myself in, tell them my part in everything or tell them I lied for Christian. Timmy is dead. Nothing is going to bring him back. I'm just trying to move on and live my life as best I can."

"I would never want you to do that. I know you, Wes, so I know you've punished yourself for what happened. I'd never want you to go to prison."

"Timmy should never have gone to prison either. Maybe we didn't kill him outright, but we all had a hand in his death."

I don't contradict him because it's true. I feel for him, but he has to live with what he's done.

"I don't talk to your brother anymore." He pauses and traps one hand with the other like he's trying to control his fist when he speaks again. "I was always in his shadow growing up...All of us were. We treated him like he was a golden god or something...So pathetic." He shakes his head, the regret etched on his face. "And now every time I think about him, I have a hard time remembering the good kid, the friend he was when we were young. Somewhere along the way he turned mean, and he doesn't show any signs of changing."

I'm not surprised by his words, but they sadden me. In a way, Wes was Christian's conscience, the only person who called him on his bullshit. If Wes has given up on him, then it's as bad as I thought. "I get it."

"He's not a positive influence in my life. And while it pains me to know I'm losing him as a friend, I'm willing to accept it for what it is. I'm moving on."

I nod, reaching out to take Wes's hand. We have a long history. And without question, there is far more good to our story than bad.

"So, the reason I drove all the way out here." He looks at me and then looks away. He's nervous. "I couldn't just up and leave town without talking to you...Didn't want to risk the chance of never seeing you again. You know I've always cared about you. And I think you also know that at some point that caring turned into something more."

"Wes." It comes out sounding like a warning. I want him to stop before he says too much, but he's not having it.

"I'd be missing out on, who knows, maybe the best chance at happiness I'll ever have if I left and never spoke my truth to you. And the truth is I've loved you even when I shouldn't have, and I love you still. Your baby, *his* baby...You know I would love him like my own."

I'm dumbstruck. Wes stands, tall and unburdened. "I'm going to leave now. I don't want to pressure you. I just want you to know that you have a place to go, a person who wants you, and someone who's willing to make a good life for you."

He leans down and kisses me on the cheek before I hear him close the screen door behind him. I hear him thank Janelle. Hear him say he's going to get some miles behind him before he stops for the night. I hear him say his goodbyes to Lawrence and listen as Ethan lets out a happy yelp when Wes does something to make him laugh.

I've been sitting there for some time before Janelle and Lawrence come outside. Lawrence hands me a cup of tea as Janelle places a piece of paper in my other hand. "He left this for you." It's a phone number and his new address. "That boy is in love with you."

Nothing else is said as the three of us sit and watch the sky turn from pink to purple to midnight blue.

* * *

SIMON

Samantha clinks a fork against her champagne flute. "A toast to the man of the hour."

I swallow my discomfort. All eyes are on me as Professor Westfield stands at the head of the table, and I'm not much for being the center of attention. Samantha's smile stretches clear across her face, as does Mrs. Westfield's. Brett smiles though clenched teeth, though I know he's probably fantasizing about doing me in with his steak knife right about now. He sees me as the guy who stole his scholarship. According to Brett, it's his year, not mine. Winnie, my West Virginia friend, leans in and whispers, "You've earned it."

"A near perfect score on the LSATs. A stellar undergraduate academic record, a degree earned with honors while conducting research, tutoring fellow students and holding down a job. And completed one year early no less!" He shakes his head, smiling. "I'm in awe of this young man. Raise your glass, everyone, and join me in congratulating this year's recipient of the Honorable James W. Crawley Memorial Scholarship."

"Here, here," Winnie chimes in, clinking her glass with mine. "I hope I'm sitting in your place next year."

Samantha sits on my other side and touches her glass to

mine. Her free hand lands on my upper thigh, giving me a reassuring squeeze. "I'm so proud of you."

How did I get here?

"I feel like I'm an ESPN commentator asking the top recruit which team he's going to play for next year," Professor Westfield jokes. "Is it going to be U Penn, Duke, Michigan, UVA, Cornell or good old Northwestern?"

"I've narrowed it down some, but I'm still not sure. U Penn is out, Cornell too."

"The two ivies? I'm surprised."

"I don't want to be in New York, I'm sure of that, and for some reason Penn doesn't appeal to me." The reason is that mere mention of the word Pennsylvania turns my stomach. I blame the Pennsylvania Department of Corrections for that. I am not going back. And I throw New York under the bus because Cornell and NYU have top-ranked MFA programs for creative writing, and Samantha has mentioned both in passing when she talks about her future. "My mother is down in South Carolina now, so Duke and UVA are still contenders, but I'd say Northwestern and Michigan are my top two."

Samantha is my girlfriend now. There's no *let's not put a label on this* with her. The distinction was made after a bout of pneumonia that literally knocked me on my ass this past January. I was basically running myself ragged between taking on extra credits and then getting my applications together. School broke for the semester, and so did I. Samantha called an ambulance for me when my fever was still running wild after four days and my wracking cough turned into a wheeze. She tells me that I said, "I have to go to work," as they were loading me onto a stretcher. I don't remember it that way, but hell, I *was* out of it. She loves that story, tells it whenever she gets the chance. It's always followed by the tale of her nursing me back to health. And she did. It was two weeks before I was fully back on my feet, and she was with me every step of the way. Samantha did my laundry, made me homemade soup, registered me for classes with the help of her dad, and lugged my textbooks back from the bookstore at the start of the semester when I was still too weak to do it myself.

I've never been sick like that in my entire life, and it did something to me. With my brother and Brandon having left for Oregon the year before, I was truly without family. I could scarcely get out of bed and I was alone. And for the first time, I was actually suffering from it, from loneliness. She swooped in, made it all better.

As I recuperated, we spent nights watching television together and talking. I saw her in a different light, I guess.

Three months later and I'm doing everything in my power to land myself in a different state. She has another year left before she graduates, so if I choose somewhere other than Northwestern, I can extricate myself from this relationship in a relatively painless way. Career wise, though, Northwestern is where I should be. I've made connections here, and since I'm not a fortunate son with a daddy on the bench or in corporate law, I need every hand up I can get.

The fact that I'm even considering another school is proof of how much I want to be free of her. And I care about her. I do. I care enough that the idea of hurting her pains me. Initiating a break-up literally fills me with dread, so much so that I play a game with myself sometimes. It's called: What if I did wind up with Samantha?

Would it be so bad? I get along great with her parents, know I'll fit right into the fold. She's good to me, has proven time and time again that she cares about me. Samantha doesn't come with the baggage of a fucked-up background like I do, and I reason that can only bode well for a relationship. Fact is, I can see how my life with her will play out, and it's not a bad life. But deep down I know it will be like a custom-tailored suit that still doesn't fit quite right.

I'm back in my room now, exhausted from the effort it took to keep the smile on my face tonight. I slip the picture out of its frame. I keep it tucked behind the one of me, Tim and Mike that sits on my desk. It's been so long that I don't know if I'd be able to see her face if I didn't have this picture to remind me. It feels ridiculous to think of her the way I do. I'm still stuck on a sixteen-year-old girl when she's not that person anymore.

But this faded picture in my hands is everything. It's a reminder that I'm capable of love, the kind of love for another person that consumes you. It's a reminder of why I can never make a life with Samantha.

When I took her home tonight, I wanted to leave her at the door, avoid the lie I've be telling her with my kisses and with my touch. She was happy tonight, happy for my success and envisioning her place in the future I have, one that is all but guaranteed now. I couldn't do it, couldn't hurt her tonight. So when she drew me into her room, when she undressed and invited me in, I went to her. I closed my eyes and saw the face of another girl, remembered the feel of someone else's skin when I held her body beneath mine.

I made love to Charlotte.

I always do.

Part Three

A SORT OF HOMECOMING

Chapter Twenty-Three

CHARLOTTE

"We should get going, Charlotte. Long drive ahead of us."

"Yeah, I'm coming."

Lawrence looks as sad and as washed out as I do. The past three weeks have been among the most trying of my life. Right up there with finding out I was pregnant, my baby' life-saving surgery, and the harrowing weeks spent last winter nursing Ethan through a respiratory infection that landed him back in the hospital.

I'd been on such a high. Half-way through my sophomore year, I'm kicking ass in school. I've made friends, a few guys and girls in my dance ensemble group mostly, and a few acquaintances from study groups. Ethan, now almost three, has weathered storms but is healthy and happy. It's like the rug has been pulled out from underneath me just when I was starting to feel so...normal.

I'm sitting in the passenger seat now, wishing we'd gone straight home after the appointment with Janelle's lawyer this morning. But Lawrence spotted a billboard for the Pablo Picasso exhibit at the Art Institute and decided we should go there as a tribute of some kind, being that Janelle had a few of his prints hanging in the house. It did nothing to lift the mood. Janelle collected funky prints for our home, bright contemporary renderings of a rooster, a horse and a bull. This exhibition was subtitled Mother and Child. Every piece, spiritual and somber, spoke to me. I could feel the pain Janelle must have endured over the years, her prayers to have a child of her own never answered.

The call from Janelle's lawyer came out of nowhere. We had to venture to Chicago for the reading of her will? My grief still felt paralyzing, like being trapped shoulder-deep in quicksand, so I didn't connect the dots until this morning. Once I did, I was ashamed of the way my heart raced. And I was being ridiculous. Me and roughly two million other people walking the streets of the city of Chicago—what were the odds of seeing him?

It figures the one time luck was on my side, it would leave me doubled over as if I'd been kicked in the gut.

"You all right?"

"Yeah...No."

"That's how I feel."

I change the subject, not wanting to reveal what's really dragging me down. "Do you think she knew?"

"Knew what?"

I look over my shoulder to make sure Ethan is sleeping. "Don't you think it's odd that she contacted her lawyer just six weeks ago? And then dies a few weeks later?"

Lawrence keeps his eyes on the road but nods. A moment later I see his left hand go to wipe at an errant tear. "You think she had some kind of premonition?"

"An aura, a premonition…I don't know. I just keep thinking she might not have been feeling well and didn't say anything." I hesitate, not wanting to say what I've been thinking. "Was I so wrapped up in my own life that I didn't notice?"

"You know she'd hate it if she heard you talking like that." He clears his throat and meets my eyes when we slow to a stop at a red light. "And the doctor said it was very likely she had no warning. She never even complained of a headache. Sometimes these things just happen."

Lawrence is no stranger to tragedy, but this has to be hitting him hard. Janelle once mentioned that his wife died years ago of a sudden, massive heart attack, and now Janelle of an aneurism. No warning whatsoever.

"She did everything for me."

Lawrence reaches over and grabs my hand. "You gave her something to live for, you and Ethan. You know that, don't you?"

I let out the breath I've been holding. "I was thinking I'd withdraw from my classes this semester, regroup a little." Referring to the strict instructions laid out in Janelle's last will and testament, I add, "Guess I can't after that sermon, huh?"

He chuckles quietly. "I don't see why you can't lighten your load a little, but taking a semester off? No, I don't suppose that would sit well with our gal."

"I don't know how I'll manage without her."

"We can do this."

"Lawrence, you love it up here. I don't expect you to upend your life for me."

"I won't be. I'll be up here most of the time, but I'll be down in Ann Arbor too. Janelle would want this…Want me to help you see it through. And Arlene is on board. She'll be a great help."

Arlene Gold, our neighbor. She's a little on the kooky side, but I do trust her to babysit. She had Janelle's stamp of approval, and that means something.

"I'm going to drop two classes, both electives. I'll do the three that contribute towards my major. I can make the other ones up later, maybe online."

"Sounds like a solid plan. Did you talk it over with Barbara?"

"Not yet. She'll probably give me," I turn again to make sure Ethan is asleep, "shit about it. I love that woman, but she is a damn pitbull."

Barbara Ryan is a pitbull, but a wounded one at the moment. Janelle's death was devastating to her as well. The two of them had forged a close friendship over the past few years, meeting for lunch at least once or twice a month whenever school was in session and Janelle was down in Ann Arbor with me.

"I don't know about you, but I feel like we need her more than ever right now."

I nod, conceding the fact. "Did you meet her kids at the funeral?"

"Yeah...Nice boys, both of them."

"Marriage is weird, right? I mean, can you imagine any guy walking away from her and those two kids. She's annoying sometimes, yeah, but she's amazing."

He shakes his head. "I shouldn't comment because I don't know what happened there, but you're not a man in my book if you walk away from your responsibilities."

Lawrence cocks a brow. "Did you just say something?"

I nod and repeat what I whispered a moment before. "I saw Simon today."

We're already back in town, just a mile or so from home, but this news compels him to pull over. "What?"

"I saw him. He was walking out of the museum. He didn't see me."

"Or his son."

He puts the car into drive and we don't speak again until after we pick Moe up at a friend's and we're back in the house. "Give me the little fella." To Ethan, he says, "Moe's hungry. You gonna help me feed him?"

Ethan has been quiet these past few weeks, grieving along with the rest of us. He's reverted to sucking his thumb again, which makes me, captain of the germ police, edgy as all get out. "Thumb out of your mouth, sweetie."

He side eyes me and goes on sucking his thumb like it's a T-bone.

Lawrence looks weary. "Some battles just aren't worth fighting."

"Roger that."

I get the distinct impression that we're not done with our conversation from before when Lawrence comes into the living room after dinner and hands me a bowl of ice cream. I love homemade ice cream but tonight it feels too thick to swallow. I forge ahead though, because I can't look Lawrence in the eye, even if it's to tell him I'm not hungry.

"So what are we going to do about this?"

Deep breath. "I can't."

"You will one day. You know that, right?" When I don't answer he says, "You're breaking that man's heart every day you don't tell him."

"He doesn't…"

I don't know what I mean to say. What? He doesn't what?

"Think of the worst case scenario, Charlotte. Worst case,

he's a rotten fool and he doesn't want to be a part of Ethan's life. No loss, right? He's not a part of his life now."

"No, Lawrence, the worst case scenario is him hating me for keeping it a secret."

"But that can happen tomorrow, or that can—no, it *will* happen when Ethan is old enough to ask questions, to demand answers."

"Don't."

"I'm just telling it like it is, sweetheart." He reaches over and rubs my shoulder. "I'm not looking to upset you. You know I want the best for you. And that boy, well…He's my heart, you know?"

When I look at Lawrence, I see that he's holding back tears, just like me.

"Me and Janelle talked about it. And while I didn't agree with your decision back then, I could understand your reasoning. But that old argument doesn't hold water anymore, now does it?"

"What are you saying?"

"I'm saying you are a woman of means."

"Oh lordy, I can't even think about that."

"I don't want to think about her giving me this house either. It pisses me off. And just for the record, I won't accept it. This place is yours."

I fix him with a hard look. "Uh, you *will* take it because that's what she wanted." I hit his knee with mine. "I don't exactly love the wilderness the way she did, and anyway, I know I can come up here with Ethan and crash whenever I want."

"It just bothers me. Makes me look at my little ramshackle place with sad eyes, I guess."

"Your cabin is perfectly fine, but she knew you'd do this place proud. And you're a fisherman…You were always meant to be lakeside." And it's true. I can picture Lawrence casting off from the shore at the edge of the property, can picture him teaching Ethan how to bait a hook. "But I know exactly how you feel. Don't get me wrong, I'm grateful and all, but I'm still reeling from this morning."

"Want a beer? I'm dying for one."

I waggle my eyebrows. "I'd love one."

"One time deal, a toast to Janelle. She'd tan my hide if she knew I was giving your underage butt a beer."

"She'd tan my hide." I laugh as he pops the cap and hands me the bottle. "What was up with that? You'd think Janelle and my dad grew up on a farm in Wyoming or something." I can't help but smile. "Life is simpler when you plow around the stump, Charlotte."

"Always drink upstream from the herd."

It takes me all of ten seconds to come up with another one of her winners. "Letting the cat out of the bag is a whole lot easier than getting it back in."

"When you wallow with pigs, best expect to get dirty." Lawrence raises his bottle to mine. "To our Janelle." Looking up, he adds, "We miss you, angel."

I take a long pull off my beer. "I'm rich."

"In my book you're rich, but I'm thinking most people would say you're just comfortable. What's important is that you're able to provide for your son. Independence and peace of mind...What a gift she's given you."

"When she said Paul taught her everything, I never would have guessed."

"He seems like a good man."

"He does, right? Solid move flying out for the service, wasn't it?"

Lawrence finishes his beer and takes the half of mine that's still left. I don't protest, even though I do like the taste of it. He gives me a pointed look. "Don't dwell on it." Lawrence knows my praise for Paul is an indirect dig at my father.

"Please don't tell me to forgive him. This was about the last straw for me as far as my dad is concerned."

He puts his hands up and shakes his head. "Wasn't going to suggest it. I'm saying don't dwell on it because you can't change him. People don't change."

"I know."

"So tell me about Simon. What kind of person is he?"

"This feels like a trap."

"It's not. I'm truly curious as to why you think this young man will react negatively."

"He'll flip! Can you imagine getting news like this?"

"No doubt it'll be a shock, for sure. It's just...I never had children, and now having Ethan in my life, I could never imagine *not* wanting him in my life. Do you understand?"

"I do."

"Then give it some thought, that's all I'm asking."

Chapter Twenty-Four

SIMON

"You clean up nice."

She's looking at me in the mirror, her chin perched on my shoulder. It's true, I look nothing like the boy I was four years ago.

Tonight is calling to mind the prom I missed back in Pennsylvania, even as I stand polished and ready to escort Samantha to her Commencement Ball. I didn't go last year when I graduated, even though I had a girlfriend, even though Samantha nagged me incessantly. But my attendance at this event is nonnegotiable. It's her big night and I will be there for her. I'll slip into the tailored shirt and the fitted suit, one of three purchased on credit when I realized I needed to dress the part I was playing.

She straightens my tie and then wraps her arms around my middle. "I'm going to have the best looking date in the room."

"You're not so bad yourself," I tease back through gritted teeth, turning around and taking her in from head to toe. In her pale blue dress adorned with just a bit of sparkle, she looks like some golden haired angel walking among mere mortals.

The sight of her should take my breath away.

"Looking good, son," Professor Westfield says as he claps me on the back. He's been calling me son since long before I started dating Samantha, but I cringe when he says it now.

Samantha's mom kisses me on the cheek and then fusses as the photographer poses the happy couple on the stairs and on the front landing. The photographer gets the four of us together then, snapping pictures that will last a lifetime.

"So, you're officially no longer a one-L. How does it feel?"

"One down, two to go. It feels good."

"Are you sure you made the right decision turning down that summer associate position? I could still make a call."

I feel my jaw tighten and breathe through it. "Interning with Judge Michaels will be a great experience. Could lead to a clerkship after I graduate and it's the type of exposure to litigation I want."

"Don't get me wrong, it's prestigious, it's just not the direction I'd take if I wanted a shot at corporate law." When I go to speak up, he nods and attempts to placate me. "I know that's not where your heart is, but you don't want to cut off avenues so early on in the game."

What he's thinking but not saying: You'd best get a job that will allow my baby girl to live in the manner she's become accustomed to.

What I'm thinking but not saying: You've been a great help to me these past few years and I do appreciate it. I know first-year law students don't get offers for associate positions at white-shoe firms, know your wealthy law school buddy did that as a favor to you. I feel bad turning it down, I do, but I don't want anything from you anymore. I don't want to get rich representing corporations or getting affluent people off when they're guilty. I don't want to get rich so I can buy a five thousand square foot home for Samantha to decorate and a lakeside cottage to boot. I don't want to marry your daughter. In fact, I'm laying the groundwork for our break-up at this very moment.

I don't have the heart to do it today, even though she's betrayed me. Samantha has told a lie of omission that I cannot forgive.

Tomorrow I'm driving nearly five hours to Ann Arbor. It's taking everything I have in me to refrain from confronting her, to hold back the rage I've felt since I found it. In a rush to get my suit from the dry cleaners, I was looking for my keys when the crumpled paper fell from her bag onto the floor. The familiar handwriting caught my eye. Ironing out the creases, my heart hammered when I took in the name and return address. Awful things began to click into place when I noticed the postmark dated more than two months ago. The envelope was empty, and a thorough search of her bag, her desk, her dresser drawers and her car turned up nothing more.

I avoid Samantha all day, giving myself time to think. She feels threatened, naturally she would, but it's still no excuse for what she's done. I'm furious but there's guilt there too. This past year I've given her something to believe in when I shouldn't have. And I feel guilty because I'm relieved. Yes, I immediately see her betrayal for what it is: my get out of jail free card. I don't deserve to feel morally superior to her. I'm well aware of the fact.

I spend the afternoon searching the internet. The same search I've done so many times before finally gets me a hit. It's a transfer of property notice, the address the same as the return address written on the envelope. Property transferred to Charlotte Mason from one Janelle Cohen, nee Mason. Her aunt, the aunt she went to live with. All this time, has she been just a few hours away? And why is the property in Charlotte's name? A search of her aunt's name reveals a death notice dated this past December, just a few days after Christmas.

Samantha knows something is off tonight. She's asked me what's wrong twice already. I assure her I'm good, and in a way, I'm better than I have been in a very long time.

Charlotte wrote to me. Nearly four years have passed and she's reaching out. It's crossed my mind that the letter might be nothing more than a long overdue, scathing rant where she tells me off over the shitty way I walked out on her, but I don't care. She's thinking of me—that's all that matters right now.

I dance with my soon to be ex-girlfriend, stay by her side as she chats up our fellow classmates, help her stay upright when she drinks too much, and drop her off at her parents' house, surprising her father when he opens the door a little past midnight.

He's a brilliant man, perceptive, and it feels like he's about to ask me a question—one I don't want to answer—when she pukes on his slipper-clad feet. *Thanks for the save, Samantha.*

"Jeez."

"Um, I guess she overdid it."

He shoots me an annoyed look. "Obviously." When I make a move to help, he waves me off. "I'll take care of her."

He knows.

I was planning to leave at daybreak but sleep is out of the question. So I'm walking Main Street in Ann Arbor as the sun rises, sipping from a cup of coffee that cost me nearly five bucks. The shops and restaurants here remind me of Chicago and Evanston: aesthetically pleasing and wildly overpriced. Quaint and charming, that's how Samantha would tag this downtown area.

I hold off until seven in the morning, and while I'm thinking it's rude to drop in unexpected on her so early, I just can't wait any longer. Her place is in a nice area, just a short distance from campus. Does she go to school here? She must. Probably just finished her sophomore year. I knock on her door, smiling because I'm proud of her. Mr. Vargas would be too.

I don't get a second knock off before a woman pops her head out from next door. "Can I help you?" When I turn, her eyes go wide. "My Lord," she whispers.

"Um, yes ma'am, I'm looking for Charlotte Mason."

She comes out into the corridor between the two units. Comes close, looks me over and studies my face in a way that's uncomfortable. Absently, she says, "She went home a few days ago."

"Home?"

The woman, who looks to be in her mid-sixties and bears a freakishly close resemblance to Kathy Bates, is suddenly all business. Dressed in workout clothes, she looks tenacious, like she could power walk laps in the mall for hours.

"Yes, home. What's your name young man, and what's your business with Charlotte?"

"I'm Simon Wade. I'm a friend of Charlotte's. She's been trying to get in touch with me, and I, uh, came to see her."

"She's been trying to reach you?" For some reason this nugget has piqued her interest.

"Yes. I got a letter. Didn't say much but it said she was living in Ann Arbor. It's important that I get in touch with her."

"It sure is," she mutters under her breath.

"Would you happen to have her phone number?"

She considers this for a moment. "Her number, no, but I can give you her address. Wait here."

I have a feeling that she does, in fact, have Charlotte's number, but I let it go. When we talk, I don't want it to be over the telephone. I want to see her in person, so the address is even better.

"Go see them, and don't give my girl Charlotte any trouble. You give her trouble and Lawrence will bust your helmet, you got me?"

Bust my helmet? I want to ask who Lawrence is, but I don't want to engage this crazy lady for one second longer than I need to. I nod, careful as I take the paper from her hand. "Thank you."

She watches me until I'm back in my car. Powell, Michigan. I map the address and see that it's way, way up north. Seven hours north. It's no matter. I'm so determined to see her that I don't care if I have to drive all day and night. So I stop at another little café, one where it looks like I can grab a sandwich, another large coffee and take a leak before I head out. It's not until I'm back in my car and biting into my egg sandwich that it all sinks in. The drawing hanging on Charlotte's front door, the odd way her neighbor eyed me, her words: Go see them...*them*.

I nearly choke, my hands shaking as I reach for some coffee to wash the mouthful down. I tell myself not to jump to conclusions, that Charlotte and this guy Lawrence make up "them"—that's who the strange woman was referring to. *Don't go imagining crazy shit, Simon. It's not possible, don't be an idiot.* I'm talking myself down, which only adds intensity to my freak out.

Instead of heading north as planned, I find myself driving back to Evanston. I need to know what was in that letter before I see Charlotte. I need to be prepared.

* * *

CHARLOTTE

"Thanks, Wes. Yeah, I'll talk to you soon."

The call ends with me feeling better than I have the past few times we've spoken. After dropping in on me last summer, Wes began writing to me regularly. For the most part he's kept things casual, but I know he would like nothing more than a place in my future. The ball is in my court. I'm always careful and on guard when I interact with Wes. I don't want to hurt him, don't want to lead him on.

I broke down and called him after Janelle died, during a stretch when I was feeling particularly awful. And he was so good to me. Even offered to drop everything and come out to help me through it. When I made it clear I wanted him to stay put, he respected my wishes but supported me with phone calls and care packages for both me and Ethan. One of those phone calls ended with him telling me he loved me. I know I hurt him when I said I couldn't be serious with anyone when I still had so much unfinished business in my own life, but that was the truth.

In the days that followed, I began to ask myself when exactly I planned on addressing that unfinished business.

I waited a few days before I looked him up online. Waited a few more days before I got serious and tracked down a contact number for him. Avoided looking at the number scribbled on the wall calendar for another week before I worked up the nerve to call. When I called and a woman answered, I nearly hung up but didn't. She took my name and number and said she'd give him the message. Two weeks passed before I tried again. Same woman answered. Yes, she gave him the message last time, yes, she'll tell him I called *again*. Clearly, I was trying her patience. I asked her to tell him it was important. The clipped way she repeated my words, *it's important*, settled it: this girl was his girl. Probably the beautiful swan who was gliding alongside Simon the day I saw him in Chicago. When a month passed with no return phone call, I'll admit I was angry.

Detached and cold, I knew the flip side of Simon Wade all too well. Did he receive my messages and then choose to ignore me? History does often repeat itself, so I wouldn't put it past him.

Studying his profile picture again, I can almost feel the cold sting of his stare, feel the pain of being judged and then dismissed by that troubled teenage boy. He set out to hurt me back then, more than once. But then he loved me, loved me with an intensity I fear I may never experience again. The man in this picture, which version of Simon is he? With his sharp suit and his gel-slicked hair, he looks every bit the future power player Simon was striving to be.

"Maybe," I speak to his image on the screen, "I don't know you anymore."

Simon is the father of my child, he was the first man I ever loved, and I haven't opened my heart to anyone since. But time has passed, a lot of time. I don't know him anymore, that's true, and he doesn't know me. Those two damaged kids back in Pennsylvania don't exist anymore. Maybe it's childish of me to continue to look back on that time as special. I can't deny that I still long for Simon, but I need to face the very real possibility that he doesn't feel the same. What we had back then, maybe it was never all that significant to Simon.

Once I let that sink in, I'm able to let go of the anger. I am ready and able to sit down and write the letter. It doesn't take three messy, tear-stained drafts like the last time. Now older and wiser, I'm clear and concise. I state the reason I decided to keep the pregnancy from him and express my sincere hope that he can someday find a way to forgive me. I let him know he's welcome to come and meet his son if he wants to, and if he does not, I'll respect that decision as well. I wish him happiness then simply sign it: Charlotte.

Reading it over, I know there's one big fat lie in there. Ethan is the most precious thing on this earth to me, so I will forever think of Simon as a coward and a jackass if he chooses not to meet his son.

I slip a recent snapshot of Ethan in with the letter. He's smiling ear to ear, with his arms wrapped around his pal, Moe. I take a deep breath when I drop it into the mailbox.

That's that.

In the days that follow, I prepare to take cover, to weather the storm I've just set into motion. When a week passes and then two, when the cold winter wind gives way to sunny days and springtime, well, that's when I give up.

SIMON

"Samantha's not at her place. Is she here?"

Eyes wide, Mrs. Westfield takes me in, backing away a step before regaining her composure. I'm sweating, my clothes are rumpled, and I've been dragging a hand through my hair in frustration for most of the four-plus hour drive back to Evanston. I'm sure my eyes have taken on a feral quality by now.

"She is, but—"

"Simon?" Samantha calls out quietly from the upstairs landing. She looks wary of me as she makes her way downstairs with slow, measured steps.

"Where's the letter?"

"What?"

"The letter, Samantha. What did you do with it?"

"I don't—"

"Come in and sit down, Simon." Mrs. Westfield's tone is meant to soothe me. "I'll get you something cold to drink…You look terrible."

"I don't want to sit." Samantha's eyes are wide when she comes to stand beside me. She moves to take my hand but my fists are clenched. I lower my voice and turn to her. "Get me that letter."

"I don't have it."

When I hit my fist into my open palm she startles, and I have to walk away for a moment to collect myself. She follows me into their living room but keeps a good distance between us. That's for the best, because if I don't start getting some answers soon I'm going to start breaking shit.

"I burned it."

I force myself to use my indoor voice, knowing that screaming and ranting won't get me the information I need. "You burned the letter?"

She looks ashamed, lowering her head as she nods. "I was looking through your mail one day. I mean, you just always let it pile up on your counter. I've been looking through it for years now. Who do you think separates the bills from the junk mail?" She shakes her head when I don't answer. Flopping down onto the couch, she lowers her head into her hands. "She called here. My mother gave me the messages to relay." Looking up, she starts but then trails off, "I just—"

I take the seat across from her. I'm tired and I don't want to plow through this muck of tangled feelings right now. "The letter, Samantha."

"It was nothing, Simon. Some syrupy ploy to get you back." When I go to stand, she puts her hands up in surrender. "I know, I know…That was yours to interpret on your own. I had no right to keep it from you. It's just that from everything you've told me about your childhood, this seemed like nothing more than a desperate girl from the boonies trying to dig her claws into the boy who made good. Your star is on the rise, Simon. All she'd need to do is look you up online to see you have a bright future, to see an opportunity."

"An opportunity?"

Samantha starts to bite at the skin around her thumb. It's a nasty habit, and one I've only seen her resort to in particularly stressful times.

"Just tell me, Samantha."

"She has a child."

Now my head drops into my hands. "Holy fuck."

"Simon, please listen to me. You and I both know this happens all the time. Who's to say she didn't get herself knocked up after you left? And now, bingo, years later she sees that a boy from her past has made something of himself. Problem, meet solution." She adds, "He looks too young to be yours. It doesn't add up."

"Oh my God. Are you serious?"

"I—"

"You *saw* him? *Him*? It's a *boy*?"

Her eyes are wide with fear. "There was, uh, a picture."

Her voice is pitched high when she adds, "Even Mom thought he looked way younger than what she claimed."

"Samantha, I'm serious, whatever you're keeping from me, get it right fucking now or I'm going to tear this house apart myself."

She's crying as she stands on legs that visibly tremble. "Wait here."

She heads back to her room, shaking her head in warning at her mother as they pass on the stairs. Mrs. Westfield stands at the entrance of the dining hall, opposite from where I am, but close enough to swoop in if needed. She knows the score—was in on it even—and now she's going to have to help her daughter pick up the pieces.

Samantha returns with something pressed against her chest. I open my hand, angry that she's still holding back from me. She puts the small square into my palm. "I burned the letter but I kept this."

Ethan James - 2 years, 10 months. It's written in Charlotte's hand. I stare at the name but can't bring myself to turn it over for some reason. When I do will myself to look at the photo, I crouch back down and take a seat on the couch, speechless. He is small, this little guy, but I don't really know what a two or three-year-old is supposed to look like. His face is what knocks the wind from me, though. It's that picture of me and my brothers. I was around five or six in that shot, but this boy looks like me, like us. There's no denying this child is a Wade.

I swallow and look up at her. "So you looked at this picture." I raise my voice to be heard. "I mean, you *and* your mother looked at this picture, and you agreed that this child could not possibly be mine?"

"I didn't—"

"He's practically my clone! You don't even know what

Charlotte looks like, so even if this boy looked absolutely nothing like me, what excuse could you possibly have for not telling me? And *she* would never lie to me. She'd never—"

"She's *been* lying to you for a long time, Simon. Let's at least get that much straight. If that is your child, then she *is* a liar." I have nothing to say, and Samantha senses an opening. She's nothing if not determined. "And why now? Why after all this time is she reaching out to you?"

I get up to leave. There's somewhere else I need to be, and I'm itching to rid myself of this arrogant, manipulative daddy's girl. "Maybe I'd know if I'd had a chance to read that letter."

Mrs. Westfield comes out and puts her hand on my arm as I'm reaching for the doorknob. "Simon."

"Please don't." I'm still too angry and disappointed to look at her when I add, "Tell your husband I said that I'm sorry and I'll call him when I can."

"Hello, Charlotte."

I practice the words standing in front of my mirror. I came back here to shower, to throw a few things into a duffel bag in the hopes she'll allow me to stay nearby for a few days, and to look at that picture again.

I hold the one of Ethan, my son, up next to it. The sandy blond hair is the same as mine, same as Mike's. The dimple in his left cheek matches the one in my own. The only difference is the eyes. He doesn't have blue eyes like us Wade boys. No, his are a warm hazel brown like his mother's. In this picture he's knee deep in snow, a black and white pup by his side who looks like a trustworthy friend. Ethan is smiling, making the dimple crease in a way that makes me long to reach out and touch his cheek.

He is mine.

There is no doubt in my mind.

As my truck grinds its way up and out of Illinois, up past Green Bay with another three hours still left to go, I busy myself imagining how it's going to be. Anything is possible. I haven't seen Charlotte in nearly four years. And I don't know what was in that letter. Was it an angry letter, or was Samantha telling the truth, that Charlotte is seeking me out? Don't know, because when it comes to Samantha, I can no longer believe so much as a word she says.

Maybe she won't be the serious, sweet girl I once knew. Maybe the years have hardened her. Maybe she's with that guy, Lawrence, or worse, married, and they're happy together. Maybe he's been playing the role of father to my son for the past few years. Worry turns to anger when I think of some faceless stranger teaching my son to catch a ball, some random guy reading to Ethan before his bedtime, soothing him when he cries.

She's been lying to you for a long time.

I'm angry, but then I think back to the day I left, the scene playing out like a movie in my mind. Her face as I shoved that paper bag into her hand. The desperate way she reached for me as I backed away from her. Her voice when she told me she loved me.

Don't do this to me. I remember saying those words. What an ass, like somehow I was the aggrieved party. What did I leave in my wake when I ran off?

What have I done to Charlotte?

Chapter Twenty-Five

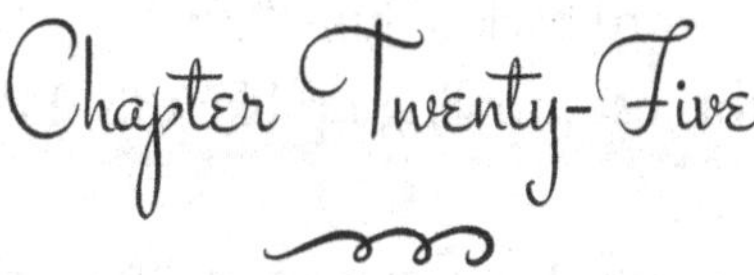

CHARLOTTE

A couple of months ago I would have been prepared, but as the weeks passed, expectation turned to uncertainty, disappointment, resentment, and then resignation.

A hurricane is raging inside of me, and though I feel unsteady, I'm acutely aware that I'm rooted in place.

Neither one of us speaks. He goes to open his mouth but then closes it just as quickly. I know I should greet him, invite him in, do something besides stand here like a statue, but I can't seem to take action.

Lawrence slows as he gets closer to the porch, clearing his throat. "Charlotte, you going to introduce us?"

I do not move or speak or breathe.

Simon turns to Lawrence and offers his hand. "I'm Simon Wade."

"I know who you are, son." Looking down at the cooler he's holding, he says, "I'd shake your hand if I could, but the trout were practically jumping into my boat today." He looks between me and Simon, then says, "Well, I'll leave you to it," as he passes through and walks into the house.

Simon takes one step closer. "Hi."

I breathe the word back to him. "Hi."

"I'm sorry for just showing up like this. I didn't have your number and I..."

When he trails off, I find my voice. "No, it's fine. I'm glad you came. It's just that I wasn't expecting you. I'm just..."

"I know, I should have..."

I cover my mouth to stifle the nervous cry-laugh that's rising up. "It seems neither one of us can form a coherent sentence." I wave him in with one hand. "Come in."

He takes a few steps inside and looks around before he turns back to me. "So, I went to see you in Ann Arbor yesterday."

"I left last week right after classes ended."

"You go to Michigan?"

"I do. And you're in law school now? Still at Northwestern?" He smiles at me and nods. Damn, his eyes are gentle, familiar. "So you finished your undergrad early, stuck to your plan..."

"Yeah, I took classes during the summer and every winter break. Kind of a lunatic move thinking back on it now. Pretty sure I was the only one-L who didn't think the workload was that heavy this year." He spells it out when he sees that he's lost me. "One-L, that's what they call first year law students."

"Oh, makes sense."

The air is heavy, choking my words and rendering me so self-conscious that I can't even walk in a natural way. And it's crazy making small talk like this when there is so much between us.

Simon's gaze follows mine when instinct draws my eyes towards the stairs. I wonder when the elephant in the room is going to stampede his way into this awkward conversation. I'd wager we have no more than ten minutes before he's up from his nap, fifteen if I'm lucky. Better to just bite the bullet.

"So, you got the letter."

He jams his hands into his pockets, shifts his weight on his feet. "Actually no, I didn't. I, um, came across an envelope with your return address. So I went there yesterday. Met your neighbor?"

"Arlene Gold?" My heart is beating double-time imagining what she said to Simon. "What exactly did she say?"

He cocks his head to the side, eyes playful. "Something about Lawrence busting my helmet if I wasn't nice to you?"

"Sounds like her." What is this? He's not mad or demanding answers. I'm so confused. "Uh, wait. What did you mean when you said you saw an envelope? Why didn't you get the letter?"

He shakes his head once. "Can that be a story for another day, Charlotte?" He swallows like he's shoring himself up. "Point is, I don't know what you said in that letter, but I did see Ethan's picture."

I take a seat on the couch, mind racing, breaths shallow. "I wish I made a copy of that letter. I spelled everything out, explained it all. Now you're here and I feel tongue-tied."

He sits down next to me but leaves a few feet of space. "Just start at the beginning."

I can feel my heart rate picking up. I thought I was so ready to do this. "I can't," I say on a gasp as the first tears start to fall.

He reaches over and takes my hand, rubs his thumb over the top of mine. "Yeah, you can, Charlotte...You kind of have to."

When I look over, I see he's facing forward and his free hand is wiping at his eyes. Yes, I do owe him this. My voice shakes when I start in. "Ethan was born on April tenth." I look away when I add, "He just had his third birthday."

He attempts a smile but it's heavy with emotion. "Did he have a party?"

"Well yes, and it was a-rockin', if you consider cake with me, Mrs. Gold and Lawrence a party."

"Anything with Mrs. Gold in attendance would be...interesting at least."

"I know she comes off a little kooky, but Arlene is great. Super smart too...She's a retired physics professor. She babysits for Ethan while I'm in class. She's been a great help since Janelle..."

"Janelle is your aunt. And she passed away this past winter." He answers my unspoken question. "Found some info online. And I'm sorry for your loss."

"Thank you. It's been really hard. I mean, Janelle swooped in back then and pretty much saved me."

He squeezes my hand. "I feel lost, Charlotte. There's so much I don't know."

"Mommy." Ethan's voice is loud and clear, stretching the word mommy out in a playful way. "Mommy, I awake," he says a moment later and then adds, "Mommy, get my Moe!"

Simon's eyes light up at the sound of Ethan's voice. He wipes his palms on his jeans, looking both excited and fearful. "Is that how he wakes up?"

"Sometimes." I go to stand. "He's sweet though, he doesn't always bark orders."

I pause then, thinking this through. I can't just bounce back into the room with Ethan and proceed with introductions. I'm scared. I need more time.

Simon seems to understand. Either that or he's running scared too. Looking to the front door, he asks, "Do you want me to go?"

"I want you to stay." The words are out before I can pull them back. "But I...I want to give Ethan a head's up on all this. He's precocious, catches on quick. Like, watch what words you use around him because he thinks he's a grown man. I mean, he spends pretty much all his time with adults, so that's how it goes and—"

"Take a breath, Charlotte. It's all right."

"I don't want to introduce you to him as Simon, like you're just some random person."

Ethan calls out in a sing-song voice, "I wait-ting."

I go on, clear-headed and steady this time. "And I think we need to talk about a few things first, don't you?"

"Sure." He looks upstairs with what looks like longing—or maybe that's just what I'm hoping for. "I'll get lost until his bedtime and then we can talk?"

Lawrence peeks his head into the living room. "You go up and check on him, Charlotte, and then I'll take over. Take the man into town, get something to eat and you two hash it all out. I'm on duty."

I check with Simon, who nods and gestures that he'll be waiting outside. "Thanks, Lawrence, you're a lifesaver."

"Here I come," I call out, taking the stairs two at a time.

My sweet boy greets me with a smile when I open the door. *Everything is going to be all right.* And I absolutely know this because I'm on solid ground now, I'm not the person I was a few years ago. I can do this, with or without anyone's help. So no matter how it all goes down with Simon, I'm going to be all right and so is Ethan.

"Hey, my love, how was your nap?"

He stretches his little body out like a cat. "Where is Paw-paw?"

"Paw-paw is downstairs waiting for you, and he wants to know something."

"What?"

"He wants to know if you'll have a boys' night with him... Help him with Moe, make sloppy Joe's, watch *Lion King*—"

"I say yes!"

"Ok, we'll go downstairs and tell him. And while you have boys' night, I'm going to go out and do some stuff."

He rolls over and snuggles his body into mine. "You can come, Mommy."

"You'd let me come to boys' night?"

"Yes," he says, and that simple word makes my heart ache with love for my son. I pray that Simon sees him the way I do. I pray that letting him into Ethan's life is the right thing to do. I pray, like I do every day, that Ethan will stay healthy and that everything will turn out all right.

I must be squeezing Ethan a smidge too tight because he begins to squirm. "I love you, baby. I'll be back in time for the second part of boys' night. I've got something I need to do."

Understatement of the year.

* * *

SIMON

I want to bound up those stairs right alongside Charlotte. My need to get a look at Ethan with my own eyes is overwhelming, but I know she's right, that a sudden, unplanned ambush isn't the right way to do this. Waiting on her outside, I feel like I have to, I don't know, drop down and bang out a hundred push-ups or something—anything to make use of the excess adrenaline pumping through my system.

It's a full ten minutes before she comes out. I'm glad for the time now, feel more centered when she opens the door and looks to me. She's every bit the girl I remember from that picture, but I can't say she looks exactly the same. There's something about her eyes that's different, more knowing. She's thinned out a bit, but it just makes the spots where she's curvy more noticeable. I can see that she's taken a minute to fix herself up. She's changed clothes and put her hair up, but she still doesn't fuss much over her appearance. Girls like her just don't need to, and I'm thinking she's finally come to realize that.

She stops halfway down the porch steps. "You still have the truck?"

"This trip might be her swan song," I say as I trot around to open the door for her. "It sounded like she was protesting the entire way up here."

"It's about as far away as you can get," she says a moment later as she snaps her seatbelt into place. "I felt like I was being exiled to Siberia when I first got here."

I shift into gear and she points me in the direction we're heading. "When was that, exactly?"

"Um, early October…Couple of months after you left."

"Was it your decision? I mean, how did it all come about?"

She looks to me. "Can we hold off on the questions until after we grab some food?" She looks down to her lap, and I notice she's wringing her hands. "I mean, I'm holding it together but I'm kind of a mess right now…Be prepared for me to start leaking like a faucet once I start talking."

"Understood." I want to tell her that my thoughts are running haywire too, but I think she knows as much. "So where do you want to eat?"

"You mind if we just get some take-out? It's a nice night, we can have a picnic."

"Ok."

"It's just that this is a small town, like microscopic compared to where we grew up. And I've always been like a roadside attraction here. And tonight of all nights, I don't need an audience."

"Roadside attraction?"

She gestures for me to make a right at the stop sign. "You know, Janelle's wayward niece...Uppity little thing from down south...Pregnant." Her voice trails off on that last word, and I don't know if it's my place to reassure or comfort her. "Pull in right here. I'll go inside," she says, making it clear I'm meant to wait in the truck. She turns back to me with an apologetic look. "It's just that with you showing up, and Ethan looking like your little mini-me...I can hear the phone lines buzzing already." As Charlotte hops down from the footboard, she adds, "Sadly, I'm what substitutes for newsworthy around here. It's the nature of being an outsider in an insular community like this."

Two guys in their late twenties, maybe early thirties, come out of the shop as she's going in. They nod and smile at her, one holding the door open and then pausing a full ten seconds just to watch her as she moves inside. Charlotte has no idea. The men trade looks that express appreciation for her form, and smile as they head back to their truck talking. Taking it all in, I'm one hundred percent sure she's the topic of their conversation. She's oblivious to the effect she has on people, on men. One thing that hasn't changed.

"I was going to go with burgers, but then I figured I should give you the full tourist experience. Cudighi sandwiches, a pasty for us to split, and some Trenary Toast for dessert."

"It smells good, so I'll just trust that you're not trying to poison me."

"If I wanted to poison you, you'd be having creamed trout à la Lawrence back at the house."

I'm so grateful that she's making things easy, that it's not strained when we talk, but I'm itching to know things and the mention of Lawrence's name triggers my need. "Is it all right to ask a question now?"

"Turn left and pull into that area." Once I put the truck in park, she says, "You want to know who Lawrence is." Gathering the bags, she hands me two bottles of water. "Come on," she hops out and calls behind her, "I'll tell you everything."

"What a spot."

It's a perfect late spring day and the sun is dancing off the ripples on the lake. You can see how crystal clear the water is. It looks like you could cup your hands, take a mouthful, and it would be the best thing you've ever tasted.

"I used to come here by myself every day after school that first year, just to sit and think. It's spectacular, right?"

"You always said you wanted to live by the water."

"I think I was envisioning a place with water warm enough to swim in. I don't hate this place, not at all, but it's unbearably cold and it feels so damn remote up here in the winter. Makes Ann Arbor seem like a tropical paradise."

She opens the containers and breaks a beef patty apart, handing me one half. "This is a pasty." She pronounces it *past-ee*. When I go to take a bite, she leans back on her hands, her own food forgotten. "So Lawrence was Janelle's boyfriend.

He's lived up here his entire life. Ethan adores him, calls him Paw-paw."

"Seems like he's a big help to you."

"He is. And I think having Ethan around has been a big help for Lawrence too. He took Janelle's death really hard."

"I bet you all did."

She nods. "Even Ethan. I never thought a child so young could grieve, but he spent hours sitting on her bed at our place in Ann Arbor, like he was waiting for her to come home. And he went back to wetting the bed and sucking his thumb. It was heartbreaking to watch."

"How is he now?"

She smiles, picking at a blade of grass. "Kids are resilient. He talks to her picture sometimes, but it's not in an unhappy way...More like he's just telling her about his day. We're all better. Lawrence and I can talk about her without breaking down. In fact, we make a point of bringing her up at some point just about every day."

"So she took you in?"

"More like she acquiesced when my dad arranged to dump me on her doorstep."

She takes a bite of the pasty and then puts it down. "I don't really care for these. Hand me the bag?" Opening the sack, she hands me a sandwich wrapped in foil and unwraps her own. "Cudighi is an Italian sausage concoction. Much better, if you ask me."

I want to press, but get the feeling I need to let her go at her own pace. A moment passes before she picks up the thread. "So yeah, I wrote you a few letters when I found out I was pregnant. I was trying to get it right, come up with some right way to tell you. Obviously I never mailed the letters, and my father, who hadn't taken an interest in my life for nearly a decade, was snooping around my room and found them."

"Shit."

"Next thing I knew, Christian was tossing me into his car and dragging me halfway across the universe. And then that was that. I was living with Janelle, a woman I didn't even know."

"Did Christian..."

"What?"

I feel my face redden. "I imagine he was angry when he found out, furious if he knew it was me."

"Yeah, he knew it was you."

"Did he hurt you?"

"Nothing out of the ordinary."

I put the sandwich down and run my hands through my hair. "What exactly does that mean?"

"He pushed me, I guess? I can hardly remember. He was the least of my worries back then."

"You're so casual about it, make it sound like it's nothing. You know how it eats at me that I never beat his ass for the times he put his hands on you?"

She twists to look at me. "It's just how it was. You can't call the cops when your brother shoves you out of the way or yanks on your ponytail. But I'm not delusional. I don't think he's normal or that we had a typical sister-brother relationship. He's not the nicest guy on the planet and my family is dysfunctional...Two things I already know."

"I always felt like you sugarcoated it for me. You'd lie when I'd ask about the bruises."

She nods once, slowly. "I didn't want you getting into it with Christian. He would have made it his mission in life to hurt you in some way. But I swear, it was only squeezing my arm too tight or me knocking into something if he pushed me. It rarely happened and it was never more than that." She looks back to the water. "And that's in the past. I'll probably never see him again in my life."

"You don't speak to them?"

She shakes her head. "I went back once, a little over a year ago. I was literally in town for two hours, no more than that. My father never even asked about Ethan. Christian didn't get off the phone to come over and say hello. It was beyond weird." She shakes her head like she's shaking off the memory. "I've made peace with it. Janelle and Lawrence made a nice home for me, took care of me the way my mother would have, I think. And thanks to Janelle, I won't ever need to go back to my father looking for help."

"Janelle gave you that condo." She looks surprised. "Public record."

"Right." She goes to hand me the remainder of her sandwich. "You want this?"

"No." I say, sitting up straighter. "I'm too hopped up to finish my own."

"Can I ask you something?"

"Sure."

"Are you mad at me, Simon? I kind of envisioned this scenario where you'd show up and be really pissed off." I don't know what to say to that. "I mean, I knew where you stood back then...I know you wouldn't have wanted me to go through with the pregnancy."

I can't address that directly yet either. "I just remember waking up that last morning we were together and being so disgusted with myself, mad at myself for being so weak."

She smirks. "And your first thought was, 'Damn, I'd better get to a pharmacy.'"

"Not my finest moment. I've replayed that morning over and over in my mind." I reach over and take both of her hands. "I just want you to know I'm truly sorry for the way I left."

Charlotte's lopsided smile does nothing to disguise her pain. "It was a pretty crappy way to leave. The worst." She slides her hands out of mine and wipes at one eye. "I didn't even think about what you gave me. I mean, I looked in the bag, but I didn't actually think to take it." The next breath she takes is shaky. "A few weeks later, the contents of that bag were *all* I could think about."

"I wish I would have known."

She lets out a cheerless laugh. "Do you? Think back and be serious. Do you *really* wish I would have told you I was pregnant when you were, what, one month into your freshman year on a full college scholarship?" She starts shoving our trash back into the take-out bag. "I'm glad I didn't tell you."

"Hey, wait a minute."

She shakes her head. "There's no way to be wrong or right about this. I understand why you wouldn't have wanted me to go through with a pregnancy at the time. I would have been crazy to suggest it. I *know* it would have been a disaster. I know that." She takes a deep breath. "You never lied to me. I knew you were leaving. Those months after you left were so hard, but in the end I decided that I couldn't get rid of our baby or hand him over to someone else to raise. And to keep him, I knew I had to let you go."

"Did you hate me?"

"Sometimes," she says without hesitation. "Sometimes I'd catch a person looking at me in a judgmental way, a few times people made comments...I'd feel ashamed and resent you for it. I wasn't too happy with you when my ankles were swollen or when I'd look in the mirror and see a walrus staring back at me either." There's a hint of a smile before she sobers. "But I had a few really bad days...Just scared more than anything."

"I'd imagine you were scared every day."

"No." She shakes her head with authority. "You think you know what scared is until something truly terrifying happens." She looks up to the sky and lets out a frustrated breath. "The sun's already setting and I have so much more to tell you."

"I'm not going anywhere."

She stares at me for a moment, probably trying to figure out what exactly I mean by that. And I don't know the logistics, the hows or the whens—I realize it makes no logical sense—but still, I already know I'm going to be where they are, where my son is.

"There's something you need to know about Ethan. There were complications with the pregnancy and we, he...He had to have surgery while he was still inside of me."

I feel my breathing slow. "What was the matter?"

"Aortic stenosis. It's a congenital heart condition where the left ventricle of the heart becomes dilated and basically dysfunctional."

"And the surgery worked?"

"So far, so good. It's amazing what they can do now. The surgery can basically alter the outcome of the condition when it's done very early. The survival rate is pretty dismal for infants when it's not detected early on." It takes a minute to register that she's rubbing my back, making soothing circles, comforting me. "It's a lot to take in, I know."

"Tell me how it happened. Everything."

"Um, ok." She doesn't stop rubbing circles on my back as she tells me about the clinic up here, being rushed to the hospital in Ann Arbor, meeting with all the fetal heart specialists, waking up from the surgery, and the long wait to see if he'd be healthy at birth. "The goal is for the balloon catheter they insert to expand the valve, which results in better blood flow, which can give the ventricle the ability to develop in a normal way. When Ethan was born, the doctors felt the size and function of his left ventricle was adequate. So while he's not entirely out of the woods, the surgery was a success."

I can't get the words out at first. I just sit there shaking my head from side to side. "I'm so sorry you went through all of that on your own."

"I wasn't alone, I had Janelle." She takes her hand off my back when she adds, "But I was lonely for you back then."

* * *

CHARLOTTE

It says a lot, the fact that I'm finding it so easy to rattle off the details of Ethan's surgery and health history. His diagnosis, the surgery, all that time he spent in the NICU? It was devastating, confusing, frightening—the absolute lowest point of my life. But I'd rather go on about it all night than to talk about us, about what's going on here right now, about how this is going to play out.

I got carried away there for a moment, telling him I'd been lonely for him when I was scared out of my wits in the hospital. And what was I thinking rubbing his back like that? I should have just gone ahead and licked his neck while I was at it.

I scoot away, trying to be subtle about it, leaving a foot or two of space between us. For all I know, Simon is here for the day and that's it. *I'm not going anywhere.* I can't let myself read too much into those words.

When I opened the door to find him standing there with

his hands in his pockets, I felt like I was in a time warp, and the feelings I had for him when I was no more than a girl came rushing back. Dressed in black jeans, a worn Cubs t-shirt and beat up Vans, he looked like my Simon, not the impeccably groomed man from his online professional profile. Taking him in, my mind went back to nights in the woods, hot days spent on the bank of the river, stolen moments in his tiny bedroom, crammed in together on his twin bed.

I remind myself that I haven't been touched by a man in nearly four years. That's all this is. The one and only date I went on with a guy from my Cognitive Psych class didn't even end in a goodnight kiss. Gah. Now my mind is on kissing, and I have to hop off this crazy train because there's a whole lot more than my feelings at stake here. I owe it to Ethan to do this right. I want Simon to be in his life. I'm not going to mess that up by throwing myself at a guy who, for all I know, has moved on. Picturing that blonde's face does the trick.

I keep talking, careful to keep the conversation in neutral territory. "Ethan still sees his specialists every six months for follow-up care, and all of his regular providers, like his pediatrician, physical therapists, pediatric dentist...they're all on site too."

"Has he had any setbacks?"

I nod my head and feel my shoulders sag under the weight of the memory. Last winter was rough. "He had a stubborn respiratory infection last year, and those can be really dangerous for kids like Ethan. He was in the hospital for a few days." When I see the stricken look on Simon's face, I feel the need to reassure him. "He's healthy, he's doing great. I just have to be careful about exposing him to infections, so I make sure every little nick and cut is cleaned and bandaged, keep him away from anyone who's sick with a cold, and he has to take antibiotics before dental work or any other procedures as a precautionary measure."

"Sam—" He stops abruptly, shaking his head. "Is he, uh, small for his age?"

"No." Why would he ask that? "He was, but now he's in the fiftieth percentile for height and weight. His doctor is really pleased with his growth rate. And he's a great eater. He loves fruit, he'll try any vegetable, he even eats fish."

"It's good to know he's doing so well."

"Yeah, between the complications and him being a few weeks premature and all, it was a rough go for a while there. I can still be overly cautious to the point of being neurotic, but I'm getting better."

"I bet you're a great mother."

I can't accept that compliment from him. It floods me with too much emotion, both good and bad. I keep rattling off facts to keep myself from saying something like: *How the hell would you know?*

"So yeah, for now he just has to see his cardiologist regularly and there's a chance he'll have some restrictions later on, like with contact sports and that kind of thing."

"Charlotte."

I get that he wants me to look at him, but it's hard. It's so hard to be around someone you've been pining for, someone you've cried over. He's been like a ghost haunting my dreams for nearly four years, and now he's right here sitting beside me. His presence feels massive. His voice, his scent—it's sensory overload.

"Hey."

He reaches over and rubs a thumb across my cheek. When did I start crying? It takes everything in me not to turn into his touch. I'm desperate for his affection, even after all this time.

But I won't make a fool of myself, not now. I straighten my posture and reach for a paper napkin to dry my eyes.

"I'm all right."

"Ok," he whispers, withdrawing his hand.

He looks up and I follow. It's getting dark. The night sky is beautiful here. There are no streetlights or lit up buildings to compete with the stars. But nightfall means a new day is coming, and I need to get busy preparing for that day.

"Simon, are you planning to be a father to Ethan in some way?" I start to say, "It's all right if you—"

He grabs my wrist. "Don't." The ensuing silence prompts me to face him. "Don't give me an out, don't tell me it's fine if I just want to meet him and then go on my merry way. There's nothing about walking away from my son that's all right." He practically spits fire repeating those last two words back to me. His eyes are stony when he asks, "Do you want me to be in his life?"

"What kind of question is that? I wouldn't have reached out to you if I didn't want you in his life."

"Why now?" I shake my head, confused by his question. "What brought on this sudden urge to reach out to me now?"

"You can be such a jerk sometimes." I wrench my hand from his grasp. "You think this was a sudden urge? You think I didn't agonize over telling you when I was pregnant, when they told me he might not survive, when I gave birth, when he finally took his first steps? You think I haven't thought about you and what was best for *you* every damn day since?"

He nods and lets out a cheerless laugh. "You did this for me, huh?"

"Are you seriously getting sarcastic with me right now?"

I stand without waiting for an answer and walk the trash over to a waste can, the paper sack with the cinnamon toast smashed in my hands and discarded, even though it's the only damn thing I like out of everything I bought tonight. When I turn back, Simon is laid out flat on the grass, the heels of both hands pressed into his eyes. I don't know if he's angry, suffering or sad. I'm all of the above, so I stop and slowly inhale a calming breath as I lower myself onto the grass next to him again.

"I want you in his life. I always did." He goes to speak but I stop him, placing one hand on his shoulder. "When I went back home last year, I also stopped by your trailer. I drove all around town. I told myself I was just reminiscing, but the truth is I wanted to run into someone, your mother or Garth or someone...anyone who might tell you they saw me." He folds his arms across his chest. He's listening. "I met the people who live in your trailer now. Your mother moved?"

"She's in North Carolina with her boyfriend. She left a few months after Timmy's funeral."

I nod, remembering those words: *There's not going to be a service, Charlotte. There's no mahogany casket, no priest, no flowers.*

"It looks different now. They don't keep it up the way you did."

He smirks. "So you're saying it fits right in?"

I ignore the remark, get to what I'm really trying to tell him. "The people who live there now are poor. They're young, but they have that look that ages you, like life has been one trial after another. They had a little boy and she was pregnant with another baby on the way. The man had a hard edge, like he was filled with contempt. And she...I don't know, she looked apologetic on his behalf even though he hadn't said or done anything. It was no more than a minute or two that I was there, but that moment has stayed with me. I can't forget him. The way he looked, it was as if love and hate and misery had wrapped and tangled themselves around him like a sick vine."

He's still flat on his back, eyes turned skyward. "What are you saying?"

"I guess that if I had to do it all over again, I wouldn't change a thing." I watch one tear escape from the corner of his eye. "I never would have trapped you there, Simon."

Chapter Twenty-Six

SIMON

She's nervous, bouncing from the ball of one foot to the other, her mind already on the big event. "I'll see you at around eight? Is that good?"

"I'll be there. You sure this is ok with Lawrence? I can always crash in my truck for the night."

"No, it's fine. Just, uh, I hope you can sleep with all the dead animals in here."

I look around again, pretending to study the obscene number of antlers adorning the walls of this cabin, but I'm stalling really. Just letting out a breath and feeling grateful that she's able to be light and to joke again, because the night has been hard on both of us.

"Does this freak Ethan out?"

"Not at all. He loves animals, but it's different up here. The people have hunting in their blood, and he spends a lot of time with Lawrence." She shrugs. "It's natural to him."

"Can I bring anything tomorrow? I mean, I feel like I should bring him a present or something."

"No," she shakes her head, "you don't need a treat or anything to break the ice with him. And I'm kind of strict about presents being for birthdays and Christmas only."

"What does he like to talk about?"

"He's three, he'll talk about anything."

"I don't know how to do this."

"Neither did I." She smiles at me in a way that makes my chest hurt. "Don't worry so much."

My head is swimming with all she's told me tonight, so I figure I'll be staring at the ceiling, processing it for hours. I'm running on no sleep whatsoever, though, and it catches up to me. I fall into a deep, dreamless state, and wake the next day with a start.

It takes a moment to orient myself. The sun is bursting through the partially open slats of the window blinds, leaving a trippy striped pattern along every surface, myself included. Shading my eyes, I take in the sparsely decorated room that is not my own, and then register two hostile opposing sounds: the ear-splitting ringtone Samantha programmed into my phone to distinguish her calls and knocking on the door that has now escalated to pounding.

Ignoring the phone, I scramble to my feet and trip on my way to the front door.

The key turns in the lock just as a curse rips from my mouth. You'd think I'd just taken a bullet instead of stubbing my big toe. Her eyes are wide as she takes me in. And then the cloying lyrics of Ed Sheeran's *Perfect* start up again in earnest. We both look back towards the bedroom. I don't know what she's thinking, but I'm sick, listening helplessly as that line about dancing in the dark rings out through the cabin. I've never wanted to sink into the ground more than I do right now.

She taps her foot, looking away from me. It blessedly stops and then starts up again not five fucking seconds later.

"You gonna get that?"

"No."

"You overslept."

"Shit."

"Simon." She pauses, and my anger flares in response to the look on her face, the one that says: You're already making promises you can't keep.

"No." I advance on her slowly. "You don't get to do that." She crosses her arms over her chest. "You made me wait three years, and before I got here, I was up for two days straight driving back and forth looking for you. You don't get to judge me right now."

The phone finally stops making noise.

I pinch the bridge of my nose, chastising myself for the bad decisions I've made recently, for taking the easy road. For better or worse, I've had a lot of time to think over the past two days.

It's embarrassing to acknowledge that I like what I see when I look in the mirror these days. I'm borderline smug sometimes, thinking myself an honest man, one who's done good and is going places as a result. I've been shutting down my inner critic, the voice that warns me against morphing into this new, upgraded version of Simon Wade. I've been enjoying the perks of being a de facto member of the Westfields' inner circle. I tell myself it's nothing, but I'm enjoying the dinner parties that Brett and the others don't have a standing invitation to, enjoying the impromptu lessons on the finer things in life. Their subtle encouragement to eat, to dress, and to converse in the company of intelligent people in a certain way has granted me access to that oh so elusive thing: I am now in the room.

Being with Samantha benefitted me, so it was easy to let her weave her way into my life. I tell myself I'm still my own man, that I'm not impressed with the trappings of this life. I climb into my beat-up truck proudly, like it's some testament to my character or a badge of honor—act as if I have a choice in the matter. Tell myself that I'm nothing like those buttoned-up pussies who look on at me with envy, even as they're stepping out of their flash rides. I'm the chosen son now. I have the connections, have the best-looking girl on my arm, have everyone thinking I'm the smartest guy in the room.

Seeing that envelope shook me up. Prompted me to make those calls, to back out of that lucrative summer associate post and then beg for the less prestigious judicial internship that I'd turned down the week before. Seeing Charlotte's name in print reminded me of who I am, of the reason I wanted any of this in the first place. She reminded me of the shithole that is my hometown, reminded me of my family.

I'm standing less than a foot from her now. Her face is flushed but she hasn't backed down. Her lips are fixed in a firm line and her shoulders are squared. Knowing Charlotte, she's told Ethan about me using a string of superlatives that I don't feel deserving of right now. I've got a clear visual of them sitting at the table waiting, a special breakfast cooked and ready for me, the guest of honor.

There's no fight left in me. I step back, drag a hand through my hair. "I'm sorry I screwed up. Is he upset?"

"He went out on the boat with Lawrence, he's fine."

"When will they be back?"

She looks at her phone. "Around eleven, so you've got an hour."

"Wait," I say as she turns to go.

"It's fine. I told him I made a mistake, that you were coming for lunch not breakfast."

"Thanks, I appreciate that."

"So you'll be there?"

I hate that she's asking me, but I've got no choice but to suck it up because I deserve it. "I'll be there." I'd do anything to turn the clock back a few hours, to ease the tension between us. "Charlotte, we're good?"

She's got one hand on the doorknob when her eyes trail back down the hallway that leads to the bedroom. "Yeah, perfect."

* * *

CHARLOTTE

Stupid girl

That's the reflex, the first thought that pops into my head when I catch my reflection in the plate glass window of the deli case. I give myself a mental slap and straighten my shoulders. Screw that noise—I don't lob insults at other people for no good reason so I'm sure as hell not going to do it to myself. Standing in line at the grocery store, I'm surprised when I have to stifle a giggle moments later, suddenly struck by the absurdity of that cheesy ringtone and Simon's look of utter humiliation. And then the emotional rollercoaster shifts right back into gear, because the thought of someone being perfect in his eyes—someone who is not me—weighs like a stone in my heart.

"Charlotte?" Leena Karvonen is standing in line behind

me. I cringe just a little, knowing she's seeing me at my worst. "How are you?"

I used to refer to Leena as the president of the welcoming committee. She's the one who called me a slut when my pregnancy first started to show. I did hate the bitch back then, but time has lessened the sting of words that once had the power to cut me deep. You don't forget, but you can move past it. That's how it is with Leena. We're not friends, and she's never acknowledged or apologized for the dig, but she's retracted her claws and shown me a better side of herself over time. Basically, I'm over it.

I do my best to shake the morning off, but a half-hearted smile is the best I can offer. "I'm good, Leena. What's new?"

"Getting ready for the season, same as everyone else."

"Are you getting a lot of bookings?"

"Busier every year. We're fully booked for July and the first half of August."

"Good on you."

"Have to take it while you can get it, right?" She glances down at the baby formula and diapers in her cart. I imagine the winters are tough on people like her. No sane person is looking to vacation up here once the winds start howling and the snow starts up. Leena cocks her head to the side. "I saw Lawrence the other day. He's looking better. How's it going?"

"We're all doing better. Thanks for asking."

"My mother said Janelle left Lawrence the house?"

Here we go. No hesitation, she just dives right in and asks about my personal business. And why does she even ask? As usual, Leena's intel is on point. "She did, that's correct."

"So are you and the baby leaving?"

"No, it's not like that. We're here for the summer and then heading back downstate for school in September."

I'm just stating the facts, but I can see the mention of me leaving for school has wounded her. Leena was more than just a smart-mouth, she was a smart girl from what I remember. Probably had dreams of going to college herself. But she stayed back to help her family, and from what I'm told, Leena and her husband have done a great job taking over the management of her parents' bed and breakfast. I smile and toss her the chocolate bar I was contemplating buying for myself, needing something to soothe my achy heart. "You could probably teach a class on small business management down at the U."

She catches it on the fly and laughs. "I'd scare them all off." But you know she likes what she's doing from the smile on her face. "It's only for people who enjoy running on no sleep, fretting over making payroll every month, and plastering a smile on their face when dealing with uppity trolls." She opens the candy and breaks off a small piece. "Some Gwenyth Paltrow wannabee asked me if our linens were organic on the phone the other day. Can you believe that shit?"

I laugh at the name used to reference outsiders. "Easy now, you're talking to a troll."

"No girl, once you've survived a few winters up here you're a Yooper."

"I whine all winter, so I don't think I've earned the compliment, but thanks anyway."

A man clears his throat behind Leena. I look up to see Simon smiling. Oh, jeez. Leena turns around and then slowly turns back to me. Her eyes are wide when she mouths the word: *Hot.*

What the hell, who cares? "Leena, that's Simon. He's Ethan's dad. Simon, this is Leena."

The cashier, an older woman I don't recognize, is taking this all in. Both the cashier and Leena are now looking back and forth between me and Simon as if there's a tennis match in progress.

"Hello." Simon shifts a bouquet of daisies dyed a peculiar shade of blue to his left hand, offering his free hand to Leena in greeting. "It's nice to meet you."

She's practically breathless in response, whispering, "Hi."

I can see my sixteen-year-old self in Leena's reaction. Simon is tall, broad and lean. His features are defined but his smile is warm. His icy blue eyes don't look distant the way they used to, now they sparkle with amusement. The overall effect is disarming.

She regains consciousness and waves Simon in front of her. "You've just got that one thing, go ahead of me."

"Yeah?"

"I insist," she says, giving him a dreamy smile. When he turns to pay the cashier, Leena looks to me and mouths: *He is gorgeous!*

I shake my head. Not to dispute the fact, but to express that it doesn't really matter. He's not mine.

"Funny running into you here," I say, waiting on him.

He takes the bags from my hands. "I was looking for a flower shop but couldn't find one. I need to apologize to this girl, figured a nice bouquet would be the ticket."

"A nice bouquet, huh?"

"Yeah." He looks down at the sorry bunch. "Blue is her favorite color."

"How do you know?"

"She used to drink blue slushees...Made her tongue and lips turn blue. She used to love some nasty cereal with blue marsh-mallows...Ate it for breakfast, lunch and dinner."

"Boo berries. Her dad should have been locked up for nutritional neglect."

"And she thinks I don't know this, but she stole my favorite t-shirt, the faded blue one I got when I saw My Morning Jacket in Pittsburgh the year before I met her."

I shrug to indicate I have no memory of this alleged theft, enjoying this back and forth entirely too much. "Do you think she'll forgive you?"

"I hope so." I open the back hatch and turn to take my bags from him. He holds them firm in his grasp, eyes searching mine. "I'm nervous about today and I could use her in my corner."

I try and fail to shape my expression into a smile. The image of him with that girl haunts me, the pain bubbling up, as razor-sharp as it was that day in Chicago. I manage to nod. "See you at the house."

Seeing how he's in my rearview mirror, I will myself not to cry on the drive home. It takes some effort. He's quiet when he pulls up alongside me, getting out of his truck at the same time, taking the bags from my car. The air is charged and my body feels weak in some zero gravity kind of way, unsure and unsteady. I don't know if I can survive being this close to him. I breathe in through my nose, out through my mouth, ditching the ha-ha-ha exhale they taught in my birthing class at the hospital. I was annoyed back then, seeing as I was scheduled for a c-section, but the relaxation techniques are coming in handy right now.

He follows me into the kitchen and puts the bags down on the counter. We see the drawing at the same time, the work of a child. There's a big head with two spindly legs sticking out from it, dots for the eyes and nose, and a smile that stretches from one side of the face to the other. It looks like an effort's been made to draw a baseball cap over the head. Next to it is a smaller version of the same figure, complete with a smile.

Simon picks it up from the table, staring at it. "He did this?"

"Yeah, this morning."

"It's me? With him?"

"Yup," I answer, trying to go about the business of getting lunch together.

He pulls out a chair and sits down. I look over to see him transfixed, eyes glued to the paper when he asks, "What did you tell him about me?"

I rinse my hands and sit down in the chair opposite Simon. "He's not at that age where he's asking any hard questions yet, so I started off by explaining that kids have a mom *and* a dad. I told him that you, his dad, have been going to school somewhere far away. It was so far that I didn't know where to find you, so you didn't even know about him until yesterday. And once you found out, you got in your car and drove up here right away so you could meet him."

"Thank you for that. I don't want him ever thinking I wouldn't have come if I'd known."

"He had me take out his baby book this morning. He wants to show it to you."

I don't tell him that Ethan actually said: *I gonna show Dad baby Ethan.* I had to excuse myself for a few moments. Just hearing him refer to Simon as Dad had me welling up, and then being hit, once again, with the guilt over Simon never having the chance to witness all those milestones, I felt a crushing sense of sadness.

"I'd like that."

I feel like telling him to brace himself, because it's going to hurt.

* * *

SIMON

She's already called me five times this morning. She has to know I'm not looking to connect with her right now, must understand that I'm furious, so I can only assume she's hell bent on pleading her case. She's too arrogant to simply admit she was wrong and apologize. I'm sure she's been thinking this through, maybe even working out a strategy with her mother since I tore out of there. I'll have to face her someday, talk to her in the very least, but today's not that day. I switched the ringer off before I left the cabin, but the buzzing sound it's making as it vibrates against the table is about as disruptive as a jackhammer right now.

"You're more popular than the president." Charlotte tosses this out before going back to the counter to finish preparing lunch.

"Hey, about before—"

"Let's not do this right now." She turns to face me. "I can't."

Her expression is a plea, so I don't press, but I'm itching to clear the air because I want to know more about her life in return. She hasn't been holed up here for the past three years. She's a college student, and a beautiful one at that. I want details on everyone who's in her life, in Ethan's life. I need to know what I've missed.

Her expression turns on a dime, eyes bright and smiling now. "What have you got there?"

I didn't hear them come in, so my heart rate skyrockets when I turn to see my son, finally getting a chance to take him in. He's hiding behind Lawrence, peering around the man's legs to get a look at me. I'm smiling even though I'm definitely more scared than he is right now. I've rehearsed this moment a hundred times over the past forty-eight or so hours, but I'm stumped now, the opening lines I've practiced forgotten.

I stand and then crouch down so I'm at his level. "Hi, Ethan...I've been waiting so long to meet you." Lawrence moves into the kitchen area, which brings my son closer. I still have the drawing in my hand, so I hold it up to him. "Did you draw this?"

"Yes," he answers. He's out from behind Lawrence now but still holding onto the hem of his shorts with one hand.

"I really like it. You're a good artist."

"That's me," he points to the little figure tentatively, "and that's Dad," he adds when he points to the large blob that is me.

"I'm Simon. I'm your dad."

He gives me a lopsided smile, and that alone threatens to crack me wide open.

"Who's hungry?"

"I could eat," Lawrence says, sliding a chair out. He reaches over and shakes my hand. "Good to see you, Simon."

"Thanks for letting me use the cabin."

He nods and smiles as he directs Ethan to take the chair between us. That one small gesture leads me to believe I have an ally in this man. Charlotte hands Lawrence a glass of water and a pill as he asks, "What's for lunch?"

"A little chicken salad."

Ethan glances my way when he says in a quiet voice, "Sawad is my favowite."

"Does your mom still put those little red berries in her chicken salad?"

"Cwanbewwies?" he asks, nodding his head and smiling. "Yeah."

Charlotte shoots Ethan a playful look as she sets the

chicken salad and a basket full of rolls onto the table. "Except now I make sure to put the cranberries in there so that Ethan won't feed his lunch to Moe." Looking to me she explains, "The dog doesn't like them."

"You've got a dog?" When he nods, I say, "You're lucky. I always wanted a dog when I was your age, but my brother Timmy used to sneeze and cough like crazy whenever he was around animals, so we couldn't have one in the house."

He looks at me, all wide-eyed innocence. "I don't sneeze."

Charlotte chimes in. "That's because you don't have allergies. If you did, Moe would make you sneeze." He laughs when Charlotte lets out an exaggerated *ah-choo*. "Where is Moe, anyway?"

"Out back chasing after something or other," Lawrence says. "Maybe after we eat, you can show your dad how you feed Moe." Lawrence looks to me. "Ethan's very responsible with the dog." Taking small bites of his sandwich, a shy smile takes shape as Lawrence continues to praise him. "He's getting real good at brushing his coat out at night, and always makes sure he has enough water and food."

Ethan looks to Lawrence. "And I teached him fetch."

Lawrence smiles and musses Ethan's hair. "That's right, you taught him to play fetch."

I'm a little envious of their close relationship, but grateful at the same time. It's easy to see Lawrence is a positive influence on Ethan. And he strikes me as a Grizzly Adams kind of wilderness man with his beard and calloused hands. He's someone who can protect his homestead. With him around, you know Charlotte and Ethan are in good hands, they're safe.

I'm reaching over for another roll when Charlotte says, "Three sandwiches...Some things never change."

I smile, remembering the way she used to tease me about

how much food I could put away. I want her to remember the good parts, the times when we were together and it was good between us. It makes me feel like she's letting me in a little, makes me feel like I belong here.

Turning to Ethan, I say, "Yeah, that's something you should know about me. I eat, *a lot*."

He laughs as he copies me, taking a big bite out of his sandwich.

"Big man, big bites," Charlotte reaches for the sandwich and gently pulls it back from Ethan, "little man, little bites. Now chew, you don't want to choke."

I watch Ethan chew his food and then mouth the word *sorry* to Charlotte. She shakes her head, reassuring me it's no big deal.

"I done," Ethan announces as he squirms his way down off his chair. "Wanna see Moe?"

"Can't wait," I answer, feeling as if I've just been handed an invitation to ride shotgun on the space shuttle.

I watch as he uses all his might to slide open the back door and then follow him onto the deck. The home backs onto an inlet where you can see the great expanse of Lake Superior just beyond. The beauty of it stops me in my tracks for a moment, and before I know it, Ethan is running at his version of full speed towards the water.

"Wait up!" I'm sprinting to catch him when he suddenly stops to pick a tennis ball up off the grass. My heart is beating double time and I'm running through scenarios of what could have just happened when I hear soft chuckling behind me.

"He nearly gave me a heart attack."

"It's nerve racking being around a toddler, right?" She takes in my wide-eyed look of panic and busts out laughing.

"Sorry, but you should see your face right now. It's not as bad when you've had the benefit of being eased into it."

"Is he all right around the water?"

"He's not reckless by nature and he listens to what he's told, but no, one of us is always out here with him. He knows he's not allowed outside unless he tells me or Lawrence first."

"That's good."

"I want to get him into swim lessons but that's going to have to wait a while."

"When do kids usually start?"

"Are you kidding? They have swim lessons designed for infants now." She shakes her head smiling. "Ann Arbor is chock-full of overachieving parents who want their kids to be skilled swimmers, champion chess players and fluent in multiple languages by the time they hit kindergarten."

"Just like home, right?"

I notice she doesn't take her eyes off Ethan when she laughs and says, "Oh yeah, just like home."

"Is it because of his heart?"

"It's really about making sure his immune system is strong. Like, he could be enrolled in preschool this coming fall, but I'm waiting on that too." She looks to me, maybe to gauge my reaction before she looks back to the shoreline. "Last winter was rough. I can't put him in a classroom full of germy kids until I'm sure he can handle it."

"We didn't start school until kindergarten, right?"

"I started preschool at four, I think."

"Well, I'm on board with whatever you decide."

The words—my first actual co-parenting statement—hang in the air. Is she going to shoot me down, tell me that I have no say?

"Thanks," she says instead, and there's no sarcasm or animosity behind it.

Ethan is finally slowing down an hour or two later. In that time, we've tortured poor Moe by making him run after our ball about a hundred times. I got a tour of Moe's doghouse too, with Ethan urging me to crawl all the way inside of it with him. He's shown me how he tosses stones into the lake, and to my relief warns, "Don't go too cwose," when I edge towards the shore. He also introduced me to the different birds that come to peck off the feeder that hangs from one of the smaller trees. The best was when he pointed to the one he called a black cap chickadee. Ethan asked me, "You know why?" meaning why they're named that, and then started calling out, "Chick-a-dee-chick-a-dee," in his little voice. When the bird started making the same sound in reply a moment later, Ethan turned to me clapping his hands with a look of pure joy. I had to fight the urge to scoop him up and squeeze him tight, this sudden, unfamiliar feeling of unconditional love coursing through me.

"Is he tiring you out?"

We both turn to her at the same time and say, "I'm not tired," which makes her laugh.

"You wanna see the hamuck?"

"Sure." I have no idea what he's talking about, but I'll say yes to anything this boy asks me right now.

"The hammock, Ethan? Are you sure you don't want to go upstairs for a nap?"

"I not tired," he repeats, this time with a little spit and vinegar.

"It's all right, I'll hang out with him."

"He's going to pass out in five minutes."

I shrug. "I've got no pressing appointments or anything."

"Ok," she says, considering something for a moment. "If you're sure you don't mind, then I'm going to grab my laptop. I'm taking two courses this summer to make up for the ones I dropped this past semester." My face must show the concern I'm feeling. She lowers her voice, reassuring me, "Losing Janelle was overwhelming for a while there, and I had to slow my pace, needed to be home with him."

"That must have been really hard."

She's lost in thought for a moment before collecting herself and nodding. When Ethan comes to tug on my hand, she says, "You're popular around here."

"Thank God."

And I truly thank God for this day, when not ten minutes later, Ethan's warm little body is curled up into mine, breathing evenly.

* * *

CHARLOTTE

He's in love.

I've never taken drugs, never had much desire or opportunity to drink, but I imagine what Simon's experiencing right now is the best high ever. When a child you love graces you with a smile, a hug or their touch, it feels like you've won the lottery. It's something you come to crave.

Simon is in the hammock with one foot hanging over the side, slowly pushing off on it every thirty seconds or so to keep them in motion. He's lulling Ethan to sleep while looking down at his face, watching as his eyes get heavy and his breath deepens. Simon is mesmerized.

I've got my laptop open, trying in vain to concentrate on the slides I'm supposed to compare for my Art History class, but there's a far more interesting subject holding my attention right now. I don't want to be caught staring in amazement at the sight before me, but it's hard to look away. Not ten minutes later, I can hear a man's deep breathing, and I know Simon has succumbed to the fresh air and the gentle swaying of the hammock. I tiptoe closer and snap a few pictures on my phone. I took a couple of the two of them playing with Moe, and one where Simon had Ethan perched on his shoulders, the two of them laughing as they chased after a cotton-tail rabbit. I want these memories for Ethan—that's what I tell myself.

"How are you doing?"

I take the iced tea Lawrence offers as I make my way back onto the deck. "I'm a mess."

"From where I'm sitting, it looks like things are going pretty well."

"It's so weird, though, right?"

"That'll pass."

"I guess."

"What's weighing on your mind, kid?"

"I just want to know what he's thinking. I want to lay everything out on the table. I want to know what his intentions are, and not in general terms."

"Think you might have to ease into all that, Charlotte, and slow down. Remember, this is a shock to his system. The man just found out he has a three-year-old son."

"Thanks." The reminder is something I don't want or need. I feel bad enough as it is.

Lawrence chuckles. "Didn't mean that the way you're taking it."

"I know."

"What has he told you about his life?"

"I've been babbling nonstop, haven't given him much of an opening."

"There's time for that."

"Is there?" I look to Lawrence. "I think that's what's bothering me. Is he here for another day, a week? Will we see him again before the summer's over, or is he going back to his life? Is he going to be a Christmas and birthday kind of father?"

"He doesn't strike me as that type, but who really knows? What's the worst-case scenario?"

"Hmm, I don't know...Maybe that he leaves here tomorrow, goes back into the waiting arms of his beautiful girlfriend, gets married and sues me for full custody?"

"Is your mind really going there?"

"Not really." I take a sip of my drink, considering the situation. "If I'm being honest, it's just the waiting arms of the beautiful girlfriend thing."

"Is this girlfriend real or imaginary?"

"Pretty sure she's a reality."

"Don't borrow trouble from tomorrow."

I nudge his foot with mine. "You're sounding an awful lot like Janelle right now, and I mean that as a compliment."

"No, Janelle would tell you not to put the cart before the horse."

"Or not to count my chickens before they hatch."

Lawrence studies me. "She would tell you that you can handle anything that comes your way. You've proven it a million times over. Best case scenario, worst case, doesn't matter...You and Ethan are going to be fine."

I mull that over, and knowing it's true gives me some much-needed peace. I smile when Barbara Ryan's battle cry comes to mind: *You'll do more than survive, you'll thrive!*

Yes, I need to be patient, but more importantly, I need to be realistic. Looking back over to where my son and his father rest together, I tell myself that I can handle anything that comes my way—I have to for Ethan's sake. I can even survive the loss of Simon again.

"Can you take a picture for me?" Simon asks, handing me his phone. "Ethan, let's get Moe in the picture with us."

Ethan runs over and takes Moe by the collar. "Come on, boy."

"That poor dog," I mutter under my breath. "Gentle with him, Ethan."

I look up to see Simon smiling at me. He's been doing that all day, looking at me and smiling whenever I catch him. *Don't, Charlotte*, I remind myself. Don't go hanging your hopes on a fantasy. Remember that other girl. Yeah, she makes him smile too.

Collecting myself, I snap a few pictures. They look like good ones, but I'm careful not to scroll back and check. I don't know if I'd be able to resist temptation, to get a look at the last photo he took. Would it be of her, of the two of them together?

"See if they're good." My tone sounds stiff when I hand the phone back to Simon.

"They came out great," he says. He spends his time, studying each one. He looks to me and hands the phone back over. "This one's the best."

I swallow. It is a great picture, a beautiful one. The lake, the red streaked sky and the setting sun as a backdrop give it a magical quality, but it's Ethan's expression that does me in. He's looking up at Simon, not at the camera, and smiling in an awestruck kind of way. Returning the phone, I avoid his eyes. "Yeah, that's a great shot. Can you send it to me?"

"Lemme see, lemme see," Ethan chimes in as he attempts to scale Simon's legs.

Simon sinks down onto the grass laughing and Ethan scrambles into his lap. "Wait a sec," he tells Ethan as he fiddles with his phone. "Let me send this one to Mommy and then I'll show you the rest."

Everything is magnified today. Simple words, but him referring to me as Mommy instead of, I don't know, your mother, has me welling up. When I repeat the sentence with the replacement—*Let me send this one to your mother*—I can't deny that it pleases me. Mommy sounds different, more intimate, better.

Again, I look back and catch him studying me. He clears his throat then, shifting his focus back to Ethan. "I'll have to send this picture to my brother Michael. He'll be so excited to see you, and he loves dogs too."

"He don't sneeze?"

Simon laughs. "No, that was my other brother, Timmy, who sneezed and coughed." He kisses Ethan's head like it's second nature—the way it is to me—before shifting him off his lap to stand. "Be back in one second. I've got a picture of my brothers in my truck that I want you to see."

"We'll meet you inside, it's getting buggy out here."

"I wanna see the twuck."

Simon looks to me for consent first. It surprises and pleases me every time he does it. And I'm sure I'm building this up in my head, but when I nod, he looks at me and smiles in a way that feels special. I physically feel the warmth in my chest.

Crouching down, he offers himself up for a piggy back ride. "Right this way," he says, and Ethan climbs aboard happily.

Simon walks back inside a few minutes later with a frame in his hand and Ethan still on his back. I'm standing in the kitchen, uncertain of my place, but he beckons me over to the couch once they settle in. I take the seat next to my son, needing to put some space between me and Simon.

"I'm the youngest, this one here," he says, pointing to a boy who looks to be about five years old. I gasp and cover my mouth, seeing the resemblance I always knew was there, but now shocked by the striking similarity. It's as if I'm looking at a sun-faded picture of Ethan. "I know, right?" Simon says, taking in my reaction. Looking back to Ethan he continues, "The one in the middle is my brother Michael. He's the one that loves dogs and cats and chickens and—"

"And por-ca-pines?" Ethan butts in, looking up to Simon smiling.

"He probably would let a porcupine stay at his place if one came knocking on his door." And Ethan clearly likes that answer. Pointing to the picture again, Simon says, "And this is my oldest brother, Timmy. See, you look like all of us. That's what happens in families."

Ethan looks between the picture and Simon. "You're wittle."

"I was little when that picture was taken. That was a long time ago. Have you got any pictures of when you were little?"

Ethan's eyes light up. "My book!" He scrambles off the couch, turning to Simon before he grabs the handrail and heads upstairs. "I get my book."

I can't help but call out, "Be careful on the stairs."

"That's like a reflex for you."

"Can't help it. I probably say *that's dangerous* or *be careful* twenty times a day." My eyes drift back down to where the picture sits. "I always thought he looked like you, but seeing that picture is…"

He picks up where I trail off. "Crazy, yeah. Now I know what people mean when they use that phrase, the spitting image."

"Yeah." A knot forms in my stomach. "Hey, maybe I'll let you do this with him alone. He loves narrating a little show and tell with his baby book, and I think, ah, I think…" He reaches over and squeezes my hand. His touch gives me strength, so I take a deep breath and level with him. "I imagine you're going to hate me in a couple of minutes. I just hope you know I never wanted you to miss out on any of this, Simon."

He nods, releasing my hand.

"I'm going to tidy up the kitchen." I direct the comment to Ethan, but he pays me no mind as he races back over to the couch, squeezing in close to Simon as he opens the book across their laps.

I brace my hands against the countertop when I hear Ethan's opening line.

"See this? I in Mommy's tummy."

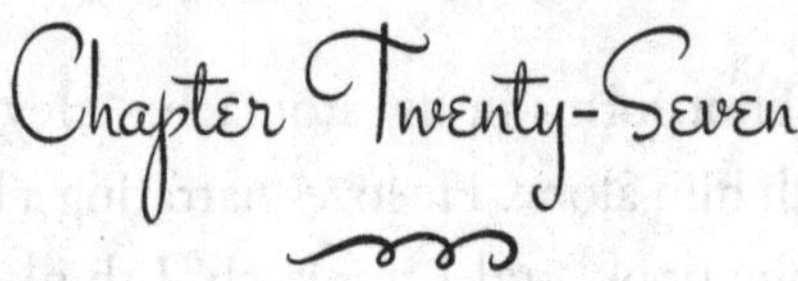

Chapter Twenty-Seven

SIMON

My dinner is tough to digest, but I put on an act for Ethan's sake.

I'm angry, but my anger isn't aimed at Charlotte—not all of it, anyway. She senses my mood, directing most of her questions and comments to Ethan and Lawrence. Sitting less than three feet away, she's avoiding me.

When Ethan lets out a giant yawn, Lawrence says, "Bath or outdoor shower, buddy?"

Ethan looks to him with drowsy eyes. "Shower."

"Come on then," he says, scooping him up.

Charlotte calls after them, "There are dry towels in the shower house." She gets up to clear the table, because sitting here with me in this choked silence-thing we've got going on is physically unbearable "Was it awful? You didn't eat much."

"No, it was good. I like salmon, I just wasn't that hungry."

She nods, her look telling me she knows my stomach is in knots and knows the reason why. I get up, scrape my plate into the trash and join her at the sink. There's a war raging inside of me. One part wants to shake her, ask her how she could do it, how she could wait so damn long to tell me. I feel cheated. Another part wants to run, the feeling of shame nearly overwhelming. I've now seen evidence of how hard the past few years have been, and I've had no hand in helping to ease the burden. And I fear that everything she said last night was true, that I wouldn't have been the least bit supportive had she told me back then. Still another part wants to drag her in close to me. I want to soothe her, tell her that I'm here now. I want to know where we go from here.

I feel lost.

Charlotte goes to speak but she's interrupted when Lawrence comes back inside with Ethan wrapped in a towel. She pastes on a smile. "That was a quickie."

Lawrence grabs a pair of pajamas from a basket of folded laundry. "He looked like he was going to fall asleep standing up." Looking to Ethan, he asks, "Mr. Gumpy or G'night Moon?"

Rubbing his eyes, Ethan mumbles, "Gumpy." As Lawrence makes his way towards the stairs, Ethan whines, "I want Dad."

Something warm blooms in my chest, something hopeful. Lawrence sets him down and prompts him to raise his arms over his head and then step one foot at a time into his pajamas. I take note of the wolverine on the shirt and the little shorts covered in the U-Michigan logo. It's a reminder of the fact that they have a life somewhere, a life that hasn't included me. But now things are different and I want in.

I look between Charlotte and Lawrence. "Is that all right?"

Lawrence shrugs. "More than all right...It's how it should be."

I chance a look back to Charlotte as I'm making my way

upstairs with Ethan, but she's facing away, eyes fixed on the sudsy water.

Ethan's asleep within five minutes but I keep reading to him, my voice getting lower the further into the book I get. I read it a second time to myself, struck by how short, simple and gentle kids' stories are. This book, about a guy named Mr. Gumpy taking a trip down the river and picking up kids and animals as he goes along, has basically nothing to it, so I can't explain why I flip through it again and then again. I could get all philosophical and ponder its themes, like the power of human connection and all that, but I think the book just makes me calm and happy—simple as that. And I'm kind of loving that Charlotte chooses books like this for him.

It's tricky getting out of the bed, shifting my weight so that I don't disrupt him, but he doesn't so much as stir. He's down for the count. I draw the blanket up over his little body, realizing with a start that I'm actually tucking my son into bed. And then I lean down and kiss his forehead, the goodnight kiss another first.

Lawrence is alone in the living room when I come downstairs.

"I'm surprised it took so long."

"It didn't, he was out before I got halfway through the book."

"Big day for him. All the excitement wore him out."

"I know how he feels."

Lawrence sees me looking around. "She went out for a run."

To escape me? I'm guessing that's the reason why. "She was never a runner when I knew her…She used to hate it."

"You still know her," he reminds me.

I nod, regretting the way I phrased it.

"She's done a great job with Ethan. He couldn't have been blessed with a better mother."

Again I nod, tongue-tied and sad at once. "Is it all right if I use the cabin again tonight?"

"Sure."

"Thanks. I'm going to head back now. Tell Charlotte I'll see her tomorrow?"

"She should be back in a few minutes." When I don't say anything, his brow creases. "I'll tell her."

I pictured this going differently. On the drive up here, I imagined this dramatic reunion, the closing credits rolling as Charlotte falls into my arms and we embrace. This feels more like a minefield—I don't know where or how to step. The air between us warms but then chills just as quickly. She ran tonight and then so did I.

Wes Keller?

After getting Ethan tucked in, I tip-toed around his room, smiling to myself as I took in the animal figures, the dinosaur collection, the blocks and the kid-sized bow and arrow. Charlotte also has an alphabet chart where each letter is paired with a picture, and a whiteboard where she's been teaching him to write his name. I chuckle when I see an abacus just slightly smaller than Ethan tucked into a corner. Knowing Charlotte, she'll have him working on linear equations by the time he's in kindergarten.

I don't see the drawings until I'm making my way out. You can tell who the subject is, because Charlotte has written the name beneath each figure, with Ethan's immature scrawl underneath. One is of Lawrence and Moe, another is of a fish. There are a few of Charlotte, and it makes me smile to see the yellow sun he draws in each picture of the two of them together. There's a family portrait too. You can tell this one's older by the quality of the drawing, and by the fact that only Charlotte has written names beneath the figures: Janelle, Lawrence, Mommy, Ethan and Moe. I wish I could have met Janelle, thanked her for all the good she's done.

The last one, the one that's taped higher than the others, looks just like the one Ethan drew of me. Admittedly, all of his figures look nearly identical, but the details on this one, down to the baseball cap, are the same. It's recent, because Ethan has done a decent job of copying the W, E and the S. I'm jealous and mad as fuck now. Easing the tape off each corner, I unleash my inner broody bastard and take the drawing with the intent of tearing it to shreds once I'm clear of the house.

Maybe I've given myself too much credit—I'm more like Samantha than I thought.

It's a few hours later when I decide to listen to the voicemails. There are six in total. She must have called right after I left her house the other day, pleads with me to come back and talk, not to do anything rash. The second came in later that night, she's weeping. The next are a series she left this morning, probably when the damn phone kept going off in Charlotte's presence. In one she forgives me. That's rich. In one of the last ones, Samantha finally breaks down and admits she knows what she did was wrong—how decent of her—and is sure "we can get past this." I don't even want to know what that means.

When the phone rings sometime around eleven, I pick up.

"Simon?" She's surprised I answered.

"I was about to call you."

She lets out a relieved breath. "I'm here for you. Always. You know that, right?"

"Samantha." I issue her name in warning, but she doesn't heed it, she presses on.

"Where are you?"

I don't mean to bark but I do. "Where do you think I am?"

She goes silent. I'm furious with Samantha, but right now my anger is over something else, or really *someone* else entirely, and I'm taking it out on her because she's the easiest target.

"I've been with him all day. I put him to bed."

"Are you at her house?"

That's all she really cares about. What she really wants to ask is if I'm in her bed. I'm tempted to lie but don't have the energy. "I'm staying in a cabin close by."

"Oh." The relief in her voice irks me. "So," she goes on uncomfortably, "tell me about him."

"He's...amazing." And it's as if I'm talking to myself now, not her, when I go on to describe him and list every great thing that happened today.

She interrupts when I'm in the middle of talking about the chickadee birds. "He sounds adorable."

"He is. He smiles a lot, seems like a really happy kid."

"Oh."

"And he looks just like me, by the way."

She sighs. "Simon, I still think—"

"If you're about to suggest that I schedule a paternity test, I'm gonna have to stop you right now."

"Just..." I can tell she's crying. "Just be careful."

I know I've done wrong by Samantha. I know I've led her on this past year, led her to believe we might have a future together. I'm disgusted with myself when I take a moment to admit that I've contemplated a future with her.

"I'm going to be back tomorrow or the day after. We need to talk."

"All right. I'll be here...I'll be here waiting for you."

I should just rip the bandage off now but I don't. She's going to be strategizing and getting her hopes up, I know that. *Don't waste your time*, that's what I should tell her, because I made my decision the moment that scrap of paper fell from her bag. There isn't a snowball's chance in hell we're going to be together again. Even if Wes Keller *is* firmly in the picture—and God, it kills me to even think it—the chapter of my life with Samantha in it is over.

Chapter Twenty-Eight

SIMON

"Couldn't sleep?" Her voice startles me. I turn to see her sitting in one of the deck chairs sipping coffee. She's bundled up in a plaid blanket with just her bare toes peeking out, hair in a messy topknot. "It's super early."

"I actually got a pretty decent sleep. I'm used to running on five or six hours."

The closer I get, the stronger the aroma of freshly-baked something gets. I barely ate dinner last night, so I'm ravenous. So hungry that I forget all the uncomfortable bullshit that's between us.

"Smells good."

"Blueberry muffins." She smiles. Is she thinking about all those mornings she snuck across the street to bring me choco-late chip or blueberry muffins? That's where my mind has drifted. She glances at the time on her phone screen. "They've got about five more minutes to go."

The house is situated facing slightly to the east, and the sun is just now making its presence known. "Do you watch the sunrise every morning?"

"No." She laughs and shakes her head. "I mean, I do like my quiet coffee time before Ethan gets up, but I'm not usually up this early."

"Couldn't sleep?" I repeat her words, looking for another smile, but I don't get one.

She blows on her coffee. "Lot's on my mind." Before I can respond, she says, "Sorry I ran out on you last night. I felt crappy when I got home and you were gone."

"It was probably for the best. I needed some time to think."

She nods. "Me too. Running helps me clear my head." Charlotte fiddles with a loose string on the corner of the blanket. "So, was I right? Were you hating on me hard after looking through Ethan's baby book?"

I hang my head, not wanting to look her in the eye right now. "I don't hate you."

"But?"

I take in a deep breath and then look to her. "Coffee first?"

She practically leaps out of the chair. "Be right back."

The few minutes she's gone gives me some time to think this through. I want to know about Wes—I'm chomping at the bit to ask her—but Ethan is the priority here. I need to keep my head on straight.

She hands me a warm muffin and a steaming cup of coffee made just the way I like it. I savor the mouthful as much as I savor the fact that she remembers this simple piece of information about me: cream, light, no sugar.

"The blueberries are fresh."

"I used to love those muffins from the diner, but this tastes so much better. Makes those ones seem like cardboard crap."

"Wild blueberries are abundant up here."

I smile listening to her, because someone else would have said that blueberries are *everywhere* or they're *easy to get*. Charlotte always had a good vocabulary. Never put on airs or anything, just always chose the word that fit best like it was second nature to her.

"We eat so many that sometimes I think we're going to turn into blueberries. Blueberry vanilla ice cream, blueberry pancakes, blueberry jam." She laughs when she sees I've already finished the muffin. "I'm getting you another."

"Thanks," I say when she comes back out a minute later. Her hand brushes mine in the transaction, her touch startling and comforting at once. I clear my throat to stave off the emotion before mumbling, "I'm starving."

"Yeah, I noticed you barely ate last night."

"It was hard."

She sinks back into her chair, wraps herself back up in the blanket. "I've pictured you looking through that album so many times. Thought about how rotten it would make you feel. Just to know you missed out on holding him, seeing him smile for the first time, getting to see him take his first steps." Charlotte looks out over the water. "I totally get it...You're angry."

"I just feel sad more than anything."

"I'm sorry. And I know those words are starting to sound empty by now, but I mean it. I wish you got to hold him when he was firstborn, got to be a part of everything."

It would be better to keep my trap shut, to keep this one thing that's been eating away at me to myself. The confession makes me sound heartless, like a total and absolute shit, and that's the polar opposite of what I want Charlotte to see when she looks at me now. I should be painting a different image for her, one that says: World's Greatest Dad. And it should be easy to take that route because Lord knows I've been lying to myself and to everyone else around me lately—so often that it's become second nature. But I don't want to lie to her.

"The other night, you said it was better for everyone that you didn't tell me, and it shames me to say it, but you were probably right." I put the muffin down, my appetite suddenly gone. "I'm ashamed to admit that I probably would have reacted like an asshole if you told me you were pregnant back then."

She reaches over, puts her hand on my shoulder. "Please don't beat yourself up over that. Please don't do that."

"I would have wanted you to get an abortion...I pretty much did suggest it back then. And seeing him now? I can hardly look at myself in the mirror. What I did...The way I treated you back then...I was so wrong."

"Do you think I found out I was pregnant and was happy about it? I assure you, I wasn't." After a pause she says, "Simon," and taps my shoulder until I look at her. "I prayed for a miscarriage more times than I can remember." She wipes at a tear. "I've never admitted that to anyone."

I reach over and catch another tear as it makes its way down her cheek. "You're a great mother, Charlotte."

"Thanks, but that doesn't change the fact that I didn't really want him until I was being wheeled into the operating room and faced with the prospect of losing him. But listen to me, I'm past that now, and I don't want you to waste time feeling bad over it. Life's too short."

"It's hard to get past it. Those pictures of him in the hospital..."

"All the tubes, the incubator...I know."

"You look so young in those pictures, but brave. I can't even imagine how scared you must have been."

"Petrified." She smiles. "Ignorance would have been bliss, I'm sure, but I was practically prepared to take the MCATs by the time I delivered Ethan. I knew the stats, the odds stacked against him." She waves her hand in front of her face. "But he was fine...He *is* fine."

"Yesterday was...everything. I still can't believe he wanted to be with me, to get to know me. It feels like a gift." I shake my head, feeling ridiculous. "I sound like an idiot."

"No, I get it. It's overwhelming."

"In a good way."

"Yeah," she nods, "in a good way."

We sip our coffee in silence for a few minutes before she looks to me and asks, "Where do we go from here, Simon?"

"I want..."

What do I want? I want to be Ethan's father, even though I'm not one hundred percent sure what that entails. I want to be near him, I want to be near Charlotte. I can't deny the pull I feel towards her, stronger now than it ever was. I want a chance at what we had, the chance to be her man again. I definitely don't want to think about Wes, about what he means to them.

"Who was calling you all day yesterday?"

She's beaten me to it.

I shake my head. "It's not what you think."

She looks away from me. "How do you know what I think?"

"I just don't want you thinking I'm attached. I'm not...attached."

"Tell me about her."

My survival instincts kick into drive. "No."

She blows on her coffee again, eyeing me over the rim of her cup. "I saw the two of you together."

"What? When?"

"End of January, I guess? I was in Chicago to meet with Janelle's lawyer."

My breath hitches. "Why?"

"You're in law school, so I'm guessing you know why I was meeting with my aunt's attorney. Are you asking why I didn't approach the happy couple, bounce over and introduce myself to your girl? While pushing a stroller?" Her laughter is laced with pain. "Yeah, that would have been awesome."

"You saw me? And you were with Ethan?"

She pulls the blanket tighter around her shoulders and nods. "I called you soon after. Not because of her, or because I felt guilty or anything...Just because it was time."

My nails dig into my palms in an effort to quell the murderous anger I feel towards Samantha and her mother. "And then you never heard back from me."

"The letter was my last-ditch attempt. When I mailed it, I told myself that I didn't expect a reply, but that wasn't true. After a few weeks passed and I didn't hear back from you, I didn't know what to think. I knew we were worlds apart, but I never for a minute thought you would just ignore me, ignore your son." She looks to me. "I'd study the picture of that slick, polished guy on your profile page, and tell myself I didn't know you anymore." When I let out a frustrated breath, she adds, "You never knew...That makes more sense"

"Her name is Samantha Westfield." Just the mention of her name wounds Charlotte, I see that. "Her father is my mentor. He was responsible for securing the scholarship for my undergrad. Sam and I, we were nothing but friends for a long time. It just kind of happened, wasn't something I was looking for."

"Friends to lovers...Sounds perfect."

"Nothing like that. And the perfect thing—"

She stands, gathers her cup and mine. "None of my business."

I grab her wrist. "I'm talking so you're going to listen." She looks down to where I'm holding her. "Me and Samantha, we were never perfect. Not even close. I lost myself for a little while there. Forgot what I wanted, who I am."

"But you picked *that* song for her?"

"She picked the song. I just didn't have, I don't know, a reason to set her straight. I've been taking a back seat and letting her drive for a while now."

"That doesn't sound even remotely like you."

"Sit down," I urge her, more gently this time. She leans against the deck railing instead, facing me. "I know what I've been through over the past few years pales in comparison to what you've faced, but things weren't easy. College wasn't what I expected. That first year I struggled the entire way through. I wasn't prepared like those other kids. Academically I felt like a total dumbass, and I was always sweating it. I knew if I didn't maintain a certain GPA then the scholarship would be gone and I'd be out on my ass. On top of that I was working nights at a warehouse because I didn't have enough money for books or living expenses. But it was the social stuff that nearly did me in. I was so out of my league. My freshman roommate's father is a chemical engineer who developed the protective coating they put on nuclear weapons, and the kid across the hall? His mother wrote that book about cleaning up your closets that's been on the best-seller list for the last decade. Those kids were rich, but more important, they knew how to walk through that world."

I look away as the feelings come flooding back with the memory of that night. "I was at a party once, a book signing or something that Professor Westfield encouraged me to attend.

He introduced me to a friend of his who happened to be on the admissions committee for Northwestern Law." I shake my head, cringing as if I'm back in that room watching the moment unfold. "So I'm trying to keep up with the conversation, contribute something that doesn't make me sound like the imposter that I am, when a server comes around with a tray of shrimp cocktail. I'd never had it before. I can still remember the look on that guy's face when I proceeded to plop the entire shrimp into my mouth, tail and all. I remember trying to smile my way through the next few minutes, even though it felt like that little piece of shell was splintering and puncturing my esophagus on the way down." That earns me a sympathetic smile, but I can't shake it off. "I was in the bathroom down on my hands and knees, wiping my vomit off the toilet seat and the floor. God...I just didn't want it to smell, you know? I didn't want anyone to know what happened."

I catch her wiping at her eyes. "Oh, Simon."

"I was afraid of being found out, of people figuring out that I didn't belong. There were two people who kept me from giving up that first year, Professor Westfield and my brother Mike."

"Mike?" I'm grateful for the topic change, and even manage a smile when she adds, "Is he still with that same boyfriend? Brandon, right?"

"Yeah, they're together. They actually got married last year."

"Wow." Charlotte reclaims the chair next to mine. "So Ethan has uncles."

"They're going to love him."

I rub at my temples then, remembering that I still need to break this news to my mother—she's going to freak—and to

Mike. But the pressing items on my to-do list have to wait. I need to make her understand.

"I used to escape to their apartment, just to get away from school."

She rests a hand over mine for a moment before gently pulling away again. "I'm glad you had them to lean on."

"I had them but then they left, moved out to Portland in the middle of my sophomore year. Brandon's father owns a repair shop and he had the opportunity to take it over. They're happy, seems like they have a nice life out there."

"Was it hard for you when they left?"

"I was used to just plugging along, so I didn't give it much thought at the time, but yeah, it was. Brandon was pretty much repairing my truck on a monthly basis, and I used that, and anything else I could think of, as an excuse to crash at their place whenever I could. They always made me feel welcome. I never had to pretend when I was there."

"It's hard for me to imagine you that way, lacking confidence."

"Why?"

She's back to picking at a string on the blanket. "You were always larger than life to me. You were strong and you knew exactly what you wanted."

"I don't know about that."

"So, the Westfield family filled the void when Mike and Brandon left?"

"In a way. They tutored me in that way of life, I guess. Professor Westfield was always showing me how to navigate, how to network and open doors for my future. He took me under his wing from day one. And being a guest in their home just made it so things rubbed off on me. Suddenly I knew how to dress for every occasion, I was a pretty decent golfer, and even knew which wineglass to use for a full-bodied red as opposed to a white." I look over to see her barely concealed look of horror. "I'm fully aware that I sound like an absolute dick right now."

"Um, yeah."

"But this is what it takes to be one of them, to get your foot in the door at one of those white-shoe law firms and climb the ladder."

"Corporate law?"

"I know it's not what I envisioned for myself, but now I don't know. I see Westfield and guys like him...They can teach and focus on the philanthropic side of criminal defense from the comfort of their homes on Lakeshore Drive, only because they made a killing early on in their careers."

"Made a killing, huh?"

"Poor choice of words."

"You want that life?" It doesn't sound accusatory when she asks, but it feels that way.

"I don't want to be poor, and I don't feel like I should have to apologize for that."

"No one's asking you to."

I rake my fingers through my hair. "I don't know what I want."

After a minute she asks, "How does Samantha factor into all this?"

My jaw clenches at the sound of her name, but if I want to know Charlotte's truth, I need to be willing to share my own.

"She was pretty obvious about her feelings from the start, but I, uh, wasn't ready for anything like that." I face Charlotte. "I was straight with Samantha, told her I was still hung up on a girl from home." She looks away, shaking her head. "Believe whatever you want, but I was a mess after I left you." It hurts to read the mistrust in her expression. "Nothing happened with her for, I don't know, two and a half years. We were just friends."

Now I'm shaking my head in frustration, because that isn't really the way it was, and I want to get it right this time. "No, we were never truly friends, it was more like I was playing a part. I didn't use her or anything, but she was Westfield's daughter. I had no choice but to be around her. My future depended on it." I look to Charlotte. "Do you know how hard it is to say all of this to you?"

It's a full ten seconds before she turns back to me. Her voice is gentle when she says, "Keep going. I need to know."

I look down to my sneakers, torn between the right thing to do and what I want to do. I don't want to stay and suffer through this conversation. I want to run, to jump into my truck, to speed away from all this. I can't take her judgement, can't bear to look weak in her eyes.

"I got really sick during my final year of undergrad. It was right after finals, a week before Christmas. I think my body just kind of gave out. A simple virus that would have put another person down for a day or two, it knocked me out of commission for close to a month. Looking back, I know the crazy workload I took on, and just all the stress and pressure of the last couple of years wore me down. I wound up in the hospital for nearly a week."

"And I bet you never called your mother or Mike to help you."

"I couldn't. That would have been ridiculous to, what, call my mom and have her blow a thousand bucks on a plane ticket to come feed me chicken soup?"

She's wide-eyed. "You were in the hospital." Then Charlotte shakes her head. "But I'm not surprised. You were always stubborn, you never wanted anyone's help."

"Yeah, pride comes before the fall."

"So, your very own personal Florence Nightingale swooped in when you were down and out?"

"It went something like that."

"I guess I should be grateful you had someone."

"It was the first time in my life when I felt alone, truly alone. And the entire family came through for me. Her mother had the spare room ready for me when I was discharged from the hospital, her father squared things away with my other professors when I missed the first few days of the spring semester, and Samantha..."

"Spoon-fed you, gave you a sponge bath?" She's trying for humor, but I can see that she's hurt, jealous, or some combination of the two.

"She took care of me."

"Did you fall in love with her?"

"No." My response is immediate because it's true and I need her to know that. "I appreciated her, saw her in a different light."

"What do you mean?"

"It's complicated." I take a few seconds, wrestling with how to put my thoughts and feelings into words. "I mean, I don't want to give you the impression that she's a bad person... She's not." Not entirely sure why I'm defending her right now. Lately she's done plenty to earn herself 'bad person' status. "But when we first met, and actually for a long time after, I saw Samantha as someone who's used to getting her way, maybe a little on the judgmental side. The way she reacted when I got sick was different, though. She was selfless and I gave into it. It was easy, and it was nice to be cared for."

"To be loved."

I hang my head. "Yes."

"So how long have you been together?"

"I've broken it off."

She sucks in a breath but then her voice comes out measured and even. "You were engaged?"

"No! Holy shit, no! We've been together since, I don't know, last January? A little over a year. And I broke it off the other day when I found out what she did. She burned the letter."

"My letter?"

"Yeah. I still can't fucking believe it. She destroyed the letter and hid the picture of Ethan. I randomly came across that torn envelope with your return address on it. I don't think she ever planned on telling me."

"God," she shakes her head, tears threatening, "I don't know what to say."

"Nothing to say, it just sucks."

"Yeah, it does."

* * *

CHARLOTTE

I'm lost in a fantasy, a new one where I dial that same phone number and bitch out the bitchy bitch-girl who practically hung up on me the last two times I called. I'm so worked up that Simon's words barely register when he says, "I have to leave tomorrow."

"Tomorrow?"

"Yeah. I'm committed to a summer internship with a judge. It starts this coming Monday."

Before I can think it through, I lodge a complaint. "That's nearly a week away." It comes out sounding accusatory and shrewish, same way that I feel. All this talk of his babe and her treachery has left me stomping down the warpath.

"I know, but I have to clear out of student housing this week and move into the studio I'm subletting for the summer." He pauses then adds, "And I need to get back to take care of a few other things."

I take a calming breath and rein it in. He's not my boyfriend, I've made no demands where Ethan is concerned, and therefore, I have no claim on his time. I do my best to sound neutral and understanding when I ask, "Were you living with her?" When in reality, the very thought of him sharing his space, his bed, his *life* with her is crushing my soul to bits right now.

"No."

He doesn't offer up more, but I'm pretty sure she's front and center when it comes to the "things" he needs to take care of.

That scene in the movies, the one where broken-up lovers say their goodbyes and exchange the belongings accumulated over the course of a relationship—will it be like that? Will she hand over his razor and a few of his books, but hang on to a t-shirt that smells of him? Will it be a tearful event? I'm now picturing Simon looking at that blond beauty with longing and regret as he hands over a box filled with cashmere sweaters and really pricey hair-care products. Gah!

"I'd come back this coming weekend, but my new boss left me a load of files to read over before I start on Monday. I think he's punishing me."

His voice shakes me out of that warped and very painful storyline. "Why would he do that?"

"I applied for this internship and I got it, but turned it down when I got a better offer. It's a long story, but I kind of had to crawl back and beg him to take me on."

"Oh."

"Can I plan to come back a week from this Friday? You think it'll be all right with Lawrence if I use the cabin again?" When I don't answer right away, he apologizes, "Sorry, I should be asking you if that interferes with your plans first, shouldn't I?"

"I never have any plans." *Way to go, loser.* "I mean, I'm spending the entire summer here."

"If I said I wanted to come and spend weekends here this summer, would that be all right with you?" I think my heart stops beating momentarily when he says, "I want to get to know him, Charlotte."

"Yeah," I whisper. "Yes," I repeat, collecting myself. "And Lawrence doesn't really use the cabin anymore, so I'm sure it's not going to be an issue if you want to stay there."

He smiles. "It's either the cabin or a tent in your backyard. This internship pays crap."

"The bears would enjoy the tent set-up."

"Way to try and scare me off." Simon reaches over then, moves a strand of hair that's fallen in front of my eyes. "I don't want to push my way in. I'm taking my cues from you."

"Do you really want to be here?"

"I do."

"Then I'm good with that. Let's just keep it week to week with Ethan, though. I don't want him getting his hopes up or counting on something—"

"You know me better than that."

"I wasn't implying that you're going to flake out on him.

I'm just saying that things happen, life gets in the way some-times. And let's face it, this is all new to you."

"You think once I'm bored—"

"Jesus, no! I just don't...I just think we need to be careful and take this slow for his sake."

What I really want to say is that I need to take it slow for my own sake. Just the thought of him being here with us, with me, has me lit up inside, excited for the possibility it presents. I need to pour cold water on those feelings, tamp down the flut-ters that took over when he did no more than move that wayward strand of hair. Even though he's telling me it's over with that girl, I don't want to hope for something that might never be.

Simon's smile could light up an entire city a moment later when he says, "Look who's awake."

Ethan eyeballs Simon, unsure what to make of him. He crawls up into my lap, burrowing under the edge of the blanket in a way that partially hides his face. He mutters back, "Hi," and then sticks his thumb in his mouth.

"That looks cozy." Simon reaches over to ruffle Ethan's hair, brushing the back of his hand against my boob with the motion. I gasp just as he clears his throat. "Ah, I'm getting another muffin." There's an apology in his eyes when he asks, "Can I get you anything?"

I squeak out, "I'm good," as Ethan mumbles, "I want my cup."

Simon jumps up. "I'm on it, buddy."

"The cups are next to the sink and the chocolate milk is on the left side of the fridge."

"Make it warm," Ethan calls after him, as if he's speaking to his butler.

"That's my dad?" Ethan asks when we're alone.

I snuggle him close. "Yes, my love, that's your daddy. He wanted to surprise you this morning so he got here super duper early."

Simon comes out with a dishcloth draped over his forearm and bows as he hands the cup over. "As requested, warm organic chocolate milk. Only the best for you, Ethan."

Ethan cracks a shy smile. "You soo-prize me."

"I did?"

"I told Ethan that Daddy woke up earlier than the sun to surprise him this morning."

The way he studies me and then smiles makes it hard to keep my head on straight. He hands me another muffin. "I did wake up earlier than the sun this morning." Handing Ethan a small piece broken off from his own, he asks, "So was it a good surprise?"

"Yes."

Simon nods, a smile stretching from ear to ear as he sinks back into his chair.

He looks hopeful.

After a day spent chasing after Moe, painting rocks, tossing stale bread to the birds and building a fort in Ethan's room when he was supposed to be taking a nap, the two of them plop into seats at the dinner table looking positively wiped out.

"No nap." I shoot Lawrence a look. "This could get ugly."

Simon raises his hand and pledges, "I promise I won't be a cranky pants."

This cracks Ethan up. "Daddy a cranky pants!"

And dinner goes by like this, filled with happy chatter, sweetness and some more laughter. It's good, so good that I have to pinch myself, remind myself that it's not permanent.

"I got this." He jumps up to finish clearing the table and shoos me away from the sink.

"All right then, I'm going to put my feet up and watch the sun set." Joking, I add, "I take my tea with milk, no—"

He cuts in, waving me out the door. "I know exactly how you take your tea. Lawrence?"

"No tea for me. We got some nice homemade peach ice cream in the freezer, though. And Ethan knows how I take my ice cream, dontcha Ethan?"

I picture him nodding with his solemn little face. "Lotsa whip cweam."

Lawrence joins me outside, resting his hip against the deck railing. "He dragged a chair over to help Simon wash the dishes."

"Yeah, he's really taken with him."

"I like him, Charlotte."

"Oh, I like him too…That's not the problem."

Ethan comes out holding a bowl with a mountain-sized dollop of whipped cream. He reaches up with two hands and gives it to Lawrence. "Here Paw-paw."

"Thank you, that's just how I like it."

Ethan nods proudly, then turns to take the kid-sized bowl Simon has made for him. "Be right back," Simon says, and returns a moment later with my tea and a mammoth bowl of ice cream for himself. "Here you go."

"Thanks."

He full-on moans when the ice cream hits his tongue. "Oh my God, Lawrence, you made this?" Lawrence, mouth full, shakes his head then tips his chin in my direction. "This is incredible. I've never tasted ice cream this good."

"I wish I could take credit for some elaborate secret recipe, but it's nothing special. Cream, eggs, sugar, vanilla and ripe peaches...That's it"

"Simple...That's why it tastes so good. Why aren't you having any?"

"I make it but I rarely eat it. That stuff will add five pounds to your hips in no time, and I have to make sure I can fit into my dance costumes come September."

Ethan's obviously gotten a second wind, taking off after Moe who is now barking up at a cluster of fireflies. Seizing on the opportunity to fling the two of us together, Lawrence makes like a leaf and leaves a moment later. Reaching down to get Ethan's discarded bowl and stacking it with his own, he says, "I'm gonna head in and do a few things on the computer."

"You're still dancing? That's great."

"I'm not majoring in it or anything, it's just a club activity. We put on a few performances a year, no big deal."

"Do you enjoy it?"

I can't help but smile. "I love it. We practice on Thursday nights and I look forward to it all week."

Looking out to where Ethan is jumping up and down attempting to catch a firefly, he says, "Then it is a big deal." A moment passes before he looks back to me. "And for the record, you look amazing. A little ice cream won't kill you." Before I can protest, he's extending the spoon my way, laden with a mixture of peach ice cream and the whipped cream topping. His eyes are fixed on my mouth. He's daring me or seducing me—I'm not sure which—but it's as if some cult leader is inviting me to drink from the fountain. My mouth opens without my permission and my eyes close when the cold rich goodness begins to melt on my tongue. "That's it," he coaxes. And when I open my eyes, that same spoon is now in his mouth. He's licking it clean.

Chapter Twenty-Nine

SIMON

I'm exhausted by the time I throw my duffel bag onto the passenger side seat and climb into my truck. It's been a long week, and longer than a week since I've been with Ethan and Charlotte. I've seen them, but a video chat is no substitute for the real thing.

At six o'clock every night I spend a few minutes listening to him talk, sing, or show me something. It hasn't been awkward the way I'd feared. No, it's been good. The calls don't last long—little kids don't have much in terms of attention span—but it doesn't matter. I just want to stay in his thoughts and keep up this connection we're developing, and it accomplishes that.

Most evenings I only get to spy Charlotte walking around the kitchen in the background, but sometimes she sits down with him and she talks to me. I pray that I'm not reading her wrong, but I believe there's a chance for us. I felt the air crackling between us that last night on the deck, and I saw the way she looked at me. I know what I feel, and I'm hoping she feels the same.

I think about the two of them nonstop. My energy is focused when I'm at work, but it's with a new sense of purpose. I'm not here just trying to prove myself, I'm here to build a future—one that can support my son. I've always had a sense of pride in what I do, in how hard I work, but now I have a child, and I want him to be proud of me someday. My perspective has totally changed.

On the ride up I have a lot of time to think. Should I tell Charlotte what I've done, that I've set the wheels in motion? I'm on borrowed time now. I'll see them first thing tomorrow morning, but then I'll be right back on the road after lunch on Sunday.

When I pull up to the cabin, I see two vehicles parked outside. The truck is clearly Lawrence's, if the hunting permit and the bumper sticker that reads: *Team SISU: We Wash our Balls in Ice Water* are anything to go by. Lawrence told me he'd leave the key under the mat like he did last time, but before I reach the porch I can see there's a note tacked to the front door.

Simon,
Come back to the house, there's a bed set up for you.
Sorry about the mix-up.

I'm sure there's some valid explanation, like Lawrence had unexpected company or something, but the note gives me hope. Maybe this is her doing. She wants me staying there, with her, with them. And I am totally on board—I want to play house with Charlotte more than anything else in the world right now. When I get there, the glow of a light on inside quickens my heartbeat.

She greets me at the door as I step onto the porch. "Hey."

"Hi." I'm half-dazed at the site of her. Dressed in pajama shorts and a tank top, she's exposing a lot more skin than I'm used to seeing, and with her hair pulled up, I feel like a magnet is drawing my lips to her neck. She's saying something, I think, but it's not registering.

"Simon?" She waves her hand in front of my face. "I'm so sorry, you must be exhausted. I was worried when I didn't hear back from you, but I guess you saw the note."

I think I get off to a stuttering start before managing to say, "Yeah, I saw the note on the door. You called me?" And sure enough, when I look down at my phone, I notice the ringer has been turned off. "I keep it on low when I'm at work, but I thought it was on. I see the missed calls now."

I'm disappointed when I see the couch has been set up for me, but I'm being an idiot. I don't expect to be upstairs with them—not yet, anyway.

"Do you want a beer?"

"I'd love one," I answer, before excusing myself to use the bathroom.

She comes back to the living room with two bottles that look like someone labeled them in their basement.

"You drink? If I'm not mistaken, you're still underage, missy."

"Don't tell Lawrence, but occasionally I do sneak one of his pricey craft brewery beers."

Upon closer inspection, the labeling looks more like a marketing ploy meant to give the bottle a home-brewed look. And then my attention is on her. Charlotte's taken a seat on the couch, right atop the blankets I'm going to be curled up in later, and she's reaching her hand up to offer me a beer, inviting me to sit beside her. I take a seat and then watch as she lifts her bottle to her lips. My eyes don't stray from that sight as I draw a long pull from my own. *Patience, Simon.* It's an absolute certainty that I'm going to replay this scene in my head later on tonight and imagine all the things I'd do with her if I could, but right now I have to rein it in.

"This is good."

"It's heavy like a stout, right? I usually can't finish one of these off, but I do like the taste of it." Charlotte takes another sip, watching as I reach back to pull my sweatshirt over and off. I lean back into the couch and meet her eyes. She glances down into her lap then, clearing her throat. "You must be exhausted."

"I'm definitely tired, but I won't be able to fall asleep yet."

Translation: *Stay here with me.*

"I knew we were having company this weekend but I didn't want you to feel like you weren't welcome, or you had to put off visiting Ethan for another week."

I'm disappointed now, realizing I won't have the two of them all to myself. "I'm glad you didn't tell me...Spending another week just video chatting would have been tough. Who's visiting?"

"A good friend of the family and her two teenage sons." She smiles when she adds, "I'm hoping to do some matchmaking."

"For Lawrence? It's a bit soon, no?"

"Lawrence is going to be sixty next year and Barbara's been divorced for more than a decade. Time waits for no man. I think Janelle would be on board. Scratch that...I know she would be."

Her expression changes. She's uneasy, starts picking at the label on her bottle. "What is it?"

"Nothing really. Just be prepared for Barbara. She's probably going to be watching you like a hawk tomorrow. If she starts asking too many questions, I promise I'll get her to back off."

"Huh?"

"Barbara, or Ms. Ryan as I was introduced to her, was the social worker assigned to me when I was admitted at Children's Hospital. She took an interest in me, I guess you could say." Charlotte shakes her head, looking both amused and annoyed. "I mean, she was relentless. She was riding my ass from day one, making sure I stayed focused, got through the GED exam, SAT prep, the college application process. I swear, there were days I truly hated the woman."

My eyes widen in surprise when she mentions the GED. Charlotte was always such a responsible student, always striving for good grades. The thought of her dropping out of high school makes my heart sink.

"She sounds great."

"Barbara *is* great, but back then I wasn't entirely cooperative or on board with the plan. There were times when it felt like her and Janelle were teaming up against me." Charlotte curls her feet up underneath her, rests her head back against the couch. "But I'm where I am today because of their nagging." She smiles at me. "Barbara is dying to meet you."

"Bring it on."

"Yeah, whatever, you've been warned."

I've drained my beer and she's barely taken two sips of hers. She takes the empty from my hand without a word and gets me another. "So, how was your first week on the job?"

"It was good. I mean, it's a good feeling knowing I made the right choice in turning down the other position."

"So this is a judicial internship, right?"

I nod as I take another sip, mentally reminding myself to slow down. "I turned down a summer associate position at a law firm specializing in patent litigation and I was worried I'd regret it. That's the kind of place where you make connections that last a lifetime."

"And you're already sure it was the right move? It's only been a week."

"Yeah, but Carl, I mean the Honorable Carl Michaels, is piling it on already. He's going to expect a lot from me, so it will be a great learning experience. And his clerk, Dan Webber, just graduated from Northwestern. We clicked on the first day."

"That's a good thing."

"They already having me sitting in to observe a trial that's starting on Monday. He's an appellate court judge. Can you imagine what that's going to be like, watching that level of litigation?"

She laughs. "Your enthusiasm makes law sound fascinating."

I poke her in the side, unable to resist. "Law *is* fascinating. It's thought-provoking, absorbing, captivating. Law is sexy, dammit."

"Whatever you say."

She's giggling now, and the sound is so freaking adorable. I want to hug her, pull her in close to me. My eyes drift down over her body, see the outline of her breasts straining against the thin fabric of her top. I don't know if it's fatigue or lust that makes me lose my sanity, but I'm having an out-of-body experience, watching from above as I reach across to drag my thumb through the condensation gathered on the neck of her bottle and then rub it across her bottom lip.

She sucks in a slow breath and I pull back. "I'm sorry," I tell her. But chancing a look back at her, I'm thinking maybe she *isn't* sorry. Her body is perched forward now and her eyes are closed. My body is primed and ready, embarrassingly so, but I know this isn't the way. "Long drive...I guess I should get some sleep."

She sighs, opening her eyes. "Yeah, get some rest. Ethan's going to pounce on you the minute he wakes up."

"I can't wait. Goodnight, Charlotte."

She smiles, pausing at the bottom of the staircase. "Goodnight, Simon."

Charlotte keeps glancing over her shoulder, checking for signs that I'm irked. Normally I wouldn't be tolerating the twenty questions routine from a veritable stranger, but this woman has done so much for my Charlotte, and in turn for Ethan. In my book, I owe her big time.

"So your mother, she's in North Carolina?"

"South Carolina."

"What was her reaction to the big news?"

"I haven't told her yet, ma'am. I was hoping Ethan could do a video chat with me when I tell her this weekend. The last time I was up here, well, there was a lot going on."

"First off, call me Barbara."

"Okay, Barbara."

"How do you think she'll react?"

"I can't be sure, but I'm guessing she'll see things in a positive light."

"I'd imagine finding out she has a three-year-old grandchild will come as quite a shock. Are you concerned about that?"

We blew past question number twenty a long time ago. Babs *is* starting to wear on me but I do my best to stay neutral.

"My mother raised three boys on her own, so she's pretty tough. I think she'll be able to handle the shock." I look over to where Ethan is playing with the older boys and smile. "I did."

"So you believe she'll react well because you have."

"I'm losing count. You've used reframing on me, thrown a little DBT in there with the distress tolerance thing, and now Roger's restatement technique. You social workers are skilled at getting people to spill their guts. Lawyers and cops should get the same kind of training."

She's delighted for some reason. "You've been in therapy?"

"Court mandated only." I'm quick to amend, "During my brother's incarceration," because while my initial impulse is to screw with her, I really don't want this woman to think poorly of me.

"Yes, Charlotte told me about your past. I'm sorry for your loss."

"Thank you."

"Do you think—"

"Enough, Barbara," Charlotte cuts in. "Will you give the poor guy a break already?"

"You're right, you're right." Looking back to me, she apologizes, "Forgive me, Simon. It's just that you've been this mystery entity for so long, and now...Well, you're here. I'm sorry about all the questions. Comes with my territory."

Charlotte reaches over, setting napkins and plates out for lunch. "Yeah, you're making me rethink my career choice."

"Not happening! The staff at MCU is counting on you to take over when I retire." It sounds like she's only half joking.

"Come inside and help me get everything ready."

I jump up first. "I'll help you."

Charlotte slumps into a chair once we're inside. "Sorry

about that. Maybe I should have held off on having you come up here this weekend."

"I'm glad you didn't. I would have been disappointed. And I like Barbara. She does ask a shit ton of questions, but her heart is in the right place."

"Here, take this out," she says, handing me a bowl of fruit salad. "Her boys are so good to Ethan, aren't they?"

"Yeah. I feel like I've been tossed to the side, though. The old man's no fun compared to the two tree climbing wonders out there."

"Never," she reassures me, placing a few serving spoons into my free hand.

I turn back to her and whisper, "I don't know about a love connection between her and Lawrence, though. I think you're way off base on that one."

"Maybe you were right, it is too soon."

Setting the food out for lunch, I'm struck by the realization that the weekend is flying by at warp speed. I haven't had much in terms of one-on-one time with Ethan. I feel cheated, but at the same time I love seeing my son so happy. The boys stayed over last night, and it was adorable watching as Ethan tried his best to imitate everything the older kids did. And Barbara's boys were great with him, including him in everything. Patient and kind, much like their mother, I suppose.

Midday is approaching fast, though, and I can feel the sand slipping through the hourglass. I think Charlotte senses my agitation when she sends the rest of them out on the boat, holding Ethan back with the promise of some time to go rock hunting with Dad. I'm skeptical he's going to give up a boat ride for that lame activity when she suggests it, but he shocks the hell out of me when he looks at me wide-eyed, clapping his hands. There's an ulterior motive—he wants the rocks so he can show the older boys how he paints them later on this afternoon—but that's okay. I'll take what I can get.

Me and Ethan are sorting through our spoils when she comes over to join us. "They're heading out on Thursday. Next weekend it's just us, I promise." Her face reddens as soon as the words are out of her mouth. "I mean, I shouldn't assume." She goes on to lip-synch, "Are you coming next weekend?" so that Ethan is none the wiser.

"I'll be here." I nudge Ethan. "Come and look at the calendar with me. Let's draw a picture on the day I'm coming back, okay?"

"You weavin'?" It cracks my heart wide open when he asks the question, even though he doesn't look too broken up. "You goin' to school?"

"No, buddy, I've got to work this week, but I'll be back in just a few days."

We take the calendar down then, count off Monday through Friday. He draws a picture of me, complete with the baseball cap I never wear, in the box for Saturday.

"I'll be here around eleven or so on Friday night, same as this week," I say to Charlotte. "I'll head to Lawrence's unless you text me otherwise."

She nods, biting her lip. "I'm sorry this weekend was so crazy."

"Don't apologize. I'm glad I got to meet Barbara."

She goes to say something else when a different kind of ringtone sounds. Ethan hops out of his chair and goes to grab the tablet sitting on the coffee table.

"Leave that for now," she says to him, but it's too late.

Ethan swipes the screen and then chirps, "Hi, Wes!"

I'd nearly forgotten about that asshole. I look to Charlotte and speak without bothering to censor myself. "What the fuck?"

Her eyes are saucers. "Keep your voice down!"

Telling my family that I have a child, letting Charlotte know I'm in the process of transferring to Michigan Law, finding out the status on her relationship with Wes—all important things I planned on doing this weekend but didn't get the chance to.

I can barely contain my rage when I hear Wes making a play for my son's affection. "Hey bud, I've missed you."

I make a mental note never to call Ethan "bud" or "buddy" ever again. Coming from that dipshit's mouth it sounds stupid. And Wes has *missed* Ethan?

Charlotte grabs my forearm when I go to stand. "What are you doing?"

"What are *you* doing? You let that piece of shit around my son?"

"Calm down."

"Don't." I shake her off and walk into the living room, taking a seat next to Ethan. My molars are nearly grinding themselves to dust, but I paste a smile on my face, taking care not to scare my child.

"Officer Wes Kellar, as I live and breathe."

"Simon?"

"That's my dad," Ethan says with pride, and I want to high-five him for the awesome timing.

I look back to see Charlotte standing in the kitchen with her eyes closed and her lips fixed in a firm line. I wonder if this is a ritual. Does he call to check on them every Sunday?

"How's life back east treating you, Wes?"

"Uh, it's good. When did you start coming around?"

Is that a dig? Is he insinuating that I've shirked my responsibility where Ethan is concerned? Before I can think of a retort that doesn't include a string of profanities, Wes asks, "Bud, is your mom around?"

Ethan looks towards the kitchen. "She right over dare."

"Is she all right?"

Now he's insinuating I might be capable of hurting Charlotte? That's it, I'm fucking done. "Don't worry, officer, I've never physically harmed anyone. That's your department, isn't it?"

With that, she enters the melee. "All right, Ethan, tell Wes you'll talk to him later. Wes, now's not a good time, okay?"

When the screen goes dark, Charlotte turns to Ethan smiling. "Hey, you want your dad to read you a story before nap time? He has to leave soon."

"I not tired."

I shake my head in frustration, mad at myself for letting my anger get the better of me. But I can't help but follow the direction my imagination's taking. I'm bombarded with images of Wes hunting for rocks along the shoreline with my son, Wes turning off the lights and locking all the doors at night to keep them safe, Wes holding Charlotte in his arms.

I choke it back. "How about a swing in the hammock?"

"Okay," he agrees, taking my hand, but a frown mars his face. Kids are perceptive.

Ten minutes pass before Charlotte makes her way across the backyard. Ethan's out cold. "I'll take over. You can get on the road."

"Are you with him, Charlotte?"

She takes her time before answering. Drags one bare foot back and forth through the grass. "No, I'm not."

That's not the whole story. "Hey, I'm sorry."

"About what?" she challenges.

"The way I acted before. I was out of line." She nods, bites her bottom lip. "But you know my history with him. You think I'm going to be on board with him being a part of Ethan's life?"

"Let's not do this now, all right?"

"Can we just talk?" Fuck, I'm so frustrated I could scream. "There's so much I wanted to talk about this weekend, and damn, we've barely had five minutes alone. Now I'm getting right back into my truck and driving for six hours."

"I knew this was going to be too hard."

"No!" I whisper scream. "I'd drive twenty-four hours straight, each way, every damn weekend just for the chance to spend a few hours with him. It's not a hardship. I'm just pissed because everything I say is coming out all wrong, I'm leaving here on a bad note, and I'll have to stew on this all week without the chance to set things straight with you."

And before she gets a chance to answer me, the entire brood pulls into the driveway, making such a ruckus when they storm out the door to the back deck that Ethan wakes up. He climbs over me, rubbing the sleep out of his eyes, his excitement skyrocketing once he catches sight of the boys.

"Forget it. I've gotta head out."

I'm fully aware that I sound like a baby, but Ethan doesn't even spare me a glance backward. Between that and Wes the Wonder Boy's call, I suddenly feel like a loser whose best friend just flat-left him for the more popular kids.

* * *

CHARLOTTE

"Are you all right?"

I sink into the couch. "That could have gone better."

Lawrence takes a seat across from me and then Barbara joins us in the living room. "The boys are painting with Ethan on the deck. They know not to let him near the water."

"Thanks."

"It looked like there was some conflict when Simon was leaving."

I roll my eyes. "For God's sake…Can we not do therapist-speak right now?"

"Okay." She smiles, and I'm grateful Barbara's never put off by my attitude, even when I turn all snarky-teen on her. "What I meant to say is that Simon looked pissed."

"Wes called right in the middle of their father-son farewell."

"I'm guessing he thinks you and Wes are an item?"

I look to Lawrence. "I think I cleared that up, but I got angry that he was angry. I mean, what right would he have to be jealous? I'm not even sure he's officially parted ways with his girlfriend." I'm so mad I could scream, but then just as quickly, I'm flooded with regret. "It just ended on a really crappy note."

Barbara asks, "Are you seeing him next weekend?"

"That's the plan."

"So next weekend the two of you talk things out. And," Lawrence adds, "don't leave things unsaid. Put yourself out there. I have a feeling he's just waiting on you to tell him what it is that you want."

Barbara shoots him an appreciative look. "That's great advice. I think Lawrence should go into the business."

. . .

"Can we start over?"

That's what Simon asks when I answer his video call on Monday night. I know he feels as bad as I do. And I want to erase some of last weekend too, but I also want to talk, really talk. That's going to have to wait, though. It's too hard to read him this way, even though I can see him on the screen. So I agree to a fresh start, and we keep our nightly chats brief and light, letting Ethan take center stage. On Thursday night we're discussing the trial he's been observing. As usual, Ethan runs over at the sound of his father's voice.

"Hi, Dad." Ethan squeezes in next to me on the couch. "You workin'?"

"I'm done for the day, little man."

"You gonna weed me a story?"

Simon looks pained but plasters on a smile. "I'll read to you when I see you on Saturday. Just two more days, okay?"

"Wait, I have an idea." I nudge Ethan aside and make my way upstairs.

I hear Simon ask, "What's your crazy momma doing?" and Ethan's giggles.

I'm back in a flash, out of breath when I flop back down on the couch. "You can have Daddy read this book. I'll hold up the pages and he can read to you. How does that sound?"

"Is that my moon book?"

"Yep."

Ethan claps his hands. "My moon book!"

"Is it your favorite?"

Ethan responds by nodding as he plops his thumb into his mouth.

I settle him on my lap and prop the screen against a stack of books on the table. "This is his favorite when he's tired. This one doesn't take too much mental energy. It's my favorite for sure."

I open the book facing out towards Simon and he begins to read the simple verse. His voice is gentle and calm, not missing a beat when I struggle to turn the pages in time. He reads it three times through before Ethan's eyes begin to flicker open and closed.

"Daddy's going to come upstairs with us," I whisper as I stand up, Ethan in my arms. I hitch him up higher on my hip and then reach down for the tablet.

Simon whispers, "Thanks. This was a great idea."

"I think we might be onto something, right?"

"I'd rather be there, but this is a decent substitute for the real thing."

"Here we go," I say to Ethan. "Under the covers."

"Again, Daddy."

"You got it, my man."

And by the time Simon gets through the short book one more time, Ethan is out.

I wriggle myself out from beneath the covers and lean down to kiss his forehead. "Goodnight, baby."

Simon adds, "Sweet dreams."

I walk to my room with the tablet and sit on my bed. Simon teases, "So, want me to read you a story now?"

"Sure." I reach over to grab a book off my nightstand. It's a parenting book, but he doesn't know that. "I'm in the middle of a good one...Tattooed biker torn between loyalty to his gang and the love of a good woman."

His eyes pop. "You? You strike me as a poetry girl, or I don't know, into Dostoyevsky or Steinbeck...Serious stuff."

"When I'm not in school, I go for romance. And it's not

mindless or anything, it just doesn't hurt my brain like most of the stuff I'm assigned to read."

"I hear that."

"I bet. I took a Constitutional Law class last year and that was the driest, most boring crap I ever had to read."

"Don't you remember what I said? Law is sexy."

"Yeah, you keep telling yourself that."

"So what *do* you do after Ethan hits the hay?"

"Oh, my evenings are very exciting. I usually have some tea out on the back deck, whip out my laptop and do a few hours of homework, mix up some muffin batter, fold laundry...You know, it's like a regular disco party here every night."

"Sounds nice, actually. Minus the homework part, of course."

"What about you?"

"Well, right now I'm sitting on my mattress, which is on the floor. The mattress also serves as my couch, dining room table, ironing board—"

"Are you fishing for pity points right now, Wade?"

"Maybe. But my summer sublets are always like this, so it's no big deal. It's a place to sleep. That's all I need."

"Is it far from the courthouse?"

"Ten minutes."

"That's good."

"Yeah, close enough to walk. Hey, so you think we'll get some time to talk this weekend?"

I nod. "We've got a lot to talk about."

"I'm sorry I freaked out about Wes." His face hardens but then he shakes his head. "I have no right to expect that you wouldn't have gone on with your life, especially since I was the one who left. It's just..."

"What?"

"Him, I guess. He's a bad guy, Charlotte."

"There's a lot you don't know about Wes. But like I said, I'm not with him…I never was."

"That's not for lack of trying on his part, though, right?"

"At least he came looking for me."

"What are you saying?"

"Nothing." I shake my head, pained. "I don't want to do this over the phone, okay?" He looks like he's going to press me on it but changes his mind. "Listen, I've got some homework to do. Talk to you tomorrow?"

"Yeah." He looks hurt, and for some screwed up reason I now feel guilty. "Have a good night, Charlotte."

The next morning I wake up to a text from Simon: *I looked for you too.*

Chapter Thirty

CHARLOTTE

Lawrence is heading down to Wisconsin to help his brother build a shed or something this weekend. That's what he told me anyway. I'm pretty sure the disappearing act is his way of forcing some alone time on me and Simon, a not so subtle attempt at matchmaking on his part.

I should text Simon and tell him to just stay here. It's ridiculous to have him driving back and forth from the cabin all weekend long when there's a spare room in the house, but I don't reach out.

I've looked at that text he sent a few days ago countless times. It shook me up, opened some old wounds.

Months passed after my father kicked me out. I wasn't expecting a search party or anything, but at the same time, I didn't anticipate a complete lack of interest in my whereabouts or welfare. Not one single person attempted to track me down. There were school records, so it's not as if I'd disappeared off the face of the earth, but still no one came for me. Not Simon, not Daisy, not my father. It's not like I was expecting my dad to have a change of heart, but damn, he *knew* where I was and still never called or visited.

Did Simon look for me? I shake off the hopeful feeling, knowing that even if it is true, he didn't put too much effort into the pursuit. After all, he moved on. He's been in a committed relationship with someone else. That's indisputable.

I'm still awake at midnight when headlights and the familiar rumble of Simon's truck announce his arrival. He came straight here. My breath hitches when I hear two gentle raps on the door. I told myself I needed some time, but I also know I left the light on in invitation. He looks tired when I open the door.

"Sorry I came by unannounced. I saw the light on."

"How was the drive?" I ask, fixing my eyes on the floor.

"Not too bad."

He's still standing on the threshold, even though I've opened the door wide and taken a step back to let him in. When I look up in question, I see that his eyes are fixed on my legs, and realize I'm wearing nothing but a tee and some boy-short undies. Did I do that on purpose too? Probably.

"Come in. I'll be right back."

"Mind if I grab a beer?"

"Help yourself," I call as I make my way upstairs.

He's on the couch, eyes closed, hair sticking out in ten different directions when I come back downstairs wearing a bra underneath the tee. I went the extra mile and added a pair of proper shorts too. The bottle of beer is propped against his thigh. I go to reach for it, thinking he's asleep, but he traps my hand and gives it a gentle squeeze.

"I'm awake."

"It looked like you were passed out cold."

"I'm surprised you're still awake."

"I guess I was waiting on you."

"I'll head over to the cabin now if you want to turn in. I just thought…Well, I was hoping that maybe if you were still up then we could talk."

I nod, my throat suddenly tight and constricted. There's so much to say that I don't know where to start. I take a seat on the couch, leaving a comfortable space between us. Simon closes his eyes again.

"I tried to find you, Charlotte, but obviously I didn't try hard enough. I didn't see a future for us back then. I wasn't coming back, and you had two more years before you could get out. Two years is a long time. I told myself it was better that way, to cut ties. Then you'd be able to move on." He shakes his head, eyes still closed. "I suffered for it. There were nights I couldn't sleep just thinking about you. I missed you more than I ever could have imagined. I don't know if you'll ever believe that, but it's the truth."

"Coming up here was really hard at first."

He looks to me. "I can imagine."

"I don't think you can. Janelle and I grew close over time, but those first few months I was walking on eggshells around her. I had no one to talk to and I was pregnant. And I mean, it's not like I was looking to make friends here, in a new school with my waistline expanding every day, but walking the halls of that place was depressing. It made me regret all the times I blew Daisy off, kept myself closed off from her."

"It's me who should have been here for you, no one else."

"But you weren't. And I'll be honest, Simon, the fact that you didn't, in your words, try very hard…God, it made me hate you at times." I wave him off when he goes to speak. "You didn't know what I was going through, I know that."

"I tried to call you but your phone was disconnected. I called Mr. Vargas, and when he told me you'd moved, I freaked out, made him promise to follow up and check on you. He got back to me. Told me you were living with an aunt. Assured me you were doing great at your new school. But I still couldn't put it to rest. I had Garth sniffing around. Even had Sienna try to pry some info out of your father, but he wasn't giving anything up where you were concerned. I searched your name online more times than I can count. But yes, at a certain point I gave up."

"You moved on."

"Yes and no. I filed you away...I guess that's the way I'd put it. Convinced myself you were living a good life somewhere. I always imagined you were in Florida, surrounded by palm trees, sand and the ocean. And I'd tell myself I was being stupid, pining away for a time in my life that didn't exist anymore."

"I never moved on."

He cocks his head. "That's not really fair. You didn't move on because the course of your life was altered dramatically. If you'd never gotten pregnant, you think you never would have moved past me? Met someone else?" When I don't answer, he presses, "Have you ever dated anyone else?"

"Guys at school have, I don't know..."

He rolls his eyes. "Expressed interest?"

"Yeah, but I'm very up front about having a child. Works like a charm when you want a guy to back off."

"I'll bet." He shoots me a bemused look. "Obviously I didn't mean it would scare me off."

I raise my palm. "I get it."

"And I know Wes Keller is doing more than just expressing

interest." Now I'm rolling my eyes. "I'm not trying to start a fight. I'm just putting it out there. He's interested in being more than just a friend. He always was."

"What does that mean?"

"It means he was into you when you were sixteen." He studies me. "But you knew that." He leans over and puts the unfinished beer on the coffee table. "The way he looked at you back then made me sick, furious. He was, what, twenty-two, twenty-three? I wanted to kill him."

"You never said anything."

"Shit that Simon can't do anything about...I had a very long list going at the time."

"Maybe that's why you were always so angry."

"Is that how you remember me?" He looks stricken. "I don't remember feeling angry when I was around you. Those few months we were together was the only time I felt...I don't know, at peace."

"You were moody."

"I still am, I guess."

"No, you're different. You talk more. There were days back then when your mood could flip on a dime and I wouldn't know why. I didn't like that."

"I'm sorry."

"I know you are."

"I could never sleep. I was always so damn worried."

"I knew Timmy being in prison was always weighing on you, but you wouldn't talk to me about him."

He nods. "It was Timmy, feeling responsible for my mom, always feeling anxious about money." He looks to me. "And I was worried about you."

"Why?"

"I was worried about something happening to you,

someone hurting you. There were nights at school that first year...I'd wake up sweating, punching some faceless stranger. My roommate probably thought I was a lunatic."

"Wow." I shake my head. "I haven't thought about that guy in years."

"Huh?"

"The diner?"

"Oh." Now he shakes his head. "I wasn't referring to that, but I guess a few of my nightmares did center around that morning." He looks to me, skeptical. "You never think about it?"

"Not really, no. According to Wes the case was a slam dunk, so the guy was going away for a long time. And then I left. I wasn't at the diner, wasn't in that town, so I had nothing to remind me."

"Better that way, I guess."

I consider it for a moment. "Maybe I don't think about the event itself, but yeah, I suppose it's changed the way I do things. I carry pepper spray in my purse, I'm careful walking around campus at night, always have my phone in hand...I'm definitely more aware of my surroundings than I would have been had it not happened."

"That's a good thing," he says, and reaches over to place one of his hands over mine before continuing. "I was talking about that lock, though. I've never been able to get the image of that lock on your bedroom door out of my mind."

The memory floods back. I'm in the cafeteria standing in line when Simon presses into me, wanting to know how it went and if my door was sturdy. He knew it was for my bedroom?

"I was blind with rage where your brother was concerned." He's lost me. "And he was just someone else I knew I couldn't take on at the time. I think a lot of my anger had to do with feeling powerless." Before I can cut in, he says, "Not confronting Christian is one of my biggest regrets."

"You thought I bought that lock because of my brother?"

* * *

SIMON

"I bought the lock because of Wes."

I stand and pace, looking for some outlet to quell the fury building inside of me. "What did he do? Why didn't you fucking tell me?"

"He didn't *do* anything."

"Right."

"He didn't." She stands and intercepts me, taking my hands. "But what you said about him before? I did know, and I wasn't comfortable with the way he looked at me back then. And I know I can't convince you that he didn't mean to cause any harm, but I believe that...I one hundred percent believe that Wes would never do anything to hurt me." When I won't meet her eyes, she drops my hands, backs away and takes a seat on the couch. "He knew I was too young, so he fought what he felt for me at the time and stayed away."

"He told you all this?"

"More or less."

"And now he feels like the time is right? He wants back in?"

"He knows that isn't happening."

"Does he?"

"He does." She draws her feet up underneath her, rests her head back. "I know you see him one way, but he's like everyone else...There's good and there's bad. He feels remorse for

Timmy. He hates himself for it. He's completely cut ties with my brother. Wes even left the police force over it. He moved away to start over."

"Let me guess...He got himself a nice little place in the Upper Peninsula."

"He's just outside Philadelphia, working for his uncle and going to school. Hey, I don't expect you to ever forgive him, and it's not my place to forgive him over what he's done in the past, but I can't bring myself to see him as a bad person."

"And yet you installed a lock to keep him out of your room when you were sixteen."

"How is it so easy for you to view the world in black and white the way you do? How do you stand there, so righteous? It may not make sense to you, but my feelings for him are complicated." I literally bite my tongue to keep from lobbing a sarcastic remark back at her right now. "You may not want to hear it, but Wes was the only person who looked out for me when I was a kid. After my mother got sick, he was the only person who stood between me and Christian's angry outbursts. Wes, not my father, stepped in and set Christian straight when he could. He made sure I had food to eat and made sure I got to school on time when the weather was bad. He took care of me." She lowers her voice. "And I've been alone for a long time. I've never led him to believe we have a future, but maybe I am guilty of keeping some sort of a relationship going with him. I have to admit, it's been a comfort to know that someone cares for me."

And then I know it's not anger I'm feeling, but jealousy over the role he's played in her life. He protected her when I couldn't. Stepped in when she needed a friend. Affirmed the idea that a man could want her, child and all.

I sink into the seat next to her but can't manage to say

anything at first. Minutes pass before I say, "I think I understand."

"Thank you."

I take her hand in mine. We sit there together in silence, both of us wrung out and spent.

Going through life leaving things unsaid is easy. Talking is hard. The kind of communicating we're doing this weekend is the kind that drains you. It's physically painful, but it takes a load off your back at the same time. To have someone you can be so open with is kind of amazing. I guess that's what people mean when they refer to someone as their person. Charlotte is my person. I believed it before but I know it now.

Even my time with Ethan is heavy this weekend. We still have times when we're goofing off or just spending quiet time side by side, but there's business to attend to as well.

I decided to prepare my mother in advance. Taking Barbara's thoughts on the matter into consideration, I agreed that springing a grandson on Mom could be a catalyst for heart failure. And it hits me, studying her face as she takes him in. This affects not only me, but every person in my life. With Mike and Brandon it's the same. Ethan insists on introducing Moe to them on the video chat and Michael smiles through his tears when his nephew recalls what I told him about our brother. "Your Timmy, he sneezed?"

I'm grateful for the strength Charlotte's steady presence has given me today.

"Is it just me, or do you feel like you went nine rounds with Tyson today?"

She laughs, pausing as a spoonful of ice cream is halfway to her mouth. "I'm about ready to pass out." She takes the mouthful then passes the bowl back to me. "I was nervous as all get out to face your mother."

"I'm glad I told her beforehand."

"Absolutely. Can you imagine how that would have gone? *You remember Charlotte, right Mom? She's got a little someone she wants to introduce to you.* That would have been horrifying."

"She was always fond of you."

"I hope she still is."

"No worries on that front," I assure her. "If I love you, she loves you."

"Love me?" Wide-eyed, Charlotte looks downright panicky.

I take in a deep breath and place the bowl on the deck so I can focus on her. "I'm sorry if that makes you uncomfortable, and maybe I should have kept it to myself for now, but I do love you. I don't believe I've ever stopped."

"I see."

"What's wrong?"

"It's just...You say you love me, but do you really even know me?"

"Come again?"

She's distancing herself, the relaxed ease of a moment ago now gone. "We were together for four months. You were with Samantha for a year. Longer than a year, actually."

"Stop with Samantha. I don't want to hear her name coming from your lips. She means nothing to me. Do you get that? I never loved her."

"What happened when you went back?"

I don't want to do this now. I don't want Samantha in this place with us. "Nothing."

Charlotte's face twists as she goes to stand. "After everything I've shared with you, you can't give me anything?"

I make it to my feet first and take her forearms, slowly pulling her up and in close to me. I keep my voice low but there's a hard edge to it that I can't mask. "What do you want to hear? Do you want to hear that she cried? That she begged? She did. And I'm a bastard because I didn't care. I fucking peeled her off me and left without looking back."

Falling back a step, I release her. What I've revealed begins to sink in.

I left Samantha the exact same way I left Charlotte.

* * *

CHARLOTTE

It's hours later when he knocks on my bedroom door. He's dressed in jeans and a sweatshirt, and I see the car keys in his hand. "Do you want me to go?"

"What are you asking me?"

"I'm just saying that if I were you, I'd want me to leave. I'm giving you the option. I'll go stay at Lawrence's tonight and I'll head out after I have breakfast with Ethan tomorrow morning."

"Is that what you want?"

"What I want doesn't matter right now."

"What was that before? Why couldn't you just tell me what happened between the two of you?"

"Because I don't want to think about her." He shakes his head, frustrated. "It was a relief to have something, a reason to cut ties with her. And now it makes me think I'm like, cold or something. That I can hurt people without really caring one way or another."

"But Samantha did something terrible to you. It's not the same. Do you really believe what you're saying right now?"

"It sounds like history repeating itself. I left her and didn't look back. Aren't you afraid I'm going to hurt you, disappoint you again?"

"Yes, I am."

His eyes close in anguish. "Do you know how much it hurts to love you the way I do?" He makes his way over slowly, drops his keys and takes a seat at the foot of my bed. "I'd never be able to live with myself if I hurt you that way again."

"I could hurt you too."

"I know that."

"Do you love me because of Ethan?"

"It's not because of Ethan. I love you *and* I love Ethan. I want you in my life no matter what." He reaches over tentatively, lays his hand over mine. My skin heats at his touch. "Open your eyes," he whispers. "Please tell me you want me in your life."

"I do. I want you, Simon."

He moves closer still. One hand skims up my thigh, landing on my hip, while the other cups my cheek. "I'll be good to you. I promise you that."

So long. It's been so long.

"I want to kiss you," he says.

They're the same words he used that first time, so many years ago. But I want more now. He sits back and watches as I reach down and peel my tank top up and over my head. I'm aching for what I've missed out on all these years, and I trust this man, so I don't stop. I shimmy out of the sleep shorts I'm wearing too, baring myself to him.

He looks me over starting at my toes, making a long, agonizing path up and over every inch of me. My instinct is to cover up, but his eyes are hungry and loving at once. "You're mine," he says, and then stands to undress himself while I watch.

His kiss is everything. It's tender, it's dominating, it's safe. "I've wanted this for so long." And his hips pressing into mine communicate his need. I slide my hand between us, wanting to feel him, remembering what it was like to have my entire body ignite like it did years ago. He moans when I make contact, and even though I know we're not ready to take that step tonight, my legs fall open for him. "You're mine, Charlotte," he repeats.

And I know it, I am.

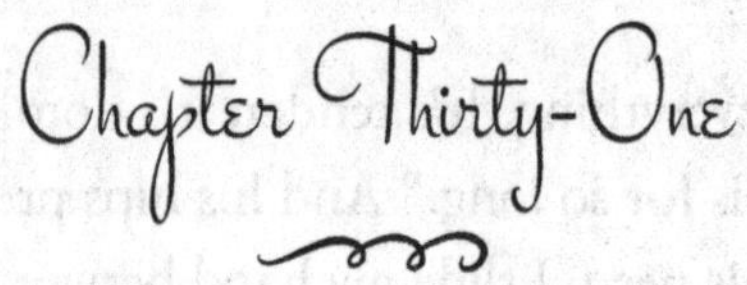

Chapter Thirty-One

SIMON

This is what it's supposed to feel like.

Ethan has just gone down for the night and the two of us are swinging in the hammock, lazy and sated. Charlotte is nestled into my side and she fits perfectly. I don't think I've ever felt so content, felt so at peace the way I do when I'm with her.

"I can't believe September is just three weeks away," she says.

"I know. I hate thinking about the summer ending."

"Are you sure you're making the right decision? I've been researching and—"

I cut her off. "You mean if I checked your computer's search history I'd find stuff like, um, the disadvantages associated with transferring in the middle of law school?"

She tickles under my armpit. "Something like that."

"And what are the downsides?"

"Obviously, you lose the contacts you've made at Northwestern." She emphasizes, "Not just the professors, but your fellow students."

Yep, that's a valid concern. Close bonds have already been forged among the first-year students, and she's right, I won't know any of my new professors.

"Transferring will make it harder to get a good internship." She looks up at me. "I imagine it would make it harder, right?"

I nod. She's not wrong. "Keep going."

"What about getting a spot on a good mock trial team, or the law journal stuff."

She's done her research. "Anything else?" She's quiet now, but I feel her shake her head against my chest. "Hey." I shift my body to the side, which isn't easy in a hammock, and coax her to look up at me. "I'm not gonna lie, all the points you've raised are valid. Socially, and just as far as, I don't know, getting to know the academic culture at a new school, it's going to be an adjustment. But it's going to be all right. People transfer all the time."

She rests her head back on my chest. "I don't think you're being completely straight with me."

"I am. Listen, Charlotte, they accepted me because they know I'm number one in my class at Northwestern. I'm going to get a spot on a good trial team, and who knows, I could be editing the Michigan Law Review before it's all said and done."

"Confident much?"

"I'm confident because I've worked my ass off, and I'm going to keep doing that. And I'll meet the faculty and students by joining groups and associations that deal with the issues I'm focusing on. I am probably going to have to do some other crap that I normally wouldn't have gotten involved with, but that'll be a small price to pay."

"Like what?"

"You know, like join the intramural flag football or hockey team or some shit...Find a way to meet students outside of class."

"You play hockey?"

"It's a co-ed league at Northwestern, so it was mostly for fun, but yeah, I played in an intramural league off and on throughout undergrad."

"Wow. I feel like I'm meeting you for the first time."

"Yeah, baby, there's all sorts of things you don't know about me."

One hand moves down my side and around my back. When she cups my ass cheek, she pulls me in closer. "Do tell."

"Hmm...Let me think." I've got a nice view down her tank top right now, and her smile is telling me she knows this. I slide the strap of her top down one shoulder as I nuzzle into her neck. "I speak fluent French now."

"Ooh la la," she whispers.

"I can fly an airplane," I add, awkwardly shifting us so that I'm now on top of her.

"Really?" she asks absently, breathy.

Rocking my hips into her, I watch her lids drift closed as her teeth graze her bottom lip. "And in my spare time, I'm a spy for the Russian government."

"That's great," she murmurs, raising her hips up to meet mine.

She shifts then, probably because I'm crushing her, and the movement sets us off balance. With a WHOOMF, we land on the grass below.

"You're lucky I landed on top," she says, catching her breath and laughing.

I run my hands down her back, resting them on her ass. "I'm just lucky in general."

"Want to take this inside, big boy?"

"At your service." But I pause, holding her in place. "Are we on the same page now? If there's some other concern you have about me relocating, you'd tell me, right?"

She shakes her head, her long hair falling in a curtain around us. "I want you there with us, Simon. I just don't want to be selfish about it."

"Selfish? You've never made a selfish move in your life. It's time for me to make some sacrifices. I'm long overdue, wouldn't you say?" She shrugs one shoulder. I haven't convinced her. "I don't think you get it, Charlotte." I raise us into a sitting position, take her face in my hands. "I wouldn't survive being apart from the two of you. I don't want to keep popping in and out of your lives on the weekends. I want to be there. I want Ethan to be close to me." Dropping a kiss on her lips, I add, "I want to be close to you."

She nods. We lift ourselves up off the ground and I watch as she rids herself of the grass and twigs that cling to her shirt and shorts. I reach over, tucking her hair behind her ear, my mind taking me back to last weekend. Lawrence was here on Saturday morning, but then arranged an overnight fishing trip with a few friends. This weekend he scheduled another trip to see his brother down in Wisconsin. I'm pretty sure he's got an ulterior motive, one that benefits me. I knew he was in my corner the first time I met him. And I'm grateful, because tonight it's as good as it was the last time, when I thought I could never feel as close to another person the way I do when I'm with Charlotte. Her sweat-slicked skin grips and then slides against mine. She opens for me, invites me into her, and then closes her eyes and sighs when I'm fully seated, rocking her hips to get closer still.

On the nights I can't be with her, I drift off to sleep in my lonely studio apartment dreaming of her. Charlotte in the shower house, Charlotte in the grass late at night, Charlotte in that cramped twin bed in her room, my hand pressed against her mouth to muffle the sweet, sexy sounds she makes. Making love to Charlotte is like nothing I've ever experienced, because the absolute best moments are when she's lying in my arms right afterwards. It's then that I feel like maybe, just maybe, my life is going to turn out better than I ever dared to imagine.

I can't get enough of her.

Charlotte wants me, I'm confident of that, but there are certain areas of our relationship where she still insists on applying the brakes. I don't like it, but I understand her logic. She doesn't want to change the way Ethan sees us together just yet, wants it to be something he sees happening gradually, wants it to be natural. So in front of him we'll hug hello and goodbye, hold hands now and then, but nothing more. One day I'll be able to wrap her in my arms and greet her with a kiss in the morning in front of our son, and he'll be able to scramble up into the bed his parents share if he wakes up in the middle of the night scared. And even though some days it's all I can do to keep from pulling her onto my lap or dragging her in close just to breathe in her scent, I know all good things come to those who wait. I can be a patient man when I have to be.

I see my life now, with more clarity than ever before.

She sags against me when she comes, and I hold her up, finishing a moment later. "You feel so good," I tell her, but what I want to say is: *You're mine, you'll always be mine.*

* * *

CHARLOTTE

"You expecting company?"

"No." I turn to see Lawrence's attention fixed out the front window.

"Maybe it's a lady selling Avon or something."

I chuckle. "Up here?"

"If she didn't look so much like Faith Hill, I'd venture a guess she's a car thief."

He lets the curtain drop as he makes his way towards the front door.

"No, Lawrence, I've got this."

I get to the door first, opening it to see Simon's girlfriend—I mean ex—standing next my car, peering down to look in the back window. "Can I help you?"

She doesn't even have the courtesy to act embarrassed or startled. "You must be the baby mama."

Lawrence steps forward but I turn to him, gesture for him to go back into the house. "It's all right, I can handle it." He looks between us, taking a moment before going back inside. I notice he takes a seat in the rocking chair right by the front window. I don't think I need protection from this woman, but it's good to know Lawrence has my back all the same.

"So I guess you already know who I am." When I don't answer, she continues to make her way around my car, closer to me. "Cadillac XT5, huh? So you're not some pauper from the backwoods like I thought you were."

The fancy car is another reminder of Janelle. She continued to drive the same F-150 she'd been driving for the last decade, but after Ethan was born, she insisted on buying us a "city" car with heated seats, four-wheel drive and every conceivable safety feature. Not one year later, she traded it in for this, the latest model, just a month before she died.

Shaking off the sting, I look over to this girl's shiny little Audi coupe. "We buy American around here."

"I certainly know Simon didn't buy that car for you. He's flat broke."

"Why are you here?"

"I guess I just had to see you for myself."

She looks me up and down, and while she's trying to hang on to this air of superiority act she's got going on, I can see the cracks in her armor. Her hair and skin are flawless, for sure, and to put together a casual-chic outfit like that I'd need a personal shopper, but there are bags under her eyes and her nails are bitten down to the quick.

She crosses her arms over her chest. "Simon is letting you ruin his life, ruin everything he's worked for. I get that he wants to take care of his son, but do you realize what he's giving up?" She doesn't wait for me to answer, not that I have any words to offer this slightly hysterical looking person. "Transferring means he loses his scholarship. Transferring means he loses an all but guaranteed job offer from one of the top law firms in Chicago. Transferring means—"

"It means he's walking away from you."

"This isn't about me, it's about Simon."

I roll my eyes. I was feeling sorry for this chick until about a second ago. "This?" I gesture between the two of us. "This is all about you."

She smirks. "You think you've won, don't you? How do you think Simon's going to feel when he has to sign for the, what, the forty-thousand or so he's going to need to get through this year alone? And another forty next year?"

I can't help but wince at that, even though she's exaggerating. I've researched that angle too. It will be thirty-two thousand in tuition for this year, and next year he'll be able to qualify for in-state tuition, which is closer to twenty-two. But she knows she's hit a nerve. If you know Simon, you know finances are always front and center in his mind. He's proud, doesn't like to owe anyone.

"He's got a free ride at Northwestern. He's at the top of his class. And you'd have him give all of that up to start over at a lesser school?"

"Michigan is ranked higher."

Why oh why am I even engaging this girl?

"If you knew anything about the field, which you obviously don't, you'd know that Northwestern is guaranteed to open more doors for Simon. At least I care enough about him not to let him destroy his future."

"I think you should go."

"Look, um, Charlotte?" She's playing it off like she isn't entirely sure what my first name is, which is laughable. I'd be surprised if she didn't know my social security number as well as the color of the underwear I've got on right now. "I get that you want him to be involved in his son's life. And he's honorable, he'd never neglect his responsibilities where Ethan is concerned." I can feel my face heating, feel a hatred that's venomous. How dare she even speak my son's name? "But he can do all of that and still stay at Northwestern. Trust me, you'd be doing yourself a favor."

"Excuse me, but aren't you the heartless bitch who failed to give Simon my phone messages? Who destroyed the letter I wrote to him? You lied to him. You never wanted him to know he has a son." I advance on her. "How can you stand here and say that you care about Simon?"

Her confident stance and expression falter. "I do care about him." She shakes her head, her pain evident. It feels like she's pleading with me to understand when she adds, "I love him."

I turn to leave because I'm shaking, and I don't want to give her the satisfaction of knowing that this confrontation has rattled me to my core. I'm on the front porch with my back to her when she calls after me, "He was going to ask me to marry him. It's true. He already has the ring."

* * *

SIMON

The lights are off when I pull up to the house. I check the time on the dashboard and then check my phone to make sure I haven't missed any messages. Judge Michaels took today off, and being the good guy that he is, left instructions for the rest of us to head out by two. It's not even nine o'clock now but everything is eerily quiet.

Are you awake?

It's been like an unspoken thing these past few weeks that I no longer head to Lawrence's cabin. I leave my stuff in a spare bedroom off the kitchen for Ethan's sake and to be respectful to Lawrence, but I've been staying in Charlotte's room.

A bubble appears, so I know she's typing back, but then it disappears a moment later.

Is everything ok?

Another minute passes before I see a light go on in the living room. As I make my way from the car to the porch, I take her in as she stands in the doorway. She's smiling but there's something off. As I get closer I can see that she's been crying, but for some reason she's trying to act like everything's good.

"Hey, what's wrong." I drop my duffle and close the door behind me before wrapping my arms around her.

Her arms feel like two spatulas as she extricates herself from my hold. "I'm fine."

"Um, no, you're definitely not. What's going on?"

She lets out a tired breath and walks to the living room, taking a seat in the chair next to the couch. Doesn't give me the option to sit next to her.

"Are you sure about this whole thing? About transferring, leaving Chicago, giving up the life you've built for yourself there?"

"Are we really doing this again? I thought we put this to bed last week." I go to take her hand, to lead her over to the couch next to me, but she wraps her arms around herself before I can reach her. "Wait, are *you* having second thoughts? You told me you were on board with me coming to Michigan. What's going on?" She keeps her eyes fixed on the floor. "If you've changed your mind, I really wish you would have let me know sooner." She gives me nothing. "Damn, Charlotte, I've already accepted my seat at Michigan."

"And Northwestern? Have you relinquished your seat there? Have you met with Professor Westfield?"

"Yes to question number one, and what does Westfield have to do with this?"

"The Westfields, *all* of them, have been a big part of your life for the past four years."

"I'm kinda sitting here baffled right now, babe." And I'm growing impatient, but I'm not going to say that out loud. "Can you just say what's really on your mind?"

"I asked you once before if you were engaged to her and you said no."

I nod. "Because I'm not engaged and I never was."

"And if I'd never reached out to you? What then?"

I'm sure I'm shaking my head because I'm dumbfounded. "How can I answer that?"

"Would you have married her?"

"Huh?"

She drags both hands along her scalp in frustration. "She paid me a visit this morning, Simon."

"Samantha came here?"

"I'm just going to ask you a question, and please, please, please...Just be straight with me. I'll never keep you from Ethan, I'll never—"

"What the hell is going on right now?"

"Did you pick out a ring, Simon? Were you planning on asking her to marry you?"

"No!" I'm pacing the living room now, so much anger coursing through me I'm afraid I'm going to blow. "Whatever she told you, it's a lie!"

I'm embarrassed when I see Lawrence standing in the hallway, hearing all of this.

"Everything all right in here?"

I turn to him. "Yeah. I'm sorry I raised my voice, Lawrence." But he's not checking in with me, he's looking squarely at Charlotte. She looks up, her face puffy and red, and nods to Lawrence. He fixes me with a stern look before turning to go back upstairs.

"After everything she's already done, why would you believe her?"

"It was more than that." I can barely hear Charlotte because she's dropped her head back into her hands. I move closer, kneel right in front of her. "She painted a picture for me of what your life is like. To be with us you're giving up a scholarship, giving up a cushy job." When I go to cut her off, she raises her hand to stop me. "Don't say it's not important because it is. And this isn't just about school. God, Simon...For me there's never been anyone else. No one. You don't have to imagine me with another man. You don't have to wonder if I'm missing him, wishing I was still living the life I had with him. I'm trying not to be jealous or insecure, but I really need to be sure you're not going to change your mind or regret this."

"Regret being with my son? Regret being with you?" I sit there, feel my hands drop to my sides. How can she think I'd regret any of this? It's a minute before I stand and walk over to the side table where I left the framed childhood picture of me with my two brothers. "I've probably lived in a dozen different places since I left Pennsylvania, between dorms, crashing with people during breaks and my crappy summer sublets. This picture has made every move with me." I sit back down at her feet as I remove the backing on the frame and take out the smaller picture that sits behind it. "This picture has come with me too. I've taken it out and stared at it so many times I've lost count. I never got over you, Charlotte. I never will."

She wipes at her eyes and takes the picture from me. She's still studying the image of us as teenagers when she says, "That girl told me she loves you. Told me you had a ring picked out and everything."

"No." I shake my head. "Her dad made a joke once that Sam had her heart set on wearing her grandmother's ring. Like, 'Just say the word, Simon, and I'll get it out of the safe.' If she's referring to that, the idea is so far fetched it's delusional."

"After she left, I was right back to doubting whether or not you truly want to be with me or if you're just doing this out of a sense of duty." She cuts me off again when I go to refute her.

"I just want you to know that I don't need you." She wipes her eyes and fixes me with a look that's sure and calm. "I want you, Simon, and I love you, but I can stand on my own two feet."

Chapter Thirty-Two

CHARLOTTE

"Are we good?"

When I nod, he pulls me in close and kisses the top of my head.

Last night Simon stayed in the guestroom. We were both spent after going nine rounds thanks to Samantha's meddling, and even though we settled everything, it still feels a little raw between us.

"I never want to do that again," I tell him.

Simon gives me a lopsided smile that melts my heart. "Me either, but what specifically are you referring to?"

"I never want to fight with you and then go our separate ways."

"Even though I was just downstairs, I know what you mean. I was itching to knock on your door last night, just to make sure we were ok."

"Same here. I needed you next to me last night."

"About that...We've never discussed—"

"Mommy, can you make pancakes?" Ethan's rubbing his eyes as he makes his way down the stairs. When he sees Simon standing in the kitchen he practically launches himself into the air as Simon swoops him up into his arms. "Daddy's here!"

"I'm here," Simon says, nuzzling his face into Ethan's side, tickling him in the process.

I turn to him smiling. "To be continued?"

With Ethan still in his arms, he moves in closer, making a sandwich out of the three of us as he presses into me. "Yes, to be continued." He alternates between blowing raspberries on Ethan's neck and then mine before whispering, "Put chocolate chips *and* blueberries in my pancakes, woman."

"My pancakes too, woman," Ethan calls out as they head out onto the back deck.

Simon has been pushing it these past few weekends, dropping kisses on me in front of Ethan, pulling me in close when the three of us sit on the couch together to read a book or watch a movie. It doesn't worry me anymore. In fact, I've come to crave the intimacy, the devotion he demonstrates towards both me and Ethan.

Last night was the exception, but not a night goes by where he doesn't creep upstairs and sneak into bed with me. I'm on birth control now, and this time I chose a more foolproof method so we're free to do what we want, but sometimes he just tucks himself in behind me and holds me close. I like that too. He's been back in my life for less than three months, I should be cautious, but I can't help but believe this is real— that Simon loves us and wants us to be together.

"What have you got planned this week?" he asks as I'm putting away the breakfast dishes.

"My final papers are due for both classes by Thursday. I'm almost done, just some edits left to do. Why?"

"My internship ends next week. I'm going to start packing up. I was thinking..."

"It doesn't make sense to bring your stuff up here. Maybe I'll head down there next week and help you. I'm sure Lawrence can watch Ethan overnight. We can pack you up and move your stuff to Ann Arbor."

"Are you all right with—"

"With you moving in?"

"Yeah. Is that taking things too fast for you?"

"I think it's the right thing to do." I busy myself drying the serving platter, avoiding his eyes when I add, "I want us to be together."

He wraps his arms around my waist and whispers, "You make me so happy, do you know that? I'm going to spend my life making you happy too."

Chapter Thirty-Three

SIMON

She looks especially beautiful today. Dressed in a simple white dress, holding a bouquet of wildflowers in one hand and Ethan's little hand in the other, I'm feeling overwhelmed in such a good way.

I've wanted to do this since not long after the day I moved in with them, but Charlotte has her own mind, and I've learned she doesn't like to be rushed. We started talking about marriage—conversations initiated by me—right from the beginning. I needed to establish my paternity legally, and I didn't see why we should wait to be married. I loved her, always had, and I knew my feelings would never change. But my girl needed some time, nearly two years as it turns out. She needed to be in it with me, living life day to day, getting through not just the easy times, but the tantrums, stomach bugs, and the disagreements that occasionally popped up between us.

We're assembled at the courthouse this morning. Judge Michaels pulled some strings and got us a private room for the civil ceremony with his good friend, the Honorable Vincent D'Angelo presiding.

Judge Michaels, a Michigan Law alum, is the one I now turn to for advice and guidance, and he's been generous with his time. It's his name and reference that secured the summer associate position I took after my second year, which led to the job offer I recently accepted.

I'm not going to lie, it's not as prestigious as the position I would have been accepting at one of the big firms based in Chicago, but along with those big salaries come six-day, ninety-hour work weeks and lots of travel. I don't want that life. I want to come home to my family every night. I want to be around on the weekends. So instead, I've opted for a well-respected firm in Michigan, one that specializes in patent and intellectual property rights law. The fact that they're also committed to taking on a set number of high-profile pro bono cases is what sold me. The reason I went into law in the first place, my brother Timmy, will never be forgotten.

It's a banner week. I'm getting married to the love of my life this morning, tomorrow I will officially graduate from law school, and on Friday Charlotte will get to walk across a stage for the first time and have an esteemed member of the faculty hand over the diploma that represents four years of her blood, sweat and tears. I know she's as excited as I am. It's a heady feeling when you realize you're about to reach a goal you set for yourself so long ago. I go back there for a moment, to all the late nights, the struggles, the worry and heartache I experienced along the way, but then switch gears. I want to focus on that peaceful feeling, the one that comes after a hard-won victory.

Charlotte brings me peace. She's always had the power to ease what raged inside of me, to comfort me. To be her family —to be her man—is an honor.

I lock eyes on Ethan, catch a moment when he's looking up at Charlotte, smiling at something his mother has said. Watching the two of them together like this feels so good it hurts.

I wonder how he'll take the news. At five years old, he's thriving. Charlotte was nervous as hell sending him off to kindergarten last fall, but he's taken to it like a fish to water. His teacher gushes over how smart he is at every parent-teacher conference, and makes a point saying how helpful and kind he is too. I feel like a proud papa bear when I walk out of those meetings, and feel the same as I watch him playing with his classmates after school. He's made plenty of friends—hell, every kid in his class was at his birthday party last month. My son is pretty much always smiling, running around with Moe or pounding away on the piano we bought second hand, you know, just in case professional soccer is taken off the table by his doctor someday down the road—Charlotte's still a bit of a worry wart. He's so easygoing and upbeat, I can't imagine he'll be anything but pumped when we decide to sit him down and tell him he's going to be a big brother.

Charlotte and I decided to start trying a few months ago, and just like last time, it happened right away. Unlike last time, though, I'm going to be by her side every step of the way.

Ours is considered a high-risk pregnancy, so we've already been to see the specialists who cared for Ethan and continue to do so. I'm not afraid the way Charlotte is. Maybe I'm being naïve, but I just have this feeling everything is going to work out fine.

I'm already looking forward to holding this child, being one of the first voices he or she hears upon entering the world, and then sitting next to Ethan, supporting him when he gets to hold his baby brother or sister. And I'll be there when Charlotte nurses our child for the first time. I finally fessed up a few months ago one night when we were looking through Ethan's baby album together. That first time I saw the picture of her feeding Ethan, I thought it was hot, maybe the sexiest thing I'd ever seen. She laughed, told me I sounded like a total perv, but deep down I knew she understood. It was more than that. She was amazing in my eyes. Ethan was bare except for a diaper, she was holding him skin on skin, and there was nothing he needed that she couldn't provide—her body kept him warm, her body protected him, her body nourished him. It's a sight so powerful, so womanly, that it never fails to take my breath away.

He's dressed like a miniature version of me today, down to the suit and tie. I've caught him looking in the mirror checking himself out a few times. He's freaking adorable, and I'm not just saying that because he's mine.

I will pledge my love and fidelity to Charlotte this morning, but those are the standard lines they feed you, just some ceremonial ritual. I'm reciting my real vows right now, in silence. I am making a vow to love them, to protect them, and to do everything in my power, for every day I have on this Earth, to deserve them.

* * *

CHARLOTTE

It's a small group, but every person in this room is meaningful.

Ethan is wiped out, the evidence of the second piece of cake his grandmother allowed smeared across his tie.

This morning he insisted on wearing a tie and a belt, just like his father. Lawrence got a kick out of that, being as how

Ethan used to insist on wearing a fur-lined trapper hat in the summertime before Simon was in the picture.

"He was born in the Upper Peninsula, so he'll always be a Yooper."

"Will I ever be one?" Barbara teases.

"Nope, you're a fair-weathered girl, through and through. You won't even come along when I take the boys ice fishing."

She heads up to see her "friend" Lawrence at least once a month, sometimes with her sons, sometimes without. They don't feel the need to put a label on it, but I hope one day they'll make it official.

"Grammy," Ethan whines, and I look over to see Simon's mother smile from ear to ear, just as she does every time he calls her name—or breathes air for that matter. "Can I have more cake?"

She looks to me and I shrug my shoulders. She only gets to spend time with her grandson in person a few times a year, so there's no way I'll ask her to play the role of disciplinarian.

"Maybe we'll share a piece. How does that sound?"

Next week he'll be back to his routine of healthy foods and adequate rest, but for now I can let it slide. It's not every day he has his entire family in one place.

I see the way Michael and Brandon look over at him every few minutes before looking back to one another smiling. They can hardly wait. Brandon's high school girlfriend, of all people, agreed to surrogate for them, and she's due to give birth to their twins in late August. That will be Simon and Ethan's first time on an airplane. Ethan is excited, but I think Simon is nervous.

Ethan has grandparents, he has uncles, he has Barbara and Arlene as de-facto aunts, and soon he'll have cousins.

He has a mother and a father who love him, and parents

who love one another. And as of today, we all share the same name.

It was important to Simon, and now it's official. Ethan is legally Ethan Mason Wade and I am Charlotte Mason Wade. My husband, the father of my child, is Simon Mason Wade.

He took my name too. It was his idea.

It's hard to shock me, but he did this morning when he said, "It's how it should be. I want the names Mason and Wade to be together, for all of us."

"You'd take a name that caused you so much pain?"

He moved in close, wrapped his arms around me from behind as I was putting in my earrings.

"I want your name because I love you." Meeting my eyes in the mirror, he added, "And love will always be stronger than hate."

A Note From Lily

A heartfelt thank you for reading *When the Night is Over*. This book was over two years in the making—a long labor of love. As each character came to life, I became more invested in their story. Simon, Charlotte, and Grace Dawson are among my favorite characters to date, but every character from this series is special to me.

Ready for more? The Blackbird series continues with:
Your Hand in Mine

Where do you go when life as you know it implodes, when everything you believed to be true is nothing more than an ugly lie?

Skylar Perillo has been living a perfectly ordinary life, but nothing is as it seems. Her life is anything but ordinary, and it's a far cry from perfect.

Leaving the one place she's ever called home is the only way forward, but it's like her mother used to say: The grass isn't always greener.

When a job as a nanny literally comes to find Skylar, she has no choice but to take it, even if it means working for the seriously uptight grump who's already gotten under her skin.

But those old pearls of wisdom do ring true, because when it comes to Leo Hale, Skylar's going to learn that you can't judge a book by its cover, and that it really is darkest before the dawn.

Also by Lily Foster

THE LET ME SERIES

Let Me Be the One

Let Me Love You

Let Me Go

Let Me Heal Your Heart

Let Me Fall

When I Let You Go

THE BLACKBIRD SERIES

When the Night is Over

Your Hand in Mine

Ghost on the Shore

All Your Life

www.ingramcontent.com/pod-product-compliance
Lightning Source LLC
Chambersburg PA
CBHW010315100726
47906CB00006B/1006

* 9 7 8 0 9 9 8 9 1 6 7 9 8 *